AF305086

BAD CREEK

BAD

PEYTON JUNE

CREEK

NORTON YOUNG READERS

AN IMPRINT OF W. W. NORTON & COMPANY
INDEPENDENT PUBLISHERS SINCE 1923

For my sister, Liv. We made it out alive.

Iris had almost finished weaving the bracelet when she remembered she had no one to give it to.

If her parents noticed the red string, they didn't bother to say anything. They hadn't spoken Glory's name once during the six-hour drive. That was to be expected. They'd barely said her name for the past year. The grief counselor claimed families often fragment after a loss. Iris thought that sounded melodramatic, at first. Now it felt like an omen.

Fragment.

As if the Garrens were made of glass.

Iris untied the string from the headrest and shoved it in the backpack with the others. Even with her headphones blasting music, she could hear her moms bickering.

April didn't think they were close enough to the lake for their favorite oldies station to be in range. Joanna was sure it was, since they'd already passed the sun-faded billboard advertising the Second Largest Crucifix in the World.

"I tried that one," April told her wife. "It was all static."

"It won't be static now. Try again."

If her moms could recycle the same harmless argument for the millionth time, maybe this summer wouldn't be that much different after all. Iris waited for them to find the station. For Joanna to laugh it off and sing along to a song by Toto or REO Speedwagon.

But Joanna didn't laugh. She swore and slammed on the brakes. A man with a tie-dyed bucket hat and reflective orange sunglasses stood in the path of their minivan. Joanna stopped the car a few inches from him. The crisis was averted, but that didn't stop the worst-case scenario from playing in Iris's head.

The man's body would roll over the hood with a thump. Shards of glass would pierce her skin. Maybe she would scream; maybe she would black out. She'd be okay, eventually. But Sunglasses Guy would be dead on impact. His orange sunglasses would fly off his face and land in the ditch. Paramedics would give them to his family after delivering the bad news. He was a single dad, of course, just to make the story more tragic. His orphaned kids would keep the sunglasses in a special place in their home so they could still have a piece of him.

Iris hadn't kept any souvenirs from her sister. Every piece of Glory was buried or sealed off in her room back in Cleveland. The funeral was a year ago, and Iris had yet to revisit the grave or step into the empty bedroom next to her own. Even though she was pretty sure Glory was the last one to have custody of their shared stuffed rabbit. Iris hadn't seen Picasso since last summer.

"Tourist," Joanna muttered. She gave a disapproving honk.

Sunglasses Guy jogged across the street to join the line outside the fudge shop. Tourists loved Michigan fudge, and Dolly's was the only place in Bad Creek to get it. The town didn't have enough residents to warrant two fudge shops. It didn't have enough people to qualify as a real town either. It was a vacation spot in a county of much better vacation spots. Petoskey had more restaurants. Mackinac had newer rental cottages. Why stay near the rocky beaches of Burt Lake, when her famous older sister, Lake Michigan, was so close?

Because this place is in my blood.

Joanna had hissed those words to her wife in a whispered argument last week. Iris had her ear to the door, listening to April suggest they go somewhere—*anywhere*—else for their summer vacation. Joanna wouldn't budge. It didn't matter if Glory was gone. The Garrens didn't just have Bad Creek in their blood now.

Their blood was in Bad Creek.

Iris wasn't sure who she agreed with. She had never imagined a summer without a week of long humid days with her best friends, riding her rickety bicycle and burning her mouth on s'mores. But she hadn't imagined a life without her sister either. Would it be disrespectful to come back without Glory? That was what April seemed to think. But what if returning was the only way to keep Glory alive? As the minivan turned onto a crunchy gravel road, Iris's insides rearranged. She feared if she didn't grind her teeth together, her heart would escape out her mouth.

The hand-painted sign for the Landings called it a "resort," but all it had were twelve one-story cabins, a sand volleyball court, a few firepits, and the marina, where the massive lake tapered into the creek that gave the town its name.

Joanna parked beside Cabin 4 and looked at Iris through the rearview mirror. This was when she usually said, *We're baaaack*, in a singsong voice, imitating a scene from *Poltergeist II*.

Instead, this time she only offered a silent smile.

"Do not leave this car empty-handed," April warned before unbuckling her seat belt.

Iris slung her backpack over her shoulder, grabbed the electric fan wedged between the seats, and stepped out.

The rental cabin hadn't changed since Joanna's childhood: same shingle missing, same broken green shutters, same wind chimes April threatened to take down every year. Same old man on the porch, waiting for them in a wicker rocking chair.

"Garrens!" he shouted.

Rex Crawford had been pushing eighty for as long as Iris could remember. His hands were the reason she knew what arthritis was, and both knees had been replaced twice, but he was still kicking. He struggled to his feet and hugged Joanna. "How're the kids?"

Rex didn't mean her daughters; he meant her students. Of course Iris was fine, and Glory was not to be mentioned.

"Lovely little terrors," Joanna told him.

Rex did his infamous wheeze-laugh. "You were quite the terror yourself."

"Still am."

There was a tiny squeal behind them. Iris flinched, nearly dropping the fan on her toes. A toddler stood on the rickety dock on the other side of Cabin 4's firepit. His chubby arms were outstretched over the edge. Ducks gathered under the worn wooden boards, fighting for a piece of bread.

The kid's mother was staring at her phone, unaware her toddler was seconds from drowning. Iris wanted to scream out, but Mrs. Baker grabbed her son just in time and went back to her phone. Still, how could she be so careless after what happened last year? She had to know. The Bakers were regulars. They stayed in Cabin 9 every year.

Supposedly, a current swept Glory away. Or she was drunk, like everyone else at the party. All explanations had to do with accidents. Tragic, but not extraordinary. There wasn't even a real police investigation. No interviews. No autopsy. It was best to accept it so they could move forward. That was what the grief counselor said. And that was what her parents believed to be true.

Iris couldn't believe it. Glory was a strong swimmer, but more than that, Glory wouldn't let herself lose control, and she was too popular to be alone long enough to disappear without anyone missing her.

Iris had been in Cabin 4 at the time. She and Gum were boycotting the party. By midnight, he was snoring on the top bunk, but Iris lay awake, expecting Glory to burst in at any moment, telling Gum to get the hell off her bed and go back to his own cabin. Her usually flawless curls would be windswept from riding in Aidan's Jeep with the top down. She'd smell of liquor and sparklers.

Except Glory never came back, and everyone expected Iris to be okay with not knowing.

But *someone* knew what had happened, and Iris had a week to find them. She wouldn't leave Bad Creek without answers.

Mrs. Baker waved in their direction. All the Garrens waved back.

Rex switched his attention to Iris. "Well, I'll be damned," he said. "She's almost a lady."

Iris numbly smiled at him. "Almost." She wondered at what age she would be considered an entire lady. Sixteen wasn't it, apparently.

"You start high school soon?" he asked.

"I'm a junior in August."

"I'll be damned. You still dancin'?"

Oh. The question hit her like a hammer to the gut, but she didn't shatter yet; she'd been taking hits all year. Anyway, it was a forgivable offense to confuse Iris with her sister. They'd looked similar enough when they were kids, sharing the same dark curls and eyes. But Glory had perfectly arched eyebrows, a sharp jawline, and a slender frame. Their moms believed all bodies were good bodies; Iris wasn't supposed to be jealous. But how could she not be jealous of an older sister with runway-model proportions and the grace of a ballerina?

Rex caught his mistake. He snapped his fingers. "No, no. You're the artist."

Nope. That was Glory too. She did it all. Glory, dancer and choreographer. Glory, painter and muse. Glory, talented and tragic.

Joanna placed her arms on Iris's shoulders. Her grip was a little too hard. Desperate. "Look what she stole from my closet," she said, changing the subject.

"I'll be damned," Rex said, studying Iris's sweatshirt.

Iris had her own Bad Creek merch, of course, but nothing beat vintage. The design was nothing special: a navy-blue anchor with the date embroidered underneath. Mostly, she loved it because it *looked* loved. It reminded her that she was part of something bigger. A legacy of women who—for one week every year—lived the same life.

Now the legacy was splintered.

Fragmented.

"Ninety-one," Rex read. "Good fishing year. Caught a sixteen-pound walleye." He dipped his knobby fingers into the breast pocket of his flannel shirt, retrieving two gold keys. He dropped them into Iris's free hand and said, "Make good choices, young lady."

He slowly descended the porch steps. Joanna offered to help. Rex waved her away. "I paid for these knees. I gotta use 'em."

When Iris opened the cabin's screen door, the corner smacked against the wind chimes, setting off a metallic twinkle.

April groaned. "I swear to God . . ."

April always had this inexplicable beef with the wind chimes. To Iris, the wind chimes sounded like the kind of music fairies would play. They'd lulled her to sleep on so many summer nights. She would even replay the sound in her head when she was home during the school year. She used to hear them in her dreams, but now she heard them in her nightmares. And in those nightmares, Cabin 4 transformed into a black hole that swallowed Iris and what was left of her family.

In real life, there was no black hole, just a hardwood floor that creaked with every step, a plaid couch with sunken cushions, and a framed grainy photograph of a black bear.

"Let's air this place out," April said.

She fluttered through the cabin, opening the windows. This was her ritual. Unlike her wife, April wasn't born a regular; she still hadn't learned to love the generations of dust. She emerged from Iris's bedroom, triumphant.

"Your stars are still up."

Her smile was even faker than Joanna's.

Iris took a big breath before she stepped into her bedroom. Usually, as she got older, the room shrank, the wood-paneled walls closing around her like a warm hug. Now the room seemed oddly empty. She noticed every cobweb, every moth-eaten hole in the gauzy white curtains. The ceiling was so high she might as well be floating in space.

Drifting into that black hole.

April entered behind her and plopped onto the queen-sized bed. "It's a bit too wet for a campfire tonight. I was thinking about heading over to Todd's?"

"The room is different," Iris said slowly. She still had her backpack on, unsure if it was safe to set it down.

"They're always updating the cabins," April said.

"No, they're not."

Rex was a crew of one. He physically couldn't keep up with the repairs for all twelve cabins, and no one expected him to. His renters forgave every splinter and stain because the Landings was a place that wasn't meant to be fixed.

"Your stars are still up," April reminded her. The light green stickers were scattered above their heads. Of course they were still up. Glory had promised they would stay on the ceiling forever. But they probably didn't glow in the dark anymore.

"Why are the bunk beds gone?" Iris asked, finally realizing what was wrong with the room.

"How about we get pizza?" April suggested.

"We can't get pizza. It's First Night."

Her mom sighed, defeated, and rolled off the bed. April was very good at giving up lately.

Iris shut the door behind her. At least the carvings on the back of the door hadn't been sanded off. She let her fingers graze over words and dates she had memorized.

I love you Jeff French 1984, one read. Right below were initials in a heart and the year 1969. And in the center of the door, *DISASTERS FOR LIFE*.

That was what they called themselves. Joanna, Paul, Beth, and Bruce. The legendary foursome. The blueprint.

Their parents.

At the bottom of the door were the most recent marks. Written in a child's handwriting, they said, *DISASTERS 2.0*, with nine tally marks.

This was supposed to be their tenth summer together.

A heavy knock made Iris jolt. She'd thought slamming the door would earn her a few moments of privacy.

"You decent?" the voice on the other side asked.

It wasn't April or Joanna.

Iris flung the door open. The boy standing there was shorter than her, with his head tilted up in a failed attempt to look taller. A worn-out white baseball cap contained his long, wispy strands of brown hair. He looked almost the same as the last time she saw him. Sure, his shoulders were a bit broader, his voice definitely deeper, but he still had a round baby face full of acne. At least one of her summer boys was unchanged.

"Hey!" Iris squealed as she hugged him. He hugged her back even tighter. *Too* tight. Like he hadn't thought he would ever see her again.

"A little late this year, huh?" he said.

Daniel Gum had a hint of a Southern accent that proved he didn't actually live in Bad Creek, Michigan. He had a whole life somewhere else. He went to a school she'd never see. He had friends she'd never meet. But in her mind, he only ever wore that stupid baseball cap and dirty sneakers. He was perpetually chewing on candy cigarettes, scheming ways to offend as many adults as possible, but never actually going through with any of his grand plans of rebellion.

"There was traffic," Iris lied. The Garrens always came in around five, but her parents had loaded the car late, as if they decided to go through with it at the last minute. She hated to think Gum was waiting for her in Cabin 3 this whole time. Iris hadn't sent him a warning text. The Disasters' group chat had been dead for as long as Glory.

"Is Aidan back yet?" she asked. Usually he would be waiting outside Cabin 4 with Gum, demanding to help unload the heaviest luggage.

"Uh . . . not sure," Gum said.

"Was his flight delayed or something?"

"I don't know, I haven't talked to him. Have you?"

She shook her head. She should have seen this coming. Glory was gone, so Aidan had no reason to hang out with them anymore.

A grocery bag of firewood awaited them outside. April must have given up on the pizza dream. After a few minutes of watching Gum rub two sticks together, there was still no fire.

"Do you need help?" Iris asked him.

He shook his head. "When the apocalypse happens, you're gonna need survival skills. First rule of survival: fire equals life."

There was a spark, but it didn't catch. Making the fire was Gum's job ever since his short stint in the Boy Scouts. Iris was in charge of prepping the s'mores, but that wasn't going well either. Every time she tried to break a graham cracker in half, it didn't split clean down the middle. The edges were jagged. Fragmented.

Maybe April was right. Maybe trying to start a fire after last night's rain was a lost cause. Maybe they should have gotten pizza at Todd's. But why come to Bad Creek if they were going to throw away all their traditions?

After a few more tries, Gum rummaged through his beat-up backpack, which was held together with safety pins and duct tape. He pulled out a camo-print lighter.

"What happened to survival skills?" Iris asked.

"Second rule of survival: use any and all resources."

Finally, there was a real flame.

She wanted to tell Gum about her suspicions right then. Gum was the only person she knew who was completely innocent. She wasn't sure it was a murder, but she was sure Glory didn't just drunkenly fall into the water by accident.

But now Joanna and April joined them with hot dogs and mosquito spray and foldable lawn chairs. Her moms couldn't bear to say her name out loud; they wouldn't survive Iris using *Glory* and *murder* in the same sentence. So Iris stayed silent.

Joanna gave one of her monologues about the Good Ol' Days and Gum gave Iris a play-by-play of his entire year. What classes he almost failed. What pranks he helped pull on the dean of his prestigious private school. The stick-and-poke tattoo some hot senior guy gave him. It looked like a gray smudge on his thigh, but according to Gum, the quality of the tattoo didn't matter if the artist was hot.

It was supposed to say *Carpe Diem,* but the *M* was illegible, so when she squinted she could only make out *Carpe Die.*

Iris didn't have any real-life updates to mention. She wasn't on the tech crew for the spring musical this year. She didn't rerun for student council vice president either. No developments on any romantic prospects. Courtney Shaw did invite her to a party. And she could have been flirting, but since last summer, Iris hadn't had the energy, and Courtney ended up hooking up with Tamia Spencer later, anyway. Gum definitely wouldn't want to hear all about the blanket cocoon Iris spent the last twelve months hiding in, watching reruns of her favorite ghost-hunting show, *Dark Unknown*.

The crackle of the fire was the same, but it didn't warm Iris up like it should have. And without Glory's perfectly curated playlist there was too much dead air. Aidan probably thought all their traditions were pointless now; that was why he hadn't come. She tried not to fault him for it. This was bound to happen eventually. Even if Glory was still around, everyone would be ready to grow up, and Iris would be left behind.

Gum was still wearing the friendship bracelet from last summer. It was so worn that the shades of blue faded into gray. Iris pulled this year's edition from her backpack and tied it around his wrist. "The zigzags are cool," he told her.

He didn't notice the other bracelets at the bottom of the bag. The red one was useless, and now the yellow one might be too. At least Gum still cared—or he was acting like he did, for her sake. Would he believe her hunch, if she told him?

"The bugs are getting bad," Joanna said after an hour. That meant she and April were going inside, and Iris could stay up as late as she pleased. First Night Bonfire only really started when the adults left.

But Gum stood too. "I got church in the morning," he announced.

"Oh." Iris tried to hide her disappointment.

"But I'll see you at the cookout tomorrow?"

Their week had a sacred order: after First Night Bonfire, there was the Second Day Cookout. Third Day was dedicated to that year's Summer Project. Fourth Day was the volleyball tourney and pizza at Todd's. Mini-golf on the Fifth Day.

Then a shopping trip on the Sixth. The week ended with the Fourth of July party at the beach. The Garrens went home the following morning.

Iris nodded. "Yeah."

Gum gave her a salute and returned to Cabin 3, directly next door.

Everything was so wrong. Why was he leaving? *She* was acting normal. Well, as normal as she could. It was everyone else who was looking at her weirdly and treating her like she had become a swirling vortex of grief. It wasn't fair.

Joanna gave Iris another sad little smile as she gathered paper plates and wrappers into a trash bag. As if to say, *See, Iris? We're back. We're doing the First Night Bonfire. At least one of your boys is here. How could anything be wrong?*

As if she didn't notice how, every now and then there would be a pause—a hiccup in the conversation, leaving room for someone who wasn't there. The void Glory left was obvious at home, but somehow it was worse in Bad Creek. Iris felt like an idiot for weaving those bracelets in the first place, for expecting any of this to be the same. It couldn't be. It wasn't a vacation without the Disasters. And they weren't the Disasters without Glory. Iris was the only one stupid enough to think otherwise.

The red bracelet weighed a thousand pounds in her bag. Iris couldn't carry it around all week. She slipped into her room, her parents in the living room behind her, chatting quietly. She wondered if they spoke Glory's name in private, when they didn't think their living daughter was listening.

She shut the door. It was breezy outside, but she was already sweating in this little cabin. She tore off her windbreaker, balling it up and chucking it against the wall. It landed beside a crooked bit of floorboard, where the wood was slightly off-color.

This was where she and Glory hid their secrets from their moms. Where they pretended they were pirates, burying precious treasure they found on the beach. Seashells, rings, and bottle caps. Whoever had last closed the lid on their hiding spot had closed it quickly. The wood wasn't secured into place.

Iris knelt and pulled away the plank. The hiding hole was about as deep as a shoebox and only a little wider than her hand. It was empty, save for one item: a red Moleskine journal with last year's date written neatly on the cover in gold Sharpie. There were a million others like it in Glory's room at home. Iris had never realized this last journal was unaccounted for.

She wasn't supposed to touch her sister's stuff without permission, but she couldn't help tearing it open and marveling at the organized chaos. Part diary, part sketchbook—Glory recorded her year in watercolors and colored pencils, poems and quotes. January was purple: pen drawings of telephone lines and street signs. April was pink: splotchy flowers labeled in Latin. The end of June was an explosion of color. There were paintings of melting ice-cream cones. Joanna reading on the dock. Gum smiling with his eyes closed, the sunburn on his cheeks immortalized in a hot-pink marker. Glory made her friends stand perfectly still for portraits instead of snapping a photo for reference. "Because the masters draw from life," Glory would explain. Then, if someone wiggled or tried to speak, she added, "Move, and you die."

Posing for Glory was always worth it. Glory made Iris's curls look like elegant ringlets. Her soft jawline belonged to a goddess from the Renaissance; her dark eyes held galaxies. She looked like someone famous. Important. That was how Glory drew everyone, especially Aidan. The sketchbook was full of him. Pages of his freckles, his crooked canines, his chipped black nail polish.

Glory must have shoved the sketchbook into the hiding place before leaving for Savi Traxler's pre–Fourth of July party. She couldn't have known she wouldn't get a chance to finish it. That the lake she swam in for seventeen summers would swallow her up.

June's colorful portraits were traded for July's muddy blacks and blues. There was no more of Iris. No more of the boys. July 1 had a house covered with ivy that must have been in a movie or something, because Iris didn't recognize it, and Glory didn't draw things that didn't exist.

July 2 was full of eyes, the same ones over and over again, looking up from heavy lids. These harsh, inconsistent lines didn't match her usual style. Glory was a perfectionist who kept her charcoal pencils at a precise point. But these marks were blunt, forceful. Obsessive, yet careless.

July 3. Her last day alive. Iris had to stare at the sketch for a moment to figure out it was not only a dock, but the one at Savi Traxler's lake house, marked by the vague form of a floaty castle in the background. The shadow in the water was new. Blurry, featureless. A single word was scratched on that page: *Waiting.*

The next one was even stranger. Glory rarely drew herself; she was far too humble to do a self-portrait. But this was clearly her. Those were her pointed eyebrows, arched up in fear. That was her mole, her one blemish, under her eye. She was underwater—her curls floated around her face and bubbles trailed from her mouth, opened in a scream. Dark hands were wrapped tight around her throat.

CHAPTER 2

GUM

Gum didn't know why sitting and standing and kneeling and eating a wafer once a week made him a good person. He was actually dead set on being what his family considered a bad person. It wasn't that Gum hated his family; they just didn't like him, and the feeling was mutual.

He looked up, squinting at the morning sun. One of the Midwest's seven wonders glared down at him. How blessed he was to be in the presence of the Second Largest Crucifix in the World. Every year it seemed to get taller, the gaunt face of the Lord and Savior carved in pine even more accusatory. Could this wooden Jesus see inside his head?

Screw you, he thought, just in case.

"Hell, Daniel, did you sleep in those clothes?" his dad said, as they both exited the car. He wasn't a tall man, but his only son was especially not tall, so the elder had a few inches on him.

Gum tried to smooth the wrinkles on his shirt. "No."

He'd barely slept at all. He'd lain awake in Cabin 3, dreading what the week would bring. Aidan had ghosted them, and Iris was all wilted. She was trying to act okay, but she was never a very good actor. Gum didn't have the power to cheer her up anymore. He felt useless.

Clarice stepped out next, effortlessly unfolding the wheelchair from the trunk. Gum missed the old nurse, Darlene, who had taught him to play poker. Clarice was thirty years younger and tried too hard to be his friend. She now carried the last person out of the car, a tiny middle-aged brunette. Though her clear blue eyes were open, she wasn't awake.

Beth Clavey could have married a rock star but had settled for her high school sweetheart: a nice, hardworking Catholic boy named Aaron Gum. Legends called her the life of a party before the accident. She was a free spirit; her energy was infectious. She lit up any room. That's what people have to say when someone dies.

Except Beth hadn't died. She'd suffered a traumatic brain injury. That's what happens when someone goes four minutes without oxygen. No one saw her fall off the dock, but luckily her twin brother, Bruce, found her in time to save her. Well, sort of. She hadn't been awake for the past fifteen years, but anyone would tell you she was the best mother to live.

As the family walked toward the church, the congregation expressed their joy to see them. Look! The Claveys still made their yearly pilgrimage to Bad Creek!

How wonderful.

How peachy.

The small talk was interrupted by someone yelling, "Are you kidding me?"

It was Gum's cousin, Hudson, wearing a turquoise shirt so bright you could see it from space. Uncle Bruce moved closer to him, and whatever he said back was too quiet for Gum to hear over the chatter in the parking lot and the obnoxious man-made waterfall at the base of the crucifix. Hudson crossed his arms, toned and tan from years of winning swim meets, before muttering something under his breath. Gum wasn't an expert lip reader, but he dabbled in swear words, and he was ninety-nine percent sure Hudson had just said, *Fuck you.*

Hudson glared at his dad for another long moment, then turned away, eyes locking with Gum from across the parking lot. Gum pretended not to notice. He knelt to re-tie his dress shoes. It had been a few years since Hudson had tried to kick his ass, but he wasn't going to provoke him. Thankfully, it was time to go inside. There was a lot of bumping and *excuse me*'s as Clarice struggled to wheel Beth into the church. She tried to secure a seat in the back, until Gum's father told her the bad news. The earth would stop spinning if they didn't sit with the whole extended family in the first pew. Mass wasn't for the Claveys to worship; it was for the Claveys to *be worshipped.* But Clarice was new. She didn't get it yet.

When they finally sat in the coveted front row, there was an empty space next to Hudson's little sister, Annie. Weird. Was he still outside, pouting? Hudson wouldn't miss Mass in Bad Creek. He got away with it back home in Kentucky, but not here. Not with Grandpa watching.

Hudson was the golden boy. The Claveys thought sunshine

shot out of his ass. Whatever they had been arguing about earlier had to be something big. Gum could only imagine the horrible deed his cousin had committed. Did Hudson want to attend the wrong Ivy League school? Did he start seeing the wrong senator's daughter?

Gum tried to forget about it. He intended to get through Mass like he usually did: pulling at the rip in his dress pants and picking crud out of his nails. The priest went on about how "no matter where we go, we always have Christ," and "we can't take a vacation away from faith." Grandpa nodded along and glanced around to make sure everyone else was moved by the identical copy-pasted sermon the priest gave every year.

Silently fidgeting didn't help Gum's restlessness. His body itched like he was allergic to the air in the church. *You barely slept*, he reminded himself. Lack of sleep would make anyone feel off. It always took a while to get used to sleeping in Cabin 3, but he'd been tossing and turning the whole night, dreading today. Dreading tomorrow. He knew this summer would be a bit awkward; he'd expected that. But he hadn't anticipated this sense of danger. This *fear* eroding his insides.

And it was getting worse the longer the priest droned on.

He tried to do some people-watching. He'd made a bet with himself last year that, by this summer, the eighty-something-year-old organ player would be dead or at least in a nursing home. Somehow, though, she was still playing away with the same big hat and long, wrinkled fingers. The boy across the aisle had a serious nose-picking addiction. The kid's dad either didn't notice or didn't care. That would never fly in Gum's household. Even during the school year, from states away,

Grandpa was watching. And so was God. Both were harder to ignore in Bad Creek. Grandpa's mustache quivered as he mouthed along to the priest's words. The eyes of wooden Jesus pierced through the stained-glass window.

Gum looked at the hanging lights on the ceiling. If they all fell, he would be a goner from where he was sitting. But there were no earthquakes in Michigan and probably no tornadoes like back home, so there was little chance they would. Damn.

When Gum squirmed in the pew, his dad gave him a warning look. It said, *Don't try anything, or I'll drop you off in the middle of the wilderness to be eaten by bears.*

His dad didn't really care about Jesus either. But Grandpa did. Gum couldn't just leave now. He'd been pretending for so many years.

"Don't know why you're so obsessed with pleasing them," Glory had said, after he was late to their sand volleyball practice because of church one summer. He'd arrived sweaty, still in his khakis and button-down shirt. And Glory, everyone's self-appointed big sister, decided this was an opportunity for a lecture.

"Not everyone has cool moms," he'd pointed out. Her eyes narrowed. He braced himself for a rant. How it was totally unfair for him to tell her to check her privilege, when his grandpa owned a freaking golf course. But her expression softened.

"Do what you have to. But you know you can't go on like this forever, so you're basically punishing yourself for nothing," she'd said, stealing one of his candy cigarettes and twirling it around her fingers. "If I were you, I'd just take the L."

But Glory didn't really get it. She couldn't. Her parents

didn't expect anything but her authentic self. She didn't even have a curfew. The Claveys didn't give love unconditionally like the Garrens. He had to behave in church to stay in their good graces. He had to live a Godly Lifestyle or risk being shunned. That unspoken threat was always hovering above him, ready to strike down at any second like a righteous guillotine.

Gum used to envy Glory.

Now he envied the nose picker.

You're fine, he told himself, though he still felt like he was going to burst out of his skin. The uneasiness kept creeping up until he couldn't help but twitch. He tapped his fingers against the pew. This was a panic attack, right? He needed to remind his brain where he was, so that he wouldn't get lost.

When he looked up, the priest was out of focus. The faces in the pews were distorted, unrecognizable. Every shadow darkened as if the sunset were here at ten a.m.

The full-body itch was replaced with pressure. All at once, gravity was doing overtime on him. What was it called when your head feels like it weighs thousands of pounds on amusement rides? Negative Gs? Or was it positive Gs? Gum stood, gripping the back of the pew. He half expected his hand to go through the wood. Nothing felt solid anymore. When he shuffled down the aisle, he thought he heard his dad ask, "Where are you going?"

He couldn't see any faces. Not only was everyone blurry, but they were empty too, soulless as cardboard cutouts or mannequins. There were at least sixty bodies in the chapel, yet Gum felt like the only living, breathing person.

He somehow burst out the front door, down the sidewalk, and into the garden with the stupid waterfall and world-record-holding crucifix. He thought he could ride this out without any witnesses.

He was wrong.

A girl about his age stood in front of the cross's concrete base, staring at him with curiosity, as if Gum were the one who didn't belong here. The color was sucked out of her skin; she was all grays and blues. Her dark hair was drenched, stuck to the side of her cheeks. She smelled like rot.

He froze. Because what the hell was he going to do? All his systems went on standby mode. This couldn't be real. Glory would never let anyone see her looking anything less than perfect. And, you know, *she was dead.*

She was heading for him. Slow, careful movements, like he was a wild animal she didn't want to scare off.

"You're not real," he said to her. His voice was an octave higher than usual. She totally didn't exist, *so why did he say that?* She cocked her head. "You're not real," he repeated with more confidence. Still, she didn't disappear. She was only getting closer. And smelling *worse.* Like moldy flesh and dirty dishes left outside in a bucket for months.

So now he was hearing things, seeing things, and smelling things. *Awesome.* Gum couldn't even hear the birds or the rustling of trees anymore. There were only the ragged breaths of Glory Garren. But she sounded more bear than girl. Each exhale was low, hoarse. The closer Glory got, the more gravity pulled Gum down. He fell to his knees.

Why was this happening? Why here, of all places? He closed his eyes, thinking, *God, I swear I'll actually start praying and stuff if you make her go away.*

She was right above him now. Gum could do nothing as she looked into his eyes and put a moist hand on his forehead.

"Hey!" someone called out.

Glory disappeared, just like that. The only proof of her was a puddle in the dirt where she had been standing and that horrible sewer stench lingering in his nostrils. But both of those could be explained by the spray of the waterfall. He must have imagined her.

Right?

Though he usually avoided his cousin like the plague, Gum felt comforted to see someone he knew was alive. Up close, the golden boy wasn't as put-together as usual. His polo was untucked, and he had ditched the expensive hair gel. Strands of blond hair hung in front of his pale eyebrows.

"What are you doing?" Hudson asked.

"I . . ." What was he supposed to say? *I thought I saw a ghost?* Hudson wouldn't believe it. Gum himself hardly believed it. "Nothing."

His brain was fuzzy, and his body felt too heavy, but he refused to show weakness in front of his dickhead cousin. Spite gave him enough energy to stand back up.

None of that had been real. He'd had a panic attack. An extra-terrible panic attack. Not sleeping enough can cause hallucinations, and the energy drink he'd chugged an hour ago had probably made it worse. He'd been thinking of her, before falling asleep. That was what probably did it. He'd barely thought of Glory for the past year, but now that he was in Bad Creek again, it was like his brain felt guilty for not mourning this whole time. Did that make him a bad friend? Probably. Did that make Glory Garren a ghost?

Of course not.

Gum didn't subscribe to his family's version of the afterlife. He couldn't fathom a loving God sending people into a never-ending pit of torment because they worshipped differently or went to first base before marriage or—*gasp*, even worse—were gay. Hell was a definite no, and heaven was still iffy. Even if people's souls (or essences, or whatever) didn't completely disappear, they went elsewhere. They didn't linger on earth.

Once you were dead, that was it. You didn't stick around. Death was like gravity, and there were no exceptions. Not if you asked real nicely; not if you demanded it. Not even if you went kicking and screaming into that good night. Not even if your name was Glory Garren.

She could get away with whatever she wanted in life, but death was inescapable. It was awful and tragic, of course. He would have preferred that it never happened. But that didn't mean Gum had to feel personally guilty about it. He started toward the parking lot, searching for some reason he could give for having missed the rest of Mass.

"Whatever's wrong with you, keep it to yourself," Hudson said behind him.

"Shut up."

Gum could see his dad's truck now, where Clarice was putting away the wheelchair. Grandpa stood next to them, watching with his hands clasped behind his back.

"I'm serious," Hudson called after him. "Don't bother. They don't give a shit about you anyway."

If the priest wasn't literally right there, Gum would have punched Hudson in his perfect teeth.

The *Dirty Diana* was in even worse shape than last summer, but the elderly speedboat refused to die. The color of vomit, with an unreliable motor and a limp pirate flag hanging off the back: this was Paul's favorite child.

Aidan helped his dad tie the boat to the rickety dock. The gray planks had cracks that worsened as the years went by, like wrinkles on skin. Just one look at them, and Aidan felt a splinter sink into his heel. Which wasn't possible. The splinter was removed a year ago. But Bad Creek didn't care if he had on thick socks and heavy boots. The memories would needle into him anyway, and they wouldn't let go. They'd tear his flesh until they hit bone.

The dock should have been replaced before Aidan was born, but the regulars at the Landings would keel over if anything changed. So they pretended to trust the weathered dock with knots that looked like bruises.

Too bad Aidan wasn't very good at pretending.

"Just rip off the Band-Aid," Paul said, stepping off the boat. His rare attempts at parenting usually included unhelpful clichés, like, *You never know if you don't try*, or *Fake it till you make it*, or *Don't eat the yellow snow*.

Paul had a sunburn so deep, it made Aidan—who never burned—wince in pity. At first glance, it was hard to tell that he was Aidan's father. Aidan was lanky and shades of gold, while Paul was stocky and pink. Yet everyone in Bad Creek swore Aidan was the spitting image of his dad when Paul was a teenager.

Paul held his store-bought cookies under his arm, waiting for his son to get off the boat already.

Aidan wasn't going anywhere.

"I'm sure your friends miss you," Paul coaxed.

Aidan pretended he couldn't hear his dad's voice over the roar of motors and someone's radio blasting country music. A Jet Ski zipped by, pulling children on an inner tube.

Yeah, maybe they would miss him, but not as much as they missed Glory. Aidan didn't have the power to leave a void like her. No one could. Even if the Disasters claimed to miss him, it would be missing the *idea* of him. The Aidan who lived in their heads stopped being real a long time ago. And now that Glory was gone, there was no point in keeping up the act.

"We had a deal," Paul reminded him.

The deal was enticing at first: stay in Bad Creek for four days, and he could fly back to his mom's house in California early. He had three days left.

The thing is, he wouldn't have agreed to it if he knew his dad would force him to participate.

Aidan groaned and stepped off the boat.

The cookout had always been his least favorite part of vacation. The old ladies felt entitled to grandmotherly chitchat and would comment on how much he had grown from last year. Little kids would run around wild, knocking into him while he tried to drip ketchup on his hamburger. He would only be safe when the Disasters formed their own camp away from the rest of the party. They would sit on the Garrens' old quilt and talk about more interesting things than the adults did. Well, Aidan would *listen* to them talk. They hardly ever asked for his input, so he'd stopped giving it.

The Richardsons rolled up in their golf cart. The basset hound in the backseat stared at Aidan unblinking, and so did its owners. Paul backed away. Aidan wasn't so lucky: Mr. Richardson clasped his old, wrinkled hands on him. Now he couldn't escape. Let the conversational chokehold begin.

The elderly couple asked him about grades (straight As) and the weather in California (exactly what you think it is). They criticized his all-black outfit, and Mrs. Richardson asked if he was still in his "goth phase" and Mr. Richardson said there were support groups for that. As always, they asked if he was "going steady" with anyone.

Bad Creek took another bite out of Aidan's brain.

This place had always been powered by déjà vu. It was a time loop. Same people. Same traditions. Same old music. Same old boats. Every summer, the line between now and then turned murky. There was a dam in Aidan's head capable of separating the past and present, but since Glory's drowning, the dam had flooded.

Are you going steady with anyone? Mrs. Richardson's voice echoed in his ear. Aidan was taken back to the last time she had asked the same question. Suddenly it was sunnier. He had that splinter in his heel. He had tried to pull it out that morning, but he couldn't, and he hadn't wanted to ruin anyone's day by asking for someone to yank it out for him. So he put his weight on the other leg.

"Uh . . ." Aidan didn't know how to answer the Richardsons back then. The wrong person could hear, and it would turn into a problem. He truthfully didn't know if he had a girlfriend. The word hadn't been said out loud yet.

Then he'd been rescued. Glory had grabbed his hand and whisked him away without a word. She never engaged in small talk. Perhaps she was excused from it because the more conservative regulars considered her moms an abomination. Aidan hated that he and his friends were always considered an extension of their parents. He had his mother's height and curls and complexion. He looked nothing like his dad, yet Bad Creek doctrine required him to be seen as a mini-Paul. Aidan couldn't imagine his mom making small talk with these people every summer. He was too young to know what really went down in the divorce, but he had to guess that Paul's obsession with this place had something to do with it. She had the right idea to stay in California. Aidan never got that option.

"Let's go to the beach," Glory had said.

"What about Iris and Gum?"

He looked to the edge of the open lawn, where the two youngest of the Disasters were already on their quilt, eating burgers and drinking lemonade. They were always an easier duo. Even if their parents didn't shove them together, Iris and Gum probably would have ended up as friends organically. But Aidan knew Glory would have never looked at him twice if it wasn't for their parents. The rest of them arrived in diapers, but Aidan's first summer wasn't until he was eight. The Disasters let him in the special club only because it was his birthright.

"They're not invited," Glory said.

There was barely anyone else at the beach.

Glory didn't bring a swimsuit, so she was still wearing a white dress with puffy sleeves. No one else had worn anything that fancy to the cookout. The campground at the Landings was "charming for its trashiness," according to Aidan's mom, even if not everyone who rented at the Landings was broke. The uber-wealthy Claveys had dibs on Cabins 1 through 3, and rumor had it the Hacknees in Cabin 10 were millionaires too, though they hardly dressed like it. The five Hacknee kids were always running around barefoot, with their mouths stained blue from popsicles.

So why was Glory all dressed up? Was this a date?

She waded into the water until she was knee-deep. She tried to trap minnows in her hands with no luck. "I would hate to be a fish," she said.

"Why?" Aidan sat on one of the towels. He didn't know if she expected him to go into the water. He dreaded how cold it would be and how awkward he would look trying to wade in without shivering. If she asked, he'd do it, though.

"Fish are stuck," Glory explained. "They die in the same place they're born."

"I mean, the lake turns into the creek—"

"Arteries, veins, capillaries . . . It's all the same blood. They're all just swimming in their future graves, on the bones of their siblings," Glory continued.

Aidan flinched. "Yeah, but then isn't the planet just kind of like a huge grave?"

Glory ceased her fish-catching duties to look at Aidan.

"Well, that's morbid."

"Sorry."

"Don't be. You're right. I don't even know what I'm saying."

She got out of the water to sit beside him, so close her shoulder touched his. Glory watched the water without speaking. Usually she was only silent when she was drawing. But she didn't bring her sketchbook with her that day, and all her grand monologues were full of doom. It was day two of vacation, and Glory already wasn't acting like herself. He hadn't noticed then.

Or maybe he hadn't wanted to.

"What were you gonna say to the Richardsons?" she asked.

"What?"

"They asked if you were *going steady* with anyone. What were you about to say?"

Aidan wanted to sink into the sand until he reached the earth's mantle. Glory was fishing for the correct answer, and he didn't know it. "I . . ."

"You could've said yes," Glory said. "If you wanted to."

"Do you want to?"

"Want to what?" She would make him say it out loud. Of course she would.

"Go steady?"

Usually Aidan made direct eye contact with people. It wasn't a conscious thing; he hadn't noticed until Gum pointed it out a few years ago. He'd called it "creepy." But with Glory, it was hard to meet her eyes because he knew if he did, she would take him over completely. He would be lost forever. This time, he let himself look right at her, and she looked at him. Yeah, he was done for.

When they kissed, it was like the splinter never existed.

But he could feel it now.

He was back at the cookout. The Richardsons were beaming at him, waiting for his answer. There was no way Glory in a white dress would swoop in and save him this summer.

Not after Aidan had ruined everything.

"I'm gonna . . . go find my dad," he mumbled.

Paul hadn't strayed very far. He was by the marina, arguing about Spielberg with a guy grilling hamburgers. Paul thought he was an expert on film because he had directed a grand total of one movie, *It Runs Below*. Yeah, some people might have called it a cult classic by now, but originally it was a box-office flop. A B movie with a bloated budget. He made most of his money from good investments and working as a script doctor for other people's movies. He used to be a Comic Con darling, but it had been years since he'd made a public appearance.

"Can we go?" Aidan asked.

Paul ignored him. What was new? "*E.T.* is horrifically paced," he argued, instead. "It's almost impressive how it made aliens boring."

"I don't know," said the other man, who Aidan was pretty sure stayed in Cabin 7. He flipped a hamburger. "I loved it as a kid."

"Oh *please*."

"Can we go?" Aidan asked again.

Paul sighed. "We just got here."

"I don't feel good." It wasn't a lie. His head ached so bad, he could have sworn chunks of his brain were missing. He'd rather be on the other side of the country, but for now he'd accept the other side of the lake.

Paul raised an eyebrow. He didn't believe Aidan, but he also didn't believe in conflict. "Five minutes," he said.

"Fine." Aidan would wait in the boat; it was the only way to avoid people. He started heading that direction, but someone blocked his path.

Iris.

She was heading toward him, still wearing Joanna's hand-me-down Bad Creek merch and her brown hair in a low-effort ponytail. Like the rest of the Landings, she was frozen in time. If this place was Neverland, she was Peter Pan. She had big grin on her face, but Aidan doubted it would last. He had broken the Disasters' biggest rule: stay friends forever. According to Iris, "Friends don't date each other." So last summer she was pissed at Aidan, and Aidan was pissed at her. Glory was somehow above it, claiming everything was fine, and Gum tended to agree with whichever sister was the loudest, so they could go back to playing their games or raiding the marina's snack bar.

Aidan didn't owe the Disasters anything. Their friendship was built on duty, based on what their parents wanted. It wasn't real. He wanted to believe he and Glory had something real, but that didn't matter anymore either. What he needed was a hard reset. To leave this place and never come back. Then the memories would go away. He could start his life over.

Still, if he didn't talk to Iris now, she would make these three agonizing days even harder. She'd show up at his dad's house on Wahbee Drive, riding the same decrepit bike. She always loved old things, especially the broken ones. She was a Landings girl, after all.

"Hey," Iris said, before giving him an awkward one-armed hug.

"Your hair's longer," he told her, which was a stupid thing to say. He should have gone with, *I missed you*, but that would have been a lie. There was so much of Glory in her face. Same big round eyes and full cheeks.

Iris flashed another quick, unsure smile. "I think you grew like eight inches."

"Speaking of eight inches," Gum began. He strolled behind her, still in the same white baseball cap, same cocky attitude. He had chips and barbecue dip sliding off his plate.

At least he could fill the inevitable awkward silence.

Iris got right to it. "You didn't come to First Night Bonfire." The smile had vanished; her dark eyes were accusing as if he'd cheated in Monopoly—which, according to Disasters' rules, was to be punished with burning at the stake.

"Daniel!" A few yards away, a man with a silver mustache motioned with a cigar. Like Aidan's dad, Bill Clavey had his own mansion on the north side, but his children and grandchildren still rented at the Landings, sweating it out with the poor folk to build character or something. Bill showed up in the Landings a few times a summer to keep an eye on his little colony on the broke side of the lake. The rest of the Claveys were standing in a row next to him, all blue-eyed and frighteningly clean. No creases or wrinkles or stray hairs. They were ready to be cast in an advertisement for Making Bad Creek Great Again.

Gum rolled his eyes. "Be right back," he said, before dragging his feet as he followed his grandfather, which stranded Aidan alone with Iris. He prayed for the Richardsons to zoom up with their golf cart again. He forced himself to stand straight, ignoring the phantom splinter pain.

"What do you think he did this time?" Iris asked. Gum was always in trouble—or, more often, *afraid* of getting in trouble. He talked a big game about breaking the rules but couldn't commit to anything. "Remember when he crawled out his window to go on a night ride with us and landed in poison ivy?"

"I thought you were the first one to get it."

"No, I'm pretty sure Gum was patient zero." She sighed. "We should do that again."

Right. Their little poison ivy cult, when they slept in a tent behind Cabin 4. No outsiders allowed. You had to show the welts on your arm to access it, as if anyone besides the Disasters would even want in. Aidan still had scars from scratching his skin raw. Unlike Iris, he didn't consider them happy little memories.

The ghost of the splinter was stabbing his heel again.

"So you're gonna be a big bad senior?" Iris continued. "More drinking and drugs and sex, huh?" That was a Rex line. He didn't say goodbye like a regular person. He gave unsolicited advice instead, like, *Have fun, kids. No drinking, no drugs, no sex.*

"I had a sip of tequila once," Aidan snorted, "and it tasted like ass."

"Wait, when? At Savi's?"

She was asking about *that night*. The night his life turned moldy and rotten. And she'd done it so casually, like they were still talking about camping.

"No," Aidan said, though his throat burned with warm liquor. His head throbbed. Now the oldies country music from the Landings was drowned out by modern pop, the bass too loud. He saw phone screens and glowsticks and the fireworks. After all, there were always fireworks in Bad Creek, even before the Fourth of July.

"And Glory?" Iris insisted.

In that moment, Glory was both dead and holding his hand, and in both universes she pulled away. Why was she pulling away? The fight wasn't that bad. They would be fine. They still had a future. They wouldn't—couldn't—just *end* like this. So where was she going?

"Hey!" he had called after her. She didn't speak as she stepped closer to the water, her red shirt disappearing into the night. Aidan couldn't see her. He could barely breathe. It was too humid. Suffocating. Still, he had followed her, calling her name, stumbling blindly.

"Do you think she was drunk?" Iris asked. "*You* were the one with her."

Aidan shouldn't have chased her. He should have given her space. They'd still had one full day left of vacation; they still had a chance to work things out.

Everything could have been so different if—

"Stop," Aidan said, both to Iris and Glory. But the memory wouldn't play out even if he'd wanted it to. When he left Michigan last summer, he'd done so with missing pieces.

Iris was unwavering. "I just want to know the truth."

The truth? Deep down, Aidan knew the truth. But his mind wouldn't let him remember. If he told Iris the things he knew for sure—the flashes of that night that wouldn't let him go—she'd fill in the gaps, and Aidan wouldn't just be Paul Ross's boy or a traitor to the Disasters.

He'd be a monster.

"You don't think it's weird that no one saw anything?" Iris added.

"No," Aidan said, a little too quickly. "I try not to think about it all, Iris."

"Well, I *can't* just act like it's not bothering me." Iris often confused *can't* and *won't*. That was how the Garren girls worked: their whims were the same as destiny.

"Then keep it to yourself," Aidan snapped. He sipped his lemonade, trying to tamp the burning in his throat. Though he looked away from Iris, he could feel her glare.

"I'm gonna find out what happened," she said. "It would be a lot easier with your help."

"It was an accident."

Aidan had been trying for a year to let it go. Let Glory go. He wouldn't let Iris pull him back in. He was done being one of her lost boys. In a few days he could forget this whole place.

Iris unzipped her backpack and pulled out a friendship

bracelet. Yellow again. Aidan didn't even like yellow, but the first time they all played a board game together he picked yellow, and now he was stuck with it.

"It can't be like it was before," he told her. "Can we stop pretending?"

He shoved the bracelet into his pocket and walked away. He didn't look back, and he didn't slow down, even though the pain in his heel made him grimace with every step.

When Iris felt overwhelmed, she used to sit on the edge of the Landings' dock and dip her toes in the creek, but that wouldn't cure her this time. For all she knew, something would pull her down by the ankles. Anything could have happened to Glory, and it wasn't fair for Aidan to act like he was the authority over the truth. He'd been her boyfriend for a whole five days.

Iris was her *sister*.

After he stormed off, Iris left too. She followed the gravel road, past Cabin 4. Gum bounced after her. In that moment she wanted to be alone, but she was afraid that if she said that, Gum would leave her alone for good.

The grove of willow trees on the other side of Cabin 12 was an in-between space. It wasn't part of the Landings, or the state park's massive trail. Years ago, the Disasters claimed it for themselves. Joanna had helped them add a tire swing.

They kept folded lawn chairs out there, along with cups and spoons they used to make "potions." They pretended they were surviving in the wilderness or had stumbled upon an enchanted forest.

Iris ducked under the long hanging branches. There wasn't much sun here, just bits and pieces of it casting irregular shards of light on the dead grass. The hideout hardly looked enchanted now. The chairs were gone. One mason jar was broken; the tire swing was nowhere to be seen.

The music from the party was drowned out by the hum of cicadas, and Gum asking her, over and over, "Are you okay?"

"I'd tell you if I wasn't."

"No, you wouldn't," he muttered, but then he dropped it, switching instead to a safer topic. "So, you owe me twenty bucks, remember?"

"What?"

"We had a bet. I said the Hacknees would pop out another kid this year. You said they'd stop at six. Guess who was right."

"Huh." Iris had hardly noticed a new baby in Mrs. Hacknee's arms. She could only think of how Aidan had looked at her like she was a contagious disease.

She didn't know where to sit without the tire swing here. She couldn't believe it was gone. Bad Creek was supposed to be a pristine snow globe, safe from danger and safe from change, but it was like Glory took all the magic with her when she'd died.

"Do you believe in fate?" Iris asked.

"Yeah. I'm psychic," Gum said. "You should probably stop betting against me."

"I'm serious."

Gum picked at the bark of the willow tree. "I don't really believe in anything. I mean . . . you can if you want though. If that helps . . ." He trailed off. But she knew where he was going. *If that helps you cope. Helps you mourn. Helps you move on.* He and Aidan both wanted her to be over it. Over Glory. Over their childhoods.

"I just don't think last summer was *supposed* to happen," Iris said, fighting the incoming tears. If she cried now, he'd only use the Sympathy Voice again. "It doesn't make sense. How could no one have noticed her . . ." She swallowed. Her body was fighting her. But she had to say it. She couldn't be like her moms, refusing to admit the hard stuff. "Noticed her drowning."

Gum kept his eyes on the tree trunk, too afraid to look at her. "It probably happened quickly, Iris." Of course, Gum knew what it takes for someone to drown. The same thing almost happened to his mom. But in that case, there were witnesses. There was closure. Even if Beth couldn't tell it herself, everyone knew the real story. There was no guesswork.

No opportunity for a cover-up.

"Do you want to head back?" Gum asked. There. He was done with this conversation.

She thought, out of everyone, he'd get it.

"You go," Iris said, and he didn't fight her like she wanted him to. Gum left, and Iris stayed in the spot where the tire swing should have been. Gum had forgotten his plate on the ground. Mosquitoes hovered around chips and a half-eaten burger.

Iris grabbed the plate and inched toward the edge of the trees. There was usually a mini-beach here, but the creek was higher than it should have been. A duck lazily floated on the dark water, perking up when Iris knelt. It flexed its wings, as if to wave hello. She wanted to believe it was *her* duck, the one with a missing foot that she had lovingly named Willem Datoe.

She broke up the burger bun and threw crumbs into the water. Before the bread could sink, Willem grabbed it. There. At least someone was having a good day today.

"You shouldn't feed the ducks."

Iris jumped. She'd thought she was alone here, but apparently her secret spot wasn't so secret. Hudson Clavey perched on the roots of a willow tree. He ought to be schmoozing with the rest of the Claveys at the cookout. He didn't belong here. The willow tree was Disasters territory.

"And you should mind your business," Iris said, tearing another piece.

"It's bad for them."

She tossed more in in. "They love it."

She wasn't going to let *Hudson Clavey* ruin her tradition.

He stepped out of the shade. He still had that smugly chiseled face, but he seemed less polished than last year. It was probably his hair. The sides had grown out, and the front was all messy, hanging over his forehead. He looked miserable. Gum had said before that Hudson hated coming to Bad Creek. Probably because he had to leave all his private school besties behind. Maybe that was why he wasn't with the rest of his family. He was protesting. Poor thing couldn't vacay in Cabo with his cronies. Must have been rough.

"They think they love it, but it messes up their stomachs," Hudson said. "It's not good for them."

"I've been feeding this duck for like ten years," she said.

"You've been killing them for ten years. There's no way it's the same duck."

Iris rolled her eyes. Just because his grandfather paid for the Second Largest Crucifix in the World didn't mean he knew better than her. Besides, he'd never tried to give her "advice" before. Their relationship was limited to taunting during the sand volleyball tournament and fighting over dibs on the paddleboat rentals. He used to try to tease her, used to ding-dong-ditch her cabin in the middle of the night. But he learned his lesson, over the years. Messing with Iris meant inviting Glory's wrath. It was mutually assured destruction.

"Whatever."

"You don't want that on your conscience," he said. Was that his thing now? Pretending to be a nature bro? As if his grandaddy didn't turn a public park into a private golf course. As if his family's sacred crucifix weren't carved out of a hundred-year-old tree that didn't consent to becoming a monument.

Hudson must have figured that, with Glory gone, he had free rein over the Landings. He was just another thing wrong about this summer. Like Aidan's defensiveness, Gum's avoidance.

"My conscience is none of your business, Clavey," Iris spat.

She tossed the rest of the bread in and left Hudson to watch Willem Datoe devour it.

She marched to Cabin 4, seething. Her first instinct was to rant about Hudson to Glory. She'd roast him to hell, and they'd giggle about all the ways they were so much better than the Claveys. But then she saw the queen-sized bed and remembered, for the trillionth time, that Glory was gone.

Another piece of Iris shattered on the dusty floor.

Cabin 4 was quiet, which meant her moms were still out, putting on brave faces for their temporary neighbors. How did her parents survive the false apologies? The Sympathy Voice? She grabbed the fantasy book she had neglected during yesterday's long drive and curled up on the lumpy plaid couch, trying to think about anything other than Glory and that freaking duck. As the sun went down, the shadows got harsher and it became impossible to see the pages clearly. She was reading the same lines over and over again, yet she refused to turn on the lamp. She wouldn't be able to focus on the words anyway. Not when Bad Creek was crumbling.

Maybe she had wasted her time making bracelets for her friends who never cared as much as she did. Maybe she was stupid to believe that whatever happened to Glory was anything more than an accident. Maybe she was slowly murdering Willem Datoe. She resisted the urge to google duck digestion and tried to focus on her book. No way was she going to let Hudson Clavey worm his way into her brain. This was one of his cruel jokes. Like when he picked her flowers when she was eleven.

Hudson was just another torment. As if she needed to feel any worse.

She was rereading the prologue when the screen door opened. Iris shut her eyes. If whoever it was thought she was asleep, she wouldn't have to admit to them she was having a lousy time. There were footsteps in the kitchen.

"Stop it," Joanna whispered. "Just stop."

"We can't ignore it any longer." That was Paul. He sounded uncharacteristically serious.

"We were *kids*," Joanna sneered.

Iris peeked from under the blanket. Her mom was in a fighting stance, while Paul leaned against the counter. His grim expression did not match his colorful floral button-up shirt.

"That doesn't mean it didn't matter," he said, not bothering to keep his voice down anymore. "That it doesn't still matter—"

"You're probably remembering it all wrong, anyway," Joanna interrupted. "You're confusing it for one of your fucking unfinished scripts."

Paul recoiled. Joanna could do damage when she wanted to. Glory inherited her wicked tongue, after all.

Paul gathered himself, staring at the faded wooden floor. "Jo. I'm trying to help."

"Well, I came here for a nice vacation, and now you're trying to bring up old—"

"Jo. Please. You're smarter than this. Can't you see you're trapped? All of us are trapped. It's not just Beth. All of us—"

Joanna let out a hysterical laugh. "You don't think I already feel guilty enough?"

There was a beat of silence. The screen door opened and April walked in with a blanket wrapped around her shoulders. Joanna's expression softened as her wife kissed her on the cheek. "Bugs are terrible," April said. "I'm in for the night."

"Was just heading out," Paul said.

April gave him a hug. "Good to see you."

"And you. Both of you." He gave Joanna a look that said

this conversation would continue, and exited the way he came. The screen door clapped shut.

Iris closed her eyes again and slowed her breathing. There were more footsteps. Someone gently removed the book from her hand and kissed her cheek. April. She tiptoed into her bedroom. Joanna promised she was coming in right behind her wife. But then the unthinkable happened. It was against all of the unspoken rules of the Landings, but Iris was sure she'd heard a click.

Joanna had locked the front door.

Iris was underwater.

The bare soles of her feet stung, embedded with rocks and twigs. Long grass tickled her exposed thighs. She wanted to stop walking, to swim to the surface, but the current was made of a million invisible hands, holding her in place. She tried to push against it, to swim toward the sunlight dancing on the shore, but she was powerless.

And she was running out of oxygen.

She couldn't shake off the slimy fingers. Though she told her muscles to thrash around, she was frozen. Helpless. She thought of Glory's self-portrait, the black claws around her neck. The fear in her eyes.

No. No no no no.

Her mouth opened. Freezing water poured in, seeping into her veins.

There was no light left.

Just when Iris was sure she was about to die, the hands released her. She wasn't underwater anymore. Though her lungs still burned; her throat was tight. At least she could breathe real air. Cicadas whined from all directions. She was sweaty. Her hair was plastered to her forehead. Had she been dreaming? She was still wearing the drawstring shorts and T-shirt she went to bed in. And now she had mud up to her knees.

Iris was truly awake now. After digging her ragged nails into her palms, she was sure of it. She didn't remember falling asleep, and she didn't remember how she got here—wherever *here* was.

A house loomed in front of her, a hideous two-story structure that was half building and half forest. Weeds jutted from the ground, climbing up the balding roof. The white paint was chipped off in large gashes, exposing a wooden foundation. A few of the windows were missing shutters, and most were missing glass.

She glimpsed the sparkling lake on the other side of the house. She'd never gone in the water at all. She was safe. Mostly. But she had no idea where she was or how she got here. Tall pine trees surrounded her from all directions. Closing her in. She was a gladiator in a coliseum, about to be eaten by some mythical beast.

There was something wrong with this place. Wrong and familiar.

Glory's drawing.

Iris recognized the house's dilapidated spire. The mess of vines. Glory had been here before. She drew this place. Why?

Iris wasn't sure if she should run toward the crumbling house or away from it.

Her blood ran cold when she felt a tap on her shoulder. She knew it. Those hands wouldn't leave her alone. But when she whirled around, she only saw another girl, barely five feet tall, with bleached bangs partially secured with butterfly hair clips. She had on a purple sports bra and matching shorts. Her neck glittered with layers of silver jewelry.

Savi freaking Traxler.

"Oh my God, girlie! I thought that was you!" Savi said, leaning in to hug Iris. She smelled like vanilla and Jolly Ranchers.

Savi was the heir to wealthy Detroit real estate investors. Bad Creek was the site of one of two of the Traxlers' summerhouses. Iris didn't know where the other one was. Florida, maybe? Every summer, Savi brought a new sidekick to stay with her. While her parents were out on their vacations-from-their-vacation, Savi and her older brother, Graham, invited their school friends for parties.

"Where are we?" Iris asked. Savi gave her a confused look. "I . . . think I was sleepwalking. Is this far from the Landings?"

"Oh my God! That makes so much more sense! You were staring at that house for-eh-ver. I thought you were possessed or something. And, I dunno, probably like a mile? I parked the Ladybug by the trailhead. I can drive you back!"

Iris agreed, not that she had much of a choice. A small opening through the trees at the edge of the meadow led to an unpaved trail. It only took a few minutes of walking through the woods until they reached Savi's adorable red Volkswagen.

Iris knew where they were now. She had been on parts of this trail before, riding bikes with Glory and the boys. She had never seen the house because once the Disasters formed their regular route, they stuck to it.

"Has this happened before?" Savi asked as they both slid into the leather seats.

"No," Iris answered. Not in Bad Creek. Not at home. And yet, Iris had made it this far. Even after Joanna locked the front door last night.

Savi cranked the radio. "Does sleepwalking run in the family?"

"I don't think so."

"I'm just asking 'cause I'm sure Glory told you about what happened at our sleepover— Sorry! I shouldn't . . . I'm real sorry for your loss and everything. I never got a chance to tell you before you guys all left, which is totally understandable! I can't even imagine . . ."

"It's okay."

Iris didn't need Savi to say she was sorry. *Sorry* didn't do anything. Condolences meant nothing, even if they were sincere. But Glory drowned at *Savi's party*; she must have seen something. She could be useful.

"What happened at the sleepover?" Iris asked.

Savi spun the pink fuzzy steering wheel. They were out of the woods now, whizzing by cottages and road signs advertising fireworks.

"I woke up and couldn't find her at all," Savi explained. "I went through the whole house. I thought she had left, until I saw her standing by the dock. I woke her up, and she had no idea how she got there. It was sooooo spooky."

Iris nodded. *Spooky* was an understatement.

When she was younger, Savi had the habit of stretching the truth, but by now she must have grown out of it. And even if the habit hadn't died, Savi wouldn't dare lie about a dead girl.

And Glory hadn't just drawn this house; she'd sketched Savi's dock too. Less than twenty-four hours before her death, Glory had captured the very place her body would be found. And apparently she'd sleepwalked to that same spot. Had she woken up at the dilapidated house too?

Iris felt goose bumps rising on her arms. She wished she had a hoodie or something. Her neck still felt cold from the memory of hands wrapped around it.

Savi slowed as they passed the only street with a stoplight. As usual, there was a line in front of Dolly's Fudge. Ladies cooled themselves with giant fans, and kids ran around with squirt guns.

"I'm so sorry!" Savi said after Iris remained quiet. "We can talk about something else if you want."

"No, you're fine! I actually wanted to ask you . . . about that night."

"Oh." It came out as a little squeak. Savi turned at the hand-painted sign for the Landings.

"When did you see her last?" Iris asked. "No one ever told us any details."

There was the crude timeline the police offered. She drowned around two in the morning but wasn't found until sunrise. Drowning can happen fast, yeah. Gum wasn't wrong about that. But she was missing for hours. The cops said these things happen all the time. But these things didn't happen to girls like Glory.

"I don't remember," Savi said. "I was pretty wasted."

"Was she wasted?"

"I . . . I don't know. I wasn't exactly keeping track of everybody. Which I feel so sooooooo bad about, Iris. Really. I'm supposed to be the host—"

"It's okay," Iris said to get the girl to stop wallowing. If it truly was a freak accident, Iris wouldn't hold Savi responsible just because it was her party. That was why the Garrens hadn't pressed charges. The cops were happy to not mess with one of the powerful families in Bad Creek. So no one questioned the cause of death. Everyone wanted to bury Glory and move on.

But what if Savi was apologizing for something else?

Iris couldn't imagine Savi laying a hand on anyone. She also never imagined her sister drowning either. Anything was possible now. And if someone was responsible for this, Glory likely knew them.

"Just try to remember," Iris said. "Anything. Walk me through the night."

"Well. Graham brought over the kegs at . . . six, I think?"

Iris pictured Savi's brother pulling out newly purchased Solo cups. Telling people as they arrived to not spill anything or break one of their mother's beloved glass dolphins.

"Rachel and I got ready upstairs until seven," Savi continued, "and that's when most people came."

Iris didn't know a Rachel. She'd probably been Savi's vacation guest that year. Maybe there were a hundred possible suspects she would never get the names of. Maybe that was why her moms hadn't sought justice. Maybe it was for the same reason no one went off on the Richardsons when they said something homophobic. Why Joanna told Iris to ignore her eighth-grade bully.

Sometimes, to survive, you have to pick your battles.

"Go on," Iris said.

"Uh, Glory didn't get there until it was dark," Savi added. "I was already pretty gone— Oh! I told her I loved her top. It was red and cropped with puffy sleeves. It tied in a bow on the bottom—"

"Was she with anybody? Did you see her talking to anyone?"

"Well, she was with Aidan, *obviously*. I think later they were arguing . . ."

"Arguing?"

Aidan wasn't one to raise his voice. He preferred to roll his eyes and mutter condescending one-liners. But Iris could see Glory starting a very public argument with her boyfriend. She would start a fight with someone in line for the movies if they had an offensive T-shirt on. She never absorbed the pick-your-battles advice. It was the best and worst thing about her.

"Yeah, and she walked away," Savi said. "She seemed *pissed.*"

"Where did she go?"

Savi shrugged. "Don't know. I was playing beer pong."

So Glory was in a *mood* at the party. She could get like that. But what if, after going off on Aidan, she started trouble with someone else, someone less forgiving?

Savi parked the Ladybug in front of Cabin 4. "We should hang out. Like, proper hang out. What are you doing tonight?"

Nothing. And everything. Day Three was when the

Disasters worked on that year's project. They treasure-hunted with Rex's metal detector. They built the tire swing. They drew maps of their own made-up island. They wrote plays and Glory made the costumes. She'd sew pinecones to T-shirts and inadvertently prick their skin with needles. But the blood was always worth it, when her moms and Paul applauded their performance.

Day Three was the best day. But it probably wouldn't be this summer. Glory was always the one who chose their projects.

"I'm busy," Iris said, fighting the spiky lump in her throat. It cut at her soft tissue, stinging her more than Glory's sewing needle ever could.

"Well, you have my number, right?"

"Uh. Yeah."

Savi was Glory's friend, not really Iris's. Glory maintained a huge social circle, while Iris only had so many slots available. Iris didn't want to waste time on half friends who were only good for partying with. She liked her friends to be soul mates. To laugh and joke but also to tell each other secrets. To trust each other with their lives. Iris thought she had that with the Disasters.

"Okay. Keep me posted," Savi said. "And you're invited to pre-Fourth, of course. If you want. No pressure or anything. I'd totally get if it'd be triggering or whatever. It's just really nice to see you again!"

The Ladybug blasted away, kicking up rocks.

Glory's last summer in Bad Creek had more missing pieces than expected. Iris should have figured that if Glory had been murdered, that would mean there were multiple possible suspects. Savi appeared forthcoming. Genuine, even, for once. Iris could cross her off the list. But Aidan . . .

Iris's stomach dropped. He was weird yesterday at the cookout. He didn't want to talk about Glory. Was that why he was avoiding the Disasters? Did he know something?

Did he *do* something?

The Claveys loved dangerous weapons. When Bill Clavey retired, he'd sold his million-dollar property in Kentucky for a two-million home in Bad Creek. He hadn't brought most of the furniture from the old house, but he'd brought every gun.

And every trophy.

They were mostly deer heads, mounted to the walls. But there was an occasional rabbit or pheasant. A single coyote was frozen mid-prowl behind the couch in the living room. Gum didn't ever like to stay at the house for long. Partly because he couldn't pass as a Clavey, partly because he didn't like sitting under the blank stares of the taxidermy.

"How old were you when you got your first one, Grandpa?" Hudson had once asked after a shooting session. They were eight that year. It was the summer after Aidan had shown up. When Grandpa Bill and Grandma Betty had first moved to Bad Creek permanently, and before Hudson was selected as the Chosen One.

"I was your age," Grandpa had said. "And I wasn't hunting game. It was a mercy killing."

"What do you mean?"

"My family dog was fading. Saint Bernard. He was down for the count anyway. It was honorable."

Gum was horrified. "You killed your own dog?"

"I took no pleasure in it, but my father gave me the rifle and told me what to do."

"I couldn't do that. I'd tell my dad no."

Grandpa's silver mustache had fallen into a frown. "I did what I had to. I listened to my father and shot my dog in the head. That was back when you didn't mouth off to your elders."

Since then, Gum had nightmares about Saint Bernards with gunshot wounds. Sometimes it was a younger version of his grandfather holding a rifle. Sometimes it was his cousin with a bow and arrow. In any case, Gum was always the Saint Bernard. He begged them not to shoot. He wanted to tell them there was no need because he wasn't even sick, there was nothing wrong with him. But everything he said would come out in desperate barks and yelps.

That was the last year he was invited to a shooting session in Grandpa's backyard archery range.

Hudson still went, often leaving Cabin 1 to be picked up in his grandfather's Cadillac in the mornings. Without AC, everyone in the Landings slept with their windows open. The sound of the old car's motor would wake Gum up—a constant reminder that Grandpa had not chosen him.

But Gum had tried to earn back Grandpa's favor. The next summer, Iris had tried to catch a wild rabbit to keep as a pet. She chased it through the weeds until it broke out of the woods, right in front of the path of a semitruck.

Gum always felt horrible when he thought about it. He'd chased Iris, who had chased the rabbit right onto the road. Cut out the middleman, and Gum was the one who had chased the rabbit to its death. And Iris almost got hit on the road along with it.

Iris had run to Cabin 4 in tears, while Gum had watched the rabbit lie there, partially flattened but holding on to life. He thought it would be more humane to put it out of its misery. Then he could bring the dead thing to his grandfather and become the favorite grandson, even if it was only for a few moments.

The second the arrow had pierced the bunny's skin, the guilt began to swarm around him. The creature twitched a final time, then its warm furry body had gone limp. Gum hadn't proudly taken his kill back to the Claveys. He hadn't deserved praise for this. Instead, he'd buried it next to a stump on the other side of the road. And he never told a soul.

The horn honked impatiently. Hudson was late today.

Gum's pillow was moist with sweat, but it was his only defense over the excruciating noise. He pulled it over his ear, waiting for Hudson to leave and start his merry little morning as the heir to the Clavey fortune. But the motor was still running. And now there was a new noise. A knock on the door. His dad didn't wait for an answer; he peeked his head in.

"Your grandfather's here for you," he whispered.

Gum's dad couldn't stand his in-laws, but he never said it out loud. It was like, if he spoke any ill will, they would *know.* Even if he wrote it on a piece of paper and burned it, they would sense his betrayal. That was why Gum had waited so long to come out to his friends, even though he knew the Disasters wouldn't care if he was gay. The Garren girls had two moms and Iris was bi and Aidan was from the magical land of Los Angeles where everyone was queer and there was no such thing as church. Gum hadn't thought any of them would react badly, but it was like admitting it would somehow result in a physical change, and he wouldn't be invisible in the eyes of the Claveys anymore. He would be a sick dog that was too far gone to save.

And that sounded way worse.

"He's here for *me?*" Gum asked his dad. It had to be some kind of mistake.

"Get dressed."

His father shut the door without any elaboration. Gum tried to scratch up a Clavey-approved outfit. He was already reserving the rest of his nice clothes for brunch and Christmas card photos at the end of the week. For years Gum had lived to win Grandpa's favor. He'd used to try in school. He wouldn't fidget in Mass, and he wouldn't talk back. All that effort hadn't mattered, though, because Gum was screwed from the beginning. He could never be what they wanted. So he'd given up on winning. He just had to do enough to stay afloat, to not make any waves.

Hudson was the better option, anyway. Hudson earned perfect grades. Hudson's swim team won state last year. Hudson talked smoother and stood straighter. Hudson *was* straighter. Even if Gum was on his best behavior, he couldn't possibly match up to Hudson.

So why did Grandpa want him today?

Outside, the sun bounced off the shimmering water. A gleaming silver Cadillac convertible was parked in front of the wooden dock. Everything was too shiny and too bright and too early.

"Good morning," Grandpa said, patting the passenger seat beside him. Empty.

Gum slid into it, feeling unworthy on the pristine white leather. He pulled at the bottom of his wrinkled khaki shorts. If Grandpa saw his thigh tattoo, Gum could kiss his inheritance goodbye.

But Grandpa didn't notice. As he drove, he rambled about something he'd seen on Fox News: alarming new statistics about young people leaving the church.

"When my father commissioned the cross in 1951, this country feared God."

Gum tried to look enthralled by the monologue about the pitfalls of his generation. He usually got away without audibly agreeing or disagreeing with the religious rants. But usually the spotlight was on Hudson. He wished Grandpa would put up the top on his car. Gum's hair was blowing all around his face, and any second Grandpa would surely point it out, demanding he go to a barber. Call him a dirty hippie or some shit.

Instead, Grandpa kept bragging about his father. How he had forged his fortune by being patient. By being loyal. By making sacrifices. And God rewarded him.

Grandpa drove painfully slow, probably so everyone could marvel at the vintage Caddy. The Landings' side of town was crowded with little rentals, but Grandpa lived on the north end, home of mansions with private beaches. They passed Savi Traxler's pink-and-blue Victorian summer home, the Dollhouse.

Glory's last moments were right off its dock. Gum hadn't been there. He was boycotting Savi's party in solidarity with Iris. They'd felt way cooler than the big kids by playing board games and eating leftover cold pizza in Cabin 4. He'd slept in Glory's top bunk, and in the morning he'd woken up to the Garren women wailing.

Gum could picture the drowning so easily, as if he'd seen it happen. Glory fell in, and a current pushed her under. She poked her head up. Her body would already be going into shock from the cold. This was when most people would panic. But, knowing Glory, she was unbothered. She thought she could get out of it. She thought the lake—like the rest of the world—would bend to her will. This was the first, and only, time she didn't get her way. The current took her again. Either her head smacked into a rock, or she swallowed too much water. Either way, one moment she was Glory Garren, queen of Bad Creek. Then she was just a corpse.

Drowning can happen quicker than you expect. In only a few minutes without oxygen, your brain shuts off. If Uncle Bruce had found his mom a few seconds later, she would have been dead for good. If he had found her a few seconds earlier, she wouldn't have irreversible brain damage. So she was in limbo, a living miracle and a lesson. Gum was taught to fear God and the water simultaneously. He had never gone into the lake or any pools or larger-than-normal bathtubs. Even when the other Disasters would dip their toes in at the edge of the Landings, even on the driest summers, when the water was only knee-high, he wouldn't go in. Glory had always given him crap for not knowing how to swim. But she'd reframe her bullying as life lessons.

"You can't let fear control you," she would say.

But maybe if Glory was less fearless she'd still be alive.

Grandpa drove past a sign for Wahbee Drive, a private lane with one resident: Paul Ross. Gum doubted he would have a chance to go there this summer. Aidan made it clear that the Disasters had died with Glory. Somehow it still felt like she was calling the shots.

If Glory can't have a good time, no one can.

Gum tried to take the thought back. It was an awful thing to think about a dead girl. He felt guilty for not feeling guilty enough.

Trees blocked the sun on the long driveway to Grandpa's house. These weren't the ragged willows in the Landings, but tall, rigid pines. As always, the Clavey estate looked like the freaking White House, with its uncanny symmetry and marble steps. Its pillars reached to the heavens, demanding that anyone who made it as far as the front door contemplate how small they were. It was as if Bill Clavey had given specific instructions to the architect, *Make it equally impressive and terrifying.* And, man, did they deliver.

Gum expected Hudson to be there, warming up. Gum figured he was only invited so the golden boy could show off with an audience. But Uncle Bruce was in the backyard by himself, sitting on the back porch drinking a beer. It was way too early in the day for that.

"Daniel! Nice of you to join us!" Bruce clapped his hand on Gum's shoulder. Hard. Too hard. Either Bruce didn't have much practice being friendly, or he was used to sturdier boys who could take the hit better. "It's past time we worked on your aim, dontcha think?" His lips looked wrong contorted into a smile. Like his son, he had a big mouth with too many teeth.

Uncle Bruce handed Gum the beer bottle. Gum almost dropped it. It was wet and cold and shocking in his hand. He glanced at Grandpa for approval. This had to be a test; they weren't actually handing him a beer. No way.

But Grandpa simply said, "In my day, drinking age was eighteen. If a man can serve his country, he should be allowed a beer."

But I'm not eighteen yet, Gum almost replied. They had to know that. Even if they forgot his birthday, they knew it came after Hudson's, and Hudson was still a minor. A mysteriously absent minor. Hudson wouldn't fall from grace after one fight with his dad. That would be insane. No, it had to be something more.

Gum took a small sip of the beer. It tasted like bread-flavored vomit, but he tried not to show it. He had to act grateful. And he kept acting grateful as they pulled out the bows. Gum had given up on archery before he was old enough for an adult-sized bow, yet they had one ready for him. Or maybe it was Hudson's. They were both left-handed.

Bruce shot arrows into the targets on the haystacks and apologized for being rusty despite coming close to the bull's-eye nearly every time. To be a Clavey was to be humble, after all.

It was hard to believe this was the man who stole a golf cart with Joanna Garren. Did he even consider her when he ranted about the "erosion of family values"? His childhood best friend was queer, but now he gladly donated to politicians who wanted people like her eradicated. Somehow, over the years, Uncle Bruce had transformed from Disaster to Clavey. How did it happen? Did he wake up one day with the overwhelming desire to get a crew cut and go the speed limit? He was all Clavey now, neatly trimmed dirty blond hair and a golf shirt worn like a second skin. When he retired, he would build his own mansion up north. And then, when his son retired, the cycle would repeat.

Bruce gave Gum instructions as Grandpa watched from the porch, though Gum didn't need his uncle to remind him where to put his fingers. He nocked the arrow in place and lifted the bow, closing his eyes. He drew back as far as he could, hoping no one noticed his muscles quivering. When it was time to aim and let go, he opened his eyes and nearly screamed.

Glory Garren was standing directly in front of the target. She looked even worse than yesterday: her skin swollen and peeling in some places, her eyes lifeless.

She's not real. He thought the affirmation over and over again. This was his subconscious. Or maybe it was God, after all, punishing him for his sins. Either way, Gum wanted her—needed her—to move. Her chest was blocking the bull's-eye. He closed his eyes again, praying she would be gone when he opened them. But, nope. Still there, gray and dripping and wearing a perfume that could only be named Essence of Horrific Corpse.

"Whenever you're ready," Bruce said, tapping his foot.

Gum had been standing with the arrow drawn for almost a minute, but it wasn't like he could say, *I'm hallucinating my dead friend right now, so, rain check?*

He pointed up on the release. The arrow bounced off the top of the target instead of on Glory.

"Again," Grandpa said from the porch, voice low and even. Bruce handed Gum another arrow. Glory kept glaring at him. He tried to will her to move. If she was in his head, he should have control of her, right? But she didn't listen. She only gazed at him from fifteen yards away, pissed like she too was disappointed in his archery skills.

The second shot soared over the target, disappearing in the line of pine trees.

"Again."

Bruce handed him a new arrow. "You're overthinking it," he advised.

Gum figured he could aim for the side of the target, but there was still a chance he would hit Glory. There were still a few dozen arrows left in Bruce's quiver. Would they keep him here all day until he hit a bull's-eye? Until he pierced Glory in the heart? They wouldn't make him do this if they knew what he was seeing. Though, if they knew what he was seeing, they'd probably have him committed.

His hands were so clammy he almost dropped the next arrow before nocking it. He pulled back, arms shaking. Glory stared at him, a smile easing onto her purple lips. She was just in his imagination. Why would it matter if he hit her? Avoiding her was going to make Grandpa and Uncle Bruce disappointed. This was a test, and they expected him to fail it. This could be his one chance to impress them. To prove he wasn't just the spare grandson.

"C'mon!" Glory yelled. It didn't sound exactly like her. It was a harsher, meaner impression. She pounded on her chest and said, "Right here! Right to me!" as if she were trying to teach him how to jump-serve a volleyball again.

"You gotta get out of your head," Bruce told him. If only he knew.

Glory was still demanding he shoot her. "C'mon, Gum! I know you want to!"

His breathing was ragged; tears welled up in his eyes. But he had no choice. He let go of the arrow. It sailed forward, fast, and made a loud squelch as it pinned Glory to the target.

Bull's-eye.

"You look like shit," Iris said. She was sitting on the picnic table between their cabins, wearing a Prince T-shirt three sizes too big. With her hair wet, and without her ponytail, she almost looked like Glory. That couldn't be lake water on her, though; she'd probably just gotten out of the shower. Still, Gum shivered.

Iris's attention turned to the Cadillac leaving the Landings. "What was that about?"

"Mandatory archery practice."

"Isn't that a Hudson thing?"

He shrugged. Usually he'd take any chance to complain about the Claveys, but not today. Not when every thought rotted into that image of Glory, with the arrow bloodlessly piercing her chest.

"Can I show you something?" Iris asked. She led him inside, where her moms were making sandwiches and dancing to an eighties pop song. They waved and smiled at Gum.

Most summers, Gum spent more time with the Garrens than with his own family. Joanna and April didn't tell him to tuck in his shirt or ask about his grades, and they didn't call him Daniel. They never made him go to church or feel guilty for existing. They would probably believe him if he said he saw a ghost today, but he didn't mention it. That'd just be cruel.

Iris practically pushed Gum into her room and closed the door behind them, before rummaging through the wooden dresser in the corner. Gum never bothered to completely unpack in Bad Creek. Not only did Iris actually use the drawers and little closet, but she brought extra pillows, blankets, candles, and her Magic 8 Ball. It was a very Garren thing to be extra-prepared, but it was an Iris thing to treat Cabin 4 as a second home.

Gum picked up the Magic 8 Ball. Part of him wanted to tell Iris about the weird shit he had been seeing. Part of him wasn't ready for the I-hallucinated-your-dead-sister conversation. Talking to Iris used to be as easy as breathing. She was always safe. Forgiving. Understanding.

Should I tell Iris? Gum silently asked the Magic 8 Ball. Every time he shook it, the twenty-sided die didn't rise to the surface.

"Your 8 Ball is broken," he said.

"It's not broken."

"Not seeing any words . . ."

"You're not shaking it right."

"I know how to shake it!"

Gum handed her the Magic 8 Ball. She closed her eyes and shook it forcefully. When she looked into the circular window where the fortune should be, her whole face scrunched up.

"You can get a new one," he said.

"I don't want a new one." She cradled it in her hands. For a second, Gum worried she was going to cry. He hoped not. Glory was the one who dealt in tears. She was usually the one who caused them, but at least she cleaned up after herself.

Thankfully Iris recovered. She placed the formerly Magic 8 Ball on the bedside table and retrieved a red notebook from the top drawer of her dresser.

"I found this," she said, laying it on the bed. She flipped through it quickly, flashes of drawings going by as she turned the pages. This was Glory's sketchbook from last year. Gum vaguely remembered the cover. He probably wasn't in this one very much. He barely saw Glory last summer. She was always disappearing and reappearing. Why was Iris showing this to him? *Oh God*, Gum thought. *Does Iris want to use this for the Project?* Couldn't they just make another group playlist or something? Did everything have to be about Glory?

"Look," Iris instructed, stopping him on one of the last charcoal-smudged pages.

The house wasn't well drawn by Glory's standards, or maybe he remembered her as a better artist than she was. People do that when someone dies. You're supposed to hype up the dead. It's like one of the main rules of Catholicism. So why was Glory so much worse in his visions of her? She'd looked at him with such contempt today. Asking—demanding—he re-kill her.

I know you want to, she had said, confirming his suspicions that everyone and God could see all the worst things in his brain.

"Have you ever been to this place?" Iris asked.

"Uh . . . no?"

It was kind of a generic house. And the drawing was so rough, all its features blended together.

"I woke up here today," Iris explained. "I sleepwalked, half a mile from the Landings."

"Have you ever—"

"No. I haven't done that before. I don't think I've even talked in my sleep. But get this: Glory was sleepwalking too. According to Savi Traxler, she tried to walk off her dock last summer." She flipped a few more pages to a double spread of a dock and a girl, who he assumed was supposed to be Glory. She looked terrified in the drawing but still better than how she'd looked that morning.

"So, that's weird, right?" Iris said.

I got you beat on weird, Iris. But he couldn't tell her. He didn't need to transfer whatever was happening to him over to her.

He couldn't deny that the coincidence was strange. What were the chances that Iris would sleepwalk to the exact same house that Glory drew? If Savi was telling the truth, it had terrifying implications. Glory mysteriously sleepwalks to Savi's dock, and only a few days later she drowns at her party. Near the same spot.

Except, it was entirely something that Savi could make up.

Savi never was a Disaster, and Gum was grateful for it. She had a frustrating tendency to lie about mundane things. She was already wealthy and beautiful; she didn't *need* to fabricate anything to get people to like her. It was always simple, inconsequential half-truths too; like she would lie about where her family went to dinner, for no reason.

But even Savi wouldn't make up something about Glory, would she?

Gum watched Iris pull her damp hair back into a loose ponytail. Now she looked like herself. Mostly. She still had this desperate look in her eyes that he didn't like.

"Can I be honest for a second?" Iris said, as if she needed permission. Garren girls were only honest, *painfully* honest. Especially Glory. She would be the first to tell you if you had a zit budding on your nose or if your joke didn't land.

Iris was honest because she was sincere. She wore her heart on her sleeve and on her face. She couldn't mask her excitement. Her disappointment either. Even when she said she was fine, Gum could tell the moment her mood changed.

"I never believed the official story," Iris said. "I think there's more to what happened. And . . . I think she's trying to tell us."

"She, as in . . ."

"You think I'm crazy."

I'm definitely crazy. But you might be too.

"I didn't say that," Gum muttered. But he'd thought it, and maybe, like the giant crucifix, she could see inside his soul.

"There's an episode of *Dark Unknown* where Max Malitz receives messages from a spirit in his sleep," Iris said. "The spirit tells him where their body was buried. And, boom, Max goes there and finds it. Ghosts have solved murders before. What if that's what's happening?"

What happened to Glory was an accident; that had never been up for debate. But Iris resisting the truth made perfect sense. Glory couldn't die like a regular person. Her death had to be special. Supernatural.

Iris's theory was batshit. Full guano. But she seemed more energized than last night. More determined. More alive. How could he take that away from her?

"I think we should go back," Iris added.

"Where? To this house?"

"Glory wouldn't draw it if it wasn't important. And, who knows? Maybe we'll find a clue. But we need Aidan first. If he cares about Glory, he'll come. What about you?"

She was looking right at him, waiting for him to say something. The Gum she knew would probably find a way to make a dirty joke right then, because the Bad Creek version of him was the comic relief. And he had always been okay with that. He preferred that.

What about you?

He cared about Glory, she just wasn't the star he orbited around. And anyway, that was all in the past. Glory was dead. She was really, *really* dead. It was too late; she couldn't be saved.

But he couldn't deny her power. Whether she was a real ghost or a new flavor of Catholic guilt, Glory was haunting him. And helping Iris get closure sounded like the best way to get rid of her. And then, hopefully, the Glory that lived in his brain could disappear for good.

So Gum said, "Okay."

Paul decorated his cabin on Wahbee Drive like a preteen with an unlimited budget. Model spaceships hung from the ceiling in the living room. Collectible cards and Comic Con meet-and-greet photos covered the walls. The kitchen wasn't much of a kitchen because there were more vintage action figures than forks and knives. Vinyl records were scattered everywhere, stacked on bookcases, leaning against shelves, some in mint condition and some scratched to hell. Paul meant to display them properly, but he hardly got around to completing anything.

Aidan had to duck under a screen-accurate model of the *Millennium Falcon* to go up the two flights of stairs to the attic, the only room free of Paul's collection of movie memorabilia. The walls were plain beige. The ceiling ran along with the slant of the roof, so the middle of the room was the tallest and the sides were short enough for some people to bump their heads.

Aidan, of course, was one of those people.

Clothes spilled out of two open suitcases Aidan hadn't bothered to completely unpack. There was no point. He only had forty-eight hours to go, and he'd planned to spend them lying on the bed with the AC on the coldest setting, listening to records so loud, he couldn't hear his thoughts. But this room was too full of memories. Distractions didn't work in Bad Creek.

He couldn't stop staring at the board games stacked haphazardly on the bookcase. The last time any of them were touched was two summers ago. On days it was too hot to be outside, the Disasters sat cross-legged on the rug playing Sorry! Aidan preferred the games where he could make decisions, not the ones where you're at the mercy of whoever shuffled the cards. The only good thing about Sorry! was screwing over your opponent, until two summers ago, when Aidan had pulled a three. He'd scooted his yellow pawn three spaces and settled it next to a red one.

"You can't share spaces," Gum had said. "You have to kill her."

Iris had butted in, "It's the rules, yeah." She'd only backed Gum up because Glory was about to send that piece home and win the game.

"Half the rules we made up," Aidan had protested. "They're stupid." He could have been referring to the sing-when-you-shuffle rule or the five-push-ups-when-you-pull-a-five rule, but really, he was protesting the no-crushes rule, and everyone knew it.

"You can't change 'em midgame just 'cause you feel like it," Gum had said.

This was the summer when his friends had discovered the crush on Glory and tried to dissuade him from doing anything about it. Glory liked Aidan back, but it would take another year for that to become official. Still, the other Disasters had acted like it was a death sentence.

Maybe it had been.

If it wasn't for Aidan, she would still be alive.

"I think the rules are outdated," Aidan had said. "We made them up when we were eight."

Glory had picked up her red piece and sent it back to start. "Well, the game's called Sorry!"

Aidan had looked at her sympathetically. "Sorry for killing you, then."

Glory took the minor defeat in stride. "You didn't kill me. The rules did."

She'd ended up winning the game anyway.

Aidan found Paul in the "screening room," aka the living room. Movie posters covered the windowless black walls. Instead of a couch, there were mismatched theater seats. Paul collected them from old theaters going out of business, sometimes driving long distances to pick them up. He had several hobbies that involved anything other than getting on with his life, and that was one of them.

Paul sat in his favorite of the orphaned chairs. It was bigger than the rest, with a blue-and-green-checkered pattern.

"Dad?"

At first Aidan didn't think Paul had heard him. His father's eyes were glued to the screen that devoured the north-facing wall. The projector was the most expensive toy in the house. Supposedly, it was better than the one at the drive-in, but Aidan couldn't tell the difference.

Paul patted the seat beside him. Aidan knew he had no choice but to obey. Since the day Aidan first met his father, Paul would sit him down in the home theater and feed him a movie that was strange or beautiful or horrible or hilarious or terrifying. It was the only way Paul knew how to bond with his son. It was also the cause of the only fight he witnessed between his parents. They'd divorced before Aidan had been born. They always seemed civil when they talked on the phone, except right after the summer he was ten. He'd overheard his mom chewing out his dad for letting him watch a scary R-rated film, though Aidan didn't think *Silence of the Lambs* was that scary.

"You need to apologize," she'd whispered to Paul during the phone call. "He doesn't understand it's wrong. He keeps defending you."

"He's allowed to like his father, Linda," Paul had said.

His mom had her cell on speaker since her hands were busy pouring cupcakes. She hadn't heard Aidan come downstairs. "I don't want him exposed to that," she'd replied.

"You mean exposed to me."

"You're not the victim here. *Aidan* is." She said it like she would rather say someone else's name: her own. She was the victim. She loved him, and then she hated him, and she couldn't be free of Paul Ross because she'd had a kid with him. And every summer since that first summer, when his mom drove him to the airport, she looked at her son like she was sending him off to war.

She thinks I'll turn into him, Aidan had realized. He decided then that he wouldn't. He couldn't. But he feared he didn't have the power to decide against his own genetics.

His mom would be elated to hear he was coming back early. She also wouldn't ask questions. She wouldn't ask about Glory.

"I looked up some flights," Aidan told his dad.

"Two more days," Paul said, not looking away from the movie. Tonight's film was in Japanese, but there were no subtitles. Paul didn't care much about dialogue anyway. He was just waiting for the kaiju to show up.

"I wanted to make sure we bought tickets in time."

On the screen, the men in suits stopped arguing to look out the window. A large eye stared back at them. Cut to a model of the city, a stop-motion, multi-headed creature lumbering between buildings. Cut to some kind of lab. Beakers of gray liquid bubbling. Two men wearing goggles probably discussing the imminent apocalypse.

Paul turned to Aidan. He probably wouldn't have bothered to face him if the monster was still on the screen. He was more interested in them than in people.

"Sometimes the hardest thing is the right thing," Paul said. "I think you should stay."

He was such a hypocrite. When times got tough, he'd bailed on his wife and son and escaped to Michigan. Now he had become the lab freak monster the scientist accidentally gave consciousness to, forced to hide away in a cave.

The last time Aidan was in this room, he was with Glory. He didn't remember what movie was playing. It was from a time when the credits came first, superimposed on landscapes and orchestral music. Glory had danced in front of the projector, spinning with ease, though she promised him she could do better if she had her pointe shoes on. If she had stretched beforehand. If the song had a different time signature. But it hadn't mattered. He could have watched her for hours, twirling with hands outstretched, reaching for something invisible, while Aidan reached for words. He had wanted to tell her he loved her then but eventually had bitten his tongue. He had thought he would get another chance later.

Aidan's phone buzzed. A text from Iris. He should have blocked her number.

Can we talk?

He didn't respond. He went to the door instead.

"Sleep on it," Paul suggested.

Sleep didn't like Aidan very much. It wasn't a relief, it was a punishment. His dreams swirled with reminders of that night ever since he'd landed back in Bad Creek.

There was the fight, loaded with the accusations he'd thrown at her. The look Glory gave him, blank and empty. Like she had fallen out of love with him right in that moment. She said, quietly, her mouth hardly moving: "What have you done?"

And then there was the void. The in-between. The act that was too painful for his brain to let him see. A heavy steel curtain in his mind wouldn't let him know the next part. He only got the aftermath, when he came to, drunk in the driver's seat of the Jeep. He was soaking wet. The car smelled like the lake. He had lost hours of time, but he could only guess where those hours had gone.

The longer he stayed here, the more he remembered. There was a reason he couldn't access those memories. He couldn't survive them.

Aidan's phone buzzed again. Iris sent him a whole novel this time, rambling about friendship and loyalty and haunted houses and Glory.

The text ended with, *I think we owe Glory the truth.*

If Iris knew the truth, she wouldn't want to hear it. But if she started digging around, what could she find? Would anyone else tell her about the fight at the party? Aidan wasn't sure if there had been an audience for it.

"Who's that?" Paul asked.

Aidan shoved the phone in his pocket. "Just Iris."

Paul leaned back in the chair. "Good."

"Are you going to buy the ticket?"

"Are you going to hang out with your friends?"

So, Paul was really going to hold his only escape route over his head. The credits were rolling now. White letters on a black screen. The movie was over, but Paul just had to let it play out. Aidan turned to leave. He wasn't going to wait until the film roll ended.

"You'll never get this time back," Paul said as Aidan was almost out the door.

Fine. Let Paul have his way. He texted Iris. She wanted

to meet tonight at the Landings. He agreed, for the last time ever. Once Aidan left Bad Creek, he wouldn't need to see the Disasters or his dad again. They all thought they knew him so well. They thought he would blindly follow the rules. But nobody knew him at all, and he intended to keep it that way.

Iris had set her alarm for 2:39, but she didn't end up needing it. She'd spent most of the night lying awake, staring at the star stickers as if their green glow could give her back some of the magic from the afternoon she and Glory had stuck them to the ceiling.

She dressed with the lights off, throwing on her sweatpants, a windbreaker, and her most comfortable sneakers. She wouldn't brave the woods without being prepared again. When she faced the house, she would be wide awake.

It didn't matter how gently she tiptoed from her room; Cabin 4 was determined to creak. She winced at every step. She hadn't planned an excuse in case she got caught. Her moms were already annoyed with her that morning when she'd returned to the Landings with Savi.

"You nearly gave Joanna a heart attack," April had said. "You can't go off by yourself with no warning."

The Disasters used to disappear for hours, and no one ever cared.

Iris closed the screen door behind her without detection. Outside, the only light came from the dying embers of abandoned campfires. The Landings always smelled of smoke at night. It seeped into her hair, clothes, and the threads of her braided bracelet. Weeks after Bad Creek, Iris would leave her sweatshirts unwashed, as if summer there could live on in their cotton fibers.

She stepped away from her cabin and onto the gravel road. Gum was late. Of course. She was alone out here, yet she didn't feel like it. She glanced back at Cabin 4. The curtains were still drawn. She couldn't hear anything but the water lapping against the dock. The longer she waited, the louder the lake was.

It almost sounded like splashing.

She held her breath, listening to the rush of water. Waiting for it calm down.

You're paranoid. You're jumping to the worst-case scenario.

The grief counselor had already told her that.

But the splashes grew more chaotic. Iris couldn't unnotice them. So, fine, she'd play the therapist's what-if game: optimist edition. What if no one's drowning? What if the splashes were just Willem Datoe, trying to get her attention?

If she hadn't already killed him.

Now there was a new sound, one that sapped her blood of all warmth.

A scream.

She knew it. She knew it. Someone was in there, struggling. Drowning.

Iris bolted toward the sound. No one was there to save Glory, but Iris would be there this time. It wouldn't happen again. She wasn't afraid of the cold, of the current. Fate would be on her side. Bad Creek would apologize for the fluke that was last year. All would be well. All would be—

She tripped over the firepit between Cabins 3 and 4 and scraped her knee on a rock. She rolled on the ground, tasting fresh-mowed grass. Pine needles clung to her hair. She couldn't slow down. This was her last chance. She ignored the sharp pain in her knee as she stumbled to the edge of the dock.

But the splashing had stopped. No. It couldn't be too late. She dipped her hands in, fighting the chill of the black water. She sifted through the lily pads, looking for a sign. But the water was black glass. Still. Peaceful. Had she imagined it?

"Iris!"

Gum stood behind her, holding the handlebars of his ten-speed bike. His mouth hung open. Iris probably looked insane, leaning over the water like that. And maybe she was.

If she didn't chill out, people would worry about her. Gum was already looking at her with the Sympathy Face, but he knew better than to ask her if she was okay this time. Instead, he went with, "Where's your bike?"

"Boathouse."

"Roger."

They walked in silence. Iris put her hands in her pockets, so Gum wouldn't notice how badly she was shaking.

Rex's cottage was across from Cabin 1, overshadowed by two ancient pine trees on either side. Directly behind was the boathouse. It was all metal siding, as simple and rectangular as a train car. Iris yanked the heavy door open and shone her phone's flashlight as she maneuvered around all the fishing junk at the edge of the floor, where shaggy orange carpet became water. Rex's boat was secured to the railings, gently bobbing as if asleep. Gum yanked on the light switch. There it was: her ancient emerald-green Schwinn bike. She checked the brakes, desperate as checking a pulse. Perfect health. Checked the front tire. Firm. Then the back tire.

"What the hell?" Iris squeezed the back one again in disbelief. *No. No no no no . . .*

"What's up?" Gum called from behind her.

The ground dropped out from under her. She fought to get out the words, but she could already feel the icy water going down her esophagus.

"My tire's flat."

She shuddered as a sob erupted from her chest. Harsh and sudden as vomit. Actually, she might puke while she was at it. Bicycle tires didn't get flat in Bad Creek. Friends didn't abandon friends. Sisters didn't die. There were no guarantees anymore. The worst-case just became worse and worse and worse.

Her face was hot. She knew her cheeks were blotchy, and the single hanging light bulb above her was illuminating every tear like a spotlight. But she couldn't stop shaking, and the tears didn't let up.

"Hey. It's okay," Gum said. Though he didn't get closer. He actually *backed up*. He was looking at her like she'd showed him all her guts.

"There's gotta be a pump, right?"

The grief counselor would love Gum, looking on the bright side like that.

He dug through a wire box but only came up with firewood and a very old instruction pamphlet for building a desk. Iris stood dumbly in place, sniffling. Catastrophizing. Finding the pump was hopeless in all this clutter. They shouldn't even go out tonight. Aidan wasn't going to meet them. It was over. It was all over.

"Okay, okay." Gum took off his baseball cap and put it back on. A weird habit he had when he was stressed. "Maybe not. But you could . . . use the other bike?"

The other bike was nearly identical to hers except for the cherry-red color. Iris gently laid her green bicycle against the wall and let her hand brush the streamers of the red one. They used to be rainbow-colored. Now they were faded, bleached from long sunny days.

Gum checked the tires for her. "Yeah, see? These ones are good."

Rex must have put air in the wrong bike's tires. He was mixing the Garren girls up again.

"How about the red one?" Gum asked. "Just once."

She nodded. The tears were already stopping, and going along with this was the only way she knew how to convince Gum they wouldn't come back.

"Just once," Iris whispered to her sister's old bicycle as she walked it out of the boathouse.

Aidan said he would meet them by the Landings' entrance sign, though his one-word text reply a few hours ago seemed less than enthusiastic. Still, Iris stupidly hoped he'd come around with enough convincing. Was Glory trying to contact them from beyond the grave? Iris didn't know that for sure. But the sleepwalking, the sketches, maybe they *were* supernatural. She just didn't have proof yet. So it wasn't lying. Not really. It wasn't lying when Max Malitz declared a creaky attic haunted on *Dark Unknown*. He didn't have proof it was spirits, but there was no proof that it *wasn't*. The show was storytelling. And Iris was storytelling here too. Glory was always better at that. She was the creative one, but without her around, someone had to pull the Disasters together.

They turned the corner, and there he was, waiting for them already, looking ghostly under the harsh white of Gum's bike lamp. Iris understood why Glory had called Aidan "pretty" instead of "hot" or even "cute." No, she'd called him pretty like a painting or a flower or a well-decorated cake. His wavy hair used to be blond when they were kids but was now medium brown. By the end of the week, the lighter streaks would come back, his tan would deepen, and the sprinkle of freckles across his nose would return.

Aidan shielded his eyes as they got closer. He looked

annoyed, but at least now he was wearing the friendship bracelet she'd made him. Gnats and mosquitoes danced under the light like a cloud of glitter.

"Where have you guys been?" he groaned. "I've been getting eaten alive for like twenty minutes."

"I brought bug spray," Iris offered.

"Let's get this over with." He hopped on his sleek black bike and pulled in front of them.

Gum gave Iris a look, like he was going to crack a joke but decided against it. Iris swung her leg over the seat of the red Schwinn. It was higher than she was used to. She steadied herself and started pedaling before she could lose her balance.

They turned toward the trailhead.

Her heart was beating too fast. They shouldn't be riding on both sides of the street like this. They also should have worn helmets. Gum's bike had a weak little lamp on the front, and Iris's windbreaker had brightly colored geometric patterns, but Aidan was in all black. What if a deer jumped out of the woods? Iris could imagine the creature's antlers stabbing into Aidan's side. He didn't even want to hang out with her. And thanks to Iris, he would bleed out on the dark road. Dead because she couldn't move on like everyone else.

At the entrance, the trail went downhill. Iris kept her hands on the brakes as she followed the boys, trying to push her intrusive thoughts to the back of her mind. But she kept seeing it. Kept hearing it. The creature's wail, the bike hitting the ground. Antlers and broken ribs and another stain on this place.

She stopped pedaling and let the red bike carry her down the dirt path. The curls not secured by her ponytail flew around in her face.

"What do you think's in the house?" Gum asked her.

Iris could barely hear him over the sound of the wind and her jacket flapping, and the imaginary accident stuck in a loop in her brain.

"I have no idea!" she called back.

"What do you want to be in there?"

"I don't know! A clue?"

It didn't matter, really. Just as long as they went. All of them.

They were going fast now. Iris gritted her teeth over every bump as the trail led them down down down. In the past, when they went downhill, they would let go of their handlebars to see who could go the longest without touching them. It was one of Iris's favorite games, even though her sister always won.

No one felt like playing it now.

The tunnel of trees blocked the moon and the stars. If a hole or a branch blocked the path, they would surely crash—

No. They wouldn't crash. Those kinds of things weren't supposed to happen here. Last summer was a fluke. It was a wrong Iris would right. Not a sign of things to come. She could be a best-case-scenario girl, starting tonight.

"What if there's pirate treasure buried there or something?" Gum said as the trail leveled out again.

"There were never pirates in Michigan," Aidan said. He loved using facts as a weapon, especially against Gum. And Gum would hit him back with something mean but nonsensical. Aidan would fold his arms and profess that he was too mature to continue this conversation. So at least that was back to normal.

"It's right up here, I think!" Iris called. She slowed and parked the bike where the trail opened up to the meadow. The house was a silhouette now, dead trees clacking against its balding roof.

Gum summarized the view. "Shit's spooky."

She should feel safer with the boys there, but in the middle of the night, she felt even more exposed. Vulnerable.

"Is this a bad idea?" Gum asked. "Isn't three a.m. the Devil's time?"

"It's past four." Aidan said.

"So we're safe, then. Fantastic."

According to *Dark Unknown,* ghosts didn't care what time it was, but Iris wasn't going to tell him that. She turned to Aidan. "Did Glory ever mention this place to you?"

"No."

"She wouldn't draw it for no reason."

"I've never seen this place."

"I just thought . . . maybe. Last summer the two of you kept disappearing."

"No one disappeared. We were just hanging out." *Without you, Iris. They were hanging out without you.*

Aidan started for the house.

She and Gum followed him into the meadow. Iris kept her phone flashlight pointed at the ground. There weren't pirates, but were there any snakes in Michigan? The thought suddenly popped into her head and held her hostage. She only saw little garter snakes in Cleveland. There had to be some here too.

Not any poisonous ones, though. But the promise of danger didn't go away. The meadow was bigger than it was yesterday morning. It just kept going, like one of those nightmares where you're being chased down a hallway that refuses to end. Was this a nightmare? Iris dug her nails into a mosquito bite on her palm until she was sure she was awake.

The house wasn't any different. It sat defiantly unchanged, though it looked flimsy enough for a strong breeze to take it apart. She was lucky that Savi woke her up before she went in. It wasn't the kind of place you'd want to roam around in with your eyes closed. Maybe Glory would have walked off the dock if Savi hadn't found her. That could be what had happened at the party. Glory had fallen asleep and stepped off the edge. But no one saved her that time.

"Iris, are you coming?"

The boys had reached the wraparound porch while Iris was still wading in the tall grass. She wasn't even halfway there. She picked up the pace, breaking into a run just to prove that her feet still worked. To prove this wasn't a nightmare. This whole night felt like the moment before a dream turned sour. The signs had been stacking up. The splashing by the dock. The flat tire. Aidan. He still wouldn't look at her. Had he always been so moody?

The mosquito bite on her hand was bleeding now. Iris wiped it on her pants. Oh. Her sweatpants were bloody already. She had cut her knee open on the rock back at the Landings. She had packed flashlights and bug spray but no bandages.

"You okay?" Gum asked her.

"Mhmmm."

The rotting front door was already cracked open. She pushed it the rest of the way. As she stepped inside, her nose was assaulted by the scent of bad eggs.

Aidan held his shirt over his nose. "What is that smell?"

"Your mom," Gum said.

Aidan sighed.

He wasn't acting that differently; she had to cut him some slack. All was returning back to normal. She just had to be patient. For all she knew, the tire swing would suddenly reappear once they were back at the Landings.

The first room was all sepia tones: brown floral wallpaper, yellow carpet. There was a square TV in the corner on a low wooden stand. If Glory was here, she'd know how old this house was. She'd gone through a phase where she got into interior design, using lingo like "mid-century modern" to describe tables.

Iris grimaced at the moldy couch next to her. Someone used to sit there. And now that couch was decaying, and so was whoever first bought it. Abandoned houses were dead people's houses. That was all this was. Not a clue. Not a paranormal hot spot. Iris shouldn't have let herself believe her own bullshit. Her plan was working. The Disasters were together. They were trying to help Glory. This place probably didn't have any real significance.

There could be strange psychological explanations for why Iris and Glory found the same house, like minerals and magnets and frequencies in the ground. The house was close to the water, after all. When Iris glanced out the broken window, she saw moonlight glittering from behind the trees. They were right at the edge of the lake. Something underneath could be the source of the anomaly. What if Glory had fallen asleep at the party and was drawn by an invisible force? That was why she walked off the edge. And whatever was in the lake bed—funky algae or bacteria—it flowed through this whole town. It could explain the noise Iris heard at the Landings. It was mucking with her senses.

And maybe both sisters were affected by it. They shared the same hereditary aptitude, like an extra-severe version of low iron.

Iris wasn't going to pitch this to the boys. First, it was a boring explanation, and second, it didn't *feel* like the answer. It didn't even explain why Aidan got so cagey whenever she asked him questions. But if he had something to feel guilty about, why would he come along with them? He'd been in love with Glory since he had come to Bad Creek. She was it for him; he couldn't have hurt her. Aidan wouldn't hurt a fly, only roll his eyes at one.

He was looking at the collection of records in the corner of the living room. Gum leaned over his shoulder. "Bruh." Gum laughed. "Why does that dude have serial killer smile, though?"

"I'm sure he was hot shit in 1950-whatever," Aidan said. "There's a bunch of them."

"Iris. Be honest." Gum held up a record featuring a black-and-white portrait of a man who looked like a ventriloquist dummy come to life. "Smash or pass?"

"Hard pass."

Aidan sat the rest of the stack of records on a dusty table. "What are we looking for, again?"

"I guess . . . we'll know it when we find it," Iris said. "Glory wouldn't have drawn this place if it hadn't meant anything to her."

She ambled into the next room, where she found a clawfoot bathtub and dirty tiled floor. Not a clue in sight. This place was more sad than spooky. Someone had lived here, loved here. Brushed their teeth in this sink and read in this bathtub. And then, one day, this place was orphaned. Now it just *existed*. Was this what Cabin 4 would become, eventually?

Stop. Breathe.

Iris had to ignore this sinking feeling. She had to ground herself. Nothing was going to happen. Bad Creek had always stayed the same, more or less. A flat tire on her bike wasn't the end of the world.

She scooted some dead leaves with her foot to better see the patterned tile floor, which must have been pretty when people lived here. Her foot bumped something soft and black. She bent to get a closer look. It was a wallet, one that had probably been here for years. She picked it up. Before she could check its contents, she caught her reflection in the mirror above the sink. Her face was eroding. Crumbling, cracking.

Fragmenting.

Her skin was full of jagged cuts, revealing a darkness inside. A nothingness. She'd been the black hole all along.

Iris screamed and jerked backward. Her head smacked the corner of a medicine cabinet. She closed her eyes briefly, rubbing her scalp to check for blood. When she opened her eyes, she dared to look at the mirror again. It was covered in grime. A long crack ran down the middle. There was nothing wrong with her reflection this time. The mirror was dirty. That was all. Brains liked to make connections. They crafted narratives even when there wasn't much to go on. She was sleep-deprived. And now she was psyching herself out.

But then hands wrapped around her throat.

Gum followed Aidan upstairs. He didn't want to be alone in this place; it was creeping him out.

The hallway on the second floor was covered with even more ugly floral print. The wallpaper peeled off in long gashes, some of it curled away like peeling flesh. Almost everything in the house had wounds. Wounds and raccoon shit.

There were a few signs of human activity. Wrappers and bottles and graffiti, including a red pentagram on one of the doors. The Claveys would think just being near one of those bad boys would damn a soul to hell, but Gum knew the star with a circle around it didn't mean anything. Max Malitz, the host of Iris's favorite ghost show, always reminded viewers that pentagrams were signs of bored teenagers, not demons.

Gum picked up a discarded spray paint can in the hallway and tossed it after he discovered it was empty. Aidan stepped around the broken glass and dead leaves.

"What'd you guys do today?" Aidan asked sardonically. "What was this summer's *Project?*"

"Nothing," Gum said.

Aidan nodded, like he'd expected that answer. "You don't actually believe her, right?"

"What do you mean?"

"If Iris was really sleepwalking, she wouldn't get this far. That's *insane.* If she somehow made it out her front door without waking herself up, she probably would have gotten hurt."

"Yeah, but . . ." Gum considered his words carefully. Aidan wasn't quick to anger like his dead girlfriend. He wouldn't blow up or make a scene. He would withdraw, and somehow that was worse.

"The same thing happened to Glory," Gum reminded him. "You don't think it's odd?"

"And who said that? *Savi Traxler?* Are we really going to pretend she's a reliable source?"

"You don't think it's kind of creepy that Glory drew this place?"

"That's not a lot to go on. And anyway, what are we supposed to be looking into? There's no conspiracy to solve. We're not the freaking Scooby Gang."

If exploring the abandoned house had been Glory's idea, Aidan would have happily gone along with it, even if she wanted them to wear costumes for the occasion.

"There's been some weird coincidences," Gum pointed out, though he wasn't sure what he was defending. The doubt inside of him was growing like a tumor. Aidan was right, as always. There wasn't a lot to go on.

If the ghost of Glory Garren was following Aidan around, it would be a different story. Aidan would have believed in it then. But that was it, right? If Glory were a ghost, she would pick someone else to bother, like her sister or her boyfriend. Therefore, Ghost Glory had to be part of Gum's imagination. And surely there was medication that could make her go away.

"Even if, somehow, Iris made it all the way out here in her sleep," Aidan continued, "and Savi isn't full of shit for the first time in her life . . . people sleepwalk all the time. It's not paranormal. Don't you see what Iris is doing? She's trying to turn this into this summer's Project. She's dragging it out instead of accepting what happened."

"You think she's lying?"

"Not on purpose. And I'm not blaming her. Don't get me wrong. It's just . . . I don't want be stuck in a loop, you know? We can't enable her. We can't play her game. Do you get what I'm saying?"

He did. He just didn't know if he agreed with it.

"Let it rest," Aidan told him. "Let her rest."

Glory isn't resting. She's harassing me.

Whether this Glory was a ghost or the sudden manifestation of adolescent schizophrenia, she wasn't going away unless they did something. And Iris was at least *trying* to do something.

Gum moved into the next room, where there was nothing but a nightstand, a metal bed frame, and a mattress that had seen better days. The walls were covered in color, contrasting with the grays and browns of the house. There were more pentagrams and genitalia, but biggest of all, written in fluorescent green: DISASTERS.

Aidan followed Gum into the room. "What the hell?" he said, shining his flashlight over each letter.

Gum's mom couldn't exactly tell him about her old hangouts, but he had heard plenty of stories from Joanna and Paul. Gum knew all the Disasters 1.0's greatest hits. Why did they leave this place out? To discourage them from trespassing? That was never a priority before.

From somewhere below, Iris screamed.

One strained shriek, followed by silence.

They both dashed for the stairs.

As Gum reached the bottom, he heard a violent noise behind him. Not Iris this time. It was a crack, followed by a strangled cry. Gum whirled around. Aidan was still right behind him, but on the third-to-last step the wood had splintered, and his leg was engulfed by the broken staircase as if their childhood fears about quicksand had come true.

Aidan grimaced as he tried to pull himself free.

"I'm fine," he said. "Go find Iris."

Then Aidan was out of focus. Enveloped into a fog. Gum's vision turned to frosted glass.

There was a cold chill, tickling the back of his neck.

Of course Glory would show up here. The house matched her new appearance, filthy and decaying and empty. She stood in the foyer, watching them. The water droplets falling from her skirt were in high definition, sparkling under the glow of Gum's flashlight. He heard each drop plop to the floor, louder than a gunshot.

She projectile-vomited muddy water out of her cracked lips, then smiled, pleased with herself. She was trying to freak him out and knew it was working, just like she knew when her mean comments were getting under his skin.

"It's already too late," she taunted. Too late for what? Iris wasn't screaming anymore, which could be a good sign or a very, very bad one.

Glory didn't elaborate. She flickered out of existence, once again leaving a puddle of water behind. Gum's brain felt heavy. Vertigo threatened him with every step.

It's already too late.

He turned the corner, not sure what to expect, not letting his thoughts even go there. The bathroom door hung open.

Iris was splayed out on the floor, still alive.

"Are you okay?" he asked her. Gum had to hold on to the doorframe to keep his balance. If Glory disappeared, why did he still feel like shit?

"It's here," Iris said.

Not *she's* here. *It's* here.

He heard a splash. The claw-foot bathtub was filling. The faucet wasn't on, but the dark water was rising anyway. *Glory,* he thought. She hadn't left, after all. But the rotting face that emerged from the muddy water wasn't Glory's. The strange girl sat up and glared at him from the tub. There was no color in the room except for her light blue eyes.

"I felt its hands on my throat," Iris added. "Like in the drawing."

"Wait, you see her too?" Gum whispered.

"See *what?*"

Gum shouldn't have said anything. He should have willed the girl away. Counted to ten and thought of his happy place. But now he was paralyzed. The girl in the tub wouldn't take her accusing eyes off him. She looked so angry. Like she wanted him dead.

"See what?" Iris repeated.

Gum tried to think of something funny to say. If he could distract Iris, he could pretend he wasn't scared. But more water was pouring out of the bathtub, smelling worse than the creek usually did. There were dead fish plopping to the tiled floor too. Iris's sneakers were drenched, though she didn't seem to notice. The ghost girl was older than Gum, maybe in her early twenties. Her bob was coated in green goo, her mouth frozen in a snarl.

Was that why Glory disappeared? To make room in the house for another rotting girl?

"Gum?" Iris asked. "What's wrong?"

"There's a girl in the bathtub."

Iris whipped her head in that direction, but before she could spot her, the girl silently dipped back under. Water stopped leaking.

"I don't see anything," Iris said.

"She's . . . gone now," Gum said, though he wasn't entirely sure. There were still dead fish and driftwood covering the floor. Iris's sweatpants were soaked up to the knees.

"I felt something in here," Iris explained. "It grabbed my neck. You think it was her?"

They needed to get out of there. Any second, the girl could reach out her decaying fingers and drag Iris down with her.

"Can we get out of this room? Please?" he whispered.

Iris put something in her back pocket. "Uh, yeah. Yeah, okay."

Once they closed the door behind them, the air felt lighter. His vision was crisper.

"What did she look like?" Iris asked.

"Like . . ."

Like Glory. Wrong hair, wrong face, wrong eyes. But same vindictive anger. The same stench. He couldn't tell Iris that. According to Aidan, that would be enabling. If Gum's visions were only delusions, he could make Iris worse. He remembered there was a French word for that. A shared psychosis between two people. Folie à deux, like the Fall Out Boy album.

Aidan was scowling like he would be graded for it. "What the fuck happened?" he demanded, having finally yanked his leg out of the staircase. Blood trickled onto his boots.

"This place is haunted," Iris said. "Gum saw a ghost."

Aidan looked at Gum as if to say, *She's your problem now.*

"Do you need me to tie a tourniquet?" Gum joked. He still had goose bumps everywhere. The awful smell had faded, but it lingered. Rust and waterlogged wood and rotten eggs.

Aidan responded with a very serious, "No," and started toward the door. "Let's get out of here."

Gum gladly followed him, but stopped when Iris said, "Wait." He looked over his shoulder. She hadn't moved, but her clothes were dry. Perhaps they'd always been dry.

"We didn't check every room," she said.

Aidan groaned. "So what? You saw your ghost, what else do you want?"

"I didn't *see* anything yet." Before Aidan could protest further, she disappeared through a doorway, going deeper into the house.

"Fucking great," Aidan said under his breath. It was directed at Gum. But Iris had always been like this, wanting to stay up one more hour. Watch one more movie. Play one more game. It was Glory who decided when the night was over.

The next room featured no dead girls, only a sagging dining room table and rickety chairs. Iris ran her hands over the moth-eaten tablecloth. She picked at the bones of dead flowers in a dusty vase, staring at them like she did her Magic 8 Ball. She moved toward the cracked glass of the patio doors, and Aidan gave Gum another glare for good measure.

"What is that?" Iris asked suddenly.

She tore the double doors open, their hinges whining in protest. At first Gum saw nothing out there but the moonlight shimmering on the lake. There was no beach, just overgrown, spindly weeds at the edge of the water, and a dead tree with gnarled roots, choked by the barbed-wire-looking vines. Iris ran up to it, grabbing at the vines, until Gum noticed the carving on the trunk.

It looked like cross with added flair. Two crescents jutted out from either side of its arms, like tree branches or antlers, too symmetrical to be accidental. Iris glanced back at them breathlessly, satisfaction creeping on her face.

Aidan crossed his arms. Of course he had to think it was too convenient. Maybe Joanna had told Iris about this place. She could have gotten the creepy cross from a movie, or perhaps she'd researched ancient folk symbols. Maybe it was from an episode of *Dark Unknown* she hadn't force-fed Gum yet.

But the dread in the pit of Gum's stomach said otherwise.

Iris shifted her phone's flashlight down the trunk. "I think there's something by the roots."

She rolled up the sleeves of her windbreaker and dug at the base, pushing aside black dirt until she revealed a tiny metal box. Light pink, with remnants of a floral design flaked with gold.

"Holy shit," she said. "Looks like a jewelry box." She used the lightest touch as she pulled open the lid, like she was an archaeologist opening an ancient sarcophagus. They said those tombs in Egypt were cursed. Gum wanted to scream, *No!* But she wouldn't have listened if he had. This was her buried treasure. She pulled out a little book.

Aidan's eyes flicked over to Gum as if to ask, *Are you falling for this?*

Iris's whole theory had started with Glory's sketchbook, which she'd found in a secret compartment in her cabin. Was that just round one, and now she was leveling up to planting "clues" in other places, creating a grander conspiracy? The drawings hardly looked like Glory's hand. Iris could have taken up art over the past year, until her skills had nearly caught up with her sister's.

Gum didn't know what to think. He was about to implode from the indecision.

Iris flipped through the book. "Looks like an old Bible." She stuck her hand into the box again, pulling out a hairbrush with hair included. Not Iris's, that was for sure. When Gum looked closer at it, the hair was fine, blond. Next, she revealed a golden pin, shaped like a flower, and a wrinkled black-and-white photograph.

"Probably some time capsule," Aidan suggested. He probably expected Gum to back him up, but Gum was too busy trying not to hyperventilate.

The photo looked torn from a high school yearbook. The subject had a big, toothy smile like an old Hollywood actress, with fluffy blonde hair framed around her pointy chin. Her eyes were intense, light with heavy lashes. She wasn't as decayed in this version. Wasn't as empty yet. But it was still her. The girl from the bathtub.

Gum wanted to puke.

"I saw her," he admitted.

Aidan looked at him as if betrayed, but rationality wouldn't help them anymore. How could Gum's brain invent this girl before he saw her photo? Aidan pretended he was more mature because he was the second oldest. Because he was from the West Coast where everyone was more "cultured." But he had it wrong. He had it so wrong.

It wasn't that Gum was picking Iris's side, anyway. He was on *Glory's* side. They all should be on Glory's side, trying to solve what happened, to get closure. To move on.

Iris snapped a picture of the symbol on the tree and started to stash the stuff into her backpack.

"Maybe you shouldn't take anything," Aidan told her.

"You think it's haunted?" Iris asked with a little too much excitement.

"Thought you didn't believe in that stuff," Gum added.

Aidan shrugged. "I don't, it's just . . . Whatever. Do what you want."

As they trudged back through the meadow, Iris demanded details. How did the bathtub girl look, sound, smell? *Awful, thanks for reminding me.*

"I don't get why you're the one who saw her," Iris said after the barrage. "I mean, it's not like you've seen a ghost before, right?"

"No," Gum said automatically. Once the lie was out, he couldn't put it back in. Iris wouldn't want to know what Glory had become. He was doing her a favor.

There was no name on the photograph. No date. They didn't know whose house it was. But it had to belong to that girl. She'd died—maybe drowned in her bathtub—and was stuck rotting along with the place.

So if this girl was a ghost, then Glory was too. But Gum saw Glory all over Bad Creek; she wasn't trapped in one spot. Why was she determined to show up at the worst times? Why was she acting so weird?

And why, of all people, was she haunting him?

No one said a word as they rode home, the sun beginning to peek through the trees. Their soundtrack became bike pedals and the chorus of mourning doves. They stayed together until they reached the trailhead, then Aidan turned and left them without saying goodbye.

Only a few souls were awake in the Landings. Fishermen filling their boats with gasoline. The Richardsons patrolling on their golf cart. Iris had pulled an all-nighter but only now realized she was exhausted. Gum dragged his bike with his eyes down, like the rising sun was too much for him. It was so bright, it looked like the lake was on fire.

Apparently Gum had seen a ghost. A real, whole specter, more than a flicker in a mirror or invisible sensations. He'd sounded terrified, but Iris couldn't help but envy him. It wasn't fair at all. She was the one who cared the most about the unseen world. She religiously watched every season of *Dark*

Unknown. She'd been the last of them to still believe in fairies and mermaids and Bigfoot. Her neck was still tender. She could even have bruises. But for some infuriating reason she wasn't allowed to see what had caused them.

On the positive side, now that Gum had a paranormal encounter, he was one hundred percent on board. They just needed to make sure Aidan was along for the ride. That could wait for a few hours, though. Iris craved her bed, even though it wasn't the usual bunk bed. She would take anything at this point. All she had to do was avoid the wind chimes and stay light on her feet.

Iris dismounted the red bike and leaned it against the boathouse. A few hours ago, the streamers had been sun-bleached white, crinkly and delicate. Sometime since then, they'd become a shiny rainbow. It could be because their color had never completely faded. The darkness from last night had been playing tricks on her eyes.

Or . . .

It was a sign. A good one, for once. It said: things would return to how they ought to be.

"Well, good morning."

Iris heard her before she saw her. Joanna was sitting on the front porch, coffee in hand, stirring it like it was a potion.

At home Joanna would wear funky patterned pants and flowy blouses expertly layered with a jacket that shouldn't match but did. She'd wear chunky heels and platform sneakers, black lipstick and blue eyeliner and a slicked bun. In Bad Creek, she was makeupless, in hoodies and athletic shorts and French braids. In Bad Creek, Joanna looked like the photos of her teenage self.

"Nice of you to join us," she added.

So she was in *a mood*.

Gum gave Iris a sympathetic look and went inside Cabin 3. His dad wouldn't be mad at him as long as his weird grandfather didn't hear about it. Iris usually could depend on her parents to be chill. Her moms didn't do discipline. That was only for their students.

It's always harder with someone else's kids, Joanna would say. But not your own. Not when they're just like you.

"We just went on a bike ride," Iris said. The proof was all there. Joanna could see the boathouse from Cabin 4. She'd probably watched her get rid of the bike.

Her mother sipped out of the cheap gift shop mug with the crack on the handle. "I would just like to be in the loop, ya know."

Iris had to stifle a laugh. Joanna hadn't let her be in the loop about anything lately, and she wasn't just hiding secrets from Iris. When April had come inside last night, Joanna had dropped the argument with Paul. Whatever their beef was, her wife wasn't allowed to know.

"It was kind of last-minute," Iris said.

"Where'd you go?"

Was this an interrogation? Iris hesitated to answer, then remembered what Gum had told her was scribbled on the wall upstairs. "Your old hideout. The house in the woods."

Joanna's eyes flicked up from the mug. "Pardon?"

Joanna had recounted every detail from her summers in Bad Creek. She'd kept journals and passed down stories orally like they were ancient legends with cultural significance. She wouldn't simply forget.

"You know, the abandoned house, right off the trail? 'Disasters' was literally spray-painted in it."

"Ohhhhh." Joanna waved her hand. "Yeah, that was just Rex's old place. Before he bought the Landings."

Iris thought that Rex only existed in the Landings. She'd never seen him anywhere else. If that was his old house, who was that girl Gum saw? The one who might have tried to strangle Iris? Did Rex know her?

"It wasn't really a hangout for us, though," Joanna continued. "We only went once."

"How did you find it?"

Joanna's mouth twitched—the same twitch she got when she was nervous but tried to hide it. Like when a waitress took her order without writing things down.

"Clavey twins found it," Joanna finally answered.

A smart lie. Iris couldn't exactly ask Beth or Bruce for more intel.

Bruce broke away from the Disasters sometime between their parents' last teenage summer and Iris's birth. The Garrens were still friendly with the Claveys, but that wasn't by choice. Everyone had to be friendly with the Claveys; it was a mandatory tax. Still, Joanna gave eye rolls at the patriotic bumper stickers on their cars. They earned no friendly waves or chitchat. And the most obvious proof: Bruce's kid was never one of the Disasters.

They'd dodged that bullet.

Beth remained a sore spot, though. Joanna was still not over what had happened to her. It must have made what happened to her daughter years later even more traumatic. The lake had tried to take her best friend and succeeded with her daughter.

"Promise me you won't go back there." Joanna's tone was serious now, like she talked to her students. "You know, old places like that probably have asbestos. And the foundation can't be safe anymore. There's got to be termites."

Her mom was being a hypocrite. She wanted her kids to be mini-Joannas, but somehow, Iris's first act of rebellion was going too far. *You and your friends did whatever you wanted on vacation when you were my age,* she wanted to scream. *You guys were smoking weed and chugging moonshine and setting off fireworks in parking lots. And I'm wrong for some light trespassing?*

"Yeah, it was gross anyway," Iris said, but she didn't intend to keep that promise. Glory had been there. Glory was the only one she owed.

Joanna nodded, pleased her remaining daughter was a good egg after all. "It's gonna be great weather for the tourney today."

Oh shit. The volleyball tournament had slipped her mind.

She retreated into her room, closing the bedroom door behind her. She wished, for the first time, that it had a lock on it. She stuffed her discoveries under the floorboard along with Glory's sketchbook. The hairbrush, a Bible, a brooch, and the photo. She left her backpack, jacket, and shoes on the growing pile on the floor, then collapsed on the unmade bed. The open window let in all the sounds from the Landings—golf carts, boat engines, and the ting of the windchimes. She had to try to get a nap in. She only had a few hours before volleyball. The blankets were all tangled under her, creating an uncomfortable lump on her butt. She groaned and repositioned them, then remembered what she had in her pocket.

She pulled out the wallet. There was a wad of crumpled

cash in there, amounting to forty-two dollars. She could still try to find the owner, but if she was going to be a rebel, she might as well keep the money. Or at least split it with the boys. She checked the ID anyway. It didn't look ancient like she expected. When she saw the photo, her heart stopped.

Bad Creek's frat-boy-in-training, Hudson Clavey, grinned smugly back at her.

Joanna Garren founded the Landings Volleyball Tournament in 1993. She'd pitched the idea to her friends in Bad Creek, and they had come up with the name for their team: the Disasters. Paul wasn't the most athletic, but he'd tried his best. Beth had played volleyball in school, so she had all the technical skills. Her brother Bruce had difficulty following the rules but no problem with aggression. Joanna had made them all work together. She'd made them a team.

After the popularity of the first year's tournament, it had become an observed holiday in the Landings. Everyone who didn't participate would spectate, lining up their lawn chairs to watch. The winners would be hailed as heroes at the Fourth of July party three days later. Each match was four-on-four, which meant the Disasters were down a player, and their best, at that.

After Iris got a grand total of forty-five minutes of sleep, she put on the same baggy T-shirt she'd worn yesterday, then searched through her drawers for her tie-dye bandanna. She glanced at her dresser mirror. Vacation wasn't even half-over and her body was worn from this place. Her hair was all frizz, and her arms were more mosquito bites than skin.

She tied the bandanna around her head, which made her look like she had bunny ears. Glory had somehow pulled off that look, but not Iris.

Besides, there was no reason for Iris to look pretty. Not here, at least. There wasn't anyone to impress. The regulars at the Landings had already seen Iris go through every awkward phase imaginable. Glory was one who had put in an effort. She had a whole curl routine, and an endless collection of skin care products. No one would notice how Iris looked playing volleyball, even if the crowd didn't have a better-looking Garren girl to gawk at anymore. Iris was supposed to be the tomboy who wouldn't dream of donning mascara in ninety-degree weather. She was supposed to be unbothered and defiantly confident even when she couldn't find a dress in her size while homecoming-shopping. Even when she watched Glory try on endless perfectly fitting options.

"You're gonna sweat it off," Iris had told Glory last year. They were almost late to the tournament because Glory had decided to put on makeup.

"This is waterproof," Glory said.

"I don't think Aidan would even notice."

"You know, it's not bad to want attention." Glory had capped the mascara tube and leaned close to the mirror to brush off the excess with her finger.

"Well, I don't want that kind of attention," Iris had said.

"You will in a few years."

"What if I don't?"

"Good, more for me, then."

Even with the mascara, Glory hadn't missed a serve.

In the end, Iris gave up looking presentable. She couldn't stay in her room any longer. She tied the bandanna like she did every year—double-looped around her ponytail—before sending a text in the Disasters' group chat, suggesting they meet on the sand court in twenty minutes. That should be long enough for Aidan to get there.

Iris still hadn't solved today's first problem. They needed an additional player. Joanna considered herself retired; April abhorred physical activity; Paul was more of a watcher than a doer these days. That didn't leave them many options.

She sent the invite to Savi Traxler before she could second-guess herself. Savi responded right away with an enthusiastic, *yasssss*. When Iris was putting on sunscreen on the front porch, Gum emerged from Cabin 3, a candy cigarette dangling from his mouth, his matching bandanna tied around his forehead. "Are you sure Aidan's coming?" he asked, stealing the sunscreen from her.

"Yes." Okay, so that was a lie. Aidan hadn't answered any of her texts that morning. But he wouldn't miss volleyball; that was their parents' favorite tradition. "I asked Savi to be our fourth."

"Oh God . . ."

"Hey! She's actually super-nice."

"You know we're gonna get our asses kicked, right?"

"I'm sure she'll be fine."

But she won't be as good as Glory. The truth was in the air between them. It didn't matter who else they invited. It wouldn't be Glory. This game, this day, *the whole week* was pointless.

No. Iris corrected herself. She'd find the truth. She'd get justice. And the Disasters would stay together through it all.

There was a sharp wail on the water. Iris tensed up, but it was just a motor. The *Dirty Diana* was pulling up to the marina. Paul called out, "Ahoy!" while Aidan silently tied the boat to the post. Iris felt instantly lighter. He'd come. He wouldn't abandon them.

Though he didn't look happy to be there. He seemed even less happy when she told him about their new teammate.

"Savi, really?"

Aidan had never displayed much tolerance for Savi's Pomeranian energy. Some people read her peppiness for fakeness, even after she'd grown out of her lying phase in elementary school. Really, there was nothing wrong with Savi Traxler. She just wasn't Glory.

"We don't need someone short and annoying," Aidan said. "We already have Gum."

"Hey! At least I know how to jump serve."

"Can't touch the top of the net, though."

"Well, it's Savi or forfeit," Iris told them, and forfeiting wasn't an option. She'd already pissed off Joanna for sneaking out. She wouldn't add "ruining the Disasters' legacy" to her rap sheet. Besides, volleyball was the least important thing on the docket today. She explained to the boys what Joanna had told her about the house—and what she *hadn't* told her.

"Sounds like she doesn't want you to get hurt," Aidan said.

"It's more than that. I have to show you guys something."

Iris didn't know how they would react to Hudson's wallet being found in the house, if they would think it's another random detail. She could imagine Aidan finding a way to sever all the connections she found.

It's a small town, he'd preach. *Probably everyone's been to that old house. What if we're the only losers who took this long to find it?*

Instead, once Iris slipped the ID out, he got serious, leaning in a little closer to whisper, "Hudson was there, that night."

"At Savi's party?" Iris asked.

"Yeah. I'm pretty sure he was." Aidan pressed his hand to his forehead, like thinking about it physically pained him.

"And now," Iris said, "we know he's been to that house."

A theory was already bubbling inside of her. Practically every person into girls liked Glory at some point. What if Hudson had a crush on her? What if he had been hiding his infatuation? What if he'd happened by that house in the woods, and flirted with her there? Glory wouldn't be into him, but she'd like the attention. And then Hudson could have witnessed Glory fight with Aidan at the party and taken that as his chance to make a move on her.

If Hudson had cornered her, Glory could've denied his advances. And then he would have gotten angry. Iris knew the type, the entitled boys who were used to getting their way. A rejection from Glory would have set him off. And she wouldn't have backed down. There would be an argument, and then an "accident." After realizing what he had done, Hudson would have called his daddy to get him out of the mess.

They couldn't talk about that now, though; the Ladybug had pulled up to Cabin 4.

Savi Traxler was dressed more like she was going to play a game of tennis at a country club than sand volleyball, wearing a pleated skort and matching halter top. Layers of jewelry adorned her neck; rows of diamonds studded her ears.

Aidan immediately scowled when he saw her, while Gum began debriefing her on the rules. "Don't trust the ref to call out-of-bounds," he said. "Rex is four hundred years old and hasn't been able to see for the past two hundred."

They didn't have time to practice. Once the Disasters and Savi had all gathered by the courts behind Cabin 11, families were setting up their chairs and blankets in the grass. Rex was in his referee shirt, talking to someone's dad as he adjusted the net.

On the other court, Hudson stood with arms crossed while his teammates joked around. He wore a T-shirt with the sleeves cut off, probably trying to advertise his biceps—which, yes, were impressive, but he didn't need to *show off*. He glanced over to Iris with a smile, as if taunting her. *Remember when I beat you for the past six years in a row?*

Or maybe, *Remember when I drowned your sister?*

Iris looked away. She didn't have proof of that yet. All her evidence was circumstantial. She could try to get more information from Savi, but Savi last saw Glory with *Aidan*, not Hudson. And Aidan had conveniently left out seeing Hudson at the party until now. Maybe he'd forgotten. Maybe he hadn't thought anything of it until they'd discovered Hudson's connection to the house.

Maybe he's hiding something. Just like Joanna.

Just like Glory.

Rex blew his whistle. It was too loud and the sun was too bright.

Iris couldn't think.

The first match blew by in a haze. She still felt like she was asleep. She wished she were still asleep. Even then, predictably, they beat the other team in only two games. One of the players—the middle-aged guy with the beard and sunglasses—was drunk, so it hardly meant anything.

Savi wasn't half bad, but they didn't need her yet. She could have lain down on the sand and taken a nap and it still would have been a landslide. They were hardly cohesive without Glory, but Aidan was tall enough to block anything at the net, and Gum's hyperactive reflexes worked in their favor as long as he didn't hit the ball out-of-bounds.

After winning the second set, Iris watched the match finishing up on the other court. Hudson's team, the Bandits, were crushing the competition. They wore black bandannas tied around their necks to match their name. It was the same group as last year: Hudson, Andy Mills, Logan Post, and Logan's older brother, whose name she forgot. They were all lake-house boys who only dared to step into the Landings to play volleyball and drink on their parents' boats, far from supervision.

When Rex declared the winner, Hudson glanced at Iris and gave her a wink and a head nod. She gave him a middle finger. This seemed to please him, because he threw his head back with a laugh and then said something to Andy, who laughed as well.

For the first time that day, Iris forgot about the house in

the woods. All she had to worry about was beating Hudson Clavey and his smug face and his smug friends. But when they lost the coin toss, she knew the Disasters were in trouble.

The first set went to the Bandits by a few points. It wasn't like her team was making that many mistakes; they were simply outplayed.

They switched to the other side of the court, where at least now they played in the shade. The next set was more tense. Gum constantly tried to fight Rex for his calls, and neither team could gain more than a one-point lead on the other until the very end.

It had to be ninety degrees outside, at that point. Iris regretted not taking a drink of water after the last game. She was getting dehydrated. Her forehead and underarms were soaked in sweat. It was almost over, though; all she had to do was make this serve and hope Hudson and his team couldn't return it. If this next point went to the Bandits they'd win, and the Disasters' losing streak would continue.

As she threw the ball in the air, she locked eyes with Hudson from the other side of the court. And it all clicked.

That was the same stare she saw in the sketchbook—those cold, unreadable blue eyes. Glory had drawn him. Glory had drawn him *dozens of times*. She'd never bothered to draw Hudson before, as she'd never captured horrifying things, like the shadowy hands. Both anomalies appeared in the same summer she'd died.

The ball barely smacked the edge of Iris's fingers and went right into the net, and then she wasn't on the court anymore. She couldn't hear her opponents' cheers or Gum complaining.

She didn't bother to answer Savi when she asked, "Hey, girlie, are you good?"

What if the hands around Glory's throat had been Hudson's? And every time Iris had felt it, was that Glory, trying to tell her?

Hudson's gaze was like gravity, pinning Iris in place. Her heart only resumed beating when he turned away, as if a spell had finally broken.

When Iris bolted away from the court, Gum chased after her. Aidan hesitated. By the time he grabbed his water bottle from the bench, he was blocked by people packing up their lawn chairs as they discussed the game. Discussed the heat. Discussed all the better times that had come before.

It was always *before* with these people. Before gas was expensive. Before *everything got so political.*

The Bandits congratulated each other with punches and dumped water bottles and discussed important plans involving Savi Traxler's boobs and Jet Skis. Hudson nodded at Aidan. His voice was broken up by the crackle of fireworks, but Aidan could still hear him saying:

Go home. You don't want to see this.

The dark lake was behind him, and so was Glory. The

whites of her eyes were big. Aidan wanted to coax her away from Hudson, but she stayed put. Clearly, she had chosen Hudson. Aidan knew she had chosen wrong.

Except that was last summer's fireworks. Last summer's moonless night. And that was the massive lake behind him, not the measly shallow creek at the Landings.

You don't want to see this.

Aidan was back on the court. Sandy and sweating. The splinter had cut though his heel bone.

"Good game," Hudson said, then walked away with the confident strut of a boy who knew he was untouchable.

Aidan's skin had prickled at the first sight of him that morning. Now there was a new memory, shining through for the first time. He hadn't put it together before, but Hudson had *been* there. Hudson was part of that missing hour too painful to access. Aidan thought the blackout was proof of his guilt. He thought Savi Traxler's bottomless punch bowl had unleashed a beast inside of him.

He was less sure of that now.

Still, that didn't absolve Aidan of anything. He could have lunged at Hudson right after he'd said those words, and Glory got in the crossfire. But if Hudson was an innocent witness, why hadn't he told anyone what had happened? The cops would believe Bruce Clavey's boy over Paul Ross's.

There was only one explanation Aidan could think of.

Hudson was also guilty.

And whatever he'd done, he wasn't finished.

Hudson had been leering over the net, like last year, but

this time his eyes hadn't been on Glory. He'd been watching Iris the same way a coyote watches a rabbit.

"Is Iris okay?" Savi asked. She had a tote bag on her shoulder, shoes in her hand.

"She's fine," Aidan assured her. He looked at her carefully, but no new memories came to him. Whatever had happened at the party likely hadn't involved Savi Traxler.

"I hope she feels better," Savi said, ignoring his answer. "Tell her to text me."

She turned and left. But Aidan wasn't free yet. Rex was waiting by the net, staring at him intently.

"Mind helping, son?" Rex asked.

Being tall meant being everyone's automatic first choice to take down volleyball nets.

"Sure."

"Next year," Rex said.

"What?" Aidan asked.

"You'll get them next year."

Aidan didn't feel the need to inform Rex that there wouldn't be a next year.

"Someone ought to beat the Claveys," Rex added.

"Yeah," Aidan agreed.

"Hope your girl's all right."

Aidan's blood practically crystallized. He wanted to fall through the sand and sink to the earth's mantle.

"She's always been too hard on herself. Just like her mother."

Oh. Rex was talking about Iris. Aidan instantly was relieved. Rex was always mixing up the Garren girls.

Even though Rex's memory was scattered, he could be useful. That was supposedly his old house in the woods. Aidan could get something tangible to present to the group so he looked like he was helping. But, of course, the truth would prove to be underwhelming, and Iris could discard the supernatural theories. She'd see who the real enemy was.

Hudson Clavey.

Aidan rolled his shoulders back, trying to reset himself. He got to work on the top loop of the net. "So, how long have you owned the Landings?" he asked.

" 'Bout . . . hm, forty-some years now. But the cabins were there before me."

Aidan already knew that. He had listened to his dad and Joanna drone on about the grand history of their beloved rundown shacks along the muddiest side of the lake. How their parents used to vacation there, and their parents before that. How on the sixth day, God created man. And on the seventh, he woke up hungover and made the Landings because that was what man deserved.

When Aidan undid the knot, half of the net dropped into the sand. "And before that?" he asked. "You lived not far from here, right? Out in the woods, by the lake?"

"That was a long time ago," Rex said. He bent over to collect the net from the ground, then carried it off.

Rex usually liked to tell stories—stories about fighting off a bear with nothing but a cast-iron skillet; his ham radio accidently intercepting CIA signals; stealing Al Pacino's car. Stealing Al Pacino's girlfriend.

It wasn't like him to shut down questions. Aidan remembered

what Iris had said about Joanna's reaction to asking about the house. She was sure her mom was hiding something.

"He doesn't like to talk about that time, dear," a voice said behind him.

Mrs. Richardson. She wore an oversized pastel shirt that read I'D RATHER BE AT THE BEACH. Her thin, veiny arms were on the wheel of her golf cart. Her husband sat in the passenger seat while their trusty fat basset hound squatted in the back. The threesome was always on wheels. It was like their bodies were perpetually fused to their golf cart. A three-headed beast, guarding the Landings.

"Uh, why?" Aidan asked.

"Because of Helena," Mrs. Richardson said, matter-of-fact, as if everyone gossiped as much as they did.

"Who's Helena?"

"His sister."

"Drowned," Mr. Richardson added.

"In . . . a bathtub?"

"No, in the lake. Poor thing. Morning of her wedding day, can you believe it?"

"Too young to get married," Mr. Richardson tutted.

"Too young to die, Maurice!" his wife told him. "Oh, it was horrible."

How had Aidan never heard of this? Before Glory there was only Gum's mom, Beth. But she hadn't died, and there was nothing mysterious about how that had happened. There were witnesses. It was an honest accident. Nothing suspicious.

But now there was another girl.

That made three. Well—two and a half.

"Wait. When did this happen?" That was Gum, standing right behind them. Aidan hadn't heard him approach. He could move so quietly the rare times he wasn't talking.

"'Seventy-two?" Mr. Richardson said.

"'Seventy-three," Mrs. Richardson corrected her husband. "After Martha was born, remember?"

"So, people just found Rex's sister there?" Gum asked.

The Richardsons wouldn't stop their merry duet. "Already dead for at least twelve hours, police said." "It was horrible!" "Poor girl." "He doesn't like to talk about it."

"Yeah," Gum said. "I bet."

After he and Aidan thanked the Richardsons for filling them in, they started toward Cabin 4. Gum, however, stopped right in the middle of the gravel road. A kid with a mouth stained blue from a melted popsicle bumped into him.

"That's three times," Gum said. "Three times someone's drowned here."

Two and a half times, but everyone talked about Beth like she was dead. Gum was no exception. If you asked him how many parents he had, he would answer, unblinking, "Just one," if he said anything at all. He got cagey at the mention of his mom, especially when Landings people said they looked alike.

Aidan could guess the causes of the first two drownings. It wasn't the truth people wanted. Regulars here foolishly thought they were protected by their neighbors, the elements. But the current doesn't care if your great-great-grandpa stepped in the same lake.

Familiarity and safety weren't the same things.

Aidan glanced back at the Richardsons zooming away in their golf cart. Then toward Cabin 4, where the Garrens were loading their minivan. Iris stepped into the backseat.

"Is Iris okay?" Aidan asked. Garren girls didn't take losing well.

"I don't know. She said she is. But she keeps saying that."

"It's just a game. It doesn't matter." Gum nodded. "I don't think we should tell her about Rex's sister," Aidan added. "She'll think it's like a curse or something. She'll turn it into a fairy tale."

Gum kicked a crushed can on the ground. "What if it is a curse?"

Aidan resisted rolling his eyes. "It's not."

Gum didn't look nearly as convinced as Aidan would have liked.

"We can't enable her, remember?" Aidan added.

Gum kicked the can again. "I guess."

"Hudson's involved. It's not a coincidence he left his shit at that house. That he was at the party."

"But the sleepwalking's a coincidence? The picture in the staircase? I saw that same girl."

"C'mon. Be logical. A ghost didn't kill her, dude."

"But my cousin did? Really? He's a douchebag, not a murderer. He's all talk. He'd never get his hands dirty."

They'd made it back to Cabin 4 by then. Paul was on the porch, keys in hand.

"It's Hudson," Aidan whispered. "You just gotta trust me."

Gum hesitated, likely thinking, *Why the fuck would I trust you?* And that'd be fair. Aidan had betrayed him by pursuing Glory. For going AWOL after last summer.

"Ready to go?" Paul asked. Now was time for lunch, how could Aidan forget? Day Four meant volleyball, then Todd's Pizza. Though Iris was in detective mode, they still had to follow summer rules. If they broke any traditions, a fairy would drop dead somewhere.

"Car one already left," Paul added. "Looks like you two are stuck with yours truly."

Todd's Pizza was a time machine stuck on shuffle: neon signs, a jukebox, World War II–era advertisements on the wall, a Galaga arcade machine, and karaoke on Thursdays. Todd's simultaneously appealed to everyone's childhood, and nostalgia brought big crowds, especially in Bad Creek.

You don't need to make good pizza if you're selling *memories*.

The Garrens were already split between the two massive booths in the corner, waving Aidan and Gum in. Aidan slid into his assigned seat in the kids' booth, next to Iris. A spring under the vinyl dug into his ass. Iris smiled. She had her milkshake now. Whatever happened to her at the game had been washed away in lumpy chocolate ice cream. Gum sat on the edge of the booth. He had managed to snag a kids' menu and crayons, and got to doodling right away.

He won't tell her. Aidan repeated the silent affirmation over and over. If he could get Gum on his side, he'd prove a huge asset. Gum had access to the Claveys; therefore, he had access to Hudson. But Gum wouldn't help if Iris steered him in another direction.

The waitress wore a bright teal collared shirt with the Todd's logo on it. "Welcome back," she said with a smile. Either she recognized them or just assumed they were returners. Though there weren't many, the first-timers were easy to spot: they were the ones who asked for directions to the beach and bought hot dogs at the expensive grocery store in town instead of bringing food ahead of time. The ones who had the current year's date embroidered on their merch. They were called the worst slur in Bad Creek: *tourists*.

When his milkshake arrived, Aidan wasn't sure what to do about the cherry on top. Glory always ate the cherry. She knew how to tie it in a knot with her tongue. She'd tried to teach them last summer in this same booth, but nobody else could figure it out.

Iris had sunk into the vinyl with her arms crossed. "I can't do it."

"Maybe you can't," Glory agreed. "Who cares? Everyone's good at something."

"Says the one who's good at everything," Gum had said.

Glory swallowed another cherry. "Everyone's talented. For example, Gum, your talent is being annoying."

"Ohhhh, you got me."

"I'm kidding. Gum, when you're not talking you're actually pretty good at noticing things. You're not a total idiot. You don't need to pretend you are to get people to like you."

"Wow, thanks."

"It's a compliment."

"Okay," Gum had said. "I'll go next. Glory, you'd be nice if you weren't such a b—"

Aidan threw a french fry at him. "Dude."

"Thank you, Aidan," Glory had said, "but I don't need protecting."

"I know but—"

"I mean it." Glory had grabbed the cherry from the top of his milkshake. "Don't hold on too tight."

On the morning before she died, Glory had revealed to Aidan that it was a magic trick. She'd tied the cherry stem with her fingers first and put it in her mouth when no one was looking. She would then make a big show of grabbing a new cherry, secretly swallow it, and show off the pre-tied stem she had been hiding under her tongue.

"I figured you'd be mad," she'd said after the confession. When he'd told her that he wasn't, she hadn't believed him. She'd always known what he was thinking.

Aidan's milkshake was starting to melt. He took the cherry off when no one was looking and tossed it on the floor.

Gum continued to draw on the back of the children's menu. It was the same coloring page since they had been born. He usually used it to play hangman or draw genitalia. But now Gum sketched the carving from the dead tree: a double cross with two crescent moons jutting out the sides.

Iris snatched the crayon from him. "Whoa, what are

you doing?" she whispered. "We still don't know what that means."

"I feel like I've seen it before," Gum said. "It's been driving me nuts."

"It could be for witchcraft. Aidan? What do you think?"

Aidan rolled his eyes. "I think you've seen too many horror movies."

"Yeah. Because of *you*. I wasted two hours of my life watching *Turtlegeddon*."

"Apparently the original from the seventies was scary," Aidan explained for the millionth time. "I didn't realize the one my dad had on DVD was the remake."

"What about the stuff in the jewelry box?" Iris insisted. "The brush? The Bible? It was, like, personal stuff, don't you think? That could be used for some kind of spell. Maybe we should ask Paul if he recognizes the symbol."

Nothing about Paul's movie was real, despite what behind-the-scenes rumors implied. The Ouija board that was used to summon the well monster didn't mysteriously move on its own. An assistant lost it. The lead actor didn't wake up to a pentagram burning on his chest. He just found out that he was allergic to liquid latex the hard way. Paul claimed he had done years of research before creating his famous monster, but that probably wasn't true either. Given that he never wrote another original script, he likely stole the story for *It Runs Below* from one of his friends in film school.

Laughter erupted from the adults' booth behind them.

"Did he ever get the boxers back?" April asked, snorting.

Joanna looked at Paul to confirm. "I think Mr. Hacknee threw them in the creek?"

April leaned in. "What about the flag?"

"Bought a new one, of course," Paul said.

"And we stole that too," Joanna squealed.

Paul coughed up his milkshake, pounding the table as he tried to recover from his laughing fit.

Aidan knew this story. The Hacknees' grandpa used to park his big-ass truck in front of Cabin 10. He was a racist, a homophobe, and a total asshole. He always flew this gigantic Confederate flag off the side of his truck. The Disasters 1.0 stole it and flew Bruce's underwear instead.

Aidan couldn't imagine his father doing something that brave now.

Iris dug around her backpack for spare quarters. This was the part where Iris and Gum argued about which Billy Joel songs to play on the jukebox. They crossed the red-and-white-checkered floor to the far side of the restaurant where the Wurlitzer sat in the corner. Aidan was supposed to go along too, but before he could follow, April spun around in her seat and looked at him. "Thank you so much for coming," she said once her daughter was out of earshot. "Really. She needs you guys. You know that, right?"

She can survive without me.

But what would she uncover without him?

Would she even look into Hudson or would she stay chasing ghosts?

"Uh, yeah."

Aidan peeled away from the booth. He couldn't stand the broken spring or Joanna and April smiling lovingly at him like he was some kind of savior.

As if he weren't part of the reason that Glory was dead.

He was pretty sure he hadn't laid his hands on her, but he hadn't helped her either. He remembered the smell in the Jeep when he'd come to the next morning. He was drenched in the same lake that killed her. He didn't even know how he got home. He must have driven back to Wahbee, drunk and cowardly.

Could new memories justify that? Maybe not. He'd been afraid to learn the truth, but now that there was a chance of partial redemption, he had to know. Then he could leave it all behind once and for all.

When Aidan got to the jukebox, Iris was still parsing through the song selection. "I think we need to find out who that girl in the photo is," she said.

Gum gave Aidan a nervous glance, and Aidan forcefully shook his head. Gum chewed on the frayed edges of his blue friendship bracelet, as if that were the only way to avoid saying something he shouldn't.

Iris's face was lit by the changing hues of the Wurlitzer, green to blue to purple. She stared at the song selection like it was a life-or-death choice. Guilt ate away at Aidan, but this was for Iris's own good. She would be happier when she had someone to blame.

What if it's you? A tiny voice whispered in Aidan's head. *What if you really are to blame?*

"We're getting off-track," Aidan said. "Don't you think Hudson was way less of dick than usual today?"

"Yeah," Iris agreed. "He tried to talk to me yesterday too."

"He skipped Mass," Gum added. "And he wasn't invited to my grandpa's for archery."

"Exactly. The Claveys might know." It was coming together now. "What if it started as an accident and became a cover-up?" Aidan suggested.

"Did they do an autopsy?" Gum asked.

That last word stung. *Autopsy.* It was hard to think of Glory covered in a white sheet, in a cold room. Being cut open and sewn back up. His chest ached.

Iris looked at Gum like he'd just stabbed a puppy. "No."

"Sorry, I—"

"Don't be sorry," she said, though she still sounded wounded. "It's a good question. It probably would have been the right idea, but no one wanted to believe it was anything other than an accident. I don't think the cops even suggested it. But . . . you guys really think it might be Hudson? She drew eyes all over her sketchbook. The same ones, over and over again. I'm pretty sure they're his."

Aidan's stomach did an Olympics-worthy backflip. He had to tell himself it was a good thing. Hudson's guilt meant his own innocence. But jealousy wasn't something that could be controlled with a leash. He felt it bite at him, sucking on his bone marrow.

Glory had drawn that house. And she had drawn *him.* Maybe Hudson had shown her that awful place. Aidan could envision it now. They giggled and twirled around the broken glass, and Hudson brushed her hair out of her eyes to lean in for a kiss. All the suave moves he used on every girl he ever wanted.

Joanna waved them over. "Pizza's here!"

That put an end to discussing Hudson. For now. Iris selected today's Billy Joel song and bounced across the checkered floor.

But before Aidan sat down to eat, he stopped at the adults' booth. "I changed my mind," he told his dad.

Paul smiled like he'd won the Parent of the Year award. "Knew you'd come around," he said.

Yeah, Paul was never going to book the flight for tomorrow. But Aidan was staying out of necessity. They could play detective one last time. Gum could get insider info from the Claveys while Iris could make Hudson nervous. Garren girls were already his type.

If all of this was Hudson's fault, maybe Aidan could sleep better. Maybe he could handle the rest of the week. Hell, maybe he could bear coming back next summer. The Disasters didn't have to be besties anymore, but they could at least be a team. Three heads were better than one, right?

Unless the heads tried to eat each other.

The scene almost looked normal.

After pizza, the three of them sat on the floor of her room in Cabin 4. Hours in the sun had deepened Aidan's freckles. Gum was red all over. And Iris was left with the memory of hands squeezing her throat. Aidan flipped through Glory's sketchbook, considering each page carefully. He barely touched the corners, as if it were an ancient holy document. Gum licked his fingers as he shuffled a deck of cards. He was bad at it. An ace went flying out.

If the bunk beds were still there, Iris could have pretended Glory was just at the beach with Savi or something. Instead, there was that hideous queen bed, too big for her faded quilt. And there were the things hidden under her floorboards. Iris took them out to study them again. The Bible, the hairbrush, the flower brooch. They had to belong to that girl. Hudson was the more viable suspect, but Iris couldn't shake the feeling that whatever had happened to the girl in the photo was connected to Glory.

"You guys want to play war?" Gum offered.

"I'm good," Iris said. Gum shrugged and turned to Aidan, who closed the sketchbook and held his hand out. He reshuffled the cards and dealt them.

Iris would have liked to play a mind-numbing card game, but she couldn't relax. They only had until the Fourth of July to solve this, and that was already four days away.

She grabbed the Bible, which sported a faded pink cover. She checked for any highlighted passages, any bookmarks. Nope. Nothing.

The boys flipped over their cards. "Hey, Iris!" Gum said without looking away from the game. "Go to First Deuteronomy. Verse twenty-three."

"Isn't that the one about crushed balls?" Aidan said.

"Wait? How'd you know?"

"You tend to reuse material. You're worse than my dad."

"Whatever. It's a classic."

When Iris got to the end of the Bible, however, her heart sped up as she saw the inside flap. There was something written in a painstakingly perfect penmanship.

"*Property of Helena Crawford,*" Iris read out loud.

Gum glanced up. Aidan smacked his shoulder.

"What?" Iris asked. "Do you know that name?"

"No," Gum answered—too quickly. He was an awful liar, and Aidan was clearly disappointed in him. How did they know something Iris didn't?

"Crawford . . . like, Rex Crawford?" Iris guessed. Bad Creek didn't have a huge population. They had to be related.

Neither of the boys answered. Gum bit his lip.

What was going on?

"Guys!" Iris snapped, trying to exert some of Glory's authority. How were they already hiding things from her? How was *everyone* hiding things from her? Iris hated being the youngest. She was always last. The last to learn the swear words, to ride a bike, to swim in the deep end. She hated the knowledge that there was more out there but she wasn't allowed to experience it yet.

Aidan shot Gum another warning glance, but it didn't work. Gum crumbled. He spoke without breathing, like if he didn't get it all out as soon as possible someone would hit him. "Okay, please don't be mad, but according to the Richardsons she drowned in the lake in 1973 I guess it was a freak thing and no one ever figured out what happened and people don't like to talk about it."

Iris set the Bible down. Her head was spinning. "Wait, but—"

Gum interrupted her. "They said so after volleyball because Rex was acting sketchy, but Aidan thought—"

"We should be looking into Hudson," Aidan finished. "There's gotta be a way to prove he did something."

"So you guys just weren't gonna tell me?" Iris tried not to let the pain show, but it was obvious. She hated the way her voice slid up when she was upset. Her words sounded so pathetic. So whiny. But she wasn't sad, she was *pissed.*

There was a beat of silence. Gum held his mouth open

like he was going to protest, but he obviously realized there was nothing he could say. He'd been caught playing both sides. Again.

And Aidan had avoided her at the cookout. Iris thought he had come around, but here he was, pulling away. He didn't trust her with her own emotions, and he must have convinced Gum not to either.

"We only have a few days left. We have to look into everything," she said. "If this Helena girl drowned—"

"That makes three times," Gum said.

Aidan shook his head. "Technically—"

"I knew it." Iris looked at the objects scattered on the floor. The Bible. The pin. The hairbrush. The picture of the girl smiling. She looked so alive. Radiating with power. She was the kind of girl who hypnotized a room. "I think if we find out what happened to her, we find out what happen to Glory."

"I agree," Gum said. "I'm sorry. It was stupid not to say anything."

Now wasn't the time to hold grudges. She needed the boys more than ever. But every betrayal was another piece of her carved out and left to rot.

"There have gotta be records of her," Iris said, trying to keep her voice even. If she sounded like she was about to cry, then that would just prove Aidan right. She needed them to know that she could be practical. That she wasn't the crybaby little sister. "It can't be a total mystery," she continued. "Even if people want to forget, there's gotta be something official, right? Old newspapers. An obituary.

What if . . . what if we checked the library? It's only four. It should still be open."

She had gone through archives at her school's library for a book report. If Bad Creek held on to its records, the library downtown would have them.

"Okay," Gum agreed. Iris had a feeling he would agree to anything she suggested right now. But Aidan's mood had soured. He collected the two stacks of cards, putting them neatly in the box. He stood, muttering something about walking his dad's bulldog. But it was just an excuse to leave them.

Iris and Gum parked their bikes in front of the brick building. The public library was across from Dolly's Fudge, so Gum had suggested they go halfsies on a bag of truffles afterward. But Iris wasn't in a very chocolaty mood. Though it was nice that Gum didn't abandon her, she knew it was self-inflicted punishment. He didn't want to be here, and he was pretending for her sake.

A bell chimed when they walked inside. The place looked and smelled like any other library: charming, but a little sad. There was a single librarian at the help desk—a woman in her sixties with spiky white hair. She was plucking away at an outdated desktop computer. Iris approached the desk while Gum hung back.

"Hi," Iris said to the librarian. "I was hoping you could help me with a research project."

The old woman looked up. "What's your name dear?"

"Iris Garren."

"Ah." She pushed up her square green glasses. "Is your mother Joanna Garren?"

"Yeah,"

"Oh yes, I remember her and her gang. They were all such little shits. I mean that in the best way." Then she went back to typing, pressing hard on the chunky keyboard, with each click being more obnoxious than the last. "So sad, what happened here, though," the librarian continued. Iris braced herself for the sympathy. "The Clavey girl . . ." *False alarm.* "I still see Bill from time to time, though. He hardly comes into town. Crazy they all keep coming back, after that mess."

"Yeah." Iris checked on Gum, who was still perusing the shelves. He was standing in the center of an aisle, reading an open book. Iris hoped he hadn't heard what the librarian had said. He always got weird about people talking about his mom. Did Iris get weird when people talked about Glory? No, she made an effort not to. It was everyone else who tiptoed around her. They were the ones who decided she was delicate. They were so wrong. She'd prove them wrong.

"What was it you needed, hon?" the librarian asked.

"Um, newspapers. From 1973. Probably the summer?"

"We have local newspapers on microfilm."

"That's perfect! Thank you."

The librarian led her away from the desk, which Gum took as his cue to follow. After digging out a few rolls of film from the set of beige drawers in the back, the librarian showed them how to load it into the viewing machine. Iris had used microfilm before, so she didn't need a demonstration on how to focus the screen but she let the woman explain anyway, since she seemed excited to show the process.

Iris was grateful the librarian didn't linger, though. Once she believed Iris had the hang of it, she returned to the desk. Iris then began scrolling through every page of the first newspaper, while Gum spun himself around in a swivel chair, playing on his phone. Iris didn't see anything of interest, just news of a new gas station being put in. Black-and-white photos of a new plaque for the giant crucifix. She read through every obituary from June. All retirees, passing away peacefully in their beds. No mention of Helena Crawford.

"So, what are we looking for exactly?" Gum asked.

Iris loaded a new film roll. "The truth no one wants to talk about."

Gum stopped spinning. "That's real fucking ominous."

"Did you know that, after the Salem witch trials, people tried to bury the story?" Iris said. "Everyone was so ashamed. It wasn't till, like, a few hundred years after, when all the accusers and the convicted were dead, that people actually started talking about it."

She'd learned that in an episode of *Dark Unknown*. Now Salem was on her bucket list. She wanted to see the old buildings for herself. She wanted to sit at Judge Corwin's dinner table and know if the tourist destination still harbored his hateful energy.

"What if it's not a shame thing?" Gum asked. "What if Rex never mentioned his sister because he's traumatized?"

"Doesn't make a difference," Iris said. She couldn't understand how Rex avoided saying her name, how he didn't drive himself crazy searching for answers. She couldn't survive fifty years without knowing what had happened to Glory. She couldn't live in uncertainty for the rest of her life.

She skimmed articles about the 1973 Fourth of July fireworks show and opinion pieces about Nixon. And then, in blocky letters—the headline she was waiting for. Iris had wanted to see it, but the words still filled her stomach with rocks.

"Found it," she said.

Gum leaned in, reading over her shoulder. "*Local Woman Drowned.*" Iris scrolled down, revealing a new photo of her. Her curls looked so silky, her eyes so bright.

"*After she went missing for two days, the body of Helena Crawford was recovered by a fisherman near Stern Road,*" Gum read out loud. "*Nineteen-year-old Ms. Crawford was a nurse in training and engaged to be married July 31st. Her initial disappearance was not reported, as her parents, Todd and Mary Crawford, believed it was simply a case of cold feet. 'But I knew something was wrong. She wouldn't just run away,' says her eldest brother, Rex Crawford. 'Lena knew exactly what she wanted, and she wanted to marry Bill. She told me the first day she met him. And she made it happen. But the last week, she hadn't been herself. Not sleeping. Not eating. Said someone was after her.'*

"*Despite the family's suspicions, Helena's passing was declared an accidental drowning. Jeremiah Clavey, local businessman and Ms. Crawford's future father-in-law, claims, 'It's easy to call Helena's passing a tragedy, but God doesn't make mistakes. He has chosen her for a grander purpose.'*"

Gum abruptly pulled away. "I can't stand this shit."

Iris finished the article for him. "*A service will be held at the family's home on Tuesday, from ten to two. Helena will be remembered for her grace, humor, and beauty, and will be missed by everyone blessed to know her.*"

So that was it. No one knew how she had ended up in the water; no one tried to find out. How could one argue with God's will? The only other thing on the page was a report on the deer population.

"So," Iris said, "she was engaged to Bill Clavey, and that's—"

"My grandpa, yeah." Gum used the edge of Iris's chair to spin himself in circles again. "Must have been before he moved back to Kentucky. It's all super-fucked-up," he continued. "My grandpa made it seem like he and Grandma Betty were high school sweethearts or something. No one mentioned a dead fiancée."

"Then the same thing basically happens to his daughter . . ." Iris always steered clear of the Claveys. She knew what they were signaling when they wore their button-down linen shirts, their tasteful beige bumper stickers urging America to return to "family values." Bill was the most frightening. He only gave Iris polite smiles, but if he didn't already assume Iris was queer, he'd still think she was Devil's spawn because of her parents.

Now she almost felt bad for the guy.

Almost.

Whatever trauma he had buried deep down didn't excuse bigotry. What she didn't get was why he moved back to Michigan after he lost his fiancée, or why he stayed after losing Beth.

Why did Rex stay?

Why did Savi invite Iris to a party on the anniversary of Glory's drowning?

Why did Joanna demand to come back this year?

Why did you come back, Iris?

She reread the article silently. She wished Rex had been a little more specific when he mentioned his sister not acting like herself. Not sleeping and not eating could have meant she was depressed. But what if she had been sleepwalking too?

"It seems like a bunch of old families," Gum suggested. "I mean, the Claveys basically founded the place and Rex has been here forever. Your mom's grandma stayed here too, right? Whatever it is doesn't seem to be targeting tourists."

Iris stared at the photo from the paper. Helena had a beauty queen's smile. Long lashes and milky smooth skin. Iris wanted to grab her through the screen and ask what had happened to her. Then it dawned on her. There was nothing stopping her from doing that.

"We should go back to the house and ask Helena," she said.

"She's sorta dead, Iris."

"I mean *her spirit*," Iris clarified. "She's already been trying to communicate with you."

"If by *communicate* you mean staring at me like she wanted to kill me, then yeah."

She sighed. He was being so defeatist. She couldn't blame him. She was still new at this trying-to-find-the-best-case-scenario thing herself. So far, all her hunches had led her closer to answers. She could feel the truth buzzing around her. So close. So close. She just had to keep reaching. Keep clawing for it. Not let her frustrations mutate into anger.

"Sometimes, in *Dark Unknown*, Max has to offer his energy to commune with spirits," Iris said. "That's why he doesn't call himself a medium. He's a *conduit*. 'Cause, it's like he's a channel for spirits to pass through."

"Maybe," Gum said, as he typed out a text. She wanted to tell him to put the phone away and pay attention, but she didn't know how without sounding like an overzealous substitute teacher.

"We just explain that we want to help her cross over to the other side," Iris suggested. "That's why she's still here. Unfinished business. She hasn't been avenged."

Gum nodded. "Maybe we do the avenging tomorrow? Aidan wants to meet us at the drive-in for a stakeout. Apparently Hudson is supposed to be there."

"Hudson wasn't alive for the first drowning," Iris pointed out. "He was a baby for the second. There's no way it's him. I mean, Hudson couldn't have made me sleepwalk."

He couldn't make her do anything. She was immune to his charms. He could give her as many dimpled smiles as he wanted and she'd still see him as he was: a spoiled asshole.

"Maybe the swim team is really a front. During practice they actually do witchcraft," Gum joked. He was deflecting, as usual.

"Please take this seriously."

He put his phone down. "I am. I just don't want to pick sides. I want to be fair to both of you, ya know? And would it be so bad to chill and watch a movie for *one night*?"

"Sure," Iris said, deadpan, not even bothering to hide her disappointment. She couldn't count on the boys, even if their intentions were good. They were too afraid, just like the rest of Bad Creek. But Iris would prove she was fearless.

She would avenge Helena. And Glory.

Even if she had to do it alone.

It was Aidan's idea to stalk Hudson, but once they arrived at the drive-in, all he did was complain. His knuckles were tense as he drove through the massive grass parking lot at two miles an hour. He had to avoid hitting families dropping their expensive popcorn, dogs barking at other dogs, and college kids smoking joints by the porta-potties.

Iris said she'd meet them there, but it would be getting dark soon. Gum worried she wasn't coming. After the library, she hadn't ridden over to Aidan's house with Gum. She had claimed she needed to stop at the Landings first. Supposedly her moms would be mad if she missed dinner. That was bull, but Gum couldn't be mad at her for lying. He was lying nonstop. Every time he got a sudden chill, he could have sworn it was Glory's breath on his neck. He still hadn't told either of them about her; he couldn't. Since he'd mentioned the ghost in the bathtub,

Aidan was sure Gum was delusional and Iris was falling down a rabbit hole.

Plus, none of this investigating had made Glory go away. Gum was starting to think closure wasn't possible.

"I don't see the Great White," Aidan said.

Hudson's giant Escalade would stick out like a sore thumb in this sea of beat-up minivans, but they weren't even sure he would be here tonight. Aunt Brenda said her son was going to the drive-in, so here they were. But if Hudson could cuss out his dad in the presence of the Second Largest Crucifix in the World, he wasn't above lying to his mom about his plans.

None of those things meant he ought to be a suspect, though. Aidan's theory was way off base. As much as Gum liked the idea of Hudson going off to prison, being insufferable wasn't a crime. Hudson hadn't done anything to hurt Glory. No one had. The lake had taken all those people because tragedy struck like lightning. It didn't need a motive.

Ghost Glory didn't have a purpose. She wasn't a saint with a heavenly message; it was the opposite. It was like all of her good traits left her when she died, and now only her ugly parts remained. Surely she was pissed about her own death, but that wasn't Gum's fault. He didn't deserve her rage. And he wasn't a first-round pick for being a messenger either. If she had unfinished business, she could take it somewhere else.

Aidan parked the Jeep in the third row of cars, a good spot despite arriving so close to showtime. He tuned the radio to the drive-in's station. The charming vintage ads were still running, so they had about five minutes to spare.

"What's even playing?" Gum asked, pulling a pack of candy cigarettes from his back pocket.

"It doesn't really matter. We have a mission," Aidan reminded him.

Right. Find Hudson. And then . . . watch him to see if he did anything murdery? It wasn't a foolproof plan, but Gum didn't have any better ideas. Iris blamed ghosts, and Aidan blamed Hudson, and Gum tried to resist the urge to shiver.

She would show up soon. He could sense her. He chewed on one of the candy cigarettes, hoping the chalky texture would give his brain something else to focus on. But there was no ignoring the heaviness in his bones.

When the big screen went black, people turned off their car lights and the muffled voice of an unenthusiastic and underpaid college kid came through the Jeep's radio.

"Thank you for joining us for another summer at the Bad Creek Drive-In," they said. "Our first film in tonight's Monster Feature, *It Runs Below.*"

Gum laughed, while Aidan sank down his seat, groaning.

Aidan got embarrassed at any mention of Paul's movie, but Gum always thought that was dumb. Gum's parents had never done anything noteworthy. His mom didn't get a chance, and his dad was perfectly content with being ordinary. The movie wasn't even that bad. It was campy. Fun. Aidan just couldn't admit that he would have liked it if it were directed by literally anyone else.

"You know I met the director once?" Gum teased. "He's so cool."

"Really, I heard he was an alcoholic deadbeat."

"Are we talking about the same guy? 'Cause Paul Ross is the smartest, funniest, sexiest man I've ever met."

"You're so gross." But Aidan was laughing.

There was a knock on the passenger door. Gum jumped. Even through the closed windows, he could feel the cold seeping in. She was here. He saw her curls in the darkness, the glimmer of water falling off her face. He blinked, and Glory was gone. It was just Iris, holding her backpack, waiting for them to unlock the door.

Get a grip, he told himself.

Gum slid into the middle of the bench seat to let Iris in. She plopped down, exasperated. Maybe she rode her bike all the way here. The drive-in wasn't far from the Landings.

"Sorry," she said. "What's playing?"

"Only a masterpiece," Gum said.

The opening scene had started: a top-down shot of a well, with the slowest zoom in history. Red names appeared in the center of the black void, disappearing with a cheesy ripple effect.

Iris giggled. "Oh, finally. True cinema."

Aidan turned down the radio. "We're not watching the movie."

"You're right," Iris said. "It's not a movie, it's an *experience*."

"I think we should split up, look for his car."

"Okay," Gum said. He preferred to not to have today's scheduled breakdown in front of his friends. He couldn't lie to their faces again.

Iris took a big swig of her water bottle. "And then what?"

"See how he acts."

"M'kay." Iris squeezed her giant bottle in the cupholder

and stepped out after agreeing on what routes they would take. The drive-in was about the size of a football field, with a dozen rows of cars all facing the same massive screen. With the three of them looking, it shouldn't take long for someone to spot Hudson and his obnoxious friends and his obnoxious car. Gum started down the first row, passing couples on picnic blankets and mothers spraying their kids with bug spray. He made it to the food truck at the end. Hudson wasn't in line.

Gum turned onto the second row. The sweat from the afternoon still hadn't dried on him, yet his hands and feet felt numb. He was starting to feel itchy too, and not just because of his sunburn from that morning, or the new mosquito bites on his arms. He could smell her already. She was here, somewhere.

Gum tried to glance into some of the cars without looking like a creep. He didn't see his cousin sitting with any of the usual suspects. When he made it to the food truck again, he thought about grabbing snacks, but a huge line had gathered around the popcorn machine's yellow glow. The girl at the end turned and looked at him. She wore a red shirt, a long skirt. Her skin was gray, and she was covered in dark, slimy water.

Oh shit.

He turned and started down the third row, trying to think about anything other than Glory. Then he made the mistake of glancing over his shoulder to check. Yep. She was following him, unseen between the rows of cars. He picked up his pace. Open car windows let in the movie's soundtrack—a low hum that got louder and louder as danger grew nearer. He knew Glory was getting closer. With every step, the ground felt softer.

Gum's legs were jellifying. He didn't know what she would do when she caught up to him.

He yanked the Jeep's door open and collapsed into the bench seat, locking the doors behind him. The radio wasn't set to the right station. Part of the dialogue from the movie came through, but the rest was static.

On the screen, the spring-breakers were discovering the haunted well behind their rental cottage. The main girl screamed, "Hello!" into the empty hole. When her voice echoed back, it sounded different.

By the second act, the voice that responded would have killed all of the main character's friends.

The Jeep shook. Glory had found him, and now she was pounding on the glass. If she was a ghost, how could she move the car? Shouldn't she be able to phase through walls and shit?

She looked even worse than before. Her eyes were too far apart, her smile too wide. Her teeth were smaller and crooked. She looked like a very wet, very gray jack-o'-lantern.

"C'mon, Gum, this isn't funny!" Her voice was low, phlegmy. She sounded like Glory with the flu.

"What do you want?"

She kept pounding. Jiggling the door handle. "Let me in!"

"Why me?" he asked, feeling betrayed by how weak he sounded.

She pulled back and stared at him. Her eye sockets were shifting around her face, like she couldn't remember exactly where they were supposed to sit.

"It's your right," Glory said. Her voice was gentle now. He

knew this tone. She always switched it up whenever someone resisted her charms. "It was always supposed to be you."

"So, what, now you want to kill me?"

"No," she said. "You'll be fine . . . if you follow instructions."

"Instructions? What do you want me to do?"

"I'll explain everything if you *let me in*."

All the blood rushed to Gum's head. His stomach lurched, like his body was rejecting her presence. It wasn't fair to judge a ghost by her looks or smell, but he couldn't stand it. His instincts knew something was wrong, just like the girl in the movie knew that it wasn't her own voice echoing in the well.

If he let her in, she would have all the power. He couldn't let that happen.

"No," he said. His voice was weak. Barely a whisper.

She pounded on the door again, growling, "Daniel Gum, you're such a pussy, it's unbelievable."

Gum closed his eyes and covered his ears. She would have to go away eventually. She would have to give up. Did ghosts get tired? Was that even what she was? Glory was the queen of insults, but she considered herself an intellectual. She'd never call him a pussy. She had better vocabulary than that.

And she was never *that* mean, was she?

"Dude, open the door!"

It wasn't Glory's voice now. It was too human. Aidan was staring at him through the window. Gum sat up; the static suddenly cleared away. Glory was nowhere to be seen, and as Gum let Aidan in, the rotten stench was replaced with scents of cigarette smoke, fresh-cut grass, and popcorn.

"I couldn't find him," Aidan said. "Where's Iris?"

"She's not back yet."

"What's wrong with you?"

His fear must have been hanging on his face. Gum leaned back in the seat and readjusted his baseball cap. "Nothing." He wiped his forehead for good measure.

He was drenched in sweat, though he was freezing, and he lowered the window for air. Glory was gone, for now, but she wouldn't leave him alone until she got what she wanted.

Until he followed instructions. Whatever that meant.

Aidan didn't press the matter further, so they waited for Iris. On the screen, the main girl discovered her first dead friend. Gum didn't watch the movie; he stared at Iris's water bottle instead, a green scrunchie wrapped around it.

"Take it."

Gum shivered all over. She wasn't waiting outside the Jeep, but he was sure he'd heard Glory's voice. Well, her *new* voice. The low, phlegmy gargle. As the breeze entered the cracked window, he could smell the stench again.

Aidan slouched in the driver's seat, face glued to his phone, probably trying to reach Iris. He couldn't feel Glory here. He didn't even flinch.

"Take it."

Louder this time, like she was speaking directly into Gum's ear.

That was all Glory wanted? Iris's scrunchie? She could have opened with that instead of all the dramatics. That was so like Glory. She couldn't just be a ghost, but the most horrifying ghost ever. She was the best at everything. She had to be the best at scaring the shit out of people too.

Fine. She could have her way.

What was one scrunchie? Iris had a million of them. When he was sure Aidan was distracted, Gum reached for the green scrunchie and put it in his pocket.

Iris had seen *It Runs Below* at least a dozen times, so she should have braced herself for the scene where the main character narrowly escaped the well. At the last second, right when the girl thought she'd made it out safely, the monster leaped out of the water and clamped its jaws around her leg.

When Iris used to watch this scene, she would marvel at the creature's design. It was fish-like, yet mammalian. A big hulking beast, yet slim enough to slither around the well. Its silicone skin looked appropriately slimy, and the choice to leave the actor's real teeth in was genius. It gave an unexpected human twist to the character. It deserved to be iconic just for that alone.

Iris used to smile when the protagonist's necklace reflected the moonlight—a nod to her now-dead boyfriend who had given it to her in the first scene. In the original script, Aidan had told her, there was no final girl. The monster killed everyone in the end. But that wasn't the version that had made it to theaters. Instead, the main character kicked the creature in the face and dropped a Molotov cocktail into its den.

Iris wasn't done searching her designated rows of cars, but now she was standing in the center of the grassy parking lot, eyes fixed on the movie. The final girl's BFF had just drowned, and though Iris saw it coming, there was no way the character did. She'd been looking forward to a fun getaway with her friends. It wasn't fair.

Iris could feel hands around her throat, pushing her deeper, deeper, deeper—until there was no light. No sound, just the rush of water into her nose. Her mouth.

She had to escape the screen—escape the creature's angry wails and the final girl triumphantly walking away from the explosion. That character eventually got her happy ending. Glory couldn't be saved in a rewrite.

Iris ran. She flew past the food truck, past the welcome sign, until there was only the road and the pines and the dull sizzle of cicadas. Her backpack weighed a million pounds, even though all that was in there was a lighter, a candle, a twenty-dollar bill, and that stupid Ouija board. She'd waited in that abandoned house for two hours, hoping Helena would speak to her. And, nothing. The planchette hadn't moved. The candles hadn't gone out.

The boys hadn't even asked her why she had been late.

Iris stopped only when her lungs gave out. The stitch in her side felt like she was being ripped in half. There were no wounds on her; physically, she was in perfect health. That was the problem. It didn't matter that she could feel the hands around her throat or see a warped reflection in the mirror. Anyone who looked at Iris would see her as an unharmed sister. The *alive* sister. No one would believe her if she said she was a dead girl walking.

She assessed her surroundings. A Mustang convertible was parked in front of the only house on the street. It was hard to make out the color in the darkness, but, in the sunshine, it was an unsavory pink. She was at the intersection of Meller and Stern Road, not far from the drive-in.

For as long as she could remember, the owner of that cabin had accumulated junk—decorations from every holiday, life-sized wooden cutouts of local wildlife, birdbaths, weather vanes, empty flowerpots, and a clawfoot tub full of rainwater. The most iconic piece in the collection was the rusted pink Mustang convertible with a long-missing top, which managed to look both regal and pitiful at the same time. Iris figured this was as good a cry spot as any. When she sat on the hood of the Mustang, the tears started flowing.

Glory had all the ideas. If Iris was the dead sister, Glory would have already figured out what the symbol on the tree meant. Who the claws belonged to. And Glory would get the boys to listen to her. She could convince anyone to do anything. Iris eventually gave in to all of Glory's plans, even when that tiny voice in her head was screaming.

It was screaming the first time they stepped into that pink convertible. Glory had led them away from the drive-in, promising a new spot to look at the stars.

Glory's interests were constantly changing, and this was the summer she'd started caring about astronomy. Before that, she had considered careers in fashion, interior design, and professional wrestling. It wasn't enough to win a medal at every art show or get every solo at her dance studio. There was always something out there she hadn't mastered. That restlessness that drove Glory to do more made Iris freeze. Freeze or run or cry.

"Don't be scared," Glory had said.

Iris had felt personally attacked by this. When you're eleven years old, thirteen feels centuries away. And Iris had wanted to prove she was as mature as her older sister.

"I'm not scared," she insisted.

Glory took her hand. "I promise. It's safe. I'm pretty sure no one lives here anymore."

"You don't know that for sure."

"You have to trust me."

That was how it was with Glory. She decided things, and they became true.

Glory was in the driver's seat and Iris sat on the passenger side. The boys were in the back. Glory had pointed to a grouping of stars that looked as random and insignificant as the rest. "See that wide U? That's the Northern Crown. Corona Borealis."

"Crayola Boringlist?" Iris giggled.

Of course Gum joined in. "No, Iris, you weren't listening. She totally said Coca-Cola Brachiosaurus."

"Actually," Glory chimed, "I said Koala Bear Nest."

"Capybara Bomb Test?" Iris offered.

That would have gone on forever if Aidan hadn't interrupted them with a whine. "Something just stung me."

Iris looked back to spot the red welt on his arm and the flying bugs around him. Around all of them.

"Iris." Glory said her name so slowly. "There's a nest by your feet."

It was only a few inches from her shoes. She had kicked it, and now five wasps buzzed around her exposed legs. The other Disasters evacuated the car, but Iris stayed frozen, watching more wasps emerge from the nest, land on her, then take flight.

What if she was allergic? She hadn't ever considered herself at risk of dying. That was something that only happened to old people, something that happened in movies. It wasn't until that moment that she had understood how vulnerable she was. That danger could appear with no warning.

Glory opened the passenger door for Iris. "Get up slowly," she directed. Iris eased out of the car without the wasps attacking. Together, they ran away from the pink Mustang, returning to the drive-in, where Joanna had taken care of Aidan's wasp sting without asking where he'd gotten it. This was back when she trusted her kids and trusted the universe to bring them home safely.

The following morning, Glory had climbed down from her top bunk and ridden her red bike back to the rusted convertible on Stern Road. Without an adult's help or protection, she'd picked up the nest and chucked it into the creek. It hadn't taken long for her to convince them all to go back.

A few days later, she'd bought glow-in-the-dark stars and spent the last rainy afternoon of vacation sticking them to the ceiling, with Corona Borealis right above their bunk beds.

Now Iris looked up at the stars, which were always so much

brighter in Bad Creek. She searched for Corona Borealis but didn't know where to look.

If Glory was here, she would know.

Maybe Glory was here. Maybe, like Helena Crawford, her soul was trapped. Maybe she would be willing to talk.

Iris pulled out the Ouija board from her backpack. It had been collecting dust in the game closet of Cabin 4, yet the plastic still glimmered like it had when she was a preteen. There were rainbows and butterflies in the corners, by the *YES* and the *NO*. April had bought it because she thought it was hilariously adorable. Aidan wouldn't play with it because "science," and Gum had refused because, "That's how the Devil gets you." So only Glory and Iris had used it, but Iris was pretty sure the "spirit" they'd contacted was just her sister controlling the planchette herself.

It hadn't worked then, and it hadn't worked in the house in the woods. Not in the living room. Not in the bathroom, not by the tree with the weird carving.

But it had to work now.

She lit the candle. It was hardly like the tall ritual candles they used in *Dark Unknown*, but Bath & Body Works had to do for now.

She placed the planchette at the center of the board and took a deep breath. "Glory, are you there?" Nothing. She closed her eyes, tried to focus on inhaling and exhaling. "If you can hear me, give a sign."

Her lungs felt thick, like they were too full. *Breathe,* she told herself. *Breathe. Then wait. Then hope, and repeat.*

A chill went through her. She shut her eyes tighter. Faintly, she could make out a new sound—a buzzing. The wasps again. Iris opened her eyes and looked behind her, expecting to find a huge nest, but there was no sign of life.

No, the noise was a car heading toward her. She blew out the candle, grabbed the board, and shoved them both into her backpack. She yanked on the rusted door handle and melted into the backseat, realizing only then she'd never grabbed the heart-shaped planchette. Was it still on the hood? Had it slid off?

But it was too late; she'd been spotted. A white Escalade had parked in front of the pink Mustang. Hudson Clavey stepped out and walked right up to her.

Shit.

"Are you okay?" he asked. He had his hands on the top of the broken front window. Iris sat up and brushed a stray curl from her forehead.

"Why wouldn't I be?" It was her first instinct. *Act cool. Act confident.* Not like she had dried tears on her face. Not like she had been talking to the wind.

"I saw you running," he said. "I wanted to make sure you were all right."

"I'm fine, thanks. You can go back to the movie."

He still didn't move, didn't blink. Just stared at her with his pale eyes. Then, once she was appropriately creeped out, he said, "I was gonna leave anyway. I don't get the appeal of horror movies."

Could he tell she had been crying? Hudson Clavey's opinion had never mattered to her, but the idea of him witnessing her fall apart sounded unbearably mortifying. Even worse than when she'd lost it in front of Gum yesterday. She crossed her arms and flicked her ponytail behind her shoulders.

Think. Say something clever.

"Horror movies are like roller coasters," Iris said. "The cycle of fear and relief releases dopamine." She'd heard that once on a podcast.

Hudson nodded, impressed. "I don't care for roller coasters either. Maybe my brain works differently."

She snorted.

Yes, Hudson. You're not like all the other boys. She couldn't believe she almost agreed with Aidan's theory about Hudson. Whatever got Glory had to be bigger than him. Powerful. Something that couldn't be contained in a vessel wearing Crocs and a hoodie boasting the logo of some bougie private school.

"What?" Hudson asked, smiling slightly.

She'd probably confused him, switching from meltdown mode into rolling her eyes.

"Plenty of people don't like scary movies," she explained. "That doesn't make you unique. I mean, it makes sense you don't like them."

He hopped over the door and sat next to her. She tensed up, then forced herself to relax. She still had no idea why he had been in that house, or why he'd been talking to Glory at that party. She had let Aidan's paranoia get to her during volleyball, but it wasn't going to happen again. She had to conduct an unbiased investigation if she was going to find the truth.

Up close, Hudson looked a little like his cousin but in an uncanny way—like Gum had drunk a Ken doll potion. They had the same round, pale Clavey eyes and little upturned pointy noses that people ask their plastic surgeons for. But that was where the similarities ended. Hudson was tall, with wide shoulders that came from being a Varsity Swim God. His hair had been white-blond as a child and hadn't darkened much since. She wondered if he got highlights. He probably did. She envisioned Hudson rolling up to a salon, asking for hair to make him look like a World War II recruitment poster.

"Why does it make sense?" he asked.

Because if you googled the word privilege, *you would find a million guys that look exactly like you.* Weird people liked horror, and there was nothing weird about Hudson Clavey. He had an image purposely crafted to be as inoffensively normal as possible.

"When you go through shit, frightening things become comforting," she said. "If you don't have any trauma, I'm sure horror is uncomfortable. It pops your innocent little bubble."

"Could be the other way around, though? Don't you think for some people it's just re-traumatizing?"

"No," Iris said flatly.

"Then why did you run?" he pressed.

She wasn't crying anymore, but her face still felt hot. "Why do you care?"

Hudson blinked a few times, like a robot malfunctioning. He thought he was adorable for admitting his fear of PG-13 movies. Just because he was admittedly very good-looking didn't mean Iris had to congratulate him whenever he managed to articulate a somewhat original thought.

"Like I said. I saw you run," he said.

She scoffed. "Stalker."

"I can only imagine how hard it's been after what happened. I'm so sorry about Glory, Iris. I wanted to tell you that."

She'd heard it nonstop for the past year. From friends, from strangers. From teachers and neighbors. Everyone was *so sorry about Glory*, but when Hudson Clavey said it, he sounded the most genuine.

She'd technically known him her whole life, but she'd barely spoken to the guy one-on-one like this. She'd known enough from his smirk and his pedigree.

Where was this coming from? Was it remorse? It had been a year, and no one had questioned Glory's death but Iris. Saying something about it now only made him look suspicious. He would have to know that. He was an asshole, not an idiot.

And probably not a murderer either.

Hudson was still waiting for her answer. Iris had been staring at his too-perfect face, trying to see if there was a real human soul behind it. "Uh, thanks," she said.

"Do you need a ride?"

Murderer or not, she wouldn't be seen in a Clavey car with a Clavey boy. Her moms would never forgive her. "Nope, I'm fine right here."

He jumped out of the Mustang without another word. He stopped in the middle of the road and turned to look at her. She noticed now that Hudson wasn't standing with his shoulders back, walking around like his daddy owned the place. He looked weary. Tired and hunched, with his hands in the pocket of his hoodie. He was Atlas holding up the world, and the world was heavy today.

Iris's heart was beating too fast. She worried he could hear it all the way from there. He picked up something from the road and handed it to her. A little pink heart. The planchette.

Hudson added, "See ya around, Garren," as he climbed into the Great White. But there was no bite in the way he'd said her last name. It was half-hearted teasing, trying to follow the old script.

It can't be like it was before. Can we stop pretending?

She only thought of Aidan's words as she returned to the drive-in. He was right; it couldn't be the same, but she wasn't the one who was trying to pretend. Everyone was hiding from her. Aidan. Gum. Her own mothers.

How had Hudson Clavey been the only one to really look at her?

It was Iris's idea to have their strategy meeting over a game of Sorry! and root beer floats, probably to assure them she was perfectly fine. She had disappeared for an hour and had a run-in with their only suspect, but she was fine. Just peachy.

Gum wasn't convinced, and apparently Aidan wasn't either. He kept giving Gum a series of not-so-subtle side glances on the drive to Aidan's, as if Iris running off was proof she was insane. Nothing paranormal to see here.

On that same drive, Iris had warned her moms she'd be sleeping over. Gum hadn't bothered checking in with his dad. He could do whatever he wanted on vacation as long as he showed up for mandatory Clavey duties.

Roy, Paul's elderly bulldog, grunted excitedly when they walked inside. He followed them upstairs, all the way to the attic. He had been fat and gray forever. He had to be at least twelve years old, but he was still doing happy little hops, and once they broke out the popcorn, he begged for a kernel. They settled on the rug in Aidan's room, and Gum threw the popcorn for Roy to catch while Aidan set up the board. He left the red pieces in the box, which he shoved under his bed, out of sight.

"I only talked to him for like five minutes," Iris said as she shuffled the cards. "I asked him why he followed me, and he said he was already leaving 'cause he hates horror movies."

That part sounded true. Hudson was always such a baby about hunting. Killing, he was okay with. But blood and guts? He couldn't stomach it. Uncle Bruce teased him about it all the time.

Aidan drew the first card—a two. He pulled his yellow pawn out of the start and drew again. "He's playing you, Iris."

Iris pulled a one and also took her pawn out. "We really don't have a lot to go on. What makes you so sure it's him?"

Gum got nothing useful from his turn.

"He acted weird at the party. And he had been at the house," Aidan reminded her. "He had been around her last summer, long enough for her to draw his eyes a million times."

The answer was obvious, but Gum wasn't going to point it out. Hudson and Glory didn't make much sense, but you don't have to be soulmates to hook up. Still, out of all of Glory's faults, she was loyal above anything else. She always did exactly what she said she would, and she didn't let anyone mess with her friends (except for her). But maybe Aidan had the wrong idea of their relationship. He thought it meant forever, and Glory had decided it was temporary.

"He's trying to lure you in," Aidan continued. "He tried to do the same with her, and when it didn't work—"

"I think he was just being polite," Iris said. "Gum?"

"Yeah," Gum agreed. "I mean, he's a dickhead, not Ted Bundy."

Gum genuinely believed that, especially since the Glory he saw wasn't desperate to cast the blame on Hudson. But then again, this was the second time she showed up right before Hudson did. First at Mass, then the drive-in. But what about at Grandpa's house? Uncle Bruce was there. Bruce and Hudson had been fighting . . .

Could Hudson's dad have learned about Glory's real cause of death? That was why he was pissed at him? Gum still wasn't sure. He couldn't focus, not with Roy whining at the door.

"Gum, it's your move."

He was barely invested in the game. All his blue pawns were still trapped at the start, while Aidan and Iris were close to scoring. He drew from the deck, finally pulling the coveted Sorry! card. He could steal either of his opponents' positions and finally be in the game. The green and yellow pawns were close together, so it wouldn't matter which one he took.

"*Take Iris*," crooned a voice right next to him. He saw her then from the corner of his eye and put his head down, staring at the board. Brown water plopped on the cardboard. Gum could feel every hair on the back of his neck stand up.

"Gum? Hello? Jesus Christ, you never fucking listen."

She was waving in his face. Her fingers were bloated and peeling, but her manicure was still impeccable. Her voice was a low gurgle, as if coming from the wrong part of her throat.

"Gum?" That was Iris now, a million miles away.

"There's only one option," Glory said. "You see it, right? You don't have much time to mess around. Clock's tickin'."

"What does that mean?" Gum said. He sounded desperate,

and he didn't care if she made fun of him for it. "You aren't saying anything!"

"Gum, who are you talking to?" Iris asked.

"It means it's not over, dumbass." Glory's smile was wider than it had been at the drive-in. Last time, she didn't have enough teeth; now she had too many. Like her face didn't remember its own design and was responding to Gum's reactions. She took the feedback but overcorrected, resulting in a toothy Muppet mouth.

"C'mon. Be serious for once," Glory sneered. "You really think it ended with me? It *never ends.* That's the deal."

Gum knocked over all the pieces on the board with one swipe of his hand. Suddenly the room grew warmer, lighter.

Glory was gone.

Now all eyes were on Gum. At least they were living eyes this time.

"Was it her?" Iris asked in a whisper.

Gum couldn't explain the truth. Aidan wouldn't believe it and Iris would be devastated. Glory wanted him to antagonize her, after all. Steal her scrunchie. Steal her pawn. Mess with her.

Iris added, "You saw the girl from the house again?"

Close enough. Gum nodded wordlessly.

"What did she say?" Iris asked.

"She said . . . that it wasn't over."

"That's literally what I was thinking!" Iris said. She was much too happy about it, like she'd successfully predicted the plot of a TV show. "It's a pattern. It's happened three times."

Aidan butted in, "Well, technically—"

Iris didn't let him finish. "Each drowning was, what, like twenty or thirty years apart? She's trying to warn us, guys. It's gonna happen again. I was right. Bad Creek is cursed."

Maybe the whole town wasn't cursed, but Gum definitely was.

The Jeep still smelled like the lake. Gum and Iris hadn't mentioned it at the drive-in, but Aidan was sure the smell lingered on him. So, of course, he had that dream again.

He came to in the driver's seat. A bomb had gone off inside his skull. He pushed open the door to puke. That was how it had happened the first time. He'd emptied his guts and crawled inside the house. He hadn't even made it up the stairs to his bedroom; he'd simply collapsed on the couch. His brain hurt too much to think about what he had done.

But in the dream, he didn't puke. And Glory was next to him. She was cold. Slimy. Dead. He dragged her body out of the car. She weighed nothing. It was too easy to carry her to the edge of the water, where a moose was wading, neck-deep. Its features were twisted, skin shredded off. It was even more decayed than Glory was. He knew something bad would happen if he got any closer to it, so he dropped

Glory where he stood. He didn't turn around to check if she sank to the bottom or not. To check if the zombie moose was still watching.

Besides, he had a lot of work to do. Suddenly he had a sponge in his hands. And soap. And a bucket of water. He began to scrub the inside of the car.

Then he woke up. Sunlight was streaming out of the round, circular window above his bed. He was safe. The truth wasn't that bad. The lake wasn't on him, that was just his own sweat.

Still, he grabbed his phone from the bedside table. Six-thirty a.m., way too early to be awake. They had stayed up past midnight.

There was a snoring lump on the floor next to him. Gum had managed to tangle himself inside of the sleeping bag, and the pillow was five feet away. And Iris . . .

She wasn't on the futon.

"She's probably in the bathroom," Aidan muttered to himself, before turning over and burying his head under the comforter. A minute passed. Another. He didn't hear the door creak open. Okay, maybe she wasn't in the bathroom. Maybe she had her moms pick her up. That girl always had a flair for the dramatic.

He shouldn't enable her. He tried to close his eyes, to go back to sleep, but Roy started barking hysterically. It wasn't his normal, excited bark either. There were whines intermixed. He sounded like he was in pain.

Aidan shot up in bed. The sleeping bag swished around as Gum untangled himself.

"The fuck is that?" he muttered.

Aidan pulled on his boots in a panic, not bothering to lace them all the way.

"Something's wrong." Now that he studied the futon again, he noticed Iris had left her sweatshirt. Her backpack. Her water bottle. Her phone.

There was no way her moms had picked her up.

Roy kept whining from somewhere outside. Aidan peered through the window. There was just the Jeep, no signs of the Garrens' van. A fog hung over the lake. The *Dirty Diana* looked ghostly, bobbing gently in a gray void. Roy was close to the dock, barking at nothing.

No, not nothing.

A figure wavered on the edge of the mist.

Iris.

That was her ponytail, her giant T-shirt hanging halfway to her knees. She stood on the dock, facing the water, rocking back and forth on her heels.

Gum peeked out the window, wiping crust from his eyes.

"What the fuck is she doing?" Aidan asked.

"I think . . . she's sleepwalking," Gum answered.

Shit.

Aidan flew down all three flights of stairs. He didn't have time to wonder why this was happening. A suicidal urge. A horrible coincidence. A curse. Didn't matter. He just knew he had to get her to safety. Even if she didn't break her legs or hit her head on the way down, it wouldn't be pretty. Unconscious people plus water were not a great combo.

When he burst outside the back patio, Iris wasn't standing

still anymore. She'd shuffled farther and farther onto the dock and into the fog.

"Iris!" he shouted.

She didn't even flinch when he called her name. She couldn't hear him. Of course she couldn't hear him. She was asleep.

Aidan ran, nearly slipping on the dewy grass. Iris was only a few inches from the edge now and she wasn't stopping.

Just in time, Aidan grabbed her by the back of the shirt. She tried to fight her way out of his grip by blindly throwing her hands around.

Aidan knew sleepwalkers could freak out when awoken prematurely. You're supposed to be gentle with them, but now wasn't the time for gentle.

He yelled directly in her face. "Iris!"

He managed to put his hands around her shoulders and give her a good shake. Her eyes fluttered open, and she gasped as if she *had* gone underwater. But she still didn't move.

The morning light flicked off. The fog dissipated, replaced with smoke from fireworks. Aidan gripped her too tight. Glory had told him not to. *You always hold on too tight*, she had said. But she wasn't saying anything now. Why wasn't she saying anything? Glory's eyes were glazed over. Still hazel, still glittering with gold eye shadow, but she wasn't really there. She felt gone. Aidan shook her again. She didn't react.

"What did you do to her?" Aidan had shouted. There was someone else standing in the darkness. In his dreams, it was the zombie moose, but he knew it really was Hudson. He stood knee-high in the water.

That was when Hudson said it. "Go home. You don't want to see this."

With a gasp, Iris broke her trance. She wasn't Glory anymore. And Aidan was in the present. Iris glanced around wildly, and stared at the lake, like she was going to ask it something.

"You okay?"

She nodded, pulled a curl behind her ear. "You shouldn't have woken me up," she said, frustrated. "I almost had it. She was trying to tell me something. I was so close . . ."

"Close to drowning, you mean?"

How could she possibly be mad at him for saving her?

She sighed. "I *felt* her, this time. I think Glory's trying to lead me."

"Lead you to your death?"

"To *answers*." She kept her eyes on the lake. The morning was downright serene, with the coos of doves and trill of frogs in the water. If she would have continued, she would have quietly faded into the mist.

Gum had caught up with them. He put his hands on his knees, panting. "What the hell, Iris?"

"I saw it, okay?" she said. "The smudge."

"The smudge?"

"What she drew, at the edge of Savi's dock. I think it was the killer. Only a few more steps, and I would have seen who it was."

"Only a few steps, and you would have gone off the edge," Aidan told her.

She shook her head. She couldn't accept it.

But a new thought was bubbling inside of him. The same unanswered question from last year. *What had he done to her?* It wasn't just smooth talking that had turned Glory so passive. Hudson had *changed her.* Somehow. By the time Aidan had gotten to her, it was too late. But it wasn't too late for Iris.

"What did he say to you, exactly?" Aidan asked.

"It's not a he. It's a . . . feeling."

"I mean Hudson." It could have been hypnotism. It could have been a weird poison that attacked the brain, transferred through touch or administered in a drink. Oh God, had Hudson slipped something in Glory's cup?

Iris gritted her teeth. "I know what I saw," she growled, before storming toward the house, slamming the door behind her.

"Give her a sec to calm down. It's just like before, ya know? It's always the same fight. You both care about Glory a lot," Gum said. He had changed into a new shirt and left his baseball cap off. His leg hadn't stopped bouncing since they'd gotten in the car. The Jeep still smelled like stale lake water, and Aidan could feel the splinter every time his foot hit the gas.

Iris had said one of her moms would pick her up, and shooed them out the door, still believing Aidan had betrayed her.

"I'm tired of fighting," Aidan said. He never wanted to fight her. He only wanted to save her, but Iris wouldn't allow herself to be saved, she'd rather chase ghosts.

"It's up here," Gum said. "On the left."

Aidan held his breath as he turned into the parking lot. Gum had asked for a ride to brunch with the same cadence one would ask to be sent to the electric chair. And Aidan didn't blame him.

Handerson's was only a short drive from his dad's house, near the shiny new golf course, in the shadow of the giant crucifix. The mansion-turned-bed-and-breakfast was one of the county's oldest buildings, yet whatever antique charm it once had was washed away in gallons of white paint after the new owners bought it, leaving a square fortress with tall windows and perfectly aligned blue shutters.

This was Clavey country.

Bill Clavey stood outside on the porch. He shook hands as customers walked in. When he noticed the Jeep, he marched up and put his beefy hands on top of the open window before Aidan could crank it closed.

"You're Paul's boy?"

He was a sturdy old man, with a thick mustache and shockingly white hair. Aidan always thought he looked like Colonel Sanders's evil twin.

"Uh-huh."

"Your family comin' to eat?" He *sounded* like Colonel Sanders's evil twin too, words soaked in a Kentucky drawl that suggested he was trying to sell something. Probably not fried chicken.

"No, Grandpa, he was just dropping me off," Gum said. He always talked to the Claveys like you're supposed to talk to cops. Respectful, but stilted. Like he was trying to avoid incriminating himself.

Bill Clavey didn't look away from Aidan. His robotic eyes didn't even blink. "Please join us! All on me, of course."

"You don't have to," Gum mumbled to Aidan.

"*I insist,*" Bill said.

Aidan stared at the man's face, trying to will a memory to float up to the surface. He had already considered the possibility that Hudson hadn't worked alone, that maybe his family had helped him get out of trouble. Maybe if Aidan spent the morning with the Claveys he would remember something else.

Aidan was ready to burn this whole town, he just needed something to strike the match. So he forced a smile, practically feeling his cheeks cracking from the falseness of it.

"Sounds good," he said.

As Bill Clavey led them into the restaurant, he pointed out the features of the building. "Real ivory on the piano. Couldn't be made today. Even *music* is offensive now."

Gum gave Aidan a sympathetic look. *It's fine*, Aidan mouthed, though he was practically vibrating with anxiety.

"Original mahogany trim," Bill continued. "They almost had it replaced a few years ago, but I wouldn't allow it."

They passed room after room of candy-colored walls, not unlike the peeling wallpaper in the house in the woods. The same house Hudson had been in. Probably with Glory.

Don't think about that.

Yet the thought hadn't left Aidan's mind since he'd learned about them. He'd asked it to leave politely, but it decided to make his brain its home. The thought slept on his brain's couch. It raided his fridge. It used his Netflix log-in.

The rest of the Claveys congregated in a private room next to the main dining hall. They sat at a huge circular table surrounded by baby-blue floral wallpaper, matching their creepy blue eyes. Gum's dad wasn't there. Aidan had hardly interacted with the guy, but compared to his in-laws he always seemed refreshingly normal. Bill grabbed the nearest server—who was already balancing drinks on a tray—and asked him for another chair for "Paul Ross's boy." When Aidan sat, they all stared curiously at him, part offended and part amused he would dare dine with *civilized* people.

After all, he was still wearing last night's T-shirt and sweats, socks that didn't match, and sandals half chewed up by Roy. He hadn't even checked a mirror this morning to know the state of his hair. Everyone else was in their Sunday best.

Hudson wasn't present. There wasn't even a place setting for him.

Hudson wasn't just late; he wasn't expected to come at all.

Aidan turned to Gum. "Where's Hudson?" he whispered.

Gum shrugged. He seemed checked out. The rest of the Claveys started to order, but Gum had his head down, messing with the napkin in his lap, tracing his fingers around the white cloth, performing the same motions over and over. A long vertical line, two horizontal ones intersecting it, then two curves, facing outward.

Something twisted in Aidan's gut.

Across the table, the nurse ordered for herself. Beth's eyes were open yet far away. She didn't react to any of the conversation at the table, and no one but the nurse acknowledged her. Paul had explained before that Beth was in a coma. Yes, her eyes were open, and sometimes she twitched. It was all involuntary. But most people in comas rested in bed. They weren't paraded around like this, just to be ignored.

Now Aidan understood the appeal of curses. If Beth was

cursed, she could be like a princess in a fairy tale who could only wake up when the beast was slain. If this was a fairy tale, what happened to her would have meant something. And there was a chance she would wake up, after the curse was lifted. After true love's kiss or the clock struck midnight.

Aidan shouldn't have given Gum shit earlier. Now he regretted calling all of Gum and Iris's theories delusional. They *were* delusional, but he could have said it a little nicer.

"So, you're Paul's boy?" asked the man on the other side of the table. Bruce Clavey. One-fourth of the Disasters 1.0. He hardly looked like the boy from the pictures in Paul's living room. He'd lost a lot of hair, for starters, along with the glimmer of rebellion in his eyes.

"Uh. Yeah."

"But you're not a year-rounder?"

Year-rounders were people who *actually* lived in Bad Creek. Most of them were stubborn elderly locals like Rex, who toughed it out in the snowy winters when all the tourists were gone and most businesses were closed. No one stayed in the mighty lake houses on the north side for most of the year.

Except for Paul. And Bill Clavey.

"No. I live with my mom in California."

"In Los Angeles?" probed the woman next to Bruce. His wife, Brenda, looked like the ladies on Fox News, with an unnatural tan and aggressively blonde hair.

"Pasadena."

"Hollywood," Bill Clavey said. He dragged the last syllable, milking the word for all it was worth. Hollywood was a bad thing, and the rest of the family was expected to understand it. He then let out a hearty chuckle. "Not much like your father when he was your age." Aidan liked to think it was true, but that didn't feel like a compliment to either of them. "How is Paul?" Bill added. His tone was light, but his eyes were accusing.

"Fine." Aidan had been lucky to avoid them at the cookout this year, but he knew he would never completely escape interviews by adults who didn't care about him.

Bill dabbed his mustache with a napkin. "Is he still off the bottle?"

Aidan gritted his teeth. "Yes."

"For how long now?"

None of your business. "It's been a long time."

"You play basketball?"

"No."

"A waste, with your height."

Even though Aidan had heard this one before, he looked at Gum, pleading for a lifeline. But Gum was still zoned out, tracing the same lines on his lap. He would often pull at holes in his jeans or chew on the fraying edges of his shirtsleeves. But this was new.

Aidan didn't like it.

"So what *do* you do?" Bill Clavey said.

"Uh . . ." Aidan was seventeen. He didn't have to *do* anything. What did these people want from him?

"Do you like movies, like your dad?" Bruce asked, then snickered like it was an inside joke. As if he hadn't been best friends with the guy twenty years ago.

"Nasty stuff in that movie," said Brenda. She had her lips

pursed, her hands to her neck, ready to clutch her pearls over the sins of *kids these days.*

"I can't believe the drive-in still plays that every summer," said the other lady: a slightly younger version of her sister-in-law. She wasn't as polished, though; not as seamlessly blonde. Her dark roots were showing. "It's a family place. But everyone's promoting Satanism these days . . ."

"It's not promoting Satanism," Aidan said.

They obviously hadn't seen the film. The monster was only summoned after the main character's boyfriend performed the séance. If anything, the film denounced alliances with the unholy, blaming the college kids for their own horrific deaths. The Claveys should have been eating it up.

"The Hollywood elite are grooming our children with the media," the other guy said. Bruce's brother Brian. He looked exactly like him, with a little less jaw and a little more hair.

Bill Clavey turned to Aidan. "Have you seen the gardens?"

Aidan didn't know what to do with the conversational whiplash.

Bill pulled back his chair, setting his cloth napkin on top of his empty plate. "Daniel, why don't we show Paul's boy the gardens outside?"

Gum silently obeyed, and so did Aidan. Bill Clavey was less intimidating without his loyal family of followers, and Aidan would rather be anywhere than in that claustrophobic room with the dry scones and blue-eyed robots staring at him. Bill led them outside the front door, toward a path with trees and flowering bushes.

That was when it hit him. Aidan had never been to

Handerson's for brunch, but he had visited in the gardens. Those were the same flowers, the same stones on the path with names of donors etched onto them.

It had been Glory's idea. He was partially relieved she'd chosen the time and place for dates, but it had felt oddly salacious to go off by themselves. He sometimes thought being with her this way was too good to be legal. No one had been frequenting the gardens that night, because only Glory Garren would want to see flowers after dark. Had she chosen that venue because she'd wanted it to be private? A secret?

Had she wanted *them* to be a secret?

"Do your parents know you're here?" Aidan had asked her as they passed under an arch covered in what he had assumed were roses.

"You mean, do my parents know if I'm here *with you?*" Glory had replied, reading his mind as always.

She was always one step ahead. He'd liked that. He had felt like she had a plan. She was his current, guiding him. But now he wondered if that had ever been a good thing, or if he was pathetic for falling for everything she said.

"You don't have to worry about my moms," Glory had said. "They like you."

"I know." Of course they liked him. They liked Paul, so they had to like Aidan. They liked Beth, so they had to like Gum. Bruce had deserted the Disasters a long time ago, so Hudson was never allowed to be liked.

"So, why are you afraid?" Glory had asked.

"I'm always afraid."

Glory smiled like he'd said something funny. "What are you scared of most?"

"Honestly? You."

She laughed, and Aidan was unsure what that meant. Was she making fun of him? Had he said something wrong, and she was finally realizing how much of a mistake he was?

"You're afraid of me? Really? You think I'm gonna bury you in this garden?"

"No. I'm more afraid of . . . being without you," he admitted.

"Aw." She knelt by a grouping of wilted blue flowers. "Well, you're gonna have to wait for me till next summer. What if you want to talk to other girls?"

"You're the only girl who exists. I'll wait for you."

She giggled. "You're so cute." She pointed at the shriveled trumpet-shaped flowers by her feet. "That's me. Morning glory."

"I think you mean midnight glory," Aidan said.

"Well, that does sound scarier." She laughed again and leaned in closer to grab the single pretty flower of the bunch.

"You shouldn't pick it," Aidan warned. "That's the only good one."

"They'll bloom in the morning. This one should be dead by now anyway." She'd pulled the flower away from its siblings and presented her prize to Aidan, pressing it into his hand.

"I should be giving *you* flowers," he'd pointed out.

"I don't believe in gender roles." She smiled then, and for a moment it knocked the wind out of Aidan.

"Wait. What are *you* afraid of?" he had asked her after he'd recovered. But she never answered him. And she had never promised to wait for him.

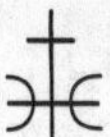

The morning glories looked different in the daylight, purple and not blue like Aidan remembered. More of them were blooming, with only a few curled up and dead.

Had Glory orchestrated the same bit for Hudson, making him promise allegiance but not offering the same loyalty? It didn't matter. Aidan couldn't be mad at her, even if she had been sneaking around with Hudson. That didn't mean she deserved to die.

But if she hadn't died, would they still be together?

Bill pulled out a cigar and pointed it at the Second Largest Crucifix in The World looming over the pines. "You know," he said, "my father commissioned the cross in 1951. He brought God back to this town."

Well, the Son of God didn't look very happy to be in Bad Creek. The massive Jesus glared down at them, demanding their reverence. And Bill Clavey was staring unblinking at Aidan. What was this guy's deal? Was he still trying to decide if Aidan was a no-good Satanist alcoholic like his dad?

"You know this place was near-wilderness before my ancestor, Cyrus Clavey, built his cabin up here?" Bill continued. "He cleared . . . must've been a thousand trees. Lived off bear meat. He brought Bad Creek into being."

"I thought Hudson would be here," Aidan blurted.

Bill Clavey took a drag of the cigar. His eyes—so bright blue they practically reflected the sun—were like Hannibal Lecter's, Aidan decided. He was sizing Aidan up, imagining how his flesh would taste. Still, those eyes didn't stir up any memories. Not like Hudson's had.

"I didn't think you were friends," Bill said, as if he knew all of his grandkids' friends. He probably didn't even know Aidan's name. He was just "Paul's boy."

Aidan shrugged. "We hang out sometimes."

"I don't think so." The old man dropped his cigar right on a bed of flowers. "Give my regards to Paul." He went back inside the restaurant without picking it up.

Aidan should have responded with, *Yes sir*, or something like that, but he didn't have any fake politeness left in his system. This guy lived right next to Paul. Why was he so curious about him? Why was he suddenly so curious about Aidan? Like he only just now existed?

According to Iris, the Claveys were victims of the "curse." Bill had lost his fiancée and his daughter to the lake. Did he also blame it on the supernatural? And since Aidan's dad was a full-blown Devil worshipper, he had to be at fault. That was the way these people's brains worked.

Aidan played back the conversation in his head, wondering why he thought he could press that far, wondering what the hell Bill's beef with his dad was about, wondering if he would ever learn how fucked up that family was and if he even *wanted* to know. He picked up the cigar and tossed it into the nearest trash can, only a few feet away.

CHAPTER 21

Okay, so this was going to be harder than she had thought. The current by Wahbee's dock was strong. The second Iris stopped paddling, the lake pushed her back as if to say, *Nope, you're not getting any more clues today. You had your chance. Come back later.*

If only Aidan hadn't woken her up this morning. She'd been so close. Only a few more steps, and she would have known what Glory had drawn at the edge of the Traxlers' dock.

In the seconds between sleeping and waking, she had felt a pull—the feeling of her heart being lassoed toward a great big truth.

After the boys had left, Iris had freed the oar of cobwebs and dragged Paul's old kayak down to the water. Ten minutes of struggling, though, and she still hadn't gone farther than a few yards. And there was another problem: She was awake. So far, Glory had only sent Iris messages while she was sleeping.

Even if Iris managed to overpower the current, she wouldn't even know which direction to go.

This was hopeless.

She almost dropped her oar when she heard a voice. "Whoa, do you know what you're doing?"

Another kayak was gliding toward her. She scowled when she saw who was in it.

Hudson Clavey was like that zit on your nose that you know you're supposed to ignore, but you really want to just pop and get it over with. She shouldn't give him the satisfaction of watching her tear him away from her skin.

"Hold the oars like this," he said. God, he was going to mansplain to her. "If you want to go left, you push your oar on the right side, and vice versa."

She started to paddle away from him, pushing as hard as she could.

"See, you got it!" He followed her, catching up easily. "Shit, didn't know we were racing."

"We're not."

It was exactly like Hudson to make this a competition. That was how he lived his life. Everything was a game, and he was always winning.

He gave her a smirk, letting his kayak coast next to hers. They were farther from shore than Iris had ever swum. Dragonflies zoomed around their oars. Glory had a phase when she was really into insects and would wake Iris up with a new bug fact. When Iris had first learned dragonflies only lived for a few weeks, it had made her unreasonably weepy. She wondered if they knew their lives were short, and that was why they were always in a hurry. People didn't get that luxury, but maybe dragonflies did. Were they happier, knowing death was coming?

"This is beautiful," Hudson said, admiring the water lilies. "It looks like a Monet painting."

Iris rolled her eyes. Was he really trying to impress her with basic art history knowledge?

She didn't know exactly what her type was yet, but it definitely didn't include Hudson Clavey. Her crushes were ultra-random and unreachable. The girl in her algebra class, for example. She had helped Iris understand the hard equations, and Iris had given her advice for dealing with her shitty boyfriend. But the two never broke up, so that hadn't gone anywhere.

There was the boy across the street who walked his family's Pomeranian after school. He'd let Iris come along sometimes, and she hadn't realized how much she liked him until he moved away. Then there was the kid with glasses who always challenged their history teacher, bringing in sources to call out inaccuracies. The whole period would turn into a debate, and it was magical to watch them take down Iris's least favorite teacher. But Iris didn't know how to even approach someone that smart, that brave.

If she had a type, it wasn't Hudson Clavey. That was what she needed to keep reminding herself.

Besides, she had a curse to break.

There were a few geese in their path. Iris hadn't paid them any mind, but as they paddled closer one of them honked and started fluttering its wings, like a helicopter bracing for ascent.

"Fuck off," Hudson told the goose.

He held up his paddle defensively. Iris didn't feel like fighting today. The birds had claimed their turf; that was fine. She'd just leave. She tried to whip herself around as fast as she could. Too fast. The kayak flipped.

Cold water seeped into her nostrils. She was only underwater for a second. But that was a second too long. Panic seared through her. Before any claws could drag her down by the neck, she grabbed on to the capsized kayak and lifted her head out of the water.

Iris frantically looked for her oars. Shit. They had floated outside of her reach.

Hudson kept yelling at the goose, but it braced its wings, honking at him menacingly. Iris gave it a massive splash, drenching it. It gave one last honk, as if to say, *This isn't over*, before floating toward the others.

Iris tried to hoist herself back into her kayak, with no luck. She felt like every minute she was in the lake she was in more danger.

"Hey, it's okay. You should be able to touch here," Hudson said, his voice soothing.

Iris stopped kicking and extended her toes until she reached the rocky bottom.

Before this summer, he hadn't wanted anything to do with her, and now he was practically stalking her. Could it be a coincidence that Hudson had run into her out here? The thought hit her as suddenly as a static shock. Glory had led Iris to the house, where Hudson's wallet had been. Then Glory had led her off the dock, where Iris ran into him.

She didn't know if that made him safe or very, *very* dangerous.

Iris tried to jump into the kayak again, but it kept flipping. She didn't have the arm strength to lift herself.

"Hold on," Hudson said, his voice still so gentle it made Iris want to cry. "There's a dock up here."

She was so panicked, she hadn't even noticed it. Unlike the big one at the Landings' marina, this was a private dock that they probably weren't allowed on. She only needed to be there for a second, to get on the kayak, then she would paddle back to Paul's and never get in this lake again. She climbed the ladder as quickly as she could despite her wobbly hands.

Hudson watched. If he planned to kill her, boy, was he taking his time. She was about to lower herself into the kayak when he suddenly said, "There's a leech on your leg."

Only then did she see the crimson dripping down the fleshiest part of her calf. Then she spotted the leech, as thick as her pinkie and half the length. Its black mouth pulsated as it sucked on her skin. The blood still inside of her body all rushed out of her head. She sat before she could faint.

That was when she noticed there were more. Another one on that leg, right above her foot, and a third on her other calf.

They were just leeches; this wasn't life-threatening. She didn't need Hudson to save her. But he switched into chivalry mode before she could tell him that. He climbed the ladder and went over to her. "Let me help," he said.

Iris ignored him and tried to grab the one on her ankle, but the tiny monster was latched tight. More blood steadily oozed around its mouth. And pulling was getting her nowhere.

Hudson guided her hand away. "You can't just yank them off like that. Let me help."

"Why are you being nice to me?"

He paused. Still hovering over her. She tried to maintain composure, but it was hard with the blood dripping down her legs and with Hudson sitting *that close.*

"Because . . . that's what you deserve," he finally said.

"You think I deserve sympathy. Well, I don't want it. Not from you, or anyone."

He sucked in his lips, but he didn't give her the Sympathy Face, at least. "You saved me from the goose. It's only fair I repay the favor. But, hey. Your call."

At least he had acknowledged that Iris had won that fight. "Fine," she snorted, but only because she'd pass out if she thought too much about the little squishy thing sucking her dry.

He went for the one on her ankle first. When he pulled the skin and dug his nails under the leech's head, Iris saw spots at the edge of her vision. Her body could accept the parasite sucking her dry, but not Hudson Clavey touching her. His hands were softer than she expected, and his eyes weren't nearly as cold as they used to be.

Just like the streamers on Glory's bike, they had changed color.

Finally, the creature came loose. More blood dripped on the dock.

"Holy shit. I couldn't even feel it the whole time," she said, to get rid of the silence.

"Yeah, their saliva numbs their hosts. You only notice after they've already got ya."

Hudson tossed the leech on the dock. It writhed around

for only a few seconds before he picked up a rock. Iris looked away when he crushed it. She didn't want to see the blood and wonder how much of it was her own.

She hoped they weren't ruining a stranger's dock. She looked behind her, hoping no one would see them there, trespassing. The house didn't match the other mansions on the north side. This one was white with tall pillars. Then she saw the targets to her left and put two and two together.

"This is your house," she said.

Hudson had lured her here. *Somehow*. Obviously, the geese and the leeches weren't paid actors, but Hudson must have taken this opportunity to bring her to his lair.

He was working on the next leech; she could feel his fingers on her, the light pressure of his nails between her skin and the creature's mouth.

"This is my grandpa's house," he said.

"Same thing."

"Not really. I'm only allowed in if I'm invited."

Like a vampire. He sure handled the blood well.

"What does that mean?" she asked.

"It means, in my family . . . everything has to be earned. It's all transactional. If you don't follow the rules, well, there's no room for mistakes."

"I think that's how every family works, though. There have to be some rules . . . some boundaries . . ."

"Let's just say, not everyone's idea of fair boundaries is the same." His hands pulled away from her, and she closed her eyes as the rock slammed against the wood planks again. "Okay, I know what you're thinking," he continued. "Why am I whining? I'm luckier than most. Trust me, I know I have a lot to be grateful for. But . . . for me, it's not worth it. And to them"—he pointed at the white building—"I'm not worth it either."

She wasn't expecting any of that. When Gum complained about the Claveys, it made sense. He didn't match them. Hudson blended in with the country club crowd—perfect polos, perfect posture, and perfect arrogance to match. This conversation could be an act to appeal to her. But if it was a lie, this boy deserved an Oscar. And if he had wanted to kill Iris, he had already missed his perfect chance.

"Sorry, that was a lot," Hudson said.

"I don't get it," Iris said. "If you never fit in with your family, why be a dick to your cousin, instead of being, like, a united front?"

"I think I realized too late . . . and I'm sorry for that. Believe me, I'm sorry for a lot of things." Why was he so determined to tell her sorry? He was never sorry when he smacked a volleyball in her face. She never asked him to be. Because she would never apologize for all the times she did the same to him.

"Well, I'm not the person you need to apologize to."

He looked up at her. Yes, his eyes were different than before. There was a little bit of warmth in the center, a drip of green that she only noticed now that she was this close to him. Iris's cheeks felt warm. What was wrong with her?

"You're right," he said. "Everything's different now. I don't believe the same things as them anymore, but the impulses are there. I still have a lot to unlearn. I'll talk to Gum."

He lifted the rock, ready to crush the last leech.

"You don't have to kill it," Iris told him half-heartedly.

"If I don't, it'll get someone else." He slammed the rock, hard. Blood splattered from every side. Some of it belonged to her. And some belonged to victims she'd never know.

The blood on Iris's legs was dry now, but her shirt and shorts were still damp—and so were the ends of her ponytail.

She and Hudson had paddled back toward Paul's without saying much. He had asked if she needed help lifting her kayak out of the water. When she'd said she was fine on her own, he had let her go. He hadn't pointed out her flushed cheeks, her shaky hands, but he must have noticed.

Every second that went by, Iris only felt more lost. Hudson hadn't shown any murderous tendencies, except to leeches. If Helena could show up in the bathtub to whisper ominous warnings to Gum, couldn't Glory appear to Iris and confirm the name of her killer out loud?

Glory seemed to be leading her toward Hudson, but she wouldn't have led her to him if he was a bad guy. Glory wouldn't put her in danger like that.

Which meant Hudson must know something.

When Iris called April to pick her up, Joanna answered. Iris's moms used to be interchangeable in many ways: both were dependable for rides to theater practice; both were good cooks and good listeners. But since last summer, Joanna had become withdrawn and quick to anger, and Iris didn't need any more drama today. She'd have rather dealt with April.

Joanna promised she'd be there in five. She sounded perky, like her old self. But there was plenty of time for her good mood to grow moldy.

She couldn't tell her mom about the sleepwalking or about Hudson. Hanging out with a Clavey boy was certainly against the rules, and going in the lake by herself was even worse. Even before last summer, that wasn't allowed.

When Iris was in second grade, April had sat her kids down and explained why that rule was created. Even the vague description of Beth's accident made Joanna upset. Iris never remembered her parents fighting about anything else.

Back then, Iris had been on April's side. She had felt plenty mature enough to deal with hearing this sad story, certainly mature enough to swim without supervision. She was a big kid who could handle this kind of stuff. And to prove it, she decided she would swim the whole length of the Landings, from the deepest end, where the measly creek swelled into the lake, to the tire swing behind Cabin 12, where the water was too shallow to fish. She'd still wear a life jacket and bring a float in case she got tired. According to Iris's seven-year-old logic, that would made her brave but also responsible.

She had walked toward the dock in her swimsuit and jumped in. Early in the morning, there was no wake from boaters, so it hadn't taken her long to swim to her precious willow tree near Cabin 12. On the lap back, she had grabbed the prettiest water lily she could find and carried it with her. She had gently set it on the edge of the dock, to keep it safe as she climbed up the ladder.

That was when she'd noticed Glory standing with her hands on her hips, waiting. Iris had figured her sister would be supportive once she understood the motivation. Instead, Glory had yelled at her like Joanna had yelled at April the day before.

"That's stupid! Sometimes rules are for a reason!"

Iris had cried like she always did when she got in trouble. But Glory had promised she wouldn't tell their parents, and she'd kept that promise.

Joanna didn't wait for Iris to put on her seat belt before asking, "So, what did you guys do?"

Joanna wanted to know which board games they played, which horror movies they watched, which junk food they gorged themselves on. Iris could have muttered a quick recap, minus the sleepwalking and Hudson. *Hudson.* Just thinking his name gave her a flutter in the pit of her stomach. She would run into him again. They couldn't go back to snarky quips whenever they passed the other.

She mentally shook herself, reminding herself that she didn't have a crush on Hudson fucking Clavey. No way things had gotten *that* bad.

"Why did you stop being friends with Bruce?" Iris asked

instead. She hadn't known she was going to until it had come out.

Predictably, her mom didn't answer right away. Iris had crossed a line somehow, and Joanna herself would cross a line if she admitted that.

"Sometimes people drift apart," Joanna eventually said.

Iris could relate. She'd had a friend in first grade who had become a stranger by the time they were in middle school. Friends could drift apart, of course. But not *best friends.* When there was a strong bond, you needed something even stronger to sever it. And the Disasters 1.0 had had the strongest bond possible—at least, that was what the stories made it sound like.

Was that really it? Could they have grown apart as they grew up? Was that already happening with Disasters 2.0? The version of Bruce that existed now didn't exactly look like someone her mom would hang out with. When had that changed?

She thought of the argument she'd overheard after the cookout. Joanna pleading with Paul, *Don't you think I feel guilty enough?*

"Did you guys have a fight our something?" Iris pressed.

"Nooooo, nothing like that. When we started college, we said we'd still come back every summer, but Bruce ended up studying abroad. Besides, life happens. We all went to work and then had kids. Bruce didn't come back for a few years."

"Was it 'cause of Beth?"

Joanna hesitated. "No, that was before Beth's accident. He started coming back after."

"And how was she, before? Were you and Beth drifting apart too?"

"She was my best friend." Joanna took a deep breath. "You don't have to be worried about your boys, Iris."

"That's not—"

"If it's meant to be, it's meant to be. You're not who you thought you would be when you were five, right? So you can't expect everyone to turn out how you imagined." There was an uncomfortable pause before Joanna gave her the Sympathy Smile. "Think you can make it past the groundhog, this year?" she added, referencing the dreaded sixth hole at the mini-golf course. They always played putt-putt on Day Five.

Usually Iris looked forward to playing every year, but beating that demented groundhog was the last thing on her mind. Her thoughts swirled with sketches of blue eyes and water lilies.

Once at the Landings, Iris changed, put Band-Aids on her leech wounds, and sat in the backseat of the van. Joanna's good mood hadn't faded yet. Her moms sang along to "Love Shack," and Iris stayed inside of her head.

When she stepped into the mini-golf parking lot, the midday sun warmed her face. She wished the morning fog had stayed, to complement the blur in her head. Instead, her armpits were wet, and her thighs uncomfortably rubbed together, and her ponytail was heavy on the back of her neck.

The boys and Paul were waiting by the plastic pirate ship in front of the entrance. The ship was older than their parents, and it looked like it. It had been much grander, much bigger, to Iris when she was a kid. Now she saw it for what it was: the paint was scraped off, and it looked stupid without any masts. It wasn't much bigger than Paul's little boat. Every year, the four Disasters lined up in front of the ship for a photo.

April didn't demand they take one this year.

They walked through the rocky arch with an open treasure chest on the side, holding the putters. The balls were in a much less impressive bucket, right next to them. Paul joked about practicing his swing lately, as if finally, after thirty years, he would beat Joanna. The adults didn't act like they had anything to hide.

And they didn't act like Glory was dead.

"Iris, did you hear me?" April asked. Iris looked up at her. Her mom had been talking to her, and she'd tuned her out. "What color ball do you want? They're out of green."

Iris looked at the selection. There were only white and red left, and though Glory wasn't here to play, Iris couldn't take her color.

"White," she said.

Her throat tightened, but she had to do this.

The pirate motifs ended once they stepped onto the sidewalk path. Hole one was carnival-themed—tiny statues of lions and elephants and juggling clowns dotted the worn turf.

Per usual, Iris went first because she was the youngest. Then Gum, who was six months older. Then Aidan, who was almost a year older than Gum. Then it would have been Glory's turn, as she was a whole year older than Aidan.

Iris did okay.

Gum hit the ball too hard for each stroke.

Aidan would have done better if he'd actually tried.

Glory was dead.

They moved on to the next hole without waiting for the adults to have their turns. Gum had the scorecard, which was probably for the best. If Iris saw the blank space where her sister's name ought to be, she would unravel even faster. Once they were two holes ahead of their parents, Aidan spoke for the first time that day.

"Hudson wasn't at brunch."

Of course he wasn't. He had been with Iris. Now would be a good time to tell them, but Aidan would be pissed at her, and Gum hardly looked like he was listening. He was doodling on the scorecard.

Iris unsuccessfully tried to hit the ball around the miniature shipwreck, then sat on the bench. "Gum, it's your turn," she told him.

He glanced up as if breaking from a trance. He set the scorecard beside her and picked his putter up from the ground. He had drawn the same shape over and over again: a double cross with crescents at the sides.

"Dude," she said, "why are you drawing this?"

He shrugged and smacked his ball right up against the plastic ship. "I don't know. I got bored."

"We really need to find out what it means," Iris said. She looked at Aidan. "Did you ask your dad?"

"Why?"

"Hasn't he done a lot of research on occult stuff?"

Paul's office was full of old books and maps and printouts from the internet tacked onto the walls. Iris hardly ever went in. That was where Paul was holed up when he was home, searching for inspiration for his second film, which would probably live in development limbo forever.

"My dad doesn't know anything, okay?" Aidan sniped. "Just drop it."

"I'm not accusing him of anything." Iris said. She loved Paul; he was like her bonus uncle. And clearly Joanna and he had gotten over their beef from a few days ago. When she turned to see how close the others were, she accidentally made eye contact with Joanna, who smiled and gave her daughter a thumbs-up.

Iris walked to the hole with the swinging log and plastic beavers. As she stepped over a stream, the white ball slipped out of her grip. It tumbled down the fake waterfall, into a muddy lagoon. "Crap."

She could return to the first hole and ask an employee for a replacement ball, but it would take too much time. Iris took a deep breath and knelt above the lagoon; the water so opaque she could barely make out the shapes of the balls underneath. She put her hand in the slimy water and tried not to think about all the bacteria in it.

The first ball she grabbed was red. She tossed it back in.

The next ball she found was also red.

And so was the next.

"Iris! Grab one before the old people catch up!" Gum shouted.

Paul called out, "Hey!"

She started using both hands, grabbing several golf balls at once. Red, red, red, red. Each was warm as flesh. They shouldn't have been warm. The water was freezing. This was a sign. It had to be.

"Please tell me," Iris whispered. There was a reason her usual ball color was out; there was a reason her Schwinn had had a flat tire.

"Please tell me," Iris begged. To the lagoon. To God. To the universe. To Glory, if she could hear her, wherever she was.

Glory would be able to solve this.

Glory would be able to solve this.

That was it, wasn't it? She understood it now. Glory was asking Iris to take her color. To take *her place.* If Iris relinquished herself to her sister, she could act as Glory's conduit. The answer had always been obvious.

Glory was the only one who could solve her own murder.

Iris plucked a red ball from the water and walked back up the hill.

"You guys," she said. "I have an idea. How to trigger it again."

"Trigger what?" Aidan looked pissed.

"The connection between me and Glory."

"How do you know it's her talking to you?" Gum asked. He pushed the swinging log to go faster as Iris dropped the red ball into position. "What if it's something else? Glory was sleepwalking. It sounds like Helena might have been too—"

"It's her," Iris said. "I can't explain it, I can just feel it."

Then she hit the ball without hesitation. It effortlessly rolled past the swinging log.

Hole in one.

Cross. Slash. Half circle. Half circle. Iris and Aidan probably didn't notice what Gum was carving into his leg with his fingernails, and he preferred to keep it that way. They were getting along, for the first time this summer. Gum wasn't going to ruin their night.

The sun stubbornly hovered above the horizon. Fluorescent orange and pink reflected on the water. Iris's Bluetooth speaker blasted the playlist Glory had painstakingly curated for them last summer. Gum had to admit Glory had good taste in music. But he still considered "accidently" kicking the speaker off the dock. Anything could summon her these days. He'd rather listen to the Richardsons blabber on about how life was better during the Reagan administration than anything related to Glory Garren.

"Savi says the party's starting at eight tomorrow," Iris said. Her feet dangled over the water, like she was just daring something to drag her under. At this point, that was probably her goal. After all, her new brilliant plan was to re-create Glory's last night alive.

And Aidan, for God knows what reason, was fine with it.

"We should go at nine," Aidan said. He was leaning over Iris's phone, reading through her messages with Savi Traxler. He too was only inches from the water. This morning he'd called her delusional, and now he was more than happy to cosign on her theory.

Gum sat cross-legged on the other side of the Landing's dock, digging his ragged nails into the skin right above his tattoo. Cross. Slash. Half circle. Half circle. He drew blood, wiped it with his palm, and started on the other leg.

"M'kay," Iris agreed. "I'll go shopping with my moms tomorrow. They're going into Mackinac anyway."

"Get a red top," Aidan said. "Puffy sleeves."

"Yeah. I know the one."

"And a white skirt."

"That shouldn't be too hard to find."

Gum should've stopped them. He should've reminded them that they already knew it was going to happen again. *It's not over*, Glory had warned. Maybe they'd listen if he admitted the truth about Glory. If he admitted he had stolen Iris's putt-putt ball. When the whispers told him to snag it, he didn't resist, even though the voice sounded nothing like Glory anymore. Now his sin weighed a trillion tons in his shorts pocket. But he couldn't confess.

And he couldn't stop drawing that stupid symbol.

He let them go on like that, until the sun had finally

disappeared behind the pines, casting the just barely visible crucifix in shadow. Still, they weren't finished. They walked the stretch of the Landings, planning tomorrow night like it was a heist. Gum numbly followed, a trickle of blood running down to his knees.

Iris and Aidan stopped when they reached their willow tree, where the water was higher than it should have been. Iris took off her sandals and dipped her feet in.

Stop stop stop, he wanted to yell. But what was the point? No one could stop a determined Garren girl. And every time the truth begged to escape his lips, he felt his throat tighten.

Aidan swatted a mosquito. "What happened to the tire swing?"

"Since when are you nostalgic?" Iris said, playfully slapping his shoulder.

"I always liked the tire swing."

"Yeah, but you just *admitted it*."

"Seriously, though. What happened to it? Was it last summer?"

"I don't know. It was already gone when we got here. Why don't we just blame the Claveys?"

Aidan rolled his eyes. They took a break from planning Iris's ritual suicide, and debated where to buy supplies for a new tire swing instead.

Gum tuned them out. He couldn't let himself listen to them acting like friends again. It was a false victory. The calm before the storm. Something was coming, and Gum worried it would be all his fault.

Cross. Slash—

"What about Gum?" Aidan said.

Gum perked up. Had they even noticed that he hadn't talked in an hour? Had he even said a word after putt-putt? Could he, if he wanted to?

"He wasn't at Savi's party that night," Aidan clarified.

"I mean, I wasn't either," Iris pointed out.

Aidan nodded. "Yeah, but we need you . . ."

Need you to be Glory.

"Gum's the only one who's seen Helena. He should go too." Iris glanced at Gum. She had that manic determination in her eyes. She looked just like her sister. "But just watch, okay? Don't interact with me at all. Be a ghost, basically."

"Take it." The words fluttered into his ear like a mosquito. Quiet, in the scheme of things, but so wickedly close to his eardrum he jumped. Aidan and Iris couldn't hear it. They were focused on the scary movie playing on Aidan's laptop, while Gum stared at Iris's broken Magic 8 Ball on her nightstand. The night had been admittedly bearable after they went inside Cabin 4. Their secret plans were not to be mentioned while Iris's moms were around.

The movie Aidan showed them was the perfect distraction: some postapocalyptic western with zombie horses. Aidan would never admit it, but he could be just like Paul sometimes. Except Aidan would act all humble as he presented whatever obscure media he'd hyper-fixated on and be shocked when everyone liked it. Eventually he'd forget to play it cool and start rambling about the cinematography and point out shots that were actually a reference to a Renaissance painting or some shit. That was the best version of Aidan.

And that was how the night had gone, brain-eating farm animals and popcorn mixed with marshmallows until Glory realized she wasn't the center of attention.

"*Take it*," she whispered. Voice low and slippery and so close it could have come from within him. The lights were off. Everyone was so focused on the movie, Iris maybe wouldn't even notice if Gum leaned over and grabbed her Magic 8 Ball. He could buy her a new one. But she had said she wanted to hold on to the original. How could he possibly do that to her?

"*Take it*."

No fucking way, Gum thought, knowing Glory would hear him. His heart raced from the small disobedience. She couldn't actually force him, could she? He still had free will.

"*Take it*," she growled. But Gum didn't move. He didn't move for the whole movie, not even to grab popcorn. He sat on his hands to avoid the urge. He watched the last hour of the movie in the reflection of the Magic 8 Ball, and when it was over, and Iris said she was too tired for another one, Gum dragged his feet through the dewy grass between their cabins. He lay on the lumpy mattress in Cabin 3 and stared out the open window, where he could still see the Magic 8 Ball on Iris's nightstand.

He didn't sleep.

His ears were ringing from hours of *take it take it take it*. He probably had permanent hearing loss at this point. His heart ached, like Glory had reached her hands inside of him and was squeezing his internal organs for fun. Gum's hands, propped under his pillow, had gone numb.

Not even his eyes had rest. He forgot how to blink. There were spots at the edges of his vision, making a vignette around the stupid fucking Magic 8 Ball.

Dawn came. Birds merrily chirped. Boat engines cranked to life. A whole night had gone by, and Gum was still stubbornly holding on to what little autonomy he had left. Popping every blood vessel in his eyes, giving himself a heart attack, for what? Pride? Since when could he afford any of that?

What was another humiliation?

Fine.

The second he relented, the invisible hands clutching his chest let go. He could blink. He could breathe. But he knew his body would rebel again if he didn't act quickly.

Gum climbed out the window. He didn't quite stick the landing, but Glory was silently laughing at him anyway, so who cared?

Iris had slept with her window open. Easy. Gum approached as silently as possible, keeping his eyes on the lump of blankets on the bed. He'd almost made it, fingers just about to lift the screen, when a corpse peeled away from Iris's door.

Just like Glory, and just like Helena, she was waterlogged, covered in algae and fish guts. She shuffled toward Iris's bed. Her head hung forward unnaturally, bobbing up and down with each crooked step. It was like her spinal cord had snapped in half, and the only thing keeping her head from toppling to the floor was her rotting skin. She wore a tattered blue dress that cut off a little past her gray knees. What was left of her hair hung in a braid, with soggy ribbons.

He wanted to scream, but Glory squeezed his throat.

"Take it."

He stayed at the window, watching helplessly, as the decaying girl with the ribbons in her hair tore through the quilts, revealing a sleeping Iris. She grabbed Iris by the neck, lifting her out of the bed with impossible strength, and Iris's eyes didn't flutter for a second.

"Take it. Take it. Take it."

And then what? You take Iris?

Glory and her ever-expanding army of drowned girls. Even in the afterlife, she had to lead a clique. *When did this one die?* he silently asked. If she really was Glory, she'd know just by the outfit. She once got really into historical costuming, probably just so she could ruin movies for people.

Glory's inhuman voice echoed in his ear. *"When it was her time."*

Ribbon Girl dragged Iris by the throat, inching toward the door. It swung open with an eerie creak. Even the cabin was an accomplice now. But what was Gum doing to do to stop it? Aidan had run to her, shaken her awake, at the dock. Gum's feet were cement as his hands lifted the screen of their own accord, snatching up the Magic 8 Ball.

Iris and Ribbon Girl disappeared out the bedroom door. They were heading outside. Gum watched them slowly approach the dock. A few more moments, and Iris would go off the edge. The water was only five feet deep there, but it wasn't impossible to drown in shallow water. Iris would go under and

Gum would just be standing here, holding the fucking Magic 8 Ball.

"It'll be her time soon."

The screen door clacked open. "Iris!" called a female voice. Joanna, barefoot in her pajamas, ran to the dock. The second her hand touched her daughter's, Ribbon Girl dissolved into muddy water.

Gum hurried back to Cabin 3, slipping through his window to watch the Garrens.

Iris still didn't wake as Joanna coaxed her back inside. Joanna looked around nervously. As if she had also seen the rotting ghost. As if she too worried it would come back.

"Can I borrow some nail polish?"

April looked up from her book—a crime thriller, as usual. The cover was splattered with red, blocky text. Iris didn't understand how her mom could casually read something like that on their porch, on the anniversary of her daughter's death.

Then again, Iris was going to a party tonight.

"Yeah...in my makeup bag. On the sink," April said, before closing the book on her lap. "Why?"

"Lost mine," Iris answered. She turned to go back inside, but her mom reached for her.

"Will you sit with me for a while?" she asked.

Joanna was out grabbing Fourth of July cookie ingredients for tomorrow. She claimed to not be patriotic, but she couldn't help but bake for a theme. She had seemed to be in a good mood this morning, and Iris hoped it lasted during their trip into the city. Shopping in Mackinac could be a slog. April always held out on buying her yearly pullover until they went to the very last store and decided actually the first store had the best options. It was always too hot and Iris's thighs chafed from walking and it was the day before the last full day in Bad Creek. She'd rather spend it with her boys in the Landings.

This year, however, she had a mission. Red top. Puffy sleeves. Flowy white skirt.

Whatever was responsible for Glory's death, she would confront it at Savi's party.

"I might have to skip making cookies tonight. We're all going to Aidan's when we get back from Mackinac," Iris said. The party wouldn't start until much later, but she had to get ready early. Glory used to prep for hours whenever she had to attend a social event. Iris couldn't just show up; she had to show up like Glory.

"You would cruelly leave your mother all by her lonesome?" April asked, smiling weakly.

It was a joke, but only to cover the painful truth. This was *the* day. The grief counselor stressed memory triggers and anniversaries, like Glory's birthday, the day she was supposed to graduate, the anniversary of her death. July third had come.

And Iris was going to a party.

Guilt squirmed around in her stomach as she ran inside and grabbed nail polish. Red. That was the color Glory would choose. One summer, Glory was convinced she was going to be a world-famous nail tech. She had painted designs on all their nails—vines and flowers and clouds and swirls. Gum had wiped his off before it had dried, stressing his family would kill him if they saw. Aidan had left his on the whole week, but he was a chronic nail-biter. The polish was shredded by the time the Garrens left on the fifth of July. Iris had reapplied a clear coat twice a day so hers wouldn't chip. Eventually, of course, it had.

She would never get those cloud nails back.

Iris returned to the porch and sat beside April. She wished she could explain why she was being extra-distant. It would be worth it, once she presented the truth to her parents. They would forgive her once they had closure.

"How'd you sleep?" April asked.

"Good."

"You don't remember sleepwalking?"

Iris's hand twitched. Bright red polish streaked across her finger.

She had woken up in her room. There were no twigs on her feet, no dirt on her quilt. Iris hadn't gone anywhere last night.

"What?"

"You were wandering out of your room right before the sun came up. Joanna sent you back to bed," April explained. "She used to do that too, you know, the first few years I came up here," she added with a nervous giggle. "She freaked me out. I thought it meant the cabin was haunted."

"When did she stop?"

"After Beth."

Iris glanced down at her nails. They looked like a bloody mess.

It's not just me. It's not just Glory.

If Iris asked Joanna about sleepwalking, would she say anything? Or would she skirt around the truth again? Glory was hiding things last year. Joanna was hiding things now.

Perhaps she always had been.

The family van pulled up in front of the cabin. Joanna stepped out and triumphantly held up grocery bags. "All right, losers, now the real shopping begins."

By store number three, Iris was ready to explode. Every time Joanna looked at her, Iris felt her temper spike higher. She wasn't sure if she even had the right to be angry. Maybe Joanna would have told her about the sleepwalking if she'd asked. Maybe she truly didn't notice all the strange coincidences. But Iris knew now that she wasn't just paranoid. Even Aidan, the eternal skeptic, saw the patterns.

Iris tore through a clothes rack, pretending to search for a T-shirt in her size. This tourist trap seemed to cater to old ladies, with cheesy slogans like *I'd rather be at the lake* in script font.

She had to bring it up. She almost did in the first shop. There was a likely chance Joanna would just gaslight her again, but if Iris didn't try, the anger was just going burn her from the inside out.

She waited until April was safely on the other side of the store, trying on sunglasses she'd never buy. Joanna nudged Iris, holding a pullover. "Is this cute?" she asked.

"Yeah," Iris said.

"But for me, though? Is it pathetic to wear tie-dye after forty? What's the Gen Z consensus?" Normally that would make Iris laugh. But when she finally looked at her mother, her vision burned red.

"Why are we here?" Iris asked sharply. Joanna's smile faltered for a second.

"This can be the last stop if you're all shopped out."

"No, I mean Bad Creek. Why did you want to come back so bad?"

Joanna put the shirt back on the rack. "It's our place. I've spent every summer here. I couldn't imagine . . . I thought you wanted to come."

"You thought I wanted to come back to the place where my sister died?"

Joanna made a strangled noise and gave Iris a pained, wide-eyed look. But Iris didn't falter. The truth was, Iris had wanted to come back too. But she had a real reason. A noble reason. It wasn't some masochistic urge to revel in her trauma. She had a murder to solve and a curse to break.

"How can you come here year after year?" Iris went on. "You revisit the place where all this bad stuff happened, without talking about it?"

"Iris," Joanna warned. Her jaw set, eyes glassy.

"What *really* happened to Beth, Mom?" Iris thought she'd cry, but she was practically yelling over the inoffensive pop music inside the store. A little girl in a stroller perked up to stare at her, but Iris didn't care. "Do you even want to know, or do you want to just keep pretending everything's fine? When were you going to tell me about the sleepwalking?" Joanna winced. But Iris was on a roll. "What else aren't you telling me? I'm not a baby anymore. You think I can't handle it, but I've *been* handling it. All alone. This *whole time.* So tell me—what happened to Beth? What happened to *your daughter?*"

Joanna swallowed. They stood in silence, at dueling stance.

For a year, Iris had dreaded the inevitable moment when she'd fragment into a million tiny pieces. But she didn't think about what would come after. That anything positive could come out of it. Her new sharp edges had the power to cut through bullshit.

"Why did we come back here?" Iris had to know what drove her mother to return to the same place where she'd lost her best friend and her daughter. Was it the same thing that brought Bill Clavey back from Kentucky even after losing his fiancée? She needed someone to finally *voice it*. If Iris knew what this curse was, she could break its hold.

April swooped in, unaware of the tension, or maybe, like her wife, unwilling to acknowledge it.

"I think the one at the first store was the winner," she said.

"I'm afraid so," Joanna agreed. She plucked the car keys from her purse and walked out of the store.

ighting didn't strike twice, which meant this wasn't random coincidence. Grandpa had rolled up to Cabin 3 again, *on purpose.*

Gum fumbled with the laces of his dress shoes. He considered declining the invite, but it wasn't like he'd get any more sleep this morning. And if he was away from Iris, he couldn't steal anything else from her. He couldn't help Glory with her plans.

He dragged himself from his bedroom. He didn't feel entirely alive when he made it to the kitchen. His dad was eating breakfast at the table, telling his wife about his unlucky fishing this trip, like she could hear him. As if one day she'd wake up and remember everything he'd said. Gum used to do that. Just like he used to pray.

"Are you going with your grandfather?" his dad asked.

The horn honked again.

"Do I have a choice?"

As if he had a choice about anything.

His father didn't answer directly. He never straight-up said Gum ought to follow the Claveys' rules, it was just implied. After all, Grandpa controlled his inheritance. He paid for his mom's medical bills and for their at-home nurse. If Gum bothered to come out, his dad would surely get a nervous look and say, *Best to keep that private.* And Gum would be too afraid to ask if it was because his dad was unaccepting or just anticipating Bill Clavey's reaction.

He had no idea what his mom's reaction would have been. She didn't react to anything, since he could remember. But his dad kept a diary of every odd blink, every muscle spasm that looked like a nod. Her reaction to certain medication, certain food. Like someday his devotion would cure her. Gum tried not to dwell on what she could have been before, because she wasn't coming back.

People didn't come back. Gum was extra-sure of that now. Glory hadn't been speaking to him at all. The girl in the bathtub, the girl with the hair ribbons—they weren't other drowned girls of Bad Creek. They were hollow effigies. Something evil was wearing their faces.

And it wanted Gum to do its bidding.

The Cadillac honked. Showtime. Gum went out the front door to see Grandpa parked in the middle of the road, smoking a cigar.

"Good morning," Grandpa said. He wore a collared shirt and fedora that matched his mustache. "I need some help in my garden today. Mind giving a hand?"

"Sure."

Grandpa drove with the top down, even though it was much too hot for it. He yapped on and on about *character*. "Kids these days don't have it. They're spoiled. They're sensitive. They want someone to blame."

Was he talking about Hudson? Gum wouldn't be promoted to Number One Grandson out of nowhere. His grades had tanked to a new low last quarter, and he'd spent the first part of the summer playing video games instead of getting a job.

If Grandpa noticed anything he'd done the past year, it would only make him unhappy. Hudson had to do something to be cast out. But not murder. The Claveys weren't the cartoonish villains Aidan saw them as.

And Glory's killer wasn't a someone. But a *something*.

"Unfortunately, in this world, you can't have your way all the time," Grandpa continued, before clearing his throat. Gum braced himself for an unsolicited Bible verse. "*Do you not know that your bodies are temples of the Holy Spirit, who is in you, whom you have received from God? You are not your own.* That's from Corinthians."

"It's a good one."

There was a Bible verse to justify anything. Usually Grandpa preferred the ones he could make about family values eroding and the culture taking over. His children and grandchildren would nod and thank him for his unsolicited wisdom. But others fought him on it.

Once, Gum had overhead Rex fighting Grandpa over his impromptu sermons. Glory had been holding Gum hostage on Cabin 4's porch, having him pose for a portrait. She'd made him take his hat off after she'd started over three times.

"Can you not draw hats?" Gum had teased.

"It's just ruining the composition," Glory answered. Serious. Glory could never admit defeat.

"So you're just going to sit by?" Grandpa's voice had bellowed. He was standing over Rex, refilling his pontoon boat with gas at the marina. Gum couldn't help but glance toward them. He was supposed to keep his eyes on the horizon. Glory always got mad when he fidgeted while she was drawing.

"They're taking over churches," Grandpa went on. "I passed one on my drive with a sign that said it was LGBTXYZ friendly. Nothing is sacred!"

"Can't say it bothers me," said Rex. "Plenty of real problems in this country. Gas is up five cents from yesterday. It used to be *five cents a gallon*."

"I remember that. And you and I both remember when this was the America our Founding Fathers fought to free. There's a holy war in our nation. What side will our children take if we don't lead them?"

Rex cranked the motor of his boat. He must have said something to rile Grandpa up, because Grandpa had stormed off, gotten in the Caddy, and left the Landings entirely. When he was gone, Glory said, "I don't know how you can stand to listen to him say homophobic shit all the time." She blew on her sketchbook to get rid of pencil shavings. Meaning she was finished. Gum was free to move.

"He doesn't know he's talking about me," he said.

"But *you* know he is."

Ouch. That wasn't something he tried to linger on. He had to compartmentalize himself to survive, while she could be one hundred percent Glory Garren one hundred percent of the time. She didn't get it. She *couldn't* get it, yet Glory was turning this into a sermon of her own. She was always teasing him for not being brave enough. It was so unfair.

"Well, outing myself isn't gonna change his mind," he said, in a whisper. But then he got madder as he spoke, and couldn't help but raise his voice. "It's not just him. My uncle's even worse, honestly. And I'm not exactly the representation that'll de-bigot-ify any of them. What do you expect me to do?"

Glory blinked. Once. Twice. It was rare he fought back on her Big Sister lectures.

"I don't have an answer," she had said, finally. "I'm just really sorry. That's all."

So Glory Garren, the Girl Who Knew Everything, the Girl Who Could Do Anything, had admitted defeat. It hardly felt like victory. Gum's throat had tightened and he knew tears were on their way any second.

Because if Glory didn't have an answer, he was surely fucked.

She had closed the sketchbook and scooted onto the bench beside him. "I'm here for you," she'd said, putting her arm on his shoulder. "We all are. I know you say you don't care what they think, but how could you not? No matter what they believe, there's nothing wrong with you. You don't have to prove you've earned the right to exist."

Grandpa parked outside the mansion and headed toward the garden. Gum had to speed-walk to keep up with the older man's long strides.

The garden was massive; a magazine had even featured it a few years ago. Grandma Betty loved to brag about it. Daylilies were her flowers of choice, all in organized sections, labeled with their scientific names and their nicknames. Frilly yellow Buttered Popcorns, fluffy pink Strawberry Candies, and blood-red Ruby Spiders with spindly petals.

Grandma Betty had died only a few years after they'd built this house, but she'd always been in the background, pouring sweet tea, wearing long dresses and straw hats. If Grandpa missed her, he didn't show it. Just like he never spoke about his drowned fiancée. That would be tacky.

"Have to trim the dead," Grandpa said. Two sets of pruning shears rested on a wrought-iron table. Using one, Grandpa clipped off a wilted Ruby Spider by the neck before chucking it into a bucket. It bled a watery purple, staining his hands.

"To help new ones grow back, right?" Gum asked. He had to show that he cared; that he also considered this an engaging bonding activity. That he was super-excited to prune a garden that would never belong to him.

"Yes. The plant is healthier once we remove the dead and the dying."

Grandpa chucked more flower guts in the bucket.

"So," he continued. "I heard you had some trouble with Mr. Bowers?"

Gum nearly dropped the pruning shears. He had assumed Grandpa didn't know about that. By the time he'd hit middle school, Grandpa had stopped monitoring his grades, so he'd thought he was safe to do as he pleased—as long as he didn't get suspended.

But Grandpa had his hands in everything. Even though he lived in Michigan full-time now, he still had contacts in his home state. He knew all of Gum's teachers. He'd probably gone golfing with his chemistry teacher, Mr. Bowers. He probably sent him the Clavey Christmas cards every year.

Gum tasted blood in his mouth. He clipped off another flower. Oops. That was a live one.

"I didn't get in trouble, no," he finally said. He wasn't claiming innocence, not really. Causing trouble and *getting in trouble* were technically two different things.

There had been no formal inquiry because Mr. Bowers couldn't prove anything. He'd just happened to find a few toilets on his lawn and four of his least favorite students running away from them. He'd given descriptions to the police, and yeah, Gum was the only boy in his school with hair that long, but Mr. Bowers had nothing on camera and the incident had occurred off-campus. Nothing came out of it, and that had made the man more bitter. But honestly, if Mr. Bowers hadn't wanted to get toilet-bombed, he should have given out bathroom passes like all the other teachers did.

Surprisingly, Grandpa laughed. A big belly laugh that sounded like it hurt. He cleared his throat, pulled a new cigar from his shirt pocket, and lit the end of it. "Of course you didn't get in trouble. I talked to Mr. Bowers on your behalf."

Then he handed Gum the cigar. First beer, now tobacco. Was this how Bill Clavey introduced his sons into the men's club? Was Hudson first because he was a few months older, and now it was Gum's turn to endure a rite of passage?

Gum took the cigar but didn't put it to his lips. He wasn't

sure how to smoke it anyway. He wasn't sure if he even wanted to try. "How'd you know I didn't do it?"

"I assumed you did it. I *hoped* you did it. Jerry Bowers has earned worse things than a few unwanted commodes on his lawn."

The prank hadn't even been Gum's idea; he'd had no idea what was happening when he got in the car with the senior boys. But Chase Wiley promised they wouldn't get caught, and Gum had a hopeless crush on him, so he'd gone along with it. He wasn't sure if taking credit now would do him any favors. This could be another test, just like with archery.

"Yeah, but he's my teacher . . ." Gum trailed off, still waiting for Grandpa to utter, *Gotcha!* He couldn't believe this was the same man who had ranted about respecting authority twenty minutes ago.

Grandpa laughed again. Who knew Bill Clavey could laugh like that? "He ought not to be. Always had a chip on his shoulder. Took it out on your uncles. Not everyone is fit to be in his position. Being a leader is not a right. It's a privilege that must be earned. *Pay careful attention to yourselves and to all the flock, in which the Holy Spirit has made you overseers,*" Grandpa added. "Do you know what that means? Only shepherds deserve a flock. And not every man is a shepherd. Mr. Bowers enacts strict policies on his students because he's a spineless worm of a man. You were right to remind him of that."

Gum's jaw hung open. He knew he ought to say something, but he wasn't sure if he had accidentally slipped into a new hallucination. Grandpa liked tradition, which had to mean liking authority too. He blabbered on and on about respect and family values. But maybe he had more of a rebel in him than Gum assumed. Maybe, with some time, his politics had softened. Maybe, someday, he wouldn't even mind a gay grandson.

"Thanks," Gum managed.

"You have good character. Sometimes the right thing to do isn't obvious. Sometimes it's unpopular. Sometimes it's even painful."

So Gum wasn't as invisible as he thought. Grandpa was waiting for him to prove himself on his own. And he had done it. Grandpa didn't suddenly care because Hudson messed up; it was because Gum had risen to the occasion.

As Gum clamped the shears around another Ruby Spider, it wiggled around as if trying to free itself from his grasp. He hadn't noticed it before, but this flower had no petals. It had *fingers*. Fingers with chipped nail polish. And Gum's shears were digging into flesh and a braided green friendship bracelet. Glassy brown eyes looked at him from where the roots should be.

Gum dropped the shears, and the arm flopped lifelessly to the ground. The flower was already dead, but the girl shouldn't have been. She was the wrong Garren.

Grandpa launched into a monologue while Gum's heart beat against his rib cage. Why was he seeing Iris now?

"Your generation is so passive," Grandpa rambled. "They want to sit on their phones and be spoon-fed how to think. They'll witness. They'll watch, but they won't *do* anything."

"Yeah," Gum said. It came out as a quick, hot breath. His hands were shaking, and he had to swallow to keep vomit from escaping.

"Every generation drifts further from the light, but that doesn't mean all is lost. There's always hope, as long as you don't accept defeat."

Gum couldn't accept what his eyes were presenting him with. This couldn't be Iris's corpse among the flowers.

Yet, those were Iris's eyes, her Prince T-shirt. Her lips parted in a scream. Skin sapped of color.

"*Go ahead,*" whispered the horse voice in his ear.

It wasn't Glory. It never had been. She was too sure of herself and had a habit of steamrolling over people, but she wasn't vindictive. That self-assuredness meant she didn't seek revenge. She'd let others' jealousy eat them alive. She didn't need to lift a finger to punish her enemies. And Iris wasn't her enemy. Gum wasn't either.

Who the fuck are you? Gum asked it.

The thing pretending to be Glory laughed in his head. "*And who are you without a shepherd to follow, little lamb?*"

His ears rung. His head felt heavy. He knew now that it would force him if he didn't relent. And Grandpa was staring at the shears in Gum's hand. Waiting.

There was only one option: Gum imagined Iris was still a flower, grabbed her cold wrist, and snipped it off.

They arrived at the Dollhouse at nine because Glory always showed up at least an hour after a party started. Savi Traxler greeted them by the road. She wore a bright purple minidress and huge hoop earrings longer than her hair. She looked oddly modern in front of her Victorian house with its delicate lace trimmings.

"Babe!" Savi hugged Iris. Her breath already hinted of alcohol. "You look so cute!"

Iris looked like an imposter.

She was pretty sure the sleeves of her red top were cutting off circulation in her arms and she had already stepped on the long skirt twice.

The sun was about to set, and it still hadn't gotten any cooler. But she had to resist the urge to tie up her curls. She would have to deal with her shoulders feeling too hot, the itchy makeup melting off her face.

The night when Glory had died was the hottest night in Bad Creek ever. According to the weathermen on the radio, this year's third of July would match the record. Another good sign.

"What highlighter are you wearing?" Savi asked. "Your skin is glowing!"

"Um, thanks. It's sweat."

"You're hilarious." Savi looked past Iris and gave a little wave. "Hello, boys."

Gum said hello back, and Aidan looked around nervously, waiting for the sky to fall.

Savi deserted them once they were all inside, going off to find out who had control of the speakers. Apparently the lo-fi beats were "too depressing," as if throwing a party on this night weren't depressing enough.

Every room inside the Dollhouse had some sort of nautical mascot: glass dolphins in the entryway, lobsters on the pillows in the living room. If Iris remembered correctly, the bathroom downstairs had towels with smiling otters and soap dispensers shaped like seashells. She could imagine Mrs. Traxler picking out the colors for the walls based on their names at the paint store—*Salmon*, *Lemonade*, *Pearl*. All happy pastels, like the clothes the Traxlers wore golfing. A cluster of party guests were gathered around the kitchen counter, adorned with glittering seafoam-colored quartz turtles.

"So, is this about how that night started?" Iris asked Aidan.

"Yeah. It's creepy, like we're back in time."

Good. The more similar, the better. If Iris relived the night like Glory had, the veil between them would be easier to lift. Hopefully, she'd receive a vision while awake, this time.

And she wouldn't run into any danger as long as her friends were around.

Iris had asked Aidan that afternoon to give her a play-by-play of that night, so she could retrace Glory's steps, but he claimed it was all a blur. He'd blocked out that whole thing. For him, it was too painful to remember. That made sense. Her moms didn't say Glory's name. It would have made sense if Iris was also too afraid to look back.

Instead, she felt *hungry*. Ravenous for the truth.

Gum pulled away from them, headed to a giant clear jug of red liquid on the counter where kids way older than them were pouring the contents into plastic cups. These must have been Savi's brother's friends. Iris hardly recognized anyone here. They weren't regulars, they weren't even tourists. They were whoever had the cash to travel on short notice because Savi and Graham Traxler snapped their fingers.

The crowd was already sloppy, chugging their drinks and pulling their friends toward the hot tub, the beer pong table, the bathroom to throw up. No one gave Iris a double-take, but she still felt . . . exposed. Just like she had when she lingered near that house in the woods.

"So, what did you guys do first?" Iris had to scream it for Aidan to hear. The music had gotten louder, faster. The bass vibrated in her ears.

Aidan's eyes darted around as if he were counting all his exit options.

"I don't know. I kinda need to piss," he said, then he was gone too, pushing through the sea of college kids.

Iris should wait there, for Gum to come back with the

mystery punch, for Aidan to come back with an empty bladder. Clearly, they hadn't gotten the memo about staying focused. And staying *together*.

Iris straightened her back. Glory wouldn't have desperately clung to her friends. She would have found the biggest cluster of strangers, slid in, and regaled them with a story. Or she would have snatched a napkin and doodled until she'd have summoned her own crowd, who would watch as she effortlessly drew portraits of onlookers.

But Iris didn't possess those powers. And she didn't know how to begin to fake it.

She started walking aimlessly, so she wouldn't look stupid standing by herself in the middle of the room. She dodged a vape cloud and smacked directly into someone's chest.

"Sorry!" She stumbled away and looked up, right into the eyes of Hudson Clavey.

He gazed at her with curiosity, as if she were a hummingbird, something small and quick that he wanted to observe without scaring away. Her heart was beating like a hummingbird's too. Maybe she should have drunk something to slow it down.

He was one of the only people in the room without a cup in hand and a friend beside him. Just like her.

"Iris." His Southern accent slipped on her name. Eye-russ. He said it slowly, unsure. Probably because she hardly looked like herself. Her lashes were goopy with mascara, and her mouth was an overwhelming shade of red.

"You don't strike me as a party person," Hudson said.

"I'm not." That wasn't a very Glory response. Iris should

have said something else. She had forgotten her lines, but the show wasn't stopping.

"Me neither," Hudson said. "I'm convinced no one actually likes parties. They're *supposed* to like them."

"You don't like bass so loud your ears bleed?" Iris joked. "God, what a loser."

Hudson flashed a smile, exposing a dimple on his left cheek that absolutely did not help calm Iris's racing pulse. "If your lifelong dream isn't becoming a Beer Pong God, you're hopeless."

She looked around. No sign of the boys. "If you hate parties so much," she began, "why are you here?"

"Keeping an eye on things."

"You mean keeping an eye on *me*?"

"Well, can't say you're hard to look at." He gave her another dimpled grin. She wondered if he could hear her heart about to explode. But he was probably only saying that because she looked like Glory.

"So if you could be anywhere else right now, where would you be?" he added.

She didn't have an answer for that. Even when she asked herself WWGD (What would Glory do), nothing came to mind.

"Usually I'd say the only place I want to be is here. Not, like, waiting on the keg stand competition to start; I mean Bad Creek." The words tumbled out as she thought them. She almost forgot Hudson was the one who'd asked her the question. "The whole year, like every year, I was waiting to come back, like I was on pause until this one week in the summer."

"But?"

"It's different now, for obvious reasons. I should have prepared for that. But also, maybe it's not because of what happened. Maybe I'm different too. Or maybe everyone else is. Or maybe this town was never what I thought it was in the first place."

"That sounds . . . hard. I'm sorry."

He was apologizing to her. Again. And every time, he seemed like he meant it. Maybe he was the only one who meant it.

Her Neverland was burning. No. *Flooded*. The magic had drowned with Glory.

"What about you?" Iris asked. She had to pivot the conversation before she started crying. "Where's your happy place?"

"I haven't found it yet."

She expected him to say something flirty, a semi-ironic pickup line, like, *Maybe you're my happy place*, with a wink. But she liked that he told the truth. That he was just as lost as she was.

He leaned in closer. His cologne smelled like cinnamon and smoke. She liked it. Was he going to kiss her? Was she going to let him?

That would be totally fucked-up. A year ago today, Glory died. It wouldn't be fair if Iris kissed a Clavey boy right now.

Thankfully, she didn't have to decide. Hudson didn't try to kiss her. Instead, he whispered in her ear. "Do you feel safe in Bad Creek, Iris?"

His breath was shockingly warm. The music slowed down, the vocals fading into an even buzz.

Do you feel safe?

She had no idea what he meant by that, and that terrified her. She held his gaze, his face so close to hers. The bass was making her thoughts jumbled.

Hudson opened his mouth to say something when someone bumped into Iris. She jerked back from him as her legs were splashed with liquor.

"Girlie! There you are!" Savi grabbed her by the arm, her red, white, and blue sparkly acrylics digging into Iris's skin. "I need to steal you!"

Before Iris could consent to being kidnapped, Savi dragged her away from Hudson. He melted into the crowd quickly, like he had never been there to begin with. He was a ghost of a boy, only showing up to frighten her and disappear without a trace.

Savi's bedroom was the least tacky in the house, though it was entirely purple. Purple carpet, a purple comforter with purple pillows, and a gauzy purple canopy with purple LED lights strung around it.

Savi headed toward the walk-in closet. "I wanted to give you something, wait here."

Iris worried she was wasting time. She needed to talk to Hudson, even if the idea of him felt dangerous. Danger was productive. Danger meant proximity to the truth.

She studied the massive photo collage on Savi's wall. There was Savi with some girl at a football game. Savi with a different girl posing with skis. Savi with Glory, holding up ice-cream cones, laughing. Glory had her braces off, and she was wearing the tiny gold necklace she'd gotten for her birthday. She was wearing red, as usual. The stars painted on her cheeks meant this was taken two years ago.

Her last Fourth of July alive.

Do you feel safe?

Iris didn't feel safe. Not when three girls had drowned here, and the ghost of one of them had promised it wasn't over. Not when she was sleepwalking. And Glory had been sleepwalking. And Joanna had been sleepwalking.

She only stopped sleepwalking after Beth. April had whispered it as if, by telling Iris, she were breaking the law. April probably knew the truth. And Joanna knew. Rex knew. And so did the Claveys. The Richardsons. The Traxlers. The fish and the ducks and the swans and the trees. All of Bad Creek knew—but her.

Was Hudson trying to warn her? Did he know something was coming?

Iris forgot Savi was still in the room until she squeaked, "Okay!" She held her hands behind her back. Oh no. Iris hoped Savi didn't have an expensive party favor for her.

"Sit. Close your eyes," Savi directed.

Iris sat on the purple bed and obliged, expecting the worst. She felt the mattress shift when Savi sat next to her. Then something soft was placed in Iris's hands. She opened her eyes and tried not to scream.

She held a stuffed rabbit. Floppy-eared, with the thread of the nose unraveling. That was Iris's fault.

They'd made the bunny five years ago. Glory had done most of the work. She'd hand-stitched the white velvety fabric into something tangible. It was her idea to give it one hazel eye, and one dark brown eye. "It's half me and half you," Glory had said, then she handed Iris the pink thread and told her she could do the nose. Iris had botched it. It was a series of knots, half an inch left from where the nose should have been. She wanted to cry. Ruining her own work was one thing, but ruining Glory's? She'd feared her older sister would never want to do something with her again.

Iris had returned the bunny to Glory and confessed her sins.

"I ruined it," she said glumly.

Glory had been sitting on her bed, with her sketchbook, in the middle of another masterpiece. "You didn't ruin it. She's adorable!"

"The nose is all crooked," Iris had muttered.

"That's what makes her interesting! I would have never thought of that. I'm too much of a perfectionist."

"You don't have to say that,"

"Iris," she had said, putting her hand in hers. "I'm serious. I love it. We'll call her Picasso."

Picasso was covered in dirt and twigs now. She smelled like the lake.

"Wh—why do you have this?" Iris managed.

"Glory must have left it here the last time she spent the night," Savi explained. "I found it in the yard all covered in dirt. The neighbor's dog must have dug it up or something. But don't worry, I'll clean it up. I figured you would want it."

"Thanks," Iris said instead of tossing it out the big window like she wanted to. The longer she held it, the closer she got to tears.

"You can leave it in my room until the end of the party if you want. Don't worry, no one's allowed up here, just come grab it when you leave. Or you can spend the night! I have PJs here you can borrow!"

Savi touched Iris's hair, running her fingers through it. Iris wanted to slap them away. She wasn't close to Savi like that, but she was here to play Glory, and Glory *would* let this happen.

"What was Glory doing, the last time you saw her?" Iris asked, staring at the photos on the wall.

"I thought I told you. I saw her fighting with Aidan."

"Fighting?"

That was not what Savi had said the first time. She'd said Glory was *with* Aidan, and that they might have argued.

Fighting sounded worse.

"Yeah, it got looouuuuuddd."

Every word Savi said lasted longer than it needed to. She was drunk, which maybe could work in Iris's favor. Savi would have no filter.

"So, Glory was yelling at him?"

Savi began sectioning off pieces of Iris's hair.

"No. Aidan. He was sooooo maaaaaad."

Aidan never raised his voice. He barely talked at regular people's volume to begin with. And even if something had gotten him worked up, he wouldn't yell at Glory. Never Glory. He'd looked at her like she was his personal savior.

"What was he mad about?" Iris asked, trying to keep her voice even.

Aidan had been angry for a while now. Iris saw the way he

gripped the wheel of the Jeep. The way he shook his head at the floor. He was holding something in.

"Well, I didn't hear the whole thing," Savi answered. Her fingers tickled the back of Iris's neck, as she began to braid.

"What *did* you hear?"

"Clavey. He kept saying *Clavey*."

Iris leaped forward, freeing herself from Savi's touch. She whirled to face Savi on the bed. "He was mad about Hudson Clavey?"

Savi shrugged. "I guess."

"And then what?"

"She stormed off."

"Where did Aidan go? Did he follow her?"

"Like I said, I was playing beer pong. Do you want to play now? You can be my partner!"

Savi jumped from the bed and dragged Iris downstairs. Iris didn't resist. Her thoughts felt like they were in a blender. She tried to pin them down. Form something coherent. A timeline:

First, Aidan had yelled at Glory about Hudson.

Then, Glory was found in the lake.

After, Aidan didn't want Iris to look into what happened. He was so sure it was an accident. But, once he'd given in, he only pointed a finger at Hudson Clavey. But if Aidan had any real dirt on Hudson last year, wouldn't he have mentioned that by now?

Do you feel safe in Bad Creek, Iris?

She steadied herself on the back of a lawn chair and stared at the grass to keep herself from puking. She had made it outside, yet she still didn't have enough air. Her clothes were dripping wet; her hair was plastered to her cheeks.

People were screaming.

"I'll fix it! They're on a timer!" Savi shouted. The sprinklers had come on, and everyone was running inside. Their shrieks had turned to giggles. Iris let the cold water cover her. Maybe it would wake her up. None of this felt real.

Do you feel safe?

She should watch her back. But watch her back for whom?

Tonight was the worst idea she'd ever had. Trying to solve this without any adult help was stupid. She should have gone to the police. But what would they do about a lost wallet, an unfinished sketchbook, and inconsistent eyewitness accounts?

Do you feel safe?

She flinched as someone tapped her back. It was too sudden, too close to her neck. The smudgy hands Glory drew popped into her mind.

But it was only Gum. His expression was hollow, like he knew everything Iris had just learned. Or he knew something worse.

"You're gonna have to see this," he said.

Iris followed Gum toward the lake, stumbling like she was drunk. She wished she were drunk. She wished she'd stop feeling her thoughts eating each other, newest feeding off the last. Hudson's eyes. Clawed hands. Aidan yelling.

"Where's Aidan?" Gum asked. "I didn't see him with you."

She shook her head. Forming words wasn't possible at the moment. It was all too much. She needed a good twelve-hour nap, then she'd be coherent.

"I'll text him to meet us here," Gum said. He whipped out his phone before she could tell him that she couldn't handle seeing Aidan.

"I was trying to find you guys, and, I don't know. I was worried you went to the water again," Gum explained. "Then I found this."

Gum stopped by a pine tree. It was sparse, colorless, dying like this whole town was. He pointed to the rough bark. Did he see the truth now too? How this place had been decaying for years without her noticing?

But no. He was pointing to the symbol carved in the tree.

"That's not all," Gum said.

He gestured to the tree's roots, where the ground was disturbed.

Iris peered into the shallow hole, feeling a lot like the girl in *It Runs Below* staring down the well. There was no monster here. Only a soggy shoebox. Inside were black sticks that someone could easily confuse for twigs, but when Iris picked them up, they stained her hands black. Charcoal. And next to them, a tiny gold earring. A comb, clumped with dark curls. A bottle opener.

All things no one would notice had gone missing. Glory went through art supplies quickly, dumping them when they served their purpose. And Glory had so much jewelry, it was hard to keep track. She used that bottle opener to open her cherry sodas. On vacation, she always had at least one bottle clanking around in her tote bag. There was enough room, feasibly, for a stuffed rabbit to fit in the hole as well.

So this was what the neighbor's dog had dug up.

Iris already felt like she was going to hurl, but when she pulled out the photo at the bottom of the showbox, she doubled over and dry-heaved. She recognized it from Glory's Instagram. It was the last selfie she'd posted.

Iris couldn't puke. She couldn't even cry.

A shadow blocked the light from the party behind her.

Aidan.

"What the fuck is this?" he said.

"It's like the box from that house," Gum said. "I think Iris was right. I think it's some kind of witchcraft thing."

Aidan didn't even glance in the box. He folded his arms. "Or someone planted it to freak us out. To lead us in the wrong direction."

"Are you still talking about my fucking cousin?" Gum asked. "Because he's not creative enough to pull a prank like this."

And Hudson couldn't force Iris and her mother and her sister to sleepwalk. He couldn't plant those dreams in her head.

"You said it was weird your grandpa was giving you a bunch of attention all of a sudden," Aidan continued, still trying to convince Gum to switch sides.

"He changed his mind about me. It has nothing to do with Hudson," Gum said.

"*Sure.*"

"Why is that so hard to believe?" Gum sounded uncharacteristically offended. Usually he could take insults well. There were times Glory obviously had cut him too deep, and he'd still laughed it off.

Aidan, condescending as ever, said, "Do you get what kind of people they are?"

"They're *my* family. You don't get to tell me what kind of people they are."

Iris rose to her feet. The proof was literally there. The symbol looked magical. Satanic. When Iris had suggested they ask Paul about it, Aidan had argued he didn't want to bother him.

"What does this look like to you?" Iris said, her palms touching the shallow cuts in the bark.

"It looks like something meant to freak us out. Like something out of a horror movie," Aidan answered.

"Exactly. And who is an expert on horror movies?"

Aidan squinted at her, dark brows furrowed. He didn't look as pretty in this light.

Helena. Beth. Glory. One for each generation. Aidan loved Glory. Paul was best friends with Beth. Paul's dad had also stayed in Bad Creek. He could have known Helena. Maybe he was mad Bill Clavey had gotten to her first. And there could have been a girl before that, and before that. An endless chain. A tradition as old as the cabins in the Landings.

As old as the lake itself.

"Are you blaming my dad for this Blair Witch bullshit?" Aidan countered. "Seriously? When everything is pointing at Hudson?"

"The only thing pointing at Hudson is you," Iris said. "I don't think he's a bad guy. Maybe we were all wrong about him."

Aidan rolled his eyes. "What the fuck are you talking about?"

"I'm just saying—"

"You've been hanging out? You've been begging all of us to relive this shit and you're sneaking around with Hudson Clavey?"

"It's not sneaking—"

Aidan interrupted her. "But you didn't tell us? The same girl that demands we tell each other everything. That we have to be some kind of hive-mind . . . He's got you, Iris. And you know what? Gum's ghost friend is right, it *will* happen again. Who do you think he'll come after this time?"

"Whoa, hold up!" Gum got between them, putting his hand on Aidan's chest. Iris didn't realize how close Aidan had gotten to her. Was he about to snap? Had he snapped with

Glory, after that fight? No. If this was supernatural—if this was *Satanic*—it would have been calculated. Aidan would have had to plan it.

But why? What did he get out of it? What was the point of drowning all those girls?

"*You're* the one hiding. Tell me the truth," Iris said, voice wobbling. Tears were streaming down her cheeks, already soaked in sprinkler water. Her body had betrayed her.

Aidan stepped back and sighed.

"When I first came here, I couldn't remember," he said. Now he sounded like the boy she knew. The one who always said *please* and *thank you*. Who used to cover his hands in Band-Aids so no one would see his warts. "The whole night had missing pieces. But . . . I remember now. Or, most of it." He took a deep breath. "She kept disappearing. I called her out on it. She kept promising me that she still wanted to be together after the summer. But I didn't trust her. I saw her talking to Hudson, and I . . ."

Iris crossed her arms to her chest. "You yelled at her."

"Yeah, I did."

"And what happened after that?"

"She stormed off. I tried to find her. I was freaking out. She was standing by the dock with Hudson, and . . . she was acting wrong. Like, she wasn't talking. Her eyes . . . she was so far away. I begged her to wake up and she wouldn't. Hudson told me to leave, and then . . ." He shut his eyes tight. "The only thing I remembered was waking up in the Jeep, already parked at Wahbee. A part of me thought it was my fault this whole time and I was blocking it out. But now I know the Claveys *set me up.* I think I caught Hudson in the act, and someone knocked me out and drove me home. That explains why I don't remember anything."

Iris could tell there was more to it. He was pausing too much, like he was putting every word on trial for its life. Gum was staring at him, mouth agape.

"How can I trust you," Iris said, "when you've been hiding shit from me?"

"Who are you gonna believe?" Aidan said. "One of your best friends or the guy who is only giving you attention because his first choice isn't an option anymore?"

Her insides flared hot. "You *asshole.*"

"I'm the asshole who's trying to protect you." She wanted to believe it. She wanted to believe that he hid the truth because he was scared and confused by the lost memories. Because the Claveys orchestrated a flawless cover-up.

"If you wanted to protect me, you would have told me the truth the first time I asked you," Iris spat. "Instead, you're trying to get revenge because you're still jealous of Hudson. And you know what, Hudson's the only person who actually seems like he wants to be around me. You haven't texted me *for a year.* Would we even still be friends if we weren't forced to come back every summer?"

Aidan swallowed. That hesitation was the proof she needed.

Iris knelt by the shoebox again, sprinkler water dripping off her hair and onto the already soggy cardboard. She pulled out the bottle opener. Aidan stepped back like she was going to use it to cut him. She almost wanted to.

"Gimme your hand," Iris told Aidan.

"I think we all need to chill out. Take five," Gum said.

She stepped closer to Aidan before Gum could try to get in between them again.

"You were right," she said. "It can't go back to how it used to be."

She grabbed Aidan's wrist, with the yellow bracelet she'd wasted ninety minutes of her life braiding. She'd had to start over midway through because she'd made a mistake and ruined the pattern. And she wasn't going to leave the flaw in there. She had thought he deserved perfection. That he was the only one who could ever be worthy of Glory.

She sawed through the yellow threads now. Aidan didn't protest. On the last chop, he flinched as the metal pinched skin. He pulled back, rubbing his wrist. A few drops of blood were rising where she'd nicked him. She wished she felt bad about it.

Then Aidan turned and headed toward the house, where he would drive away in his Jeep. Guilty. Like last year.

She watched until the square taillights faded from view.

Gum broke the silence. "So, uh . . . do you want to ask one of your moms to pick us up, or . . ."

"No." Iris wiped sticky tears off her face. "We're doing what we came for." She glanced at the dock. Empty. Savi had probably warned the guests about going near the water, or everyone could sense it was haunted. Good. The fewer witnesses, the better.

"Iris," Gum said. "I think we should call it a night. It's late."

No. She wouldn't have Gum betray her too. But he was always like this, flip-flopping between taking risks and being cautious. Between appeasing Iris and appeasing Aidan.

"I'm not giving up," she said, starting for the lake.

He grabbed the back of her shirt.

"It's not Glory," he told her. "Not really. I've seen her. She's not . . . right."

She jerked away from him. "What?"

"I saw Helena in the bathtub, okay? I didn't lie about that. But I saw Glory too, only I don't think it's really her, and I think she wants to hurt you."

Iris's nails dug into her palm. She felt a mosquito bite scab break loose. Unfortunately, she *was* awake. "When did this happen?" she demanded.

Gum looked at his shoes. "You mean like the first time?"

"*The first time?*"

"I get how it sounds . . . but listen, it's been a few times, okay? At this point she barely looks like Glory. She's controlling them all, Helena, maybe my mom, and at least one other. I don't know how far back it goes, but it's just going to continue. I don't know how to stop it. Whatever it is—whatever is *pulling* you—you can't listen to it—"

"And I'm supposed to listen to *you*? Suddenly *you're* the expert on Glory?" She was yelling, but she didn't care.

Gum backed up. He'd rather she stayed the Disasters' crybaby little sister. Now that her tears had turned to daggers, he couldn't stand to look at her.

He said, "That's not what I mean."

"I thought you were on my side."

"I'm trying to be. But she won't let me. I can't stop it."

"Can't or won't?" She couldn't believe this shit. She laughed. What else was there to do? He looked at her like she was insane, like she'd finally fully lost it. But her head never felt clearer. "It's always someone else's fault, right?" she said. "You just can't commit to acting like a friend. I needed you this whole year. You guys just ghosted me. How can I keep acting like it's fine?"

"I'm not expecting you to!"

"Yes, you are! Every time I feel a little sad, you give me that look. Everyone does! It's like I'm breaking a rule by acknowledging it. That's how this place runs. Smiling, and moving on, and keeping the cycle going. Everyone relies on it. But not anymore. I'm going to break everything. I'm going to get justice for Glory. For all of them."

She took his bracelet off with one swipe. It came off the easiest because Gum's was the easiest to make. Their friendship was the easiest. They could continue where they left off, even when things got messy last year.

They always recovered. No matter what.

But they wouldn't recover from this.

Gum looked broken as the threads hit the ground. He was crying now too, and his mouth hung open like he was about beg for another chance. But he couldn't undo these days, when he had pretended to care. She was sick of all their lies.

Iris couldn't stand here with Gum acting like she was the monster. The boys had abandoned her. They were *always* going to abandon her. Maybe she was a dragonfly after all, hyperaware of the few hours she had remaining. The end was always on the horizon.

She grabbed the shoebox and ran until she couldn't hear the pulsating beat of the speakers or the slurred cheers from the party guests. She sat at the edge of the curb and tried to formulate a text that would result in the least number of questions.

Be there in five, April responded. And then, *Are you safe?*

Do you feel safe, Iris?

Iris took a deep breath. And another. And another. But she still couldn't get any air in. Every inhale poured more water down her throat.

Full of sand and fish and algae and bones.

Gum was used to his mouth getting him in trouble.

He'd picked the worst time to confess the truth about Glory. He should have waited until Iris was calm, or at least had gotten out of those wet clothes. He was so stupid. What did he think was going to happen? He stalled by the dying pine tree, tracing the symbol, over and over again, waiting for the tears to subside. *Okay, think.* There had to be a way to fix this.

How did Glory resolve their fighting? Sometimes a threatening look, a good old-fashioned public shaming. But she didn't always need to use intimidation. She just had special gravity around her that sucked everyone in. They would have followed her to the end, if she'd asked. And she knew it. That was why Gum couldn't stand her sometimes. She was so much braver than he was. So *sure* all the time. Glory was a reminder of what he could never be.

He kicked dirt in the empty hole where the shoebox had

been, then set off to find Iris. He still didn't know what to say, if she would even want to listen to him. But he had to try to explain it, before "Glory" took over again. She could punish him all she wanted. He had to save Iris. Somehow.

He circled the lawn. There was no sign of her among the trampled cups and broken chips. He passed drunk kids looking for their friends, hollering for their rides. Girls holding other girls' hair back as they puked on the lawn. He went back inside.

What if . . .

The thought nagged at him as he searched through empty rooms.

What if she went in the water? What if she's already gone?

He was loitering in the kitchen when he couldn't ignore it any longer. Savi had a black garbage bag, was picking up shards of colored glass. R.I.P. to the rainbow dolphin sculpture.

"Have you seen Iris?" Gum asked her.

Savi stared up at him.

"Her mom already picked her up, like, twenty minutes ago."

"Oh." That meant she was safe, at least.

"Find a new ride," Savi said. "Party's over."

She scooped up the dolphin's decapitated fin.

Gum's dad didn't answer his phone this late. A call would just go right to voice mail.

He could try to get his bike from Aidan's house, but it was probably still locked in the garage. Aidan wouldn't even want to see him. He thought Gum had chosen Iris's side, but Iris thought he'd chosen Aidan's—when all Gum wanted was to be on the side of *preventing anyone else from dying.*

He called the only other person he could think of.

Grandpa picked up after a few seconds.

"Hi," Gum said. "Could you pick me up from the Traxlers' house?"

There was a beat of silence. Gum braced himself for the passive-aggressive Bible verse. But Grandpa only said. "I'll be there in a few minutes," before hanging up. The call was so brief, Gum couldn't figure out if his grandfather was pissed or not. Apparently he would find out in a "few minutes."

He waited on the curb. It had been an unforgiving, humid night, but now he shivered. His arms were covered in goose bumps. A breeze went in one ear and out the other, whispering a simple instruction.

"Look down."

Iris's green bracelet. She must have ditched it when she got picked up. The last symbol of the Disasters 2.0 lay on the side of the street like roadkill.

Gum almost cried again. His blue one was still by the tree. Next to Aidan's own cut bracelet, and where Glory's things had been buried.

"Take it."

"Absolutely the fuck not," he said out loud. He had no allegiance to this thing in his ear. It wasn't Glory, that was for sure. It didn't want good things for him or for Iris. The sisters always had their spats, but it never lasted long. Glory wouldn't go on a crusade against Iris, and she certainly wouldn't enlist Gum to help.

How many of Iris's things had he taken? He had almost lost count. After the Magic 8 Ball, he'd snagged her half-empty bottle of green nail polish. And he hardly even felt guilty about it, in the moment.

How many of Glory's things were in the shoebox by the tree?

Charcoal sticks. Comb. Earring. Bottle opener. Photo. Whoever put them there had probably killed Glory and the others.

And now Gum was the one taking things.

A sinking feeling in his stomach told him resistance was pointless. The last time he tried to refuse, it didn't go well. But he still had to try, right? *Can't or won't?* He was going to find out.

He had to keep walking. The farther he got away from broken bracelet, the easier it would be to ignore. He lifted his foot, but he couldn't step forward. His muscles didn't obey his brain. He was stuck in place, pushing against his own body.

"Take it."

It sounded like an animal, something defying nature to speak. He turned around, but he couldn't see her. Was she afraid to show herself, now that he knew it wasn't Glory?

"Take itttttt."

The voice was coming from inside of his head. It had infiltrated his bloodstream, and now it wove through his tendons, seeping into the marrow of his bones. His ears started ringing. Suddenly Gum's body wasn't his anymore. His hands moved without permission, putting the bracelet in his back pocket.

Scrunchie. Golf ball. Magic 8 Ball. Nail polish. Bracelet.

There was a completeness to it. This would be the last one. He felt no relief at the realization, only dread. He needed to be chained to a tree or something until the Garrens left the state, because Gum had figured out the next part. He knew where this was going.

Glory didn't die because she was murdered, but it hadn't been an innocent accident either. It was something invisible and watching and hungry. And clearly it had decided Iris was next, and Gum, for some reason, was chosen as the one to complete the deed.

The numbness faded as quickly as it came. He was released from its grip, for now, free to run away from the scene of the crime. So that was what he did, though his limbs felt alien. He was as wobbly as a newborn fawn. Lightning bugs flashed around him.

The Disasters used to have a competition to see who could catch the most. Iris would always lose the game because she spent too much time poking holes at the top of her lid so the bugs could breathe. Gum learned years later that poking holes killed the bugs faster, something to do with sucking the moisture out of the jar.

Glory was the insect expert, so she must have already known that Iris was better off not trying to save them. But no one had the heart to tell her.

The bugs were drowned out by a new flash of light, brighter than any car headlights had the right to be. They were tinted slightly blue because the Cadillac was a car that demanded to be recognized.

It slowed to a stop, and Grandpa—dressed like he was going to Sunday brunch at one in the morning—patted the empty seat beside him wordlessly. His eyes were blue and glowing, like his Caddy's headlights, but there was no disappointment in them. No shock. Gum prayed Grandpa was going to spin teen drinking as a rightful coming-of-age activity, now that he was suddenly pro-rebellion.

Grandpa drove away fast. Fireflies smacked the windshield, their butts glowing yellow for a few seconds after impact. Gum sank into the leather seat, hugging his arms to keep warm. He felt chilly on the inside, and every time he breathed, he smelled the worst of the lake. Like he had his nose to a fish carcass.

Gum made sure his face was turned, so Grandpa couldn't see the dried tears or the aura of death latched onto him. She was still clinging to his shoulders, like a demonic backpack.

"Where are your friends?" Grandpa asked. "Paul's boy, the Garren girl?"

"They left before me."

"Without you?"

"Yeah."

"What happened?" His voice was gentle, like he wasn't even mad. For once, it felt like Gum didn't have to answer if he really didn't want to. This wasn't an interrogation; no one was keeping score.

"It was bound to happen eventually," Gum said. "It was a big fight about a lot of things. And . . . I guess we're not friends anymore."

He chose his words wisely, avoiding any mentions of murder or sort-of-ghosts or shredded strings or bloody wrists. The details didn't matter. Glory had once said he was good at noticing things, but introspection is worthless when no one wants to hear the truth. Aidan had decided it was over before it was, while Iris had never acknowledged an end. Gum had seen both sides of the tightrope. Even in heaven, he couldn't forget about how close hell was.

"Oh," Grandpa said. "Well, that's too bad."

"You never liked them."

Hudson was always flocked by identical-looking boys wearing identical-looking watches. Future graduates of Duke and Vanderbilt. Technically, those boys were Gum's classmates too. And sometimes he could almost pass as one of them. But it was like speaking in a language he wasn't fluent in.

The Disasters weren't ideal company, according to Grandpa's politics. Aidan was new money from the deviant land of Hollywood. The Garrens' careers in education were humble but respectable. Grandpa had said teachers are the backbone of society. Jesus *loved* the teachers. But a gay teacher? Couldn't have 'em indoctrinating the children.

Gay grandson? Hell, no.

"I knew you'd outgrow them," Grandpa said. "Eventually."

This didn't feel like outgrowing. Inevitable, yes, but devoid of a silver lining. It was only darkness and lightning-bug guts.

The car slowed down. They had turned the wrong direction, and now were on the dead-end private drive.

"I thought you were taking me back to the Landings," Gum mumbled.

"Tonight isn't getting any cooler. Why suffer in the heat? There's a bed for you here."

Grandpa thought he was being generous, but he couldn't see that Gum was shivering. It had to be eighty degrees outside, but air-conditioning sounded like a death sentence.

Still, Gum smiled. He didn't want to look ungrateful, because he wasn't. If he was on the other side of the lake, he was away from Iris.

Grandpa opened the front door and flicked on a lamp. Gum

was suddenly aware that he'd never been invited to Grandpa's house after dark. It wasn't nearly as unnerving at night. The reflective white surfaces weren't as stark. Shadows obscured the heads of stuffed trophies on the wall. If Gum didn't look too closely, it was as if they weren't there.

He followed Grandpa through the hallway decorated with their yearly portraits, blown up and displayed in identical white frames in order of most recent to oldest. Everyone was lined up in the same spot each year.

At the end of the hallway was a photo from before any of the grandchildren. Grandma Betty sat on the chair, her husband right behind her with his right hand on her shoulder protectively. The boys were on either side of them. Teenage Bruce had a full head of hair and his chest puffed out, trying a little too hard to look tough. Brian was much younger, with a dorky, painfully dated haircut. Beth was sitting on the chair next to her mother.

Whenever Gum looked at an old picture of her, it was as if he were glimpsing another universe, one where she got to live her life as she pleased. One where she wasn't a stranger. Where the future contained endless galaxies of possibilities. He'd never know what she had been like then, or what she could be like now, even.

Grandpa gazed at the photo a little too long. Probably thinking the same things. Then he looked at Gum. His expression hardened. "Did you see your cousin at the party?"

"Yes," he admitted. He had no allegiance to Hudson. If his cousin had gotten in trouble, well, tough shit.

"Did he speak with you?"

Speak sounded like a crime. Like breaking a vow. Something punishable.

Hudson had only spoken to Iris. Gum had seen him, out of the corner of his eye. Hudson kept scooting closer to Iris with unexpected ease. And Iris, in return, had kept twirling her hair, smiling at the floor. Gum couldn't stomach it, but he hadn't wanted start a fight he knew he could lose. He had turned away before he caught anything they'd said.

"No."

Grandpa smiled. There was nothing hostile about it.

"Take the first bedroom," he directed. "Breakfast is at eight, and don't bother making the bed. Cleaners will be here at nine. Good night."

The guest room was exactly like he'd expected: tasteful but bare, a large beige box with polished wood furniture. It would have looked like something straight out of catalog if there weren't a taxidermy rabbit on the nightstand.

He knew it couldn't be the rabbit from years ago, the one he'd pierced with the arrow and buried on the side of the road. Still, Gum's veins crystallized at the sight of it. He wasn't sure if God would be disappointed because he had taken a life or because he had been such a baby about it.

He picked up the taxidermy rabbit and shoved it in the closet, so he wouldn't have its glassy false eyes staring at him.

The closet was empty save for a few bare hangers and a black duffel bag tucked into the corner. Gum resisted the urge to peek inside. It would be unwise to snoop. Grandpa was friendlier than ever. Gum had earned his trust and respect.

He shouldn't mess that up.

Besides, there was nothing suspicious about the bag. It wasn't his business.

Still, Gum was stuck in place, staring at it like the meaning of life was just behind the thin layer of canvas. His whole body shivered. Glory had never left him. She was just better at hiding inside of his bones. Her invisible, frozen fingers forced him to kneel. Forced his shaking hands to unzip the bag.

He didn't want this. But it was getting harder to separate her desires from his.

He recognized the contents of the bag. After all, they had been stashed under his bed in Cabin 3. He tapped each one, counting them. Scrunchie. Golf ball. Magic 8 Ball. Nail polish.

And now: a broken green bracelet.

Movies were nothing like real life. They didn't depict humanity; they depicted how humanity *wants* to seem. In real life, there was no clear plot. No purpose. And there wasn't closure at the end. There were no satisfying answers. No lessons learned.

And no remakes.

It didn't matter if Aidan knew Hudson had something to do with it. An anonymous tip to the police couldn't work against a Clavey. If Iris wanted to walk into the lake, Aidan wasn't going to stay. Gum could watch her drown to prove his loyalty.

Aidan was tired of trying to prove things.

It was three a.m.—the perfect time for a bonfire. Aidan prayed Iris's demons were real, so they could snatch him up and drag him to a hell better than this one. He ransacked his room for things to sacrifice to the flame: board games, letters, bandannas, Polaroids, pressed flowers, and watercolor paintings. He didn't need them anymore.

When they were all gone, he could start over. Aidan would be eighteen very soon. If his dad cared to see him, he could take a goddamn plane.

Because Aidan wasn't ever stepping foot in Michigan again.

Once he finally collected everything, found the gasoline, the matches, and lit the fire, the sun was threatening to rise. Pink morning peeked from behind the pines.

He didn't feel any remorse when the first board game burned. He wouldn't have felt anything when Iris cut the bracelet off if she hadn't taken a layer of skin with her. He hadn't bothered to put a bandage on it. He wanted to watch the wound close, so he had proof that his body could heal. That all of this would just be scars someday.

As he threw in the cardboard packaging of Sorry! into the fire, the back door opened. A robed silhouette leaned against the kitchen doorway. Paul, taking Roy out one last time before going to sleep. Sunrise was his dad's regular bedtime. But after Roy took a dump in the yard, Paul stomped through the grass in his fuzzy slippers.

He had his serious face on, and not the one he had when someone made a disparaging remark about Christopher Nolan films. It was *the face*.

Iris really did it, Aidan thought for a horrible second. *She drowned herself to make her point.*

Because Paul had only looked at Aidan like that once before.

Last summer, exactly a year ago, Aidan had woken up inside the Jeep. He had vomited onto the driveway three times.

Though every step had felt like a blow to the head, he'd managed to collapse on the couch. He'd woken up again, dry-heaved, and crawled up the three flights of stairs back to his bed. He had only slept a few hours when his dad had banged on the door, which he'd opened before his son could sit up and adjust his eyes to the morning light.

"I have . . . news," his dad had said, before awkwardly sitting on the bed's edge.

Paul had shaken his head, then. He'd been crying. Before then, Aidan hadn't seen his father shed a tear, besides when he watched movies. Aidan felt a tickle in his gut as if a million centipedes were hatching inside.

"There was an accident."

Paul had given the details sparingly. Either he didn't know too much or he thought it was better that way. She was found in the water, in the early hours of the morning. She was already gone when the rescue services had pulled her out.

Gone. Passed away. No longer with us.

There was a funeral, but Aidan skipped it. He'd been in a different time zone by then anyway. He had been flying to and from Michigan by himself since fourth grade, but this time he had a chaperone. His mom hadn't wanted Aidan to be alone on the flight back. Maybe she'd expected him to be too much of an emotional wreck to navigate the airport. His dad was never an option to come with.

She'd bought two red-eye tickets so she could sit beside Aidan and give him reassuring pats on the hand, as if to tell him it was okay to cry. But he hadn't cried. He'd vomited six times in the bathroom instead.

Now, as his father trudged forward in his slippers and bathrobe, Aidan braced himself for more bad news. He'd promised himself ahead of time that he wouldn't let guilt overcome him. He had already burned all memory of Iris. He didn't even care what happened to her now. He should have done the same with Glory; he should have burned away all feelings for her.

Not let them fester.

After the wound on his wrist healed, there would be no proof the Disasters had ever existed.

But Paul didn't hesitate this time. He didn't say anyone was gone.

He waved around a worn piece of paper.

"Who drew this?"

He held a coloring page from Todd's Pizza. Under the glowing of the flames, the crayon-drawn symbol looked ominous. Apparently Aidan had missed an item for the pyre, probably because it had found its way into a trash can first, judging from the wrinkles and cheesy stains all over it.

"You need to tell me right now who drew this," Paul said. There was something desperate about the way he spoke.

Aidan backed closer to the flame.

"Gum did."

He didn't think it mattered. Iris thought it was something spooky, ripped out of a *Dark Unknown* episode. And maybe it was, but that stuff wasn't real. And even if his dad was into it, he didn't believe in it. Paul's interest in the occult was artistic. Fodder for his movies.

"We found it on a tree. By this old house," Aidan added.

"What house?" Paul demanded. For the first time, Aidan felt like he was about to get in trouble, like his dad was *actually* mad at him.

And for the first time, the sloppy drawing didn't feel as meaningless. Not when his father held it like it was a bomb.

"The Crawford house in the woods. And again at Savi Traxler's."

Paul inhaled, almost afraid of the answer.

"I don't know what it is, though," Aidan added.

Paul folded the paper. "It's a sigil. A *contract*."

"Whoa, what are you talking about?"

"A pentagram can summon anything, but it's generic. It's child's play. The real stuff, you can't find books on it. They're gate-kept for a reason." Paul used the same pretentious cadence as when he discussed movie lore, but his hands were shaking.

"So you think this is for real?" Aidan said.

"Did you know, in Wichita, every twenty years a girl is found dead in a tree?" Paul sometimes spoke in a scattered way, forgetting the connecting pieces. This all sounded like plot scraps from his projects, but he still had his serious face. A serious face for a serious . . . what?

For a serious curse.

"And this was carved on some tree in Wichita?" Aidan asked.

"Not this one. There are probably a million variants. There's a reason movies just use pentagrams. Point is, don't fuck with this stuff. Okay?"

"Or what? What'll happen? How do you know what this is?"

"Research," he answered. Voice flat. "Just to be safe, tell

Gum to stop drawing it, and you try to forget you ever saw it, okay?"

Aidan nodded. But he wasn't going to let himself forget. Never again.

Paul tossed the paper into the flames and trudged back inside. Aidan still had more to burn, but a few moments after the coloring page was thrown in, the raging fire collapsed on itself.

Iris was right.

The truth was about as comforting as being buried alive. Part of Aidan wished he hadn't heard it. That he'd gone back to California after all—confused and lost and angry. Now he wasn't confused. He wasn't lost.

All that was left was anger.

He thought of Hudson leading Glory to the water, to her death. The trancelike state she'd been in. Aidan had figured it had been poison. Hypnotism, even. But he saw the truth now, how she'd been charmed by his spell. But in his imagination, Glory was Iris.

He couldn't save Glory, but he could still save Iris.

The car keys were on the kitchen counter, as always. Aidan grabbed them without a second thought. It was a cold morning; he should have put on a jacket. Without the fire, his bare arms felt exposed, but his insides were ablaze.

He drove without blinking or loosening his knuckles from the steering wheel.

The Landings were busier than usual. There were more cars, more families carrying coolers, more kids running around in goggles and floaties. *Oh right.* It was the Fourth. Later tonight, everyone would gather at the beach for fireworks.

He parked in front of the marina and waited. It didn't take long for Cabin 1's door to open. There he was, the good old American boy who'd sold his soul to the Devil when he already had everything. Hudson walked out with his head down, hands in his pockets. Hoodie pulled over his blond hair. He thought he was incognito. He thought he was getting away with it.

He was dead wrong.

Aidan left the keys in the ignition and followed Hudson on foot until the boy disappeared behind the thick trees on the other side of Cabin 12.

Aidan gave it a few seconds before continuing. He ducked under branches to find Hudson in the shadows, facing the Disasters' willow tree, its long spidery limbs hanging over the edge of the shallow water. His hands danced across bark, tracing the carved slashes of a sigil.

Aidan pushed him; not hard enough to knock him to the ground, but enough to get his attention. Hudson whirled and, once he had the proper look of shock on his face, Aidan punched him in the jaw.

Hudson went down immediately, but Aidan wasn't finished. He had stupidly tucked his thumb in on that first blow. It felt broken. He had never thrown a punch before. He had never dreamed of starting a fight with anybody. But not even in his worst nightmares would Glory be dead.

All coherent thought washed away. Aidan didn't stop; he couldn't stop. The current inside of him was too strong. And, strangest of all, Hudson didn't fight back. He only put his hands over his face, blocking the next hit.

Hudson pressed his back against the tree trunk. "Stop, let me explain!"

There was nothing to explain.

Another punch. Aidan's fist made satisfying contact with Hudson's cheek.

"It wasn't me! Okay? Jesus Christ, can you listen for two seconds?"

Absolutely *not*. Hudson wasn't getting away with it anymore. Aidan wouldn't accept any excuses. He wasn't done. Maybe he wouldn't be done until Hudson was dead too.

A hand grabbed the back of Aidan's shirt, trying to yank him away. He fought against it. No one was going to stop him. No one else called the shots here.

Now arms grabbed his torso, hoisted him up, and threw him to the ground. Two men had invaded the secret cove of trees: Bruce Clavey and the other one, his nearly identical-looking younger brother, Brian. Both were older clones of Hudson. Both were in league with the enemy.

Okay, this might be bad.

The Claveys weren't only popular and powerful, they were literally in league with the Devil—or at least a demon. Paul hadn't clarified exactly what. Clearly, though, the Claveys were the bad guys. If Aidan hadn't bleeped on their radar before, he'd just put a huge target on his back. So far, it looked like they only sacrificed girls. But who was to say they hadn't murdered other people?

Yet Bruce was barely concerned with Aidan. He scowled at his son, not bothering to help Hudson up to his feet.

"We're leaving in ten. Clean yourself up," he barked.

Hudson stood, wiping his bleeding mouth. While the Clavey men marched toward the cabins, Hudson remained, glaring at Aidan.

"I know what you did," Aidan told him. "*Everyone* will know what you did."

"I'm not the one you need to worry about."

"Fuck you and your whole family."

"Hudson!" Bruce called. He didn't sound that far away.

Hudson leaned in close. Blood still dripped from his lips; his left eye was starting to look puffy. Aidan could get another hit in, if he was quick.

Then Hudson whispered, "If you care about Iris, don't let my cousin get near her."

Aidan almost laughed. Like Daniel Gum could ever be a threat to anyone other than himself. Hudson looked like he wanted to say more, but Bruce snapped his name again, so he turned and left.

Technically Gum was one of *them*. He was a Clavey by blood, but not by practice. He was too dedicated to the role of the black sheep to actually listen to these people. Save for his eyes, he hardly looked like any of them. His hair was too dark, too unkempt. He was too tiny, and too hyperactive, totally out of place with the Claveys' calm composures, noses tilted up so they could look down on everyone else.

Yeah, Gum was the one who had drawn the symbol on the napkin. Paul thought there was significance to that, but Gum had found it with the other Disasters. He wanted answers just like the rest of them.

The heavy air sizzled with the promise of lightning. A lot

of people would despair if it rained today, but Aidan prayed for the storm of the summer. For tornadoes and hurricanes. For Armageddon. Bad Creek didn't deserve a peaceful Fourth of July.

He needed to find Iris, to apologize for last night. He needed to get to her before Hudson did.

Aidan waited until the cars from Cabins 1 and 2 speeded away, then sneaked around the side of Cabin 4, to Iris's window. A phone with a lime-green case sat on the floor, connected to a charger. A patchwork quilt was balled up on the bed. There were stars on the ceiling. Muddy Converse and tie-dyed shirts on the floor.

But no Iris.

For a second, Iris thought maybe she was in heaven. She caught glimpses of the pink sky and shiny white pillars. Of an angel, lifting her up, up, up. Then the angel shook her, and she realized she wasn't in heaven at all.

She was in water up to her waist. Her toes sank into the sand. Minnows bumped against her calves.

Iris had sleepwalked into Hudson Clavey's arms. He hadn't let go of her yet, and she wasn't sure if she wanted him to. They were alone, but the Clavey mansion on the north side was right behind them. Observing.

She couldn't see any of the cars in the driveway or the archery range at this vantage point. The dock was out of sight too. There were too many trees blocking them in. This was the side of the property she had never seen.

Iris wished she could have woken up in her bed. She wished

the only times Hudson touched her weren't to save her from the lake. She wished she was sure she didn't have to be saved.

"Iris, oh my God. I'm so sorry." *Sorry*. Again. Hudson Clavey had spent this whole week apologizing to her, and he still wasn't done. "You need to leave. You need to leave Bad Creek. Now."

"No," she said. It came out as easy as an exhale. Running wouldn't help her find the truth. She would rather die than have another year without Glory and answers.

There was a weird shadow under Hudson's eye. A bruise forming.

Iris shouldn't let herself care. She shouldn't let her heart clench at the idea of Hudson hurting. But her heart and her brain were always wrestling for the wheel—she had to let one of them drive, eventually.

"What happened to your face?" she asked.

"I'm fine," he said. "You're the one in danger. You need to leave."

"No." She pulled away from him. The shore was only a few yards away. This is where Glory wanted her to go. She wasn't going to throw away her chance.

"It's trying to get you to stay. But . . . it's not in your favor, Iris. You can't listen to it."

"But I'm supposed to listen to *you*?"

Hudson, the boy who didn't give a crap about her until Glory died. The boy with the endless apologies.

Her Disasters had failed her. They thought they were saving her by keeping secrets, and now Hudson hadn't proved to be any different.

"Did you kill my sister?" she finally asked.

"No."

She knew he'd say that because she'd known that was the truth. Part of her had known since he'd spoken to her in the convertible.

"But you know who did," she added. "Don't you?"

Hudson hesitated, listening to the whine of an engine getting closer and closer. A car was coming up the impossibly long driveway. They wouldn't be alone for much longer.

"We can't talk about this here. Please. They're gonna be back soon." He offered his hand to her, but she didn't take it. Just because she believed him didn't mean she could rely on him.

Iris felt the weight of her clothes as she trudged forward toward the shore. Now her socks were all wet and sandy. She inspected her legs. No leeches this time.

"I couldn't tell you," Hudson said, talking quickly. "I didn't think it would have helped anything. But it's not over, Iris. It wants *you*. It was always supposed to be you. I was going to explain at the party—"

"You didn't tell me shit at the party."

"But you found the tree, right? I thought it would be better if you figured it out yourself. You wouldn't believe it, coming from me, but we're out of time. You need to get out of—"

"I'm *not* leaving."

"Fine," he said. "But at least go to your cabin. Breakfast is starting soon. My grandpa usually chats with the photographer before we start pictures, so it should give me a short window before I have to be back. Could you meet me in the boathouse? I'll explain everything, I swear. Just, please, don't let anyone see you—"

"My dear, you're far from the Landings."

Bill Clavey stood behind them, hands clasped behind his back. His mouth was turned in an easy smile, but there was no twinkle in his blue eyes.

You're far from the Landings. Like she wasn't allowed here, on the north side. This wasn't her *place.* Yet Bill looked at Hudson as he said it. This wasn't his place either.

"As much as I'd love to welcome you inside, I'm afraid we have a prior engagement. Hudson, the photographer will be here soon."

Right. It was the Fourth of July. Gum was always gone that morning for the Claveys' annual portrait session. Was Gum here already? She couldn't see much past the trees. She looked around for signs of others watching them.

A few feet away, there was a white marble bench. It looked like a cross between a throne and a tombstone. The back had a complicated design carved in it, filled with shiny gold: intersecting lines and curves. It was a grander, more complicated version of the cross symbol she had seen before. Only this wasn't hastily carved in wood. This one required more time. More effort. More cash. The Claveys wouldn't allow this to appear here for no reason.

Iris took her eyes off of it. Suddenly the lake felt safer than this beach.

Hudson said, "I can drive you."

"There's no need," his grandfather told him. Bill looked at Iris with a tiny tilt of the head. "I'm sure my son Bruce could give you a lift back."

Now they were definitely talking in code, and it spelled,

Don't let Hudson be alone with Iris. Had he heard what they were talking about? Had he spied Hudson lifting her from the water?

We can't talk about this here, Hudson had said.

Iris wasn't safe in Bad Creek. And judging by how nervous he acted in the presence of his grandfather, Hudson didn't think he was safe either.

She had finally figured it out.

First, she had woken up by the house in the woods. If Savi hadn't stopped her, she would have kept going to the edge of the yard, right into the lake, in the same spot where Helena had been found. Before Aidan had woken her up two days ago, Iris must have been on her way to Savi's house, where Glory had drowned. And now she'd woken up here, at the Clavey house. This was where Beth had had her accident.

Iris wasn't being led to Hudson. She was on a tragedy tour, waking up where the other girls had drowned.

But if Beth was supposed to be a victim, wouldn't her things be secretly buried, marked by a barely noticeable series of quick slashes on wood? Not a marble throne. Not a *shrine.*

Bruce was rounding the corner. She needed to get out of there.

Hudson was breaking the rules—breaking them for *her.* That had to mean something. Aidan thought Hudson had been demoted because he'd done something bad. What if that was the other way around? What if he had stopped following the rules of bad people?

Bad people, who wanted Iris to get in their car.

"That's fine. I was gonna walk over to a friend's. I think I left something at Savi's last night," Iris said. It was a solid lie, but her delivery was shaky.

Bill wasn't falling for it. "I insist. Bruce, mind grabbing the keys for the Cadillac?"

Iris tried to channel Joanna's threatening smile.

"It's fine," she said through gritted teeth, the promise she wasn't afraid to bite a man. When Iris went into the city with her friends, she carried pepper spray. Actually, she carried bear spray. It was stronger—and illegal—but her moms would rather her break a dumb law than be dead. Unfortunately, she didn't have her bear spray now. She didn't even have shoes on.

Bruce looked at his father, awaiting instructions.

"Well, all right," Bill said after a moment.

He let her walk past them, toward the house, because that was where the road was. Where witnesses could be. Iris didn't run—that would alert them too much. She only checked behind her shoulder.

Hudson was watching her.

She couldn't trust anyone anymore. Her friends had been lying to her. Her mom had been lying to her. And her gut had been lying to her too. She'd been *so sure* Glory was leading her to answers, when all along she was being led into a trap.

Iris didn't know if she could trust Hudson completely, but there was one part she believed wholeheartedly. She needed to get away. Away from this house. Away from these people.

When she reached the road, she started running, a blur of green whizzing past her. She had spent sixteen summers feeling protected by these trees. She'd never thought to wonder if the woods were on her side. The trees. The lake. The creek.

The other regulars here. Big families with big names and big houses.

The Dollhouse's yard looked unfamiliar without an armada of teenagers' vehicles parked around it. Iris knocked on the door, hoping Savi wasn't too hungover to give her a ride back to the Landings. She wished she could text her, but her phone was still in her bedroom, plugged into the charger.

Graham answered the door.

"Iris Garren," he said. She wasn't sure if Savi's brother even knew her name. He would have known Glory's, sure; she was the one who came over here. Graham looked shocked to see Iris back so soon. Or, shocked to see her alive.

The Claveys were in on it. Why not the Traxlers? Who was to say last year wasn't planned? The Traxlers could have signed off on their home being the venue for the next drowning.

"What's up?" Graham asked. "Savi's still asleep. I can wake her up, but—"

Iris backed away, tripping on the adorable cobblestone sidewalk as she ran toward the road, her bare feet scraped and bloody. Graham might have called her name, but she didn't turn around. She didn't know where to go now. She stopped running to catch her breath. The Dollhouse wasn't far from Wahbee. She could see if Aidan was awake—and then what?

Paul could still be one of them.

Iris hadn't moved for a minute now. She was frozen in the middle of the road, crying and shivering and so, so unsure. She was a stupid deer waiting for a truck to hit her.

According to Gum and Hudson, Glory wasn't the one leading Iris in her sleep. It was an imposter. Iris didn't know the boys like she thought she had. And apparently she didn't know her own sister either. All this time had worked against her; all this history only blinded her more. But she wasn't wrong about everything.

Helena was the victim of a curse.

So was Beth.

So was Glory.

And Iris was supposed to be next.

Breakfast was red, white, and blue. Blueberries in the pancakes. White, sunny-side-up eggs, and cranberry juice that stained everyone's teeth. They would have to brush them again before pictures.

Gum had slept like a dead man on that big comfortable mattress. When he'd woken up, his vision blurred between blinks. He'd found his aunts and uncles at the bottom of the palatial staircase, beaming at Gum. "Happy Fourth," they'd all said, with the same reverence they would say *and with your spirit.*

Fourth of July was big in Bad Creek. It was *the* summer holiday—meaning, an excuse to get drunk and light things on fire. Paul spent thousands on Bad Creek's fireworks show, but the Claveys were the most patriotic. What was more American than getting the whole family together, lining your blue-eyed spawn up nice and close, and sending the heavily edited photos out to everyone you know? That was what the day was really made for.

If Gum had known everyone would be here already, he would have searched for a hairbrush and devised a way to sneak back to his cabin and put on the crisp white outfit hanging in the bedroom. The dress code for the Claveys' yearly portrait was specific: khakis and button-downs for the men and dresses for the women. Nothing too dark. Nothing too saturated. White and beige and baby-blues preferred. In the first year of her marriage to Uncle Brian, Aunt Jody had the gall to wear bright red false nails. Her husband had recommended she put her hands behind her back, but Grandpa had insisted she remove her nails on the spot.

She had explained she couldn't. That had to be done at a salon, apparently. But that wasn't an excuse for Grandpa. So she tore them off one by one, with her in-laws and the photographer watching. She'd cried—Gum didn't know if from pain or embarrassment. Either way, she'd learned her lesson. Her nails had been plain for every portrait since then.

Gum muttered, "Happy Fourth," back to his aunts and uncles. His dad wasn't there. He never came to Clavey activities, besides church. But Clarice was wheeling his mother into the foyer. They both wore white dresses. Gum slipped into the living room, where the little girls were giving their dolls haircuts on the rug and Hudson slumped on the couch. He wore a white button-up dress shirt identical to his father's, but without his trademark perfect posture. He kept his head down as if no one would notice the purple splotch on his cheekbone. His left eye was swollen. His khakis were wet up to the knee.

The photographer would have to do a lot of Photoshopping this year.

Gum wanted to ask, *What happened to your face?* but words weren't possible for him at the moment. His mouth felt soft and heavy.

Five-year-old Annie started crying because her six-year-old cousin Faith had "ruined" her doll with the uneven haircut. She ran up to her brother, as if Hudson had any authority to do anything about it. "She's a *collector's* item," Annie squealed through tears.

Uncle Bruce stepped in to the room, and Annie stopped crying. "Breakfast's ready," he announced. Everyone gathered at the table, finding their seats with ease. Even the girls went right to their wooden chairs without fighting or pushing or complaining.

Gum took the last empty spot at the end of the long dining room table. A taxidermy hawk loomed directly above his head, its wings open and talons ready like it was going to snatch up his pancakes.

The conversation was muffled, all words static, senseless background noise. Gum scarfed down four pancakes, hoping that would make him feel like a person again. He was thirsty but avoided the red juice. Faith dropped her cup on herself, and the stain looked like she'd been shot in the stomach. Aunt Jody scooped her up to change her outfit, promising Grandpa she'd brought a backup. Grandpa gave her a slow nod. He trusted her now.

And apparently he also trusted Gum. He had won a seat at this table, but he didn't know if he deserved it. If he even wanted it.

The duffel bag was still in the closet.

Gum hadn't let himself think about it last night. Or maybe "Glory" hadn't let him think about it. The discovery felt like something from a dream. Gum spent breakfast pushing it away, convinced he had imagined it.

And then breakfast was over. The aunts collected plates; the girls scattered to play with toys or their iPads or anything that wouldn't get their dresses and hair bows dirty.

"Daniel, mind coming to the trophy room?"

That was Grandpa, his hand on the back of Gum's chair.

Gum nodded. It wasn't like he could go back to the Landings. The Disasters were done, so Gum might as well stay here.

If he was allowed inside the coveted trophy room, that meant he was moving up another rung. There were places to go with the Claveys. If Aunt Jody could maintain Grandpa's approval, Gum could keep passing these tests. He could be one of them, especially without his "friends" in the way.

Grandpa unlocked the heavy-looking wood door with a brass key and invited Gum to enter first. Though the walls were paneled with dark wood, it wasn't cozy, like the cabins at the Landings. There were too many false eyes staring at them. Two dozen deer heads covered the mostly empty room. There were cushy chairs gathered around a small table, a bookshelf, and a tray with glass bottles of amber liquor. It looked like where Gum imagined men traded land and planned wars back in the olden times.

He thought Uncle Brian was right behind them, but when the door closed, it was just Grandpa and Bruce. Damn. Like his wife, Brian was desperate to please. That was tacky to the Claveys, but Brian had always been nice to Gum, acknowledging him even when no one else did.

Bruce gave Gum another unnatural pat on his shoulders. His hands were thick, meaty, callused from golf but not anything that could constitute actual labor. Grandpa lit up a new cigar, to make the room's stale tobacco smell even worse. Without windows, there was nowhere for the smoke to go but into the red carpet and the hides of the deer heads.

"So, my boy, how are you feeling about today?" Grandpa said. *My boy*. Gum had never been called that before.

"Fine, I'm not hungover or anything," Gum answered. A lie, sort of. He hadn't drunk that much last night, but since he'd woken up his thoughts were sloshy and hard to pin down. He probably looked just as awful as he felt.

Bruce snorted. "Well, that's a good start."

"I have to apologize to you, Daniel. Really," Grandpa said. "You deserve the same decorum as the rest of us. It's not fair to spring this on you, but this cycle's circumstances have been"—he glanced at Bruce, a purposeful side-eye—"interesting. Please, sit." Grandpa held his palm out, gesturing to the gathering of big plush chairs.

Gum obeyed, trying to match his posture to Bruce's. Calm, confident, and unmistakably masculine.

"I know you're bursting with questions," Grandpa continued. "I'm surprised you haven't mentioned anything sooner. But it's understandable; I haven't been the warmest to you. And for that, I am sincerely sorry."

"Uh, okay," Gum said.

Grandpa took a big hit of the cigar, closing his eyes as the end of it lit red. Then he leaned back in the big chair. "God created man to serve him. But he gave us free will. We can blame the Devil all we want, but at the end of the day, we are responsible for our shortcomings. Sink or swim, man is to blame. Don't you think?"

"Sure."

"God can help us find the right path," Grandpa continued. "But sometimes God needs help. And only the best of us is capable of giving him that extra boost. In return, we share some of his power." Grandpa cleared his throat, seeming to settle into his story. "Now, God is three. The Father, Son, Holy Spirit. But that Spirit is broken into even smaller pieces. That Spirit can speak to us, *through* us. And that Spirit speaks to some more than others. Equally, some places are more attractive to the Spirit. More . . . conducive to its needs—are you following?"

"Yeah," Gum mumbled. He wasn't following at all. Saying *God loves some people better* kind of negated the endless, boundless love Jesus was supposedly all about.

Grandpa kept going. "The Spirit spoke to our ancestors. My father. My father's father. His father. Because they listened—because they opened their hearts—we've received endless blessings, and there is a special throne in heaven for them now. And there will be for this whole family, because of their sacrifices. Because of mine. Because of *yours*. You're part of a legacy. You've been chosen."

In any other circumstance, Gum would have considered this Chosen One talk to be total nonsense. It was some Manifest Destiny bullshit his family had forced themselves to believe in.

If Grandpa thought God was responsible for his privilege, he wouldn't have to feel guilty when he thought about kids with cancer or refugees or his daughter who would never wake up.

But something *had* been speaking to Gum. Grandpa was right about that. Even after a long night's rest, it was still there, clinging to his back. He'd only gotten more accustomed to the chill in his spine. Confused it with a fever or a hangover.

"You haven't been trained to hear its call, but you've done well so far. And now it's time to receive its blessings. How does that sound?" Grandpa said.

"I don't know," Gum admitted. "I'm not sure what you want from me."

He hoped the black duffel bag Bruce was pulling out of the cabinet wasn't the same one from the bedroom. That he had only imagined Iris's things in there. He prayed that this was a psychological episode that had some kind of cure.

Let me be hallucinating, please, God. Let me be seeing shit.

"Tonight we bury the lures by the water," Grandpa said. "They will bring the offering right to you."

"By *offering*, you mean . . ."

Iris. That was who it wanted. *Offering* was a polite way of saying *sacrifice.* He could even imagine Grandpa correcting Aunt Jody on it. *Sacrifice is so barbaric,* he'd say. *We are evolved people. We're civilized.*

Grandpa continued, "You will hold the offering underwater until the Spirit has drunk its fill."

Until she was dead. Until she was just like Glory.

The room was spinning; Gum's ears were ringing. He looked at the blood-red rug, which must have cost a fortune.

He thought the gold details spelled out a word at first, but when he squinted at it, it was that shape carved into the tree. Cross. Slash. Half circle. Half circle. Gum was sitting right in the middle of it. He got up from the chair, and backed away until he hit a set of antlers.

"It's not easy. It's not supposed to be easy," Grandpa continued. "When the Spirit selected my fiancée as an offering, I wanted to refuse at first. I didn't think it was fair. But I remained faithful."

Helena Crawford. The way she'd glared at Gum from the bathtub. She must have known what family he belonged to.

"It was hard, *very* hard. I cared for her," Grandpa rose slowly. He was talking in a gentle voice, as if soothing a crying infant. "That's the point. It had to be a true act of devotion. She wouldn't be a good sacrifice if I didn't care about her, right? But I obeyed, and the Spirit kept its promise. I found love again with your grandma, and she had a full life. All my investments have done well. All my children and their children are healthy, happy, and successful."

"What about my mom?"

She wasn't healthy, happy, or successful. She was on hold. In limbo. Gum never tried to blame God or fate or Bruce, who had been there when she'd fallen in. Bruce had pulled her out of the water, after all. He'd saved her life. Gum never questioned that story. He thought the worst thing about his family was their politics. He couldn't imagine they were murderers. And certainly not the Devil-worshipping kind.

"Beth is ... a reminder of what happens when we do not keep our end of the bargain." For the first time, Grandpa faltered. The light in his eyes flickered for a moment, but he quickly regained composure. "But we serve a forgiving Spirit. We were given another chance. Each heir only has to make the offering once, and the whole family will receive blessings for the next generation."

"But you already did it to Glory, right? Why take Iris too?"

"She didn't count," Bruce said.

Grandpa glared at his son, then gently told Gum, "There was a . . . complication, last summer. The ritual has to be repeated."

This was wrong. So wrong. But there was something right about it too. Everything his grandfather said was both foreign and familiar all at once. As real and natural as gravity.

But natural didn't equal right. Doing something for decades didn't make it any more okay.

Gum grabbed on to the wall, fighting off vertigo. "No way I'm going to murder my best friend."

"Your best friend who left you at a party?" Grandpa pointed out.

"That was my fault."

Grandpa shook his head. "The secular culture will try to place blame. *Rejoice and be glad, for your reward is great in heaven, for so they persecuted the prophets who were before you.*"

"But this is fucking evil."

"Is the lion evil for killing the antelope? That lion needs to survive. If it doesn't kill, it starves."

"We're not lions. We're people."

"We're more than that," Bruce said.

"What if I say no?"

"You can't," Grandpa said casually. As if they were arguing about what they'd have for dinner. "*Anyone who speaks against the Holy Spirit will not be forgiven, either in this age or in the age to come.* Matthew twelve. Do you know what that means? If we fail again, we'll all be damned for eternity."

"I'm already going to hell."

"You don't get it," Bruce sneered. "If *you* don't complete the ritual, it will take one of ours again. Maybe more, this time. Trust me, you don't want to trade a Garren girl for your family. In the end, blood is thicker than water."

Grandpa cleared his throat. "The photographer will be arriving soon." He motioned to leave, and Bruce dutifully followed. "I'll give you a moment to collect yourself," he added, closing the heavy door.

Before Gum could make a run for it, the lock clicked.

Gum banged on the door for a good five minutes, screaming all their names. But not one of the Claveys came to his rescue.

Someone had to let him out eventually. He should plan a surprise attack, but he doubted he could overpower his uncles. He'd never been in a fight. And he'd be outnumbered. Even if he somehow made it out of the room, he had no plan.

He wished the Disasters were here, so he could tell Iris she was right about magic and tell Aidan he was right about Hudson. Gum thought he understood that part now. Hudson had killed Glory not because he was evil, but because his situation was. It all was riding on the golden boy's shoulders, and once he had completed the deed, he'd wanted nothing to do with the Claveys anymore.

Hudson had even tried to warn Gum. But why couldn't he have just come right out and said it? And if Glory was this generation's sacrifice—the "offering"—why did it have to happen again so soon? What had gone wrong last time? Why did Iris have to die?

Gum stared at the duffel bag. His family had been watching him this whole week. They claimed he didn't have a choice. It was Iris or all of them. Grandpa could have been lying about that, but he hadn't lied about anything so far. He had faltered at the mention of his daughter—the sacrifice that wasn't supposed to happen.

There had to be another way. An Option C, where Gum didn't have to kill anyone.

After twenty, maybe thirty minutes, in which Gum did nothing but pace like a caged animal, the door clicked open. He expected Grandpa or Bruce, his second-in-command.

But it was Aunt Jody, with a big smile and a plate of apple pie. "Hungry?"

She was only a little more than a decade older than Gum. He remembered the wedding. Everyone had whispered about how revealing the back of her dress was during the ceremony. She'd ended up wearing a sweater during the reception. She had cried the whole night.

Now she was tastefully covered. Her dress had sleeves; the hem hit just below the knee. She laid the pie on the table along with a plastic fork and an American-flag-patterned napkin. The pie looked hilariously juxtaposed next to the taxidermy and creepy red rug.

"So, were you fine with all this, when you married Uncle Brian?" Gum asked her.

She blinked, like she was buffering. Then her smile

returned. Big bright veneers that didn't fit her small features. "Every family has its quirks."

"Does my dad know?"

"That would be up to Beth to explain," Jody said. "But . . . well, you know."

"No. I don't. What really happened to her?"

Maybe Gum could get her on his side. Maybe she thought she'd been fine with marrying into a dynasty of killers but at last she was experiencing second thoughts. Gum needed an ally. He needed someone with intel, so he could devise Option C.

"Grandpa was in the middle of explaining it to me when he left," he added. "I can't make a choice until I get the full story."

Jody looked at the door like she wasn't sure if that was allowed. Then smoothed her skirt.

"Your grandfather can finish when he comes back, then."

"Can't you just to tell me?" Gum asked.

"No, I'm . . . not the best person." Aunt Jody was too far gone, but there was one other person who might help. One Grandpa didn't have on a leash. At least, not anymore.

"Can I talk to Hudson? Maybe he can help me feel better about all this."

"Let me see." She scurried out the door, locking it behind her. Jody was too afraid to go against Grandpa, but she also seemed afraid of Gum. The way Grandpa had put it, everything was riding on him. If he didn't follow directions, he could blow up the dynasty. They all knew it, and they were terrified. Maybe ending them all was the moral thing to do. It would save future lives, wouldn't it?

Unless the Spirit attached itself to a new family.

Gum shivered. He felt so cold. Cold from the *inside*. He leaned in close to a cluster of candles, rubbing his hands near them. It was probably a fire hazard to have that many candles in a windowless, wooden room. How thick were these walls? How thick was the door? If it caught on fire, could Gum escape, granted the smoke didn't get him first?

That wouldn't be such a bad thing. That could be the third option. Option C.

If he was the chosen one, and he died before the ritual was supposed to happen . . . would that break the cycle? Would the Claveys get to survive, and Iris too?

He could live with that. Rather, he could *die* for that. Burning in this room sounded like a bad way to go, but there was no good way, was there? Going out like that could be a giant *fuck you*. He could be remembered as a hero, and not a wishy-washy coward.

He picked up a candle. There was no right choice here, but at least this would be his. And he didn't have much time to make it.

Then a new kind of chill rolled up his spine. The smell of tobacco was replaced with the rotten corpse stench. His hand let go without his permission and the candle was snuffed out on its way down, dripping wax on the rug.

The Spirit was here with him, and it wasn't pretending to be Glory anymore. Even if Gum found a loophole, it wasn't going to let him disobey. One by one, all the remaining candles went out, plunging the room into darkness.

On any other day Iris would be dry by now, but this was the coldest July morning ever. A ceiling of gray clouds blocked the sun. She shivered the whole walk to the Landings.

When she finally reached Cabin 4, there were no lights on inside and no fresh coffee smell. Her moms were still asleep. They'd been asleep the last Fourth of July, when Rex had pounded on their door with two cops behind him, holding their hats to their chests like they were saluting the flag. Apparently that was the protocol for telling someone their daughter drowned.

Iris changed out of her wet clothes. She purposefully chose the least holiday-appropriate colors she'd packed: a black shirt, jeans shorts, and her mother's bright geometric windbreaker. If Iris ended up floating in a body of water at some point today, at least she would be easy to spot.

Hudson would be waiting for her in the boathouse soon.

She still hadn't decided if she wanted to show up. Whatever was after her—whatever was pulling her in her sleep—was about to make its final move. She had to leave Bad Creek. But how would she explain that to her moms?

She really needed her big sister right now.

Iris had already looked over Glory's sketchbook at least ten times, flipping through the pages in case she'd missed something. She had studied it like she was cramming for a test but had no idea what the big essay question would be. Now she laid it on the bed and rifled through the pages in reverse. The scream, the hands, the dock, the house. And those eyes.

Hudson Clavey's eyes. Glory drew what she saw, and sometimes she could see things better than others. See *people* better. Glory had sketched Hudson's eyes with her usual elegant hand, but the lines were short. Sharp. Urgent. Like her subject would disappear if she didn't work fast enough. When Glory drew something over and over, it was because she was unsatisfied. The likeness wasn't right, or the story wasn't right.

Glory never got a chance to finish the last set of eyes; the left one was still fuzzy—an undefined smoosh of graphite. Iris was the one who had to figure out Hudson Clavey.

She left the sketchbook on the counter with a note for her moms beside it:

Out with the boys.

Will be back before fireworks.

Though Iris didn't know when she would be back. *If* she would be back.

She thought writing out her intentions would make it true. She really did want to return before the fireworks. The Garrens had missed them last year. They were too busy. There were towels and soap and sunscreen to shove into suitcases. Pillows to scream into. Funeral homes to call. Iris added a *Sorry* in case her promise didn't end up true. She grabbed her bear spray and her phone. If one of the boys called, she would answer.

Probably.

When she stepped out, it was ten degrees colder than when she first entered the cabin. It should have been getting hotter later in the day, but Bad Creek was done following rules. Or maybe this place was done *pretending* to follow the rules. Iris stuffed her hands in her pockets, fiddling with the bear spray.

The boathouse was unlocked; the door hung slightly open. Inside, Iris found Hudson Clavey on the carpeted floor. He wasn't far from the edge where Rex's pontoon boat was docked. The water looked darker than usual.

Hudson turned and gave her a grim smile. "I can't stay long. If I'm not back in time for pictures, they'll be looking for me."

Iris shut the door behind her. Now only a sliver of light shone through. She waved her hand above her head, feeling around for the dangling string that acted as a light switch.

Hudson's face looked worse than before; the red on the left side was darkening into purples and blues. His eye was half-shut—fuzzy, like Glory's unfinished drawing.

Iris's heart twisted into a knot. She wanted to know who had hit him. If he could have possibly deserved it.

"I told you I didn't . . . *do that* to Glory." Hudson spoke like he thought Iris was armed with something more lethal than bear spray. But he didn't look away from her, though she could tell he would have liked to. "And that wasn't a lie. But I'm not innocent either. If you hate me, I get it, that's fair. Just, hear me out . . ." He placed his hand on the wooden railing and took a deep breath.

"For as long as I can remember, I've known I'm supposed to kill a girl in Bad Creek. I don't know why it has to be a girl or why it has to be here. I don't think they know either, or care. My family has served this . . . *thing* forever. I don't know how far back it goes. But my grandpa's grandpa served it. They call it the "Spirit," like the Holy Spirit. Every generation, someone else has to pass the torch. Someone has to keep it happy. I always knew it was wrong. But they also told me something bad would happen if I refused."

He stared at the black water, breathing loud, almost heaving. Like it physically pained him to get it out.

"Okay . . ." Iris said, though there was nothing okay about it. It was more of a push to keep him talking.

"It's supposed to be someone you're close to. Someone you care about," Hudson continued. "A real sacrifice. Isaac and Abraham, you know? So I didn't let myself care about anyone. I tried to keep my distance, every summer. But you don't get to choose—it chooses for you. Kinda like how you don't get to choose your feelings."

"And . . . you liked Glory," Iris realized. It made sense. Glory, all bouncy curls and cherry lipstick and manicured hands covered in watercolor paint. Her light could be seen from space.

He gave her a wounded look, his jaw slack. "No! Jesus, *no*. I never had a crush on Glory. I liked *you*. It's always been you."

Iris laughed. She couldn't help it. She had suspected human

sacrifice already, but Hudson Clavey pining for her all these years? That was too much.

"I'm being serious, okay!" He was practically yelling now. "I've liked you forever. But you've always hated my guts. And I let you. I thought if I hid my feelings, if I let you hate me, it'd keep you safe."

"So to keep me safe you killed my sister?" she spat. "How *romantic*."

"I didn't kill her, Iris. And this isn't me trying to make a move on you! I'm trying to save your life. You can keep hating me after this. I don't care."

But clearly he did care. And she couldn't deny that she did too. The bear spray wouldn't protect her from that.

Hudson continued with his confession. "My family could tell the Spirit was stirring," he explained. "That it was hungry again, and though supposedly *it* chooses, really my grandpa did. He was hounding me about *offering the Garren girl*. Like it was predestined it had to be one of you two. I refused to make either of you a target, but everyone had decided it ought to be Glory. I thought I could buy time and figure out a way around it, but they kept pressuring me. Then *it* was pressuring me, so I played their game. I gathered the lures—"

"Lures?"

"Personal items. Little things she touched often. It could be anything, as long as one of them has hair on it. I had to get her alone a bunch, so I could steal stuff from her. I think she started catching on. I tried to tell her what was going to happen, but every time I opened my mouth . . . I couldn't. It wouldn't let me."

When his hands went to his throat, Iris recognized the drawing of hands around Glory's neck. Silencing her scream.

"I wanted to tell her at the party," he continued. "After trying for the whole week, I finally got it off my back. But it was too late. My dad, he probably knew I was second-guessing it. He buried the lures that night. And once the lures are buried, the offering marches to the altar . . ."

"Altar? You mean the tree at Savi's?"

He nodded.

Offering. Altar. It all sounded cult-like. Something from an episode of *Dark Unknown*—distant enough that she could still call it entertainment and discuss it with her friends. Cults were from worlds where people were bad guys and good guys. Victims and perpetrators. Not sisters and neighbors.

"I tried to stop her from going into the lake," Hudson said. "I really did, and then Aidan showed up, and I told him to leave, but he wouldn't *listen*. They'd been following me. My dad, my grandpa, they knew I wouldn't go through with it. My dad knocked Aidan out. I thought he was dead. Everything happened so fast. And then, next thing I knew, Glory was in the water. I was supposed to . . . hold her under while the Spirit feeds. It's like a baptism, that's how they explained it. But when I refused, the Spirit got angry, and my grandpa got scared . . ."

His good eye flicked up to look at her. "My dad ended up doing it."

There it was. She had her answer. Bruce Clavey had murdered Glory Garren. Well, part Bruce and part *Spirit.*

Iris knew it was true by the look on Hudson's face and the

unsteady crack of his voice. But the truth wasn't enough. She needed more than answers. She needed justice. She needed it like oxygen. Like water.

"What do you get out of it?" she asked. Her mouth was bone-dry.

"Nothing," he said, right away. Then he corrected himself. "Well, it's supposed to keep us rich and healthy and happy. But that's a load of shit. My dad took out a third mortgage on our house. He's in crazy debt, and so is my uncle Brian. Aunt Jody can't have another kid, but they're still trying. Grandma died of cancer, and Grandpa's had trouble with his heart. It's not giving us anything, at least anymore. But we're *owned* by this thing. My dad also refused when it was his turn. When the Spirit chose his best friend as the offering, he found excuses not to come back here."

"You mean . . . your dad was supposed to kill my mom?"

There it was. That was why Joanna's sleepwalking stopped when Beth had nearly drowned. That was why the original Disasters broke up.

"Yep. The Spirit got impatient, so it took his sister instead. Well, *partially*. It didn't intervene when my dad tried to save her. It left Beth alive as a reminder of what would happen if we disobeyed. My grandpa—the Spirit—it's hard to separate them now. But I think both of them really wanted another Garren this time around as revenge."

If Joanna knew she'd been in danger, that her daughters were in danger, she wouldn't have kept coming to Bad Creek. Unless the Spirit wasn't only pulling on Iris. It was tugging at everyone who ever visited. Demanding, *Stay, stay, stay.*

She imagined it as a swirling, lifeless black hole of a creature, feeding on the Bad Creek regulars generation after generation, Disaster after Disaster. This town reared its residents as fruit to be devoured each harvest, bred over and over in the same convenient spot. They would forget their lost ancestors, they would ignore the rust and the rot, they would call the stench of death nostalgia.

She backed farther from the water, feeling stupid for smooshing her face in her sweatshirts and quilts, wishing every night when she went to bed she would wake up in Bad Creek among her trees and her dock and her summer boys.

"It's trying to keep control, but it's dying." Hudson explained. "It's losing power with every generation and it has nothing left to give. It only takes. My grandpa can't see that, and my dad is so obsessed with regaining his favor, he doesn't care what he becomes."

"So you're stuck serving this thing forever?" Iris wondered if there was ever any truth to the Spirit's initial promise of prosperity, or if it was always a trick.

"Don't worry about me," Hudson said, shaking his head. "It's after you."

"I thought Glory was the *offering?* Why would it still want me?"

"To fuck with me, probably. Like my dad the first time, I disobeyed. The ritual needs to be committed by an heir from *this* generation. So Glory didn't count. Or maybe it's just greedy. I don't know. It's like the rules keep changing."

"And now they're trying to make you go through with it?"

"No. It gave up on me. I was its first choice, but I'm not the only possible male heir."

Gum.

The carpeted walls were closing in on her. No. No way. It couldn't be this bad.

"Gum wouldn't hurt me," Iris said. But Gum hadn't been himself. He'd seemed quieter. His jokes rang hollow. And his hands were always moving, drawing. Cross, slash, two crescent moons. The last thing she'd said to him was that she didn't want to be his friend anymore.

"Have you had anything go missing?" Hudson asked.

Yesterday she couldn't find her nail polish. And when she'd changed in her cabin, she had expected to find her green scrunchie wrapped around her water bottle, but it wasn't there. It could be a coincidence . . . but.

There were no coincidences in Bad Creek.

"My family can't afford another fuckup," Hudson told her. "They'll find a way to make him go through with the ritual."

And Iris would be dead, and Gum would be a killer. Just two more skeletons piled into this fucking town's closet.

"What if we killed it?" Iris suggested slowly.

"It's more of a whisper of a thing," Hudson said. "It barely has a solid form. Only when it's in water. And even then, it's ancient. My family thinks it's a god."

"You said it was losing power, though, right? There has to be a way."

"Maybe. It's just, I don't think anyone's tried to kill it before."

"That doesn't mean it's impossible," Iris decided. The Spirit could be relying on their fear. But if Iris smashed its familiar cycle, could it survive?

She had to end this. For Glory. For Beth. For Helena. For all the girls before. She did not want to add her name to this legacy. She wouldn't be another scratch on a post. A photo buried and forgotten. It wouldn't feed on her.

It would never feed again.

The Spirit wouldn't let him set the house on fire, but at least it let him walk around in circles.

Pacing was how Gum made decisions. So far, he'd been able to skirt by without making any big ones because everything had been conveniently pre-decided for him. All he had to do was endure the choices others made on his behalf. This situation was no different. The path was laid out for him here, and there was no alternative.

Was he really going to risk his entire family for Iris, the girl who hated his guts now? Gum didn't have the Disasters' favor, but he could still have the Claveys'. He was an asshole either way, but at least serving this Spirit would leave him with a support system.

He stopped mid-circle. No. That was insane, right? He couldn't be a killer. That was just the Spirit getting in his head. He couldn't tell the difference between his thoughts and the

Spirit's. *Demon.* That was a better word for it. This wasn't something holy.

This was a curse he had inherited.

Curses were afflictions that singed even deeper than bone and gray matter and neurons. There were no medications, no cures. Not even dying would end them, because curses weren't bound by mortality. And the worst ones were transmittable.

The door unlocked again; the dark room was flooded with light. Though Uncle Bruce was technically his captor, Gum was relieved to see him. If the Claveys forced his hand, then whatever happened technically wouldn't be his fault.

Bruce eyed the untouched plate on the shelf. "I see Jody left some pie."

Gum had almost thrown the porcelain plate against the wall, but he hadn't wanted to find out if the demon allowed that act of rebellion. He couldn't stand the sensation of it—the lurch in his stomach when it took control. He would do anything to avoid it again.

"Somehow, she keeps getting worse," Bruce added, smiling like they were having a normal chat. Like they ever had a relationship where they would crack jokes about their relatives. Bruce had brought clothes with him. Khakis and a white button-down shirt. He instructed Gum to change.

Family pictures were happening, after all.

Gum obeyed because, if he didn't, the Spirit would probably make him.

Bruce grabbed the duffel bag of Iris's things and guided his nephew by the shoulders, down the long hallway of photographs.

"I know this seems hard. I'm not going to lie to you. It was," Bruce said. "After Beth, I was so angry at the Lord. But even the prophet Jeremiah questioned God's love. *Why is my pain unceasing, my wound incurable, refusing to be healed? Will you be to me like a deceitful brook, like waters that fail?*"

Bruce squeezed Gum's shoulder too hard. "But God hadn't left Jeremiah, even during his crisis of faith. And he didn't give up on me, when I failed to answer his call. The forgiving Spirit blessed us with a compromise. Beth lives. She lives through him. And he gave me another chance to prove my devotion."

They were back in the dining room, where Bruce set the bag on the table, next to the bouquet of day lilies. When Bruce said *another chance*, was he talking about Glory? Gum didn't ask for clarity. His words kept slipping away.

"True devotion is unpopular," Bruce continued. "Look at the state of the culture nowadays. People get offended when you want to save children from predators poisoning their minds with the sin of pride. They get offended when you love your God. When you love your country." He sounded just like Grandpa. He looked like him too. Could Gum turn into them? The thought sounded horrifying, but what if the peace Bruce spoke of wasn't bullshit? What if he really felt free?

Gum was so *tired*.

They made it to the front yard, which was decked out with American flags. The aunts were fussing over the girls' hair bows. Grandpa had his sand-colored suit jacket on now, hands behind his back as he watched over the photographer fiddling with a tripod.

"It's a cloudy day," the photographer said. "We got lucky."

The Claveys were always lucky.

"Do you know Luke?" Bruce asked. "*An angel of the Lord appeared to them, and the glory of the Lord shone around them, and they were terrified.* What did the angel say?"

Gum did know this one. It was a Christmas classic. "*Do not be afraid,*" he answered.

"And also, *peace to those on whom his favor rests,*" Grandpa chimed in. Gum flinched. He hadn't seen his grandfather move from his spot in front. "Not everyone," Grandpa continued. "Only those who are worthy."

"I did not have to be afraid," Bruce whispered. "Of myself. Of the Spirit. I understand that now. You don't have to feel alone, because you're *not* alone. You feel it, don't you? The call? Like electricity in your soul."

Gum nodded. He *did* feel it, though it hardly felt like the innocent kind of electricity that powered light bulbs. No, it was the kind that accompanied thunder. The kind that started forest fires and racked up body counts.

"It feels like heaven when you let it in," Bruce continued.

"And heaven is for the deserving," Grandpa added.

Gum was on the precipice of deserving it. There was a tightrope ahead of him. If he fell, both sides offered a different type of damnation.

"I battled for a long time," Bruce added, "but, honestly, it's all worth it once you submit. You'll find peace."

The rest of the family shuffled into their positions. Hudson appeared out of nowhere, falling into his place on Gum's right. His outfit was pristine now, but his face remained swollen and purple. He offered Gum a sympathetic look. Clearly Hudson had felt no peace since he'd killed Glory. He had submitted to the spirit, but not to the Claveys.

Gum wanted to ask him if he regretted it, but the photographer was already coaching them. "Ladies, cross your legs at the ankle."

Clarice adjusted Beth's legs, then wheeled her into position before scurrying out of the frame. Clarice had already learned the rules. Maybe they'd keep this nurse after all.

Beth is what happens when we do not keep our end of the bargain.

Grandpa's words seared into him again. Maybe that wasn't even Gum thinking about it, but the Spirit reminding him. If he failed, someone else would drown anyway. Or worse: they would be trapped, like his mom. Grandpa had promised that the whole family would suffer. If the Spirit could possess Gum, it probably had the power to strike down whomever it pleased too.

The photographer was careful to match their positions to the previous photos, and Gum smiled like the rest of them. It hurt to keep it going for the first few minutes, but eventually he couldn't feel the muscles in his face straining. He didn't feel anything at all.

If Iris was meant to be the sacrifice, who was he to go against fate? It was God's will, and Gum's will certainly wasn't more powerful than his. So why stall any longer? There was no option C because there was no option A or B.

There was no option at all.

Bruce had promised it would be beautiful, after a while. He would submit eventually, so why pretend he could fight it? It would be easier to accept himself if his family accepted him, and the only way to do that was to accept the Spirit—holy or not.

When the photographer announced he'd gotten the shot, the family dispersed. The girls were free to ruin their dresses, and Hudson was free to sulk somewhere else. Instead, he grabbed Gum by the elbow, hard.

"They've told you, right?" Hudson whispered. "What are you going to do?"

There was no time to answer. Gum was being whisked in another direction by another will, but this time he didn't resist. Bruce had the duffel bag again. He threw it in the Great White's trunk, next to a shovel.

What kind of people drive their boats in the rain?

Aidan had already passed two pontoon boats of regulars sipping beers, who had cheered as the *Dirty Diana* had zipped passed them.

He hoped his hunch was wrong. Each time he saw anything even remotely human-shaped, he felt sick. But each time, it was a rock or driftwood or an abandoned paddle. Never Iris. When he confirmed it wasn't her, his heart surged with relief, but then fear would sink in again.

He had completed his loop around the lake's perimeter but there was still no sign of Iris. He even stopped by the spooky abandoned house. He could see the decaying siding peeking out between the pine trees. Nope. Still no Iris. The *Dirty Diana*'s motor was begging for a break, but he wouldn't allow it. Not until he was sure. He turned around. He'd check again.

His phone buzzed in his pocket. Probably Paul, discovering

the boat missing. Time for him to play concerned parent. Aidan whipped out his phone. It wasn't his dad.

Iris's name was on the caller ID. He stared at it in disbelief and then, before the last ring, he accepted the call. Iris's breathless voice chimed in on the other end. "I was worried you wouldn't answer," she said, sounding very much un-drowned.

"Where the fuck are you?" It came out harsh, but it was a bit hard to steer and talk while rain was beating down on him. Thunder rumbled nearby. A kid zoomed by on his Jet Ski, unbothered.

"At your house," Iris answered. "Where the fuck are you?"

"On the lake . . ."

"Oof. Bad idea. The lake is canceled. This whole town is canceled. Haven't you heard?"

"Am I still canceled?"

"Depends on who you ask. I don't think Hudson's face is very pleased with your fist right now."

Hudson. He had told Iris about the fight. Which meant . . .

"Are you with him?" Aidan asked. He pushed the speedboat to her limit. He could see Wahbee's dock. "He's not safe," he added. Iris had called him, which was a good sign. It meant there was a chance she would listen.

"I'm perfectly safe . . . ish," she said. "When are you coming back? We need to talk."

"Docking in two minutes. I know you're super-mad at me, and you were right about most of it, but please, *please* trust me. You need to get away from him."

"I think I see you!"

He could see her too. Iris exited the back patio waving,

with Roy on her heels—and someone else too. Someone blond and buff, whose pastimes included archery and drowning girls. Clearly Aidan hadn't punched him hard enough.

The *Dirty Diana* slowed before crashing into the dock. Aidan tied the fastest knot in his life and ran up to them, preparing his sore knuckles and dislocated thumb for another round. But Iris jumped in between before he could get another swing in.

"I saw him carving it in the tree, Iris," Aidan yelled.

She shook her head. It was fine if Iris didn't forgive him; he didn't need her forgiveness. He only needed her to believe him.

"I didn't carve it. I was going to scratch it out before you beat the shit out of me," Hudson said sardonically. "Look, I'm sorry for not saying anything sooner. I'm trying to make up for it now."

Aidan wanted to say, *Cold-blooded murderers don't deserve redemption arcs*, but thunder roared suddenly, loud and merciless. As Roy barked at the sky, Iris suggested they go in before anyone got struck by lightning.

Hudson sat in a corner of the living room, surrounded by a wall of famous movie masks. Most people were overwhelmed by Paul's memorabilia. They either loved it or hated it, but they always gave their opinion. But Hudson looked unphased. He didn't take his eyes off of Iris as she explained what had happened this morning. What Hudson had told her.

Aidan still wanted to hit him.

"But we're gonna kill it," Iris concluded. "Before it kills me."

"You mean, before Gum kills you?" Aidan asked.

It sounded just as ridiculous as when Hudson had suggested it.

Hudson spoke for the first time in an hour, pulling out books from his expensive-looking brown leather bag. "I snagged these from the trophy room. My grandpa used to be big on journaling. I don't know if the Spirit has any weaknesses, but it would probably be in here."

"So, you've seen this thing?" Aidan asked. "What does it look like?"

"Like a monster." Hudson didn't elaborate. *Monster* was the vaguest term ever. It could be a red Devil with a forked tongue or Cthulhu or freaking Bigfoot. What it looked like wasn't important, but Aidan needed something to visualize. He stared at the mask on the wall, the green, amphibious creature from *It Runs Below*.

"My dad knows about it. I think he has for a while," Aidan said. Another thing Iris was right about. But she didn't rub it in.

"Joanna knows something too," Iris replied. "Do you think Paul will help us?"

Aidan shrugged. Last night Paul didn't want to share, just gave vague ominous warnings. But Aidan wouldn't accept non-answers now.

He headed to his dad's office. He was supposed to knock before entering, but he pushed it open without hesitation. The room was dark, thanks to blackout curtains. He flicked on the lamp. No Paul. He peeked out the office window. The Jeep was in the driveway, but not the truck. Crap.

Aidan turned to leave, but the state of the room made him pause. It looked like the office of the most disorganized FBI agent ever. There were piles of empty take-out boxes. Open books stacked on top of each other, crinkled and stained from half-empty coffee mugs. Newspaper clippings tacked to the overflowing bulletin board. One had a photo of a smiling girl, a reprint of the one they found at the old mansion. Helena Crawford. Then another newspaper clipping, and another. Some with more faces. All with the same word highlighted over and over: *drowned*.

Paul Ross was a man of many talents. He was a writer, director, a part-time father, ex-husband, dog-lover. He was a collector of miniatures, of vinyl records, of Hawaiian shirts.

And in secret, apparently, Paul Ross dabbled in detective work.

Aidan called his dad. It only rang once.

"Ahoy, there," Paul answered.

"How long? How long have you known?"

Paul sighed on the other end. Like he had seen this coming. "It was a hunch, until yesterday. I thought I was protecting you by keeping it secret. That's what Jo and I decided, but . . . didn't do much good, huh?"

"Explain. *Now*."

"Right after you kids were born, Beth was hysterical this one night. We were all gathered around our cabins, having a bonfire, like normal. Beth said Jo was in danger and Bruce was a traitor. We all thought Beth was having some kind of episode. Like, she was mad at her brother for being avoidant. He hadn't been around much. He studied abroad and then was on a business trip or a honeymoon or something. Then one summer, he came back, but that set Beth off, for some reason. Her husband said she'd been acting strange lately, worried about demons taking her baby. I brought this up with Bruce and he assured me there was nothing to worry about. But then, the next morning, Bruce pulled Beth out of the water. She'd tried to kill herself. That's what we were told. But we never got a clear answer, because it wasn't like she could tell us her side of the story anymore."

His voice cracked, like he was crying or about to. "Not even a week later, an anonymous donor sent me a check for my film funding. I cashed the check, but, well, part of me knew it was blood money. It was a bribe."

"You think the Claveys sent it?"

"Yes. I thought they were embarrassed by their daughter's mental health crisis. But I couldn't stop thinking about how she was so afraid. She was sure something was coming after her because of something Bruce had done. It never sat right with me. After I moved back here, I found a few guys online who had experiences with generational curses. They showed me what patterns to look for. It wasn't until last year—until Glory—that I took it seriously. Before Beth was Helena Crawford, and before her was Marjory Stevens, Joan Aubers, Hattie Robinson. All accidental drownings. It's impossible to know how far back it goes. The archives in Bad Creek aren't the best. Small towns like these don't make the news often. And, well, that's the point, right? Evil loves small towns. There's a lot of fuckery the locals will accept. So the bodies will pile up, and no one bats an eye."

"So you're just gonna do nothing?"

"This morning, after we talked, I knew I couldn't sit on this any longer. I thought I'd try to report it."

There was a pause. Static. Faint voices in the background.

Dread churned in Aidan's stomach. "Dad, where are you?"

"I'm at the police station."

Fuck. If anyone had seen enough horror movies, it was Paul. And he knew the only consistent rule was: all cops are useless.

"They won't believe you," Aidan told him.

"I brought some evidence with me. Figured the Claveys might have more if we can secure a warrant, but, uh. They're holding me here. I can't talk much longer."

"They're holding you?" Aidan's stomach dropped. "Are you under arrest?"

"Not yet. Officially. But don't worry about me."

That only made his panic rise well above sea level.

"It's after Iris," Aidan whispered so Iris and her brand-new bestie Hudson couldn't hear. "I think the Claveys are planning to feed her to it tonight."

Not the Claveys. *Gum.* But Aidan still couldn't believe that part.

"The detective is coming back," his dad said quickly. "Stay put. Hopefully I'll be home soon. Don't let Iris near the water."

"But—"

"And, Aidan? I'm so sorry for making you come back."

The line went dead.

Aidan stared numbly at the phone for a moment. All this time, he'd thought his dad had given up. He was dead wrong. But this wasn't how he wanted to find out. And though Paul was brave for going after the Claveys, Aidan couldn't take his advice. He couldn't stay put.

He was tired of sitting around and accepting what was handed to him.

He was going to kill this fucking thing.

Aidan stepped out of the office. Iris and Hudson were sitting close together, reading over leather journals, looking downright cozy. It made Aidan's skin crawl.

Iris perked up. "Did you talk to him?"

"Yeah, but he's . . ." Aidan picked at crud on the kitchen counter. "He can't help."

Iris stepped over, leaning into one of the barstools.

"What's wrong? What did he say?"

"He went to the cops. Apparently he's been following this thing for years and he picked now to do something about it. But they're holding him there."

"What do you mean, they're holding him?" Hudson demanded.

He glared in Hudson's direction. "He says it's fine, but . . . what if the Claveys are trying to pin it on him? They tried to buy his silence when Beth drowned, but it didn't work." He ran his fingers through his hair. "Fuck."

The Claveys controlled Bad Creek. They owned the golf course and a bed-and-breakfast and the Second Largest Crucifix in the World. They probably owned the police.

"I'm sorry," Hudson said, from across the room. "I didn't know what they were planning."

Aidan rolled his eyes. "*Sure.*"

"It'll be okay," Iris said, gently putting her hand on Aidan's back. "We'll get Paul out."

Hudson nodded, as if he thought *we* included *him*. He said he was on their side, but how did they know that for sure? He could be a spy.

"Wouldn't your family be pissed that you're helping us kill your pet monster?" Aidan sneered.

"It's not our pet," Hudson corrected. "We're the ones serving it."

"So, basically, you're its bitch?"

"Aidan," Iris warned. "Please, play nice."

But Aidan was done playing nice.

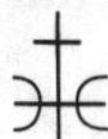

The storm pounded against the windows. The rain probably gave them more time to read the journals Hudson had so generously supplied. They should have been grateful. Still, Aidan jumped whenever thunder bellowed.

They were still reading when the storm subsided and the sky faded into a calm gray. He could barely decipher the messy cursive of his assigned volume; a few buzzwords stuck out. *Sigil. Heir. Offering. Lures.*

Bill Clavey wrote about other people like they were pests, or NPCs in video games. He wrote with the ego of a cult leader. Though this journal was dated in the 1970s, Aidan couldn't stomach the blatant sexism sprinkled throughout.

"This guy would probably kill a girl even without a demon telling him to," he complained with a shudder. "I don't think we should worry about Gum." He glared at Hudson, who sat on the floor on the other side of the room, as if he were doing Aidan a kindness by avoiding the furniture. "Who's to say it won't be your dad again?"

"It's against the rules," Hudson repeated. "My dad's afraid

to piss it off. And it's getting really desperate. It's going to throw everything it's got and hold on even tighter. It can get in your head. Make you do things . . ."

"So, you're saying Gum doesn't have a choice?"

"He doesn't *think* he has a choice."

"Isn't that the same thing?"

"Not really."

"Oh shit!" Iris uttered suddenly. She'd been lying on the carpet, but now she scrambled into a sitting position. "It hates smoking."

"At least the demon is anti–Big Tobacco," Aidan muttered.

Iris ignored him and read, "*Its skin sizzled and cracked from the heat, even inches away. I vowed to give up smoking to demonstrate my devotion.*"

"He's such a hypocrite," Hudson sneered.

"Guys," Iris murmured. "What if it's afraid of fire? What if we burn it? I mean, it makes sense, right?"

"It's not going to show up until you're near the water, Iris," Hudson stressed. "It's the only place it—"

"Has a physical form, I know," Iris finished. She tore through the pages again, like she'd missed something important.

"Let's just send Iris into the water as bait and throw a Molotov cocktail at it," Aidan suggested. He meant it as a joke. Obviously this literal demon couldn't be beat the same way as the monster in his dad's stupid movie.

Except Iris looked up. "Your dad has a bunch of fireworks stashed in the garage, right?"

In a few hours, Paul was supposed to drive the hoard of fireworks to Burt Beach, where Bad Creek put on their official fireworks display, generously donated by the big old families from the north side. Paul's contribution was always one of the largest—not that he was especially patriotic, he simply liked it when things went *boom*.

"That . . . honestly might work," Hudson said.

Iris popped up and clapped her hands together. "Let's do it!"

"Are you guys being serious?" Aidan asked. There was no way this ancient terror could be destroyed that easily. Why hadn't someone tried it before? Because they were afraid to challenge it?

Or because this was a terrible idea?

Iris was adamant. "Let's explode this fucker. We should load up on fireworks. Maybe get gasoline—"

Iris surged forward like she had the sudden urge to vomit. She bent at the waist, arms hanging lifelessly at her sides. Then, just as Aidan was about to ask if she was okay, she unfolded herself. Her face relaxed; her breathing slowed. She stumbled away from them, head lolling with each step.

She looked like she was sleepwalking.

"Iris!" Aidan shouted, lurching to grab her.

"She can't hear you," Hudson said. "The lures must've been buried. We're too late. It's starting."

Gum was sure the mud would never come off. It was in his ears, his mouth, his armpits. This was the easy part, according to Grandpa, but Gum already felt blisters forming from his bad grip on the shovel. His whole body would be sore tomorrow, though he couldn't conceptualize that yet. Tomorrow felt like a myth. There was only now: the mud flicking onto his face, Grandpa watching from a lawn chair with a sweet tea in hand, and Bruce standing behind Grandpa, alert as a guard dog.

The rain had stopped, but the sky still looked unsettled. Gum couldn't hear cicadas. From where he was standing, he couldn't see any birds on the water either. All the ducks and swans and geese knew better than to be in the Landings today.

The sigil already marked a willow tree. The *Disasters'* willow tree. Where they'd played freeze tag and curated playlists and told secrets and climbed until it was time for dinner. And now its bark was mutilated. The roots had snapped under his shovel.

We haven't climbed here for years, Gum reminded himself. And the tire swing was gone for a reason. This tree could do nothing for him, so he didn't owe it sympathy.

"That's enough," Grandpa said once Gum had dug a good three feet.

Bruce slipped something else into the duffel bag: a photo. One Gum recognized. Iris had her mouth open in a laugh and her arms were up, wrapped around her friends' shoulders. But Gum and Aidan were cropped out.

Bruce instructed him to cover the duffel bag with dirt. He obeyed. Giving in was starting to get easier. Eventually he would walk with his uncle's same self-assured ease.

"Now we wait," Grandpa said. He swished the ice cubes around his mostly empty glass.

"For what?" Gum asked.

"The offering."

"For Iris, you mean."

"Yes, the Garren girl will be drawn to the lures."

Gum shouldn't have said her name. She wasn't Iris; she was the *offering*. She was his ticket into the club, for good.

If she was in her cabin, it would only take a few minutes. There was a chance she was already at the beach for the Fourth of July party. They would have privacy here; no one would see or hear anything.

Still, Gum worried about witnesses. There would be a commotion, water splashing. Gum wasn't sure if he was strong enough to hold her under for long. But Grandpa had made it clear that he and Uncle Bruce couldn't help.

"It's not that I didn't love my first fiancée," Grandpa mused. "I loved her dearly. But there are more important things. It's hard to imagine. But you'll see."

Gum didn't love Iris like that, but there was no use explaining it to Grandpa. He shouldn't love her anymore at all. She was done with him. That should have made it easier.

Gum perched against the tree trunk, facing the water instead of his family. The sky was darkening prematurely. No sunset, just colorless clouds choking out the sun. Maybe the fireworks would start early this year.

A few hundred people would be gathered on the beach on the other side of town, playing cornhole, throwing Frisbees, and eating burned hot dogs. A few days ago, he too had a simple existence where he could busy himself with the same concerns as the rest of the world. He wouldn't get that back. This was the price to pay for being God's favorite, according to Bruce.

Gum didn't feel like anyone's favorite. He was a flimsy cardboard cutout, easily yanked around by any strong wind.

A black form waded in the water now. Too big to be a duck. Probably a paddleboarder.

"What if someone sees us?" Gum asked.

"They won't," Grandpa said. Maybe the Spirit could control that like it controlled Gum. It could have caused the awful weather and the disappearance of all bugs and birds.

"You said last year there was a complication?"

"Your cousin failed to live up to the Spirit's wishes." Grandpa glared at Bruce. "Someone else had to carry out his duty."

Oh. So Hudson hadn't done it, after all. That hardly changed Gum's situation.

He threw a rock in the creek. It didn't make a splash, didn't make a single sound. It sank silently, without any fanfare. He threw a heavier rock. Still nothing. Not a ripple. The green water looked grayer now that he squinted at it. The grass he sat on was all crumbly and brown. Hadn't it been alive a moment before?

The wind picked up, snatching the willow's long leaves with it. Gum's hair whipped wildly around his face. The gust roared in and out of his ears, his mouth, his nose; it stung his eyes until he closed them. He gripped his knees hard, afraid he would blow over and sink into the water.

When he thought the worst of it was over, he dared to open his eyes. The dark mass was approaching the shore. It wasn't a paddleboarder.

It was a monster.

It shouldn't have been this hard to find matches.

The fireworks were loaded into the Jeep. Aidan had snagged the big guns: the M-80s. Which weren't real M-80s. They were probably M-200s. Paul had bought them off A Guy.

The gasoline was in the shed near the firepit, but the matches weren't near it. Aidan had just used them this morning, yet they were nowhere to be found. His hands shook as he dug through a drawer of dead batteries and receipts and USB cords. Gum usually had a lighter on him, but Gum wouldn't be much help right now.

Aidan thought, stupidly, that Iris couldn't figure out how to unlock the front door while half-asleep, but she must have managed. Just like the matches, she'd disappeared. She was probably already down the driveway. Aidan wasn't sure if he should try to beat her to the lures or follow closely behind. It would take a second to get the fireworks in position and throw the gas on the demon. And then there were the Claveys. Hudson had made it clear that they were desperate. They weren't going to permit any errors in the ritual.

And they were *gun people*.

Aidan had no plans, no proper weapons, and his only ally was Hudson.

"Found 'em!" Hudson hollered from the other side of the kitchen.

They raced to the car without another word. Would Iris take the road or cut through the woods? She could shave off time if she took one of the trails. They already knew where the lures were. The symbol had been carved into the willow behind Cabin 12.

"I can drive," Hudson said. Aidan knew he probably looked like a total mess. He was shaking all over. But he could still operate a vehicle. If anything, it would give him something he could control. So Aidan glared at him.

Hudson put his palms up. "Or you can drive. That's cool."

The windows had been left open, so the driver's seat was drenched from the rain, though Aidan had more to worry about than wet pants.

The engine roared to life. Aidan slammed on the gas and did a donut in the yard.

Thankfully, Iris hadn't gotten very far. She shuffled, zombie-like, in the center of the road. Every step looked like a second away from stumbling.

Aidan pulled up beside her, yelling her name, but she didn't even look in his direction.

"She won't snap out of it," Hudson said.

"So we just let her walk right into danger?" Her face looked so gray, sapped of any life or color. She didn't look asleep—she looked dead.

"The Spirit won't appear until she's close to the lures," Hudson said.

"So we let it eat her soul? Sounds fucking fantastic." It was far too risky. Aidan wanted to snap her out of it now. Every second she was in this state was another second she was closer to the end. Even the air around her felt stale. Doomed. Aidan added, "I don't get how you can just be fine with this."

"I'm *not* fine with this," Hudson snarled at him. "But this is what Iris wanted. I trust her plan."

Ha. Hudson could say he was against it, but at the end of the day, whatever happened to Iris wouldn't hurt him. He'd survive, and he'd only benefit if that thing got to feed again.

"It can't be this easy, right? If it can burn, why hasn't anyone done it before?" Aidan pointed out.

"Because they were too scared of destroying the family dynasty."

"But you aren't?"

"I'd rather die than become like them."

"You're not the one in danger of dying."

"I won't let anything happen to her," Hudson said, his face grave.

"Oh, fuck off with that chivalry act."

"It's not an act."

"You let Glory die!"

Hudson didn't respond to the accusation right away. They passed the parking lot for Burt Beach—which was full of cars, as expected. The chilly weather wasn't going to stop the Fourth of July festivities, even if it were actual Armageddon. Even if a nuke dropped from the sky right now, Bad Creek would still celebrate Independence Day.

"Yeah," Hudson admitted. "I'm sorry."

"I tried to stop them," Aidan said. "But . . ."

"My dad hit you with the butt of a gun. Knocked you out. I thought he was gonna *kill* you. I thought he would kill me, honestly. He still might."

That explained why Aidan couldn't remember. Why he'd woken up feeling like his head was full of mud. But a clear conscience didn't matter if he couldn't save Iris.

They were almost at the Landings now, and Iris didn't slow down. What would happen if Aidan grabbed her, threw her in the car, and then drove far, far away? The next generation could figure out the monster themselves.

But if they made it to the other side of the country, would Iris snap out of it, or would she keep walking, closer and closer to this town that wanted to kill her? Probably. Even if she wasn't in a supernatural trance, Iris worshipped this place.

It wasn't her fault. It was a perfect storm. Whether from this "spirit" or their parents, there was the constant pressure to return. To forget the bad stuff and relive the good instead. Over and over and over again. Even Aidan had returned. He wasn't any better.

But Aidan wasn't going to sit back and follow the rules anymore. He remembered Glory at the diner, telling him, *You always hold on too tight.*

Well, today he was going to hold on tighter than ever.

Gum felt seasick. He wasn't even in the water yet, but the ground rocked under him. Sitting didn't make it better. Neither did putting his head between his knees.

For a second he forgot where he was. He couldn't see all that well. His thoughts were spiky and dangerous, each one ripping at the inside of his brain.

Offering.

Burial.

Monster.

The nausea overtook him. He closed his eyes and tried to think of being anywhere else. Being any*one* else.

Bruce lifted Gum up by the armpit and told him to kneel.

Kneeling reminded him of Mass, so he pretended he was back in church. He pretended the worst thing on his plate was the uncomfortable pew. He imagined the lights—swinging, falling, and finally smooshing him.

Until he made the mistake of opening his eyes. The creek was black, with a reddish sheen. He had time-traveled, somehow, back to biblical times. The Nile had turned to blood.

Gum had never admitted this to his friends, but he hated horror movies. He would look away during the scary parts yet still had the masochistic urge to peek through the blanket over his face. He forced himself to witness the gore even though it disturbed him.

He now forced himself to look at the monster floating in the water, supposedly a piece of God himself.

If that were true, then this was God's ugliest piece.

It had thick moose-like antlers full of cracks and little round holes as if infested with worms. Its gray face was almost human at the top, but the bottom was elongated and flaking off so much, its mouth had become a void. No teeth, no tongue. Just a gaping hole. Its shoulders were burly, bruised yellow and purple. Long arms ended in black talons. It smelled like decay and looked like roadkill. This Spirit was falling apart at the seams—a zombie that had rotted too long, animated only by the magic of devotion and the eternal urge to keep eating. Keep killing.

This was what Gum had been seeing for the past week. Not Glory. It had always been this wretched thing.

"Ah, here we are," Grandpa said. His knees wobbled as he got up from his genuflection.

Grandpa invited Gum to stand as well. "Daniel," he said. "The offering is ready."

Grandpa pointed to the ground, where a cottontail rabbit approached, somehow clean despite all the mud from the afternoon rain. Gum had seen plenty of rabbits in Bad Creek, but he knew it was *the* rabbit.

The one he'd killed years ago.

Relief washed over him. There, he had buried his chance to impress Grandpa. Now was time for his redemption. All this drama about drowning his friend was probably a metaphor. It wasn't about killing Iris; it was killing the part of him *that cared*. Gum wasn't exactly cool with murdering animals. He ate meat and all, but that was a faraway thing. Someone did that dirty work for him. And though he wasn't thrilled by the idea of killing this rabbit again, he'd get over it. He would have to get over it. Grandpa was watching.

The Spirit was watching.

It was bobbing waist-deep in the water, leaning forward to gain a better view. Its dark eyes sagged, pus-filled and bloody around the sockets.

Gum picked up the rabbit by the back of its neck. He didn't know the proper way to hold it. He figured it was like a kitten, where you can pick it up by the scruff. He didn't want to hurt it any more than he had to.

It didn't squirm as he carried it toward the edge of the water. The first step was freezing, but the next one was easier, and Gum waded in until the creek reached his waist. This was the deepest he had ever gone. It wasn't nearly as terrifying as it should have been. Maybe Bruce was right about the relief that was waiting for him. Maybe heaven was real, and it would still take Gum in.

He looked at the rabbit he held—it was a twitchy little thing. One of a hundred million easily replaceable mammals.

If this one died, there would always be another. Who would be able to tell the difference?

Then the rabbit became a girl.

She wasn't in his arms anymore, but standing in front of him, his hands around her neck. She wore a dress with a high collar and giant skirt. She looked like one of those women in photographs from the Civil War era. Then she shifted into another girl. Straight nose, dark eyes, a different old-timey dress. Then she had ribbons in her hair, becoming the broken neck corpse, who'd led Iris from her bed. Then she was the one from the bathtub. Helena. A light bob and big teeth and thin fingers that she had probably used to play piano or the harp or something. She probably had hobbies and secrets and fears that were lost to time now.

The rabbit became his mother, the version of her that only existed in the portraits. Awake and vibrant. A whole person he would never know. But something about the defiant smile on her lips told him she could have been what he needed.

And then the rabbit was Glory, imperfect but sure of herself, daring anyone to just *try* to beat her. She wasn't a nice girl, but she wasn't a cruel one either. And she didn't deserve this.

But most of all, it was Iris. Always screaming at the top of her lungs, afraid no one heard her. Loyal and desperate, with the least self-conscious laugh he had ever heard. Her heart lived outside her chest, raw and exposed and on the verge of bleeding out at all times. She was delicate. A total crybaby. And yet, she was the strongest person he knew.

"Daniel," Grandpa warned.

Iris never called him Daniel. She called him Gum, because

something about his first name wasn't right. The professors at school wanted to call him a Clavey, and he liked to remind them that he wasn't. He was all Clavey now, in the khakis and a tailored shirt, pretending girls were prey. If he caught his reflection, he probably wouldn't recognize it.

"*Daniel.*" Grandpa's impatience was audible. Though its beastly face couldn't emote, the Spirit was also displeased. Gum had waited far too long. Hesitation wasn't part of the ritual.

But Gum couldn't be part of the ritual.

He let go of the girl—the rabbit—the promise that he could ever find his family's version of salvation. Iris blinked like she was waking from a long sleep. Gum pushed her away as the Spirit lunged for them.

Aidan was no stranger to monsters. He'd been spoon-fed horror movies since he could remember, and Paul's house was full of vile creatures. Posters and action figures and masks. Maws of teeth and glowing eyes and knives for hands.

But this thing—this *Spirit*, as Hudson called it—made him stop in his tracks. Hudson was next to him, crouched behind the cover of trees, dumping out the fireworks, while the thing waded toward Gum and Iris.

"*Get down*," Hudson hissed. Aidan went to his knees and pulled the matches from his pocket. He checked to see if the Claveys had noticed him. Nope. They were too focused on coaching Gum, who was standing in the too-dark water, holding Iris by the throat.

Aidan's vision flashed to a nearly identical scene. Trade early evening clouds for a black night. Trade the Landing's muddy creek for the lake on the north side. Trade Gum for Hudson. Iris for Glory. But that *thing*. It was the same.

Its eyes were too sunken to tell, but Aidan could swear it was looking right at him.

He thought his brain just hated him enough to conjure extra-horrifying images for his nightmares. But no, it was part of the memory. This was the moose-creature he had seen in his dreams. He'd faced it on the night Glory drowned.

This time would be different. This time he was prepared. He wouldn't relive it again—no one would. Aidan struck a match, but the wind picked up, and flame was snuffed out. *Damn it*. He grabbed another one, keeping his gaze on the beast in the water.

He tried another match. Hudson shifted, so his body would block the wind. Okay, so he wasn't useless after all. But still, the match wouldn't light. And now there was screaming on the shore.

"Do you understand what you've done!" shrieked Bill Clavey. The creature was moving fast, and he couldn't see Iris or Gum anymore.

Shit. The water here wasn't much higher than mid-thigh usually. This was bad. This was really fucking bad. Iris was practically unconscious and Gum didn't even know how to swim.

The Spirit roared, and violent waves rolled away from it in every direction. Aidan backed up, but he wasn't quick enough. He grabbed two of the M-80s before the rest were engulfed in brownish red water. The waves stained the rocks in front of him, leaving behind deep red clumps.

Was that . . . blood?

Aidan felt like he was going to be sick, but he pushed it down.

"I'm going in," Hudson said.

"But—"

Hudson didn't hesitate. He jumped into the bloody water. The Spirit let out another earsplitting bellow that rattled Aidan's bones.

Two fireworks left. Two chances. And Aidan's aim was garbage. How was he supposed to throw anything at the beast now, when it was moving away, and the waves were five feet high? Another one came crashing onto shore. Aidan's boots were drenched. All he could see in the water was the Spirit's rotting antlers.

Aidan checked for the gasoline can. Gone. Taken by the waves. They were screwed. The sinking feeling in his chest told him they'd lost already. This thing had been eating souls for hundreds of years. Even if he could throw the firework in the right spot, even if he could get the timing perfect, the matches were busted.

But Iris believed they had a chance. And who was Aidan to get in the way of a Garren girl? He tried again. He wouldn't go down without a fight.

The match wouldn't light unless it wanted to. He knew objectively that he didn't have any say in the matter. But he pretended for a second that he could bend fate to his will. That was how Glory had operated. Her ice cream never melted. The mosquitoes left her alone.

Glory had the power to command, and Aidan needed to borrow it. He tried again, praying, manifesting, *demanding* the match to light.

And the universe, fate, *Glory* finally answered him.

CHAPTER 40

ris went under long enough for her nostrils to burn. Once she came to the surface, her body was hers again. Until this point she'd been frozen; her eyes wouldn't even let her look around, to check if Aidan and Hudson had made it here, and to count how many Claveys were standing by. To check if they were armed.

There was splashing. Voices overlapping. She saw the Spirit's lumpy back now. It must have gone after Gum when he'd pushed her aside. As much as Iris appreciated her friend refusing to sacrifice her to a demon, that wasn't part of the plan.

A wave hit Iris in the face. It tasted like rust.

The creature had chased Gum deeper into the water, and the monster was too far from shore for Aidan to douse the thing in gasoline. Did they even bring the gasoline?

No no no *no*. Another wave hit Iris in the face, and she almost went down again. There shouldn't be waves like this here, and they shouldn't taste bloody. The water swirled around her. She accidentally swallowed some more. Though she tried to spit it out, she couldn't get the taste off her lips.

"Do you understand what you've done!" Bill Clavey shouted. On the shoreline, two bodies waved frantically, one white-mustached and sturdy, the other leaner, blond, and balding. But none of them dared to go in.

The beast paid no attention to Iris now. It was twenty feet away, circling Gum, who struggled to keep his head above the water. When Iris searched the trees, she finally spotted the plaid sleeves of Aidan's flannel shirt.

She had to lead the thing in that direction.

"Hey!" Iris yelled at it.

It didn't flinch. It wasn't concerned with her. She was nothing—only a sacrifice. She didn't even have the dignity of being a self-sacrifice. She wasn't real unless a Clavey did the deed.

"Iris!" Hudson swam up to her, blood-tinted water splashing around him. He tried to yank her toward the shore.

"Wait," she said. "Pull me under."

"What?"

"Only for a second. *Do it.*"

His one good eye looked unsure, darting between her and the Spirit, which was five seconds away from pouncing on Gum again.

"*Hudson,*" Bill sneered. He wasn't yelling anymore. "You can make this right."

Iris actually agreed with him on that.

"It's the only way," she pleaded. She cupped her hand to his face. "Please."

Hudson grabbed her by the shoulders and gently tipped her under.

Iris was good at holding her breath. She felt like she had been holding it in for the past year. But the water slapped her, colder than it ever had been. She'd slip into shock eventually. But she had to stay. Stay, stay stay . . .

Hudson lifted her back up.

The Spirit was heading toward her now; Iris heard its ragged breath, it was salivating at the promise of another meal. She almost froze at the sight of its face and the blood-soaked claws it used to push the water out of its way.

Glory would be pissed to know the Disasters had lost the volleyball tournament again. She would be more pissed if this monster got to live and Iris didn't.

She'd say, *Iris, really. It's embarrassing.*

And she would be right, as usual.

Iris looked to Hudson. "Again," she commanded. She closed her eyes and held her breath as he dipped her under the surface for the second time.

She'd thought this place sacred, once. She'd thought the Disaster's traditions were magic. First Night Bonfire was an ancient ritual and friendship bracelets were blessed amulets. Really, they only had power because Iris gave them power. And this beast only had power if she decided it did. This creature—God or Devil or somewhere in between—was *pathetic*. It was already dying and trying to take others down with it. Unfortunately for the monster, Iris was the most powerful creature here. Powered by her grief. Her rage.

Iris gasped for breath again. The Spirit was five feet away.

"Now!" she shouted, hoping Aidan could hear her. Hoping Gum had found the shore. Hoping the beast still believed it could have her. It was Hudson's hands that pulled her under, but it was Iris's choice. *She* would outsmart this thing, these people. Bad Creek wasn't a place for saving. It was a place for breaking. Iris wouldn't fragment. She'd be the sledgehammer.

Hudson had pushed her deep enough that her head brushed against the bottom. Soft, slimy seaweed cushioned her descent. She opened her eyes: Hudson had gone down with her. His blond hair obstructing her view, backlit by a red, white, and blue lights on the surface, bright as the sun. Her limbs were all twisted around with his, trying to hold on another second. Another minute.

They weren't alone. Dozens of eyes stared back at them. A girl with ribbons in her hair, flowing around her like a jellyfish. And another, with a Hollywood smile. And another, with strikingly blue eyes. *Beth*. She gave Iris a wave before making way for the last girl.

Even dead and underwater, Glory's makeup was perfect, curls swirling around with the grace of a mermaid's. Iris grabbed her, clutching her sister for dear life. But then Glory was rising, bringing Iris with her. Glory's mouth was moving; voicelessly saying, *It's okay, Iris. You can let go. You can breathe now.*

Iris let go.

When she finally came up for air, there was no splashing, there were no waves. The water was as red as a wound. Dead fish floated peacefully around them. Iris pushed one away and realized that wasn't a fish. It was a *talon*. And that one was an arm, that one was a nose. These were bits of the beast, exploded.

Fireworks continued from a faraway place on the other side of the lake, one where no one knew about monsters because they didn't want to know. There were no signs of Bill or Bruce Clavey.

Hudson hugged Iris. He didn't mention the girls below the surface. Maybe he'd never seen them. "Holy, shit," he breathed. "It's over."

It's over. It's over. The Spirit was destroyed. Iris was not. Glory was still very much dead.

But she would be the last one.

Aidan ran to the muddy beach, hoisting Gum out of the water. Gum was gasping like he'd swallowed too much. Maybe he had. The blood, though, was a bigger concern. He had a scratch on his forehead, but the worst of it was on his arm. Three long slices, starting below his shoulder. The Spirit's talons had gotten into him.

Iris trudged toward shore as fast as she could. She had cheated her fate. She was okay, somehow. Gum had to be okay too. The Disasters deserved a win.

Aidan took off his flannel and tried to wrap it around Gum's arm, but his hands were shaking. "It's fine, you're fine. I know how to tie a decent tourniquet," he said. Gum laughed like it was a joke. Iris hoped the gashes didn't really need a tourniquet.

Hudson glanced back at the water, like he was waiting for the beast to pull itself back together, then said, "We should call 911." He pulled his phone out of his pocket and swore. "Shit." He tried to swipe the screen, but it wouldn't light up. Aidan offered his phone to him. Iris was a little selfishly pleased to see them cooperate.

She helped Aidan pull Gum off the flooded beach and walk him out of the cropping of trees. "Iris," Gum called. He looked like he was going to say sorry.

"It's okay," she told him. She ought to say sorry too, for last night. Cutting off the bracelet was a little melodramatic, even for her. They all owed each other apologies at this point. Better to call it even, instead of keeping score.

Meanwhile, Hudson hung back, talking to the operator. He didn't mention the thing that had actually inflicted the cuts. "Yes, Bill and Bruce Clavey," he said into the phone.

"I thought you were a rabbit," Gum told Iris, laughing dryly. He was delirious. She hoped it was because of the absurdity of the situation and not blood loss. He was bleeding through the flannel already, and Iris didn't know if it was a dangerous amount.

He pointed his good arm forward. "She was a rabbit too."

There was a girl on the Landings' dock. She looked like she was thinking about jumping. Iris was about to warn her not to, but there was something funny about her. She didn't *match*. The shadows hit her differently, like she was affected by an unseen light source. Then Iris realized that it was one of the faces she'd seen underwater.

She stepped off the dock, disappearing the moment before she hit the surface.

Right behind her was another girl. Then another. And another. All taking their turns. Some diving, some cannonballing. Then she recognized one: older, unmistakably lovely.

The young woman from the house in the woods. Rex's late sister. *Helena.*

She gave them all a big smile, then cannonballed in.

And then there was Glory. Actual Glory, not a trick from the beast. It wasn't a hunch. It wasn't blind hope. It was really her, watching Iris with a close-lipped grin. It was the look Glory would give her when she thought her little sister wasn't that bad, after all. A silent approval she was too cool to speak out loud.

Iris had fought the universe until it had let her make new rules. Ones where she got to say goodbye.

Glory dived off the dock like she always did. Gracefully. Unafraid. Swimming to the next place, wherever that was.

It took thirty-one staples to fix him.

Gum hadn't count them all; the nurse had just declared the number, and he had chosen to believe it. Fact-checking sounded like too much work anyway, especially under the haze of painkillers. He couldn't wait for them to wear off. For his brain to be his again. It had been far too long.

When the cops came into the hospital room, Gum told the story the Disasters all quickly agreed on, before the red-white-and-blue fireworks were replaced with red-and-white ambulance lights. It was all the truth, but in this version, the deity the Claveys worshipped wasn't actually real.

Therefore, its claws hadn't injured Gum.

"What kind of knife?" the cop asked.

"A big one?" he answered.

"A kitchen knife? A bowie knife?"

"I don't remember."

That last line got him through most of the interrogation. *I don't remember.* It was hard to argue with a kid in a hospital bed. The cops thanked him, wished him a speedy recovery, and were on their way, leaving through the flimsy curtain.

When his dad finally came in, he didn't look all too concerned. The doctors probably had already told him his son would be fine. Surgery went well. Future mobility of his arm shouldn't be affected. He needed rest, and he could go home with the extra-strong meds if the right waivers were signed. The staples were to be removed at a later date.

Gum knew he looked like hell. There were wires everywhere. His forehead and entire right arm were covered in bandages. Surely there were dark circles under his eyes, and he had to smell like death. He didn't know how many hours had passed since he had arrived in the hospital. It felt like it should be daylight outside, though he didn't have the luxury of a window.

His dad sat on the chair beside the bed, leg bouncing. "Feelin' all right?"

"Yeah, they let me do drugs." Though they weren't quite doing the job like they were a few minutes ago. All of him ached, especially his head, where he only had two measly little sutures.

Still, his father laughed at the floor. His leg was still bouncing. It was the same thing Gum did when he was nervous. "Sorry I wasn't in sooner. I have . . . news."

That was what Gum had been afraid of. What if the Spirit had pulled itself together and snuck into their cabins, slicing all the Claveys' throats?

"Good news or bad news?" he asked.

"I'm just gonna say it. Rip off the Band-Aid."

"I don't think the doctor would want you to do that."

His dad cracked a smile but didn't laugh. "They've arrested your grandfather and uncle Bruce."

Gum was relieved, though that wasn't a guaranteed victory. The Claveys could afford any kind of bail. They could flee the country and never face trial. And there were others wrapped up in it: his six-year-old cousin wouldn't understand why her dad was in jail tonight. And then there were the aunts and Brian, who had known but hadn't stopped it. Gum wasn't sure if he owed them anger or sympathy. He almost hadn't stopped it either. He'd almost let it corrupt him too.

Gum was starting to wonder if Hudson was even the one who killed Glory in the first place. When he thought about it, it made less and less sense. And he was starting to see more meaning in all the weird things Hudson had said this summer.

"Did you know?" Gum managed to ask his dad. "I mean, what they've been doing?"

"I knew they were rotten, but not this kind of rotten."

"They never let you be part of the family because they knew you wouldn't go along with it," Gum said as the epiphany came to him. He was afraid that if he didn't put it into words, it would slip away. "Because you're better than them."

"Maybe." His father could never take a compliment. He shifted in the chair. "There's more. It's ... big. This one's the good news."

Gum could use some good news. There were so many loose ends, still. This Spirit might be destroyed, but there could be others, or more pieces of it, living in different little towns, controlling different families. Then there was this giant hospital bill. Clearly Grandpa wouldn't be helping them out with money anymore.

Worst of all, he worried his friends would never speak to him again.

His dad looked like he had been crying and any minute now the tears would flow again, which didn't feel like good news, until he said:

"Mom's awake."

Gum had thought the girls at the end of the dock were a false memory. When he had eventually passed out, he had the strange, wobbly remnants of dreams. Rabbits and antlers and black water. His hands, wildly fighting toward the surface. At one point his arm was gone, replaced with the Spirit's bloated, gray limb, ending with sharp talons.

He'd chalked up the strangest of his memories as part of those dreams. But now he knew one part that was real. There were girls jumping off the dock, and there was a reason his mom hadn't been with the rest of them. The Spirit held no claim on her soul any longer. The difference between her and the other victims was that she had a living body to return to.

He let his dad believe it was a miracle, though.

"We were at the beach, watching the fireworks, and she taps me on the shoulder like it's nothing," his dad explained as they walked down the hospital's long hallway, dodging nurses with carts and people looking for rooms. "Then we got the call about you and ... Well, she's here now. They've been doing tests. It won't be a full recovery. Even with physical therapy, there'll be lasting paralysis, but—"

"Is she talking?"

"She hasn't stopped asking for you."

Gum wished this weren't happening so fast. The fluorescent lights were aggravating his headache. He needed time to take a nap, to rinse off the bloody water in his memory. Of course, his father was eager to see his wife again, but Gum didn't know exactly who he'd be meeting. He didn't know his mom, even if all his life he had ached to travel to a universe where he did.

He wasn't sure if she retained memories from the past sixteen years, otherwise, she'd remember her son as a one-year-old. Infants didn't have to meet very high standards. They could cry and shit their pants and vomit all over you. As long as they were cute, they were forgiven. Teenage Gum didn't exactly check every box. His mother was probably expecting a Hudson type. Great report cards and medals and potential girlfriends and potential college acceptances waiting for him. He didn't want to disappoint her.

Then they turned the corner, and there she was. Though Gum had seen her face nearly every day of his life, she looked different now that she was emoting. Her eyebrows furrowed as she talked to Uncle Brian. She looked annoyed. A new expression for her.

She noticed him then, and her face melted into warmth. Gum wasn't sure if he deserved it, after all those times he'd walked right past her. He stopped two feet from her wheelchair. He still hadn't thought of what to say. He didn't need to. She put her arms out, pulling him into a hug. She was awake. She was hugging him, and it didn't feel real.

"Brian said they tried to get you too," she whispered, her words a little slurred. It wasn't like she sounded different than what he'd expected, because he hadn't expected anything. He hadn't let himself imagine her voice. He had never imagined this moment at all. Hope wasn't a luxury he could afford. "He said you killed it."

It was more of a group effort. If Iris and Hudson hadn't distracted it, if Aidan hadn't exploded the thing, Gum would have been torn to pieces. That was a lot to explain, and his throat was all tight, so he just said, "Yeah."

"That's my boy."

She pulled back to look at him, her smile only faltering when she noticed the stitches on his forehead. She brushed some hair out of his face, and he stopped trying to fight the tears.

He had survived the worst day of his life, and now he got the best, single moment. He was tired, and starving, and had total mental whiplash. But he let himself accept it. The Spirit had detached from his spine; he wouldn't have to do anything he didn't want to.

And now he had his mom. She was a Clavey, but maybe she was a Clavey the same way he was. Maybe, like Gum, she kept her eyes open during prayer, waiting to see if anyone else had their eyes open too.

There was a big difference between having a formerly famous parent and a currently famous one.

On the sixth of July, strange vehicles loitered the driveway. Locals wanted to know if it all was true; reporters wanted exclusive interviews. They asked Paul if he had any prior suspicions about his next-door neighbors: the Killer Claveys.

Bad Creek, Michigan, a village of 500, is the home of the World's Largest Crucifix, and reclusive horror director Paul Ross.

That was how the first article began.

Aidan laughed out loud when he read it. First of all, it was the Second Largest Crucifix. And *reclusive* was a new word. Paul called himself retired. Aidan's mom called him washed-up.

"Reclusive?" Paul also commented, chewing on his egg roll. "Does that sound good-mysterious or bad-mysterious?" He had used the cars crowded in their driveway as an excuse to pay an exorbitant fee for delivered Chinese food.

"I think it fits your brand," Aidan said. Paul was under no suspicion, but his name had been dropped in a few articles. Maybe in a few months he'd be in a documentary. They'd name it something gimmicky like, *Bad Creek: A Real-Life Horror Movie.*

"You know I'm proud of you, right?" Paul asked suddenly. There was a beat of silence; neither of them knew what to do with the confession.

"Thanks," Aidan said. "I'm . . . proud of you too?"

Paul's research had surprised him, just when he thought he knew his dad. Maybe it had taken Paul too long to change, but some people never did.

Aidan kept reading. There were lies in the article, and most of them he had helped to tell. A few pissed him off. Social media was sure that this was proof of the Illuminati, of an organized secret army of baby-killing Devil worshippers. They conveniently ignored the evil in plain sight.

"They weren't even sacrificing souls to Satan," Aidan pointed out. "It's the opposite. The Claveys acted like it was God's will. It's not fair to blame this on the Devil."

"Trends are cyclical. 'Bout time we have another Satanic panic."

Aidan told himself he was checking for any news on the arrests, but it'd be months before any trial. There was already plenty of physical evidence revealed to the public. The same symbol from the carvings was found in a few places around the Clavey estate. There were Bill's journals. And then there were more than enough witnesses. The Claveys had been united when all was going well, but once arrests were made, they had turned on each other.

For once, Brian Clavey had plenty to say, as he was likely getting some kind of legal immunity. He confirmed that his brother killed Glory. Though, he added, he had believed the Spirit would bring back Beth, to reward his loyalty.

The other victims didn't receive nearly as much attention, unfortunately. Even though Glory's name appeared in every article, she was more a fact of the case than a whole person.

The world wouldn't know about her near-perfect putt-putt scores, or the way she scrunched up her face when drawing. Aidan was probably the only person who knew she couldn't actually tie a cherry with her tongue. Maybe she would have told him more secrets, had she lived. Revealed all her embarrassing flaws. Explained the magic tricks. Maybe she would have told them to someone else. She probably never intended for Aidan to be her only love. They weren't supposed to be forever. Yet Aidan couldn't forget her, even if that meant remembering Bad Creek.

Aidan closed out of the article to finish his lo mein. He had a text from his mom, asking how much longer he planned on staying in Michigan.

He typed out, *Until my friends leave.*

She sent him a thumbs-up emoji.

He hadn't seen them the last day and a half. Iris had a lot of explaining to do for her moms, who also needed time to process and grieve all over again. And Gum was in the hospital that first night. He'd sent a few vague texts about how his mom was doing, while Iris sent updates every time she talked to the cops.

He had almost lost them both to that horrible family. He had been right about Bad Creek being stuck in a time loop but wrong about his role in it. He wasn't at the mercy of whoever shuffled the cards. At any point, he could have said no. No to games of Monopoly or campfires that lasted too long. He could have asked Iris to make him a different-colored friendship bracelet. But now that it looked like it might be over, he wanted it back. Well, parts of it.

Aidan scratched at the back of his leg. Yesterday he had convinced himself it was a bug bite, but today there were bright pink welts snaking up his calf. Poison ivy, of course. He couldn't leave this place unscathed.

What if we had a bonfire tonight? Aidan sent in the group chat. There was no response for a few minutes. Maybe he had the wrong idea. No one had the energy or the urge to hang out again. They really were over, and the Fourth was just an extra helping of trauma they'd have to heal from separately.

Then a text from Gum: *Blowing up a demon wasn't enough??? Ur turning into a pyro.*

And one from Iris: *ok!*

A wave of a relief hit Aidan. It wasn't over. It never was.

Sometimes things just happen. It's not always the universe giving signs.

Iris had to remind herself of that while she tried to hook her bicycle to the back of the van for the third time. It was like the bike demanded to remain here. *Stay, stay, stay*, it said. Like the Spirit had. Like the regulars at the Landings when they'd heard the news that the Garrens would definitely *not* be returning next summer. Or ever, probably.

Joanna held a quiche on her hip. To the untrained eye, she was having pleasant small talk with the Richardsons, but she kept glancing back at her wife and daughter like she was thinking about homicide.

"This thing looks like it's fifty years old," April grumbled. She was trying to see if she could retrieve instructions for the bike rack on her phone but wasn't finding anything useful. Rex had let them take the bike, along with the rack. But instructions weren't included.

Tomorrow morning, when they returned the cabin key to Rex, Iris would ask him to help secure the bike, and she would give him back Helena's stolen possessions.

"I have to ask," April said to Iris, "why not the green one?"

Because the green one had a flat. Because Iris had always liked the red bike better anyway. Because even if she was leaving Bad Creek, she still wanted a part of Glory with her.

"This one has streamers," Iris said.

"Understandable."

After Joanna escaped with another Tupperware of Mrs. Richardson's baking experiments, they funneled into Cabin 4. They were leaving in the morning. "First thing in the morning," according to April. But they still had tonight.

"Did you put on lotion?" Joanna asked.

Iris had been absentmindedly scratching her leg. At some point, between giving statements to the police, a rash had developed. "Uhhh . . ."

Joanna sighed and dug through the pile on the living room table until she found the lotion—which did little to help Iris's poison ivy—but the gesture was appreciated. While Iris loaded the milky stuff over her splotchy leg, April sat on a suitcase, struggling with the zipper. Joanna sat on the couch, rubbing her knees anxiously. That was what she did when she needed to have "a talk."

She waited for Iris to finish applying the lotion and patted the plaid cushion beside her. "I should have told you before. I should have told everyone. And maybe then . . ."

"It's not your fault," April said.

Joanna nodded, still clearly battling herself. She squeezed Iris's hand.

"I told you the Clavey twins found that house," she continued. "That was a lie. *I* found it, but it hadn't felt like me because I was asleep. The summer before my senior year, I woke up standing in the middle of this meadow, and Bruce was watching me. I didn't know what that meant, in that moment. Now I guess I do."

It was supposed to be Joanna. She was the first girl who got away.

"Of course, Paul wanted to see the house for himself," Joanna continued. "He loved creepy stuff. I did, usually. But I hated that place. I couldn't get the way Bruce looked at me out of my head. Like I was prey."

"Did he try to—"

"No. Never. Bruce avoided me after that. Avoided this place altogether. For years Beth presented all these weird excuses for him. He just didn't come back with the rest of us. For years. And then one summer—God, it was so cold. You had a horrible colic and stayed in the cabin the whole week. Beth had been acting . . . off. We were having a bonfire, like normal, when she flipped out. Said the reckoning was coming. That she was going to have to pay for Bruce's sin. The next morning, Bruce pulled Beth out of the water."

Joanna stopped to take a breath.

"When she had her accident, I wasn't surprised. Just like when I woke up with Bruce behind me. It all felt so inevitable. But I never said anything. And I kept coming back. After the accident, Paul started to get suspicious. He noticed all these weird symbols. He tried to get me to look into it, to question the Claveys, but . . ." She shut her eyes and squeezed Iris's hand again. "I couldn't let myself see it. Even though, in my gut, I knew it was always going to come for me. Even after last year. I couldn't imagine just leaving it all behind. I felt *tethered* to this place."

"It pulled me to the water," Iris said. "It's probably always been pulling us back here. With all the other regulars."

The Spirit had to keep them as its consistent food supply.

"I'm so sorry," Joanna choked.

"It's okay," Iris said.

April gave Joanna kiss on the forehead. "You don't need to be forgiven."

"Still," Joanna said. "I want to be better. More present. I've been so terrified of what I'd see if I really looked back. But I haven't been looking forward either."

"Me too," Iris admitted. She didn't need Joanna to apologize, but it felt good to hear her speak her grief out loud. The Garrens didn't have to be three islands, each surviving alone, anymore.

Joanna gave a pat to Iris's knee and stood. "Do we have any firewood left?"

"I'll get some," Iris said. Usually, when they ran out, the Disasters would borrow wood from another cabin. Or steal from the Claveys. She stopped by her room and looked under the floorboard. Glory's things were already packed up. All that remained was Hudson Clavey's wallet. Iris put it in her pocket and headed toward Cabin 1, where the Great White was parked out front. The door opened, and Hudson stepped out carrying a suitcase.

He smiled when he noticed her. The bruise under his eye was worse, but still, Iris's heart did a little flutter.

"Hey," she said. "You guys are leaving?"

"Yeah."

The cabin door opened and a little girl came barreling out, dragging a baby-blue roller bag. Hudson's mom was behind her, looking at Iris with suspicion. Years ago, she'd threatened to call the cops on Iris and Glory for playing music too loud on the dock. And now Iris got her husband arrested.

"Want to go on a walk with me?" Hudson asked, despite his mother's glare.

"Sure."

They made it to the end of the gravel drive, past the Landings sign. Iris didn't know what to say, or what would happen between them now that she was leaving and never coming back. She was grateful that Hudson spoke first.

"I don't think my sister knows what's going on," he said. "She's mad she has to go to public school next month."

Iris gasped. "You guys are gonna be mingling with the poors? I'm so sorry."

"It's great, actually. I'd prefer to go to a school where no one knows me."

"You'll regret that when you try the food. It's all stale brownies and cold broccoli. Not filet mignon and crème brûlée."

"Oh shit, really? If I don't get my daily crème brûlée, I'll spontaneously combust."

They turned onto Meller Road. Iris smelled grilling

burgers. Turns out, news of the Killer Claveys wasn't going to stop anyone from barbecuing. Then she spotted the Mustang, in all her Pepto-Bismol-pink elegance, and they sat on its hood. The sun was setting now, but the metal was still warm from baking all day.

"I have a confession to make," Iris said. "I may have accidentally stolen your old wallet." She pulled it out of her back pocket and presented it to him.

He took one look at it and said, "Keep it."

"There's like fifty bucks in there. I owe you for saving my life."

"You saved your own life, Iris. I would never have tried to kill it. I didn't think there was a way out."

He scooted closer to her; her thigh was touching his shorts. They were the kind of preppy pastel shorts she usually would have made fun of. Hudson might have denounced the Claveys, but he was still dressed like he had to go golfing at a moment's notice.

"I hate your shorts," she told him, trying to distract from the sudden intimacy.

"That's fair." She waited for him to roast her outfit, call her out for her socks not matching. Instead, he took her wrist and lifted it up. He gently brushed his fingers against her braided red bracelet. She had needed something to do with her hands during the unending blur of yesterday, and she still had a lot of red string left over.

"Will you make me one of these?" he asked her.

"I thought about it," she said. The bracelets had always been exclusive to the Disasters. But who cared? The rules could be rewritten. "Do you want one?"

"Would that make us officially friends?" he asked. He still had his hand on hers.

"Is that what we are?" she asked him breathlessly.

He looked at her and didn't turn. He leaned in closer, and Iris's dragonfly heart was traded for a rabbit's. Fast, strong, but too small to support her body. Her heart was going to explode. Her blood would seep from out of her pores, from out of her fingernails and ears and eyes, and then he would finally see her as this pathetic, bleeding thing who wanted too hard. Who cried too loud.

"Iris?"

"Yeah?"

"Can I kiss you?"

Iris put her lips against Hudson's, then remembered she was supposed to close her eyes and tilt her head. He put his hands on the back of her neck, pulling her in closer.

When they came up for air, he smiled at her as if to say, *Finally.* Her brain felt gooey, like a marshmallow that melts off the stick before it can turn into a s'more. She melted into him like one too. The next kiss was more desperate, like both of them thought the other would die if they stopped.

They broke away as a golf cart zoomed past, startling them. Iris grinned at him. They probably weren't seen, but she didn't care either way. Let them all start rumors about the Garren girl and the Clavey boy breaking all the rules.

"We're gonna have a campfire. You should come," Iris said.

"Can't. We're leaving."

"Now?"

He nodded. "Yeah, my mom's probably looking for me. Will I see you again?"

"Yeah. Just not here."

Iris pulled out her phone and had him type in his number, texting him so he had hers. Then they walked back to the gravel road, hands clasped. The big white Escalade's engine was running, Hudson's mom impatiently waiting behind the wheel. Hudson squeezed Iris's hand before he let go of her and got in the passenger seat.

"Send me your address," Iris told him with a wink. "I'll mail you a bracelet."

Even though it had rained for most of yesterday, this was their biggest bonfire yet. Flames licked the edges of the firepit rocks. April was too scared to get close enough and roast her marshmallow, so Iris volunteered. Usually she helped prep the graham crackers and chocolate, but Aidan had taken over for her. Iris was now the marshmallow cooker. Gum poked at the flames and threw in more firewood. Every few minutes there would be a sudden pop, and embers flew into the air. Someone would utter, "Whooaaa," and tell Gum to stop messing with the fire, but he never listened, and Iris loved him for it.

After lightly toasting a marshmallow for April, Iris worked on Beth's.

"How do you like it?" she asked.

"Well done."

"She likes it charred," said Paul. "Or claims to. I think it's an individuality complex."

"You don't even like marshmallows," Beth said. "You're not allowed to criticize."

"Do you know what they're made of?" Paul teased. "I'd be happy to remind you."

Joanna smacked Paul on the shoulder. "God, Paul. Let people enjoy things."

Iris waited until the marshmallow looked crispy enough before pulling it out of the flame. She already knew marshmallows were cornstarch and ground-up bones. That was what this place was too—sugar and death. But the Disasters were together. Mostly. There were absences that hung in the air, but no more secrets, at last.

Their parents didn't stay outside long. The mosquitoes were too bad, and the Garrens had a long drive tomorrow morning. Besides, they knew the tent between Cabins 3 and 4 was reserved for the ones with raging poison ivy rashes. Iris and the boys had aired out the cobweb-covered sleeping bags in the boathouse.

"So, what's the verdict?" Gum asked.

"My moms were thinking Myrtle Beach next summer," Iris answered. It was inexpensive and drivable. Most importantly, it was new.

"I'm down. Not sure about the beach part, but I like turtles."

"It's *Myrtle*," Aidan corrected.

Gum pointed to the bandage on his forehead. "Sorry, I'm literally concussed? Mind being more sensitive?"

Aidan pointed his marshmallow stick at Gum. "Shut up."

"I'm feeling a bit threatened by that weapon in your hand, actually."

"Good."

"Iris, I'm starting to think they locked up the wrong guys."

"You're not nearly as funny as you think you are," Aidan said, but he was smiling. It had been his idea to have a make-up bonfire tonight. To have another go at their Poison Ivy Quarantine. Aidan, who'd wanted nothing to do with them a week ago, was now proudly wearing the new bracelet she'd woven him.

"I gotta admit, I've always hated yellow," Aidan had said when she'd tied one of the red ones around his wrist.

They squeezed into the tent—which had felt much bigger when they were younger—and played the same game of war for hours. There were jokes, and fears admitted, and accusations about who had farted and, *Oh my God what was that noise did you guys hear that?* Once they were thoroughly delirious, they zipped themselves up inside their sleeping bags and Iris hugged Picasso tight. Savi had dropped off the stuffed rabbit this morning before saying goodbye.

When all was quiet but the hum of cicadas, Gum said, "I can't believe this is our last Poison Ivy Quarantine."

"Yeah," Aidan agreed. "It's weird."

"Rex is letting us take a bike. I probably could take the tent too," Iris suggested. "I'll bring it wherever we go next summer."

"Promise?"

"I promise." And Iris meant it, though her heart ached. She was on the verge of an ending. She couldn't stand endings. That was why she skipped the last episodes of her favorite sitcoms and started them over instead. Finality meant an imperfect cutoff, a frayed edge, ruining the comforting loop.

But there would always be something wrong. She would always have poison ivy or leeches or a raw mosquito bite she wanted to scratch. She would always be scared and messy and missing Glory. But she'd be okay.

Without this place, they wouldn't be the Disasters anymore. Maybe they could be something else. Something more. Not beholden to the rules of their parents, or the curse they'd inherited.

After all, curses could be broken.

ACKNOWLEDGMENTS

Whenever I get my hands on a new book, I read the acknowledgments first. Those last few pages are proof that books don't just spawn fully formed. They're the Oscars speeches of publishing.

Now it's finally my turn.

Thank you to my agent, the brilliant Miriam Cortinovis, for seeing how far this book could go (and letting me keep the Fall Out Boy reference).

Thank you to my editor, Kristin Allard, who made my Disasters as messy and angry as they ought to be. And thanks to the rest of the team at Norton: Hana Anouk Nakamura, Rebecca Munro, Delaney Adams, Lara Starr, Naomi Duttweiler, and my copy editor, Dave Cole.

Thank you to Colin Verdi for illustrating this book's killer cover.

Thanks to my WTMP mentors, Jenni Howell and Jamie Howard. Team JHow for life!

And to R. L. Stine, for ensuring I grew up a freak; Radical Face, for sad ghost music to write to; and my camp girls, who taught me how to make friendship bracelets. I can never give enough thanks to the librarians. Y'all are the backbone of this country.

Thank you to Gabe Never and Isabel Burke for surviving that hideous draft from 2016. Max Nalow, owner of the biggest brain in Cleveland, for reading every version. Jimmie Carroll for Bad Movie Club and good advice and the most disturbing fan art. To Aunt Jen, for being the best Seattle tour guide and introducing me to oh so many magical stories at an early age. To Grandma Cathy and Grandpa Jim, for my first red Schwinn. My dear cousins, for enduring Vacation Bible School and firework burns on the barn roof. Em, please take this as an apology for slapping you in Barnes & Noble when we were middle school.

Thank you to Aunt Nikki, the family historian, for late-night cabin chats. To my mother, Sara June, for supporting my haunted doll collection and letting me steal your vacation lore. To Brooks Hinton, roomie, bestie, you may be a beta reader but you're an alpha in my heart. Here's to endless Brother Summers. Thank you to Olivia Pelletier, aka Kundo, for childhood afternoons skinning our knees in bicycle crashes. Can't believe how much we've changed. Can't believe how much we haven't.

To Austin, my beloved, for pulling the overheating laptop out of my wretched hands at two a.m. and reminding me I can always write more tomorrow. Without you, this book would have rotted me from the inside out.

My sister, Liv Leatherman, for believing before you even read the damn thing. I know you'd solve my murder in like three days, tops.

And thank you to Grandma Suey, queen of the Landings, all-time putt-putt champion. You always promised there's a great big world outside of my hometown. I found it. I found it.

So far, Scarberry, Nebraska, had more cows than people. Lenny stopped counting the cattle after three hundred something.

"Two more minutes," Evan said.

How was civilization two minutes away? Was their Airbnb actually hidden in some underground bunker? The last thirty miles had just been withered cornfields, cows, and her trusty Oldsmobile, the *Silver Bullet*. Lenny couldn't remember the last time they'd passed another car or a man-made structure other than a crumbling barn or lonely silo. The too-blue sky felt dangerous. She could already tell Scarberry would be the scariest stop on their trip, and that abandoned prison in Ohio had given her nightmares for weeks.

After two minutes exactly, Evan directed her to turn left, onto a dirt road. As dust collected on the already-filthy windshield, he closed the passenger window, faking a cough. "Ugh. Car probably looks trashed."

"Isn't that a good thing?" Lenny offered. "Won't that make the establishing shot more *authentic?*"

Evan rolled his eyes.

Authenticity. That was their branding. That was what made *Odd Kids* better than their rivals, *Dark Unknown. Odd Kids* was real. Raw. *Authentic.* Evan had used those words to pitch their summer-long road trip to their parents. He'd said that they had to go alone, the two of them. No parents. No extra crew carrying bulky film equipment. Just Evan and Lenny and the *Silver Bullet* on the open road. If they could survive it, Lenny's parents would let them do YouTube full-time. No more surprise college visits. No more pamphlets shoved under her bedroom door.

Authenticity was also the same word that got sponsors interested. Yes, they hadn't caught Bigfoot on tape yet, but wasn't it fun watching these relatable teenagers fall in love while squatch-hunting?

Authenticity.

Sure.

Evan pointed his camera out of the window. "This is it."

Yeah, Lenny could tell from the massive UFO in the front yard.

The saucer was about the size of the *Silver Bullet.* It sat on a tilt, like it was frozen at the moment it crash-landed. Nothing about it looked authentic; the chipped coppery paint and the NO CLIMBING PLEASE sign didn't exactly give off Real Alien Spacecraft vibes.

Behind it was an unassuming farmhouse and an old-fashioned windmill. The farmhouse was white—well, it looked like it *used* to be white—but was now a dusty beige with a red roof that had seen better days. Lenny had expected it to be larger, or at least have a fresher paint job. Maybe the owners of Reed Ranch kept the place dilapidated as part of their brand? But what if Evan was right? What if Scarberry was just a tourist trap after all?

No. Lenny tried to shed the thought. This was the place. It had to be.

She parked the *Silver Bullet* on the side of the road (that was the one good thing about small rural towns: you could park anywhere for free). When she stepped onto the dead grass, she resisted the urge to cover her nose. The smell of manure was bad enough while on the road, but now it was overwhelming.

"A whole three days of smelling cow shit," Evan said. "Awesome."

"It's not that bad," Lenny lied.

They were an hour early, just enough time to get the opening monologue in. They popped open the trunk, covered in worn-out stickers from small towns with big legends: Loveland, Point Pleasant, Dover. There were cutesy illustrations of skunk apes, lake monsters, wolf-people, goat-people, and a faded I WANT TO BELIEVE on the bumper.

Evan practiced his lines under his breath while Lenny adjusted the tripod and placed duct tape on their mark, right in front of the saucer.

"Tuck your hair back," Evan said, instead of brushing the loose strands behind her ear like he used to. It had been forever since he'd tickled her waist while pinning her mic to her shirt. She'd giggle and slap his hand away. Pretend she didn't enjoy his teasing.

Now they were professionals.

Evan clicked Record before coming to stand next to Lenny. She watched herself in the viewfinder and pushed her bangs into place. She looked so tiny next to Evan. It's not that he was freaky tall; he just had inhumanely perfect posture. Lenny was easily eclipsed by his height, by his self-assuredness, by her own slime-green *Odd Kids* T-shirt.

She was a speck of a girl. Blink and you'd miss her.

She took a deep breath and recited the monologue she'd written in their motel room last night. "Strange lights floating above a barn, cattle mutilation, eerie shrieks at night, and sightings of a pale creature lurking in corn fields. In the summer of 1961, this small town had more than a few strange occurrences . . ."

Evan jumped in, "Though Scarberry, Nebraska, isn't far from Highway 80, you won't find it on a map. With a population of only thirteen hundred, most of its inhabitants are farmers. But one of those residents might also be an extraterrestrial."

He delivered the lines Lenny had written perfectly, but she could practically hear him fighting the urge to roll his eyes on that last word—*extraterrestrial.*

They hadn't done an alien episode in over a year, thanks to Evan. According to analytics, aliens weren't trendy. Their channel got better engagement with cryptids and poltergeists. In fact, the next stop on their road trip was supposed to be Harrows House in Arizona, where, allegedly, a demon with a baby face and hooves had been haunting a family for generations. That was where they had originally planned to be today.

But they had also planned to be together forever.

"For the next seventy-two hours, we'll be staying at Reed Ranch, where it all began. The creature known as Old Lucky hasn't been spotted since that fateful summer, but recently a subscriber sent us proof he's returned." Lenny paused so they could later superimpose the low-res clip on the screen, before asking, "Was this little town the location of an alien invasion sixty-five years ago?"

"Or was it all a hoax?" Evan finished. He looked at her and smiled, his eyes crinkling behind his glasses. "Ready to check it out?"

After she nodded, he gave her a kiss—a tradition from their very first video. But that onscreen kiss had actually meant something. Now documenting their "love" for 400,000 subscribers was just a formality.

Lenny secretly hoped a fan would see through the façade. Someone would zoom in on her lying face and analyze the way his lips barely grazed hers. They'd freeze on a single frame of evidence, just like their show often did when dust on the lens looked *almost* like a ghost.

"Let's run it again," Evan said. On every stop on their trip, they had nailed the monologue on the first take, but he wanted backup footage, "just in case." He had taken more B-roll in the past two weeks than he'd had in the two years they'd been doing *Odd Kids*. Either he was getting more paranoid, or Lenny was just noticing it for the first time. Since when was she determined to see the worst in him?

"You kids with the TV show?" a voice called.

A man with an impressive white handlebar mustache stood next to the saucer, wearing a sweat-soaked gray shirt and blue jeans tucked into his boots. It was eighty-five degrees outside; he had to be boiling. Lenny's bangs were soaked with sweat, and all she had were bicycle shorts, her tie-dye shirt, and sneakers.

"Yeah," Lenny answered. *Odd Kids* wasn't technically a TV show, but it was easier to let old people think that. Explaining YouTube to someone who couldn't work a flip phone would prove exhausting for both parties.

"Any, uh, parents with you?" the man asked.

"We're both legal adults," Evan said. Barely. Evan had turned eighteen in the fall, Lenny the week of graduation. That was a month ago. A diploma, adulthood, and a career handed to her all at once.

The cowboy nodded before spitting black goo into the grass. Tobacco. Evan recoiled, letting out a little scoff. He was terrified of anything getting on his brand-new sneakers. His other pair got ruined at their last stop. It had been a classic possession case, except the victim just happened to be a cat. The owners were a bigger headache than their supposedly cursed pet. No one had bothered to mention they were remodeling their haunted house's attic, and Evan had knocked over a can of fresh paint. At least the paint had been a rusty color, so, in the video, they could pretend they'd discovered a bucket of real human blood.

"I'm Jared, by the way. Ranch hand for Miss Reed. I'm s'posed to take ya to your room."

The way he'd called his employer "Miss" made him sound like a time traveler from the Old West. He matched the defunct atmosphere of the rest of the place too. If it wasn't for the bulky satellite on the house, Lenny could have sworn she had accidentally teleported to a pre-television era. The subscribers were going to eat this up.

"Awesome, thank you!" Lenny said.

Evan scowled. If he had it his way, they would run the monologue again. Or better—they'd be in Arizona, investigating demonic infant cries.

"I'll show ya where to park," said Jared.

After they shoved the equipment back in the trunk and hopped in the *Silver Bullet*, Lenny slowly followed the cowboy down the dirt driveway.

"Now would have been a good time to use the body cam," Evan muttered. The "body cam" was just a GoPro on a harness, but Evan liked saying the name out loud. Lenny had accidentally dropped it over a haunted bridge a few weeks ago, and he hadn't shut up about it. She'd taken the blame for that. And she'd take the blame for Scarberry too. The manure smell. The weird old guy. If this leg of the trip went south, it would be her fault.

It won't, Lenny told herself. *This is where you're meant to be.* She knew it deep in her bones.

She tried to change the subject. "Jared seems nice."

Evan rolled his eyes. "Yeah, if you like serial killers."

"If we get murdered, we'd go *viral*," Lenny muttered under her breath.

Evan gave her an accusatory look as the cowboy pointed out a patch of dirt, where three cars were parked. Lenny rolled down the window, catching Jared midsentence.

"—and right over here is the parking lot. There's a nice spot under a tree for ya."

"Thank you."

She backed into the spot, praying it wouldn't rain. The fluffy white clouds above them were growing denser, and the *Silver Bullet* didn't do well with mud.

She tried to shake the thought. *It won't rain. It won't rain.* She was only manifesting good things now. Foretelling the worst-case scenario was Evan's job, not hers. She couldn't let herself turn into him. But it was probably too late for that. It'd been *two years.* They were intertwined now.

"I can help with bags," Jared said, sloshing the chew in his mouth. Against Evan's silent protests, Lenny let him take some of their luggage. The three of them carried two roller suitcases each as they followed a dirt path through the yard.

Jared was definitely judging all their bags. He must have thought they were shallow city slickers or something. Some suitcases were for equipment: thermal cameras and REM PODs and EMF readers. The rest were stuffed with T-shirts sent to them by sponsors and fans alike. Lenny wore most of them as pajamas after filming, since she wasn't supposed to repeat outfits for videos.

The smell of manure was even more pungent closer to the source. Beyond a metal fence on their right, black dots marked grazing cows across a field that seemed to go on forever, like an infinity mirror. This place was over a hundred acres. When Lenny had typed that stat into her notes, it had felt like an imaginary number. She hadn't really realized just how much land it actually was.

"Gift shop," Jared said, tilting his head toward a white

one-story shed to their left. A faded mural of a green alien gave them a peace sign as they walked past.

"Are you kidding me?" Evan groaned. He lifted his white sneakers to reveal a glob of manure.

"Watch where yer steppin,'" Jared advised, too late. Lenny suppressed a giggle.

Now they were getting closer to a red barn. *The* red barn.

Lenny stopped in her tracks. This was it—this was the spot where the iconic photo from 1961 was taken. She'd had a poster of the Scarberry Lights above her bed since she was in middle school. She knew the slant of the barn roof, the crooked square window, but in person, it was a darker red than the grainy black-and-white poster implied.

This was the place she dreamed of every night.

Her heart was buzzing. The next time lights appeared above the peeling roof, she would see them. And she would record them. Proof at last. Screw Evan for not believing in this place, for not believing in *her*. It would all be worth it soon.

They reached a small line of trees, their first respite from the harsh sun. *Thank God.* She didn't want fans to point out any sweat stains when they eventually posted this week's video.

The trail ended with five train cars, all a different color. Each had one window and one door, a welcome mat, and an unlit string of UFO-shaped lights hanging off the flat roof.

Jared gestured to the blue one at the end. "You're in the caboose."

Of course. It was the smallest one—about the size of an

RV. They'd asked for two beds, but Lenny doubted now there would be enough room.

"Outhouse and showers to the right," Jared added after handing Evan the keys, pointing to a cinder-block building. It looked like the kind of structure you'd find in a park or on a hiking trail.

Evan gripped the keys. Being on a break didn't mean Lenny forgot how to read his mind; she knew what he was thinking: *Outhouse? The hotel I booked in Arizona had an actual bathroom. And a hot tub. Why would Lenny make us change course last-minute for a shittier story with shittier accommodations?*

While Evan unlocked the door, Lenny turned to thank Jared—but he had disappeared already. She made a mental note to catch up with him later for an interview. If anything was going on in this place, a ranch hand would have seen something. And this guy, with his mustache and chew, would be a great character for their show.

Evan tore off his ruined sneakers and left them outside.

The caboose's interior didn't look much different from the cheap motels they were used to: beige walls and white blinds, simple wooden dressers, and a dull carpet. But this one had a table lamp shaped like a boot with spurs, and right above the loveseat there was a painting of a cow being beamed up by a flying saucer.

Evan dug through a suitcase on the floor, grumbling to himself, until he pulled out his inhaler.

"You good?" she asked, watching him breathe in deeply. He touched his chest between swigs of it, like he had to check if his lungs were working.

"Fine," he snapped. This was the first time he'd used it since they hit the road. He claimed to only bring it as a precaution. Just like the first-aid kit, the flares, and six jugs of purified water.

"I'm sure they have a hose or something to clean off your shoes," Lenny offered.

"I don't care about the shoes," Evan muttered. Oh no. He got quiet when angry. Evan had never yelled at her. Yelling didn't get results, and Evan was all about results. If he could give a printout of the stats of their relationship, he would.

Dreading the silence, Lenny unpacked her own clothes for the next three days (with backups in case she fell into a pit of manure or something).

"There's probably a map at the gift shop," she said after a few minutes. Evan loved maps. If Lenny hadn't convinced him to create a YouTube channel about the paranormal, he probably would have made his own about maps.

The attempt wasn't just for him, though. The website had called the place a gift shop *and* museum, and Lenny was curious about the museum part. She figured their host would be there. Typically, owners loved to be the spokesperson of places like this. They invited *Odd Kids* for help with hauntings, yes, but also for *exposure*. But Lenny had yet to speak to the owner of Reed Ranch. The bookings were all handled on the website; she hadn't even known the owner was a "miss" until Jared had said so.

At least *Odd Kids* was supporting a woman-owned business.

"I figured we could get some interviews lined up," Lenny added.

"Don't you have a *key witness?*" Evan sneered.

Ah, yes. The only person Evan resented more than the

host of *Dark Unknown* was the nameless emailer. Subject line: "Reed Ranch. June 3rd." Its contents had made Lenny reroute the road trip and completely ruin Evan's life.

But when *Odd Kids* had released a short teaser of the clip, it had garnered more than enough interest to justify an investigation. The subscribers would be happy that their faves stopped in Scarberry.

Evan was just being a baby because he didn't get his way.

"Still no reply," Lenny admitted. "Don't think they'll want to talk."

"That doesn't seem sketchy to you?"

"Plenty of witnesses choose to stay anonymous."

Some people's jobs were reporting paranormal encounters, some people lost their jobs for talking about them. Even if they didn't find the mysterious emailer, the town had to have other witnesses. There was something off about this place. She'd felt it during the drive, and she felt it even more now. The big, open sky was suffocating. No cameras were rolling, but Lenny was sure she was being watched.

"It's a hoax, Lenora." Evan usually called her by her given name to tease her, but right now he sounded like her grandmother. He didn't even like that word, *hoax*. He preferred kinder descriptions like *unsolved* or *incomplete data*.

Apparently, *hoax* was a weapon reserved for the cases Lenny cared about the most. So she hit him back with something just as sharp: "Or maybe, some people care more about the truth than fame."

Then she grabbed the handheld camera and slammed the door on the way out.

Claire had worked only one job in her life, but sometimes she felt responsible for everything but the Earth's rotation around the sun. Her gig at the gift shop was a Russian nesting doll, containing infinite occupations within. Plumber when the toilets clogged. Firefighter that time someone's cigarette lit the dry grass ablaze. IT expert when the Wi-Fi crashed. Therapist when lonely tourists wanted to vent.

Today, Claire was an astrophysicist.

"The military already has the technology. They just don't want civilians to know about it," said the skinny white dude sporting a patchy mustache and smudgy tattoos on his forearms. "They want you to think it's a UFO so that China isn't suspicious of our spacecraft."

"Wow, that's crazy," Claire said, deadpan. She'd learned quickly that this was the best response for his type. A rebuttal would just make the mansplaining worse. Agree too enthusiastically, and he'd start flirting, even though he was at least five years older than her and the pride flag on her name tag should have been enough for him to get the hint.

"They're not even called UFOs anymore. They're called UAPs," Mustache Bro said, contradicting himself. "I can show you an article."

Reed Ranch didn't get a lot of skeptics. Locals thought it was tacky to discuss the Beast of Scarberry and with their little tourist trap far from a real city, visitors had to show dedication to make the long drive—dedication that nonbelievers typically didn't possess. Yet, every now and then, people like Mustache Bro managed to show up.

Claire's cousin, Bri, was lucky to be stocking shelves right now. Her wiry arms were full of shiny alien plushies. As always, she was eavesdropping. She gave Claire a knowing look from the other side of the store, one that said, *Do you need rescue?*

They always took turns saving each other. From annoying customers. From school bullies. From watching bad TV shows alone.

The thing was, Claire didn't completely disagree with today's skeptic. Though she knew her hometown had never been visited by a UFO (or UAP, or *whatever*), she couldn't say that while on the clock. Reed Ranch's official position: no one can truly know what happened in 1961. But aliens make for easy logos.

Mustache Bro pulled out his phone and read aloud some article disproving the photo of the Scarberry Lights. The same black-and-white image on his screen hung on the wall behind her, surrounded by a collage of old newspapers with headlines like MYSTERY, CONSPIRACY, UNKNOWN and INVASION, followed by gratuitous exclamation points.

"See how the grain around the light looks different from the rest of it?" Mustache Bro pointed out, shoving the phone in her face. "It's edited. And not even edited well. Pre-Photoshop."

"Wow," she said flatly. "Crazy."

Shifts like this, Claire guessed that if someone took her pulse, they wouldn't find one. Maybe she'd feel more alive if she finally screamed at one of the tourists. Not even words. In her fantasy, she stared directly into the eyes of some poor soul and let out an unholy shriek. It'd go on for hours. It'd blow the flimsy gift shop apart. Take off the last of the farmhouse's shingles. Send the windmill into orbit. Claire would be the worst tornado Scarberry ever saw. She wouldn't stop until the town was leveled.

But she was still holding the scream in. Saving it for when she really needed it.

When a car door slammed outside, Claire glanced out the dusty window. Not a new customer, just Mr. J. Porter for the third time this week, clipboard and sweat-stained button-down and one of his trademark patterned ties. The first horseman of the apocalypse wore pineapple print today. How *quirky*.

Mustache Bro had moved on from the photo of Reed Ranch and onto the "totally fake" first moon landing, but Claire kept her eyes on Mr. Porter as he stepped onto the back porch. She hoped Aunt Maeve wouldn't even open the door. The offer wasn't going to get any better, and the way he'd worded it last week hadn't even sounded like an offer but a threat. Almost everyone on this side of town had sold their property already. Mr. Porter probably thought it was only a matter of time before the Reeds would fold too.

Thankfully Bri hadn't seemed to notice the unwelcome visitor. Aunt Maeve and Claire had agreed not to tell her about the first offer. Or the second. Bri had been through enough the past year; she didn't need to worry about losing the only home she knew on top of everything.

Mr. Porter was still lingering on the porch, rocking back and forth in his loafers with poorly hidden lifts. He knocked, more aggressively this time. But the door didn't open. Either Maeve was holding out or wearing her noise-canceling headphones in the bath again. Eventually Mr. Porter gave up and hopped into his shiny new sedan. Armageddon avoided.

For now.

There was a weak ding as someone new entered the gift shop. The girl was about Claire's age, with dark hair cut into a messy shag. She was short, like five-two at most, wearing a rainbow tie-dyed shirt. *Odd Kids* was printed in neon green on her chest.

Lenny Gilson.

Shit.

Claire expected the other one to follow behind Lenny. The Boyfriend—Claire didn't remember his name—did most of the talking in the videos yet managed to avoid *saying* anything. For all she cared, he was Mustache Bro in a different font. But Lenny came alone. She browsed the shelves like she was at a real museum. Her ringed fingers touched every magnet, every postcard. She even stopped to read the glass-covered original newspaper article where William H. Lamb broke the story to reporters.

Supposedly, Willy Lamb had been parked in a field with his high school sweetheart when they saw strange lights in the rearview window. That was how all these things started, right? A wholesome heterosexual couple getting it on in the backseat until something spooky happens. They rush toward the lights and what do you know, they're right above the Reeds' barn. And conveniently, Willy's girlfriend happens to be carrying a camera with her in nineteen-fucking-sixty-one. She gets the lights on film but fails to take a picture of the ten-foot-tall, long-necked, red-eyed creature that lunges from behind the barn and attacks Willy. The oh-so-brave and chivalrous Willy breaks free and hops back in the truck, but not before the creature takes a big munch out of his shoulder (no evidence of the wound or hospital record). Bleeding and terrified, Willy tries to start the truck, but no dice. The battery's mysteriously dead. They're trapped with a monster.

But then, in a shocking twist, it . . . disappears. Just like that. Allegedly it killed off half the cows at Reed Ranch, but didn't bother finishing off Willy and his girl. So anticlimactic. The story was already bonkers, Willy Lamb ought to have at least ended it with an alien abduction.

No UFOs were spotted. No aliens were captured. Didn't matter. People came in droves to get a glimpse of the lights themselves. Every cow that died that summer was blamed on the town's new pet monster: Old Lucky.

It was bullshit, of course, but the legend paid the bills. Well—it used to. Claire was working on it.

Lenny took a photo of the newspaper and kept moving. Claire forced herself to look away. She had to follow the plan: *Send the footage. Lay low. Play host if you have to, but nothing more.*

Eventually Lenny caught up to Bri, who was sticking barcodes on the back of novelty license plates.

"Hi," Lenny said.

That was all it took for Bri's ears to turn red. She covered them like she could feel them getting hotter. Ever since she'd lost her hair, her ears were her biggest insecurity. *I look like an elf,* she'd said. Claire suggested she wear a hat, but Bri professed that she wasn't a hat girl. She wasn't a short-hair girl either. Since the chemo, she was a hopeless girl. Without her long locks and sun-kissed complexion, she was basically worthless. It didn't matter how much Claire told her the pixie cut was cool and the perpetual bags under her eyes made her look like a very mysterious vampire and plenty of people were into that.

Bri stared at Lenny, eyes glazed over like the taxidermy in Randy's Diner.

"You work here, right?" Lenny asked her.

"Mm-hm," Bri said. Usually she had more words, but she was absolutely star-struck. Shit. At seventeen, Bri was only a year younger than Claire, but sometimes that one year felt like five.

"Cool. I'm Lenny. I do a show about strange phenomena across the U.S." Her words were overenunciated and extra springy. She probably delivered the exact same pitch to every tourist trap she visited. "I'm staying in one of the train cars out back."

Mustache Bro detached from the counter, muttering about tinfoil hats as he left the shop.

Bri nodded with her mouth hung open. *Stay calm.* Claire wanted to telepathically zap the words into Bri's brain. *Stay on script.* Bri said nothing. Just blinked, still holding the price gun pointed at nothing.

"I was hoping to get some interviews about what's been going on here," Lenny added. "There's been no substantial evidence since the lights of '61. But I heard there was another event a few weeks ago."

Substantial evidence? Who talked like that? Even when the cameras weren't rolling, this girl played the part.

"Uh . . ." Bri looked to Claire. She had forgotten her lines already. Claire had personally booked the room for *Odd Kids*, made the bed, sent Jared to greet them when they rolled in. She had done everything but rehearse with Bri.

"Yeah. Yeah but, Claire saw it too. You should ask her."

Lenny's big eyes flicked to Claire. *Crap.*

Lying wasn't part of the plan. Well—not lying to *anyone's face*. Bri was supposed to be the star actor around here. Claire could handle the story and camera work, but she wasn't about to do any improv. As Lenny made her way toward the counter, possible headlines flew into Claire's brain. FAMED RANCH FALSIFYING ALIEN ENCOUNTERS! DISGRACED FAMILY SELLS RANCH POST YOUTUBE EXPOSÉ!

No. Claire couldn't let that happen. She wouldn't let the rumors win, let those bullies like Mr. Porter with their suits and their business cards convince Aunt Maeve to hand over her family's land.

Claire had a new occupation: Alien Invasion Witness.

Lenny pulled out a little notepad and gel pen from her

crossbody bag, jotted something down, then stared up at Claire with her huge doll eyes, green highlights glittering in the inner corners.

"Hi. I'm Lenny. My boyfriend and I do a show about unexplained phenomena."

"Claire. I think I've seen one of your videos."

Bri put her head down, staring blankly at the price gun.

"Someone sent our team some crazy footage from earlier this summer . . ." Lenny began. "It wasn't really clear, but it looked like something was walking on the barn roof."

"Oh really?" Claire managed. She suddenly felt like the alien. Exposed. Observed. She half expected Lenny to pull out a scalpel and dissect her right there.

"Can I show you?"

Claire nodded. This was a flawed interview tactic. If Claire were *really* a witness, wouldn't showing her a video just make her testimony biased? These YouTube people didn't bother with the scientific method at all. Claire had nothing to worry about; there was no way *Odd Kids* would find the truth because, honestly, they didn't care to find the truth. They just needed to produce their clickbait so they could peddle merch to ten-year-olds. These vloggers were just as much liars as Claire was. But Claire, at least, had a worthy cause.

Lenny played the video on her phone. For the seven hundredth time, Claire watched a cluster of white pixels scurry along the roof of the red barn. If you squinted, it looked *kinda* like a four-armed alien. The creature then disappeared as a flash of light burst into the black sky.

God, Claire was good. Still no obvious faults. She'd watched enough of those fake ghost shows with Bri to know you just needed one clearish frame, and the rest could be obscured with motion blur. She'd only started fooling around with the pirated editing software a few weeks before, but she figured that if she'd taught herself code when creating Reed Ranch's website, it couldn't be *that* hard. To the average believer, the clip was convincing. Totally worth the hours distorting a free 3-D model, rigging it, animating it, tracking it to the barn roof, and scouring forums to figure out why the goddamn export wasn't working. It was a shame she couldn't claim it as her own. This would have been a great portfolio piece if she ever actually committed to film school.

"Do you think it's Old Lucky?" Lenny asked. She pronounced the name of Scarberry's patron mascot with reverence.

"Must be," Claire said.

"Do you have any idea who could have taken the video? It looks like it was filmed here."

Claire sucked in a huge breath. "We get a lot of tourists."

A double lie. The only person to come into the gift shop today was Mustache Bro.

"Could you check your guest list? See who would have been around at the time?"

Damn, she was persistent.

"Um. Maybe?" Claire said. "I can ask my aunt, but it's probably a privacy thing."

The light dimmed in Lenny's shiny doll eyes for a second, but her big smile didn't faulter. "Of course. And I respect that. Totally. Have *you* had any other strange occurrences while working here?"

Claire relaxed her shoulders. "Weird things happen all the time," she said, returning to the familiar script she used on enthusiastic UFO chasers. It wasn't as if Aunt Maeve had ever trained her on what to say. When Claire was old enough to make change, she was put in front of the register, and from there she figured out how to keep the believers satisfied. The biggest rule: Keep it vague. Let the audience fill in gaps on their own. Never deny, but try not to add any new lore. Remind them the magnets are buy one, get one half-off.

Lenny nodded enthusiastically. She set her notepad on the table. Her handwriting was so messy, it might as well have been in another language. "Would you maybe want to talk about your experiences for a video? I mean, after your shift of course."

This wasn't part of the plan. Once *Odd Kids* made it to the ranch, Claire was to remain invisible. Bri could step in as the believer. Get a few selfies with her heroes. Make sure the influencers left with enough to put in their trashy little videos to summon more UFO chasers.

"I work late tonight," Claire lied.

"Oh. The sign said you close at four."

"I help with the ranch too."

Another lie. She had very little responsibility for the cattle. That was Jared's domain.

"Maybe Bri can show you around," Claire offered.

Bri perked up. "Yeah. Yeah of course. My shift's almost over. I can give you the official tour."

"Cool," Lenny said. "Thank you. That'd be sick."

It felt like a natural end to the conversation. She waited for

Lenny to back away from the register, make plans with Bri. But she locked eyes with Claire again.

"Maybe talk tomorrow then? Before your shift?" Lenny asked with unflinching eye contact. There was something desperate about her. Whether she believed her own bullshit or not, she *cared*. She cared like this was life or death.

"Sure," Claire agreed.

So what if she embarrassed herself on-camera? It wasn't like she had a reputation to protect. And if Lenny didn't get enough witnesses, *Odd Kids* could bother Aunt Maeve. And that would ruin everything.

Aunt Maeve didn't know about Claire's master plan. It was easy getting Bri and Jared on board, but Maeve would've said it was too risky. And she would be wrong. She didn't have the savvy to keep this place running; she was afraid to get her hands dirty.

Claire had been born with her hands dirty.

She had indefinitely postponed film school. She had zero friends left (besides Bri) and nothing but time. She was the only one who could do something.

"I'll give you guys my number," Lenny said. "Just text me when you'll be available. I can come to you if you live close by."

"I live here."

"Oh, awesome. I'll see you soon then."

Guilt crept in, but Claire pushed it down.

Lenny was eating it up. Which meant the rest of her subscribers would. *Odd Kids* would get ad revenue for publishing Claire's work, and a new generation would care about the Scarberry Lights, battling to secure a room at the ranch. Buying up merch. Paying for tours.

Everybody won.

Out of all the jobs Claire had worked, saving her family was the most important. And if that meant convincing this influencer that an alien lived in her backyard, then she would be happy to oblige.

"**A**re you being safe?"

"I'm always safe, Dad."

Lenny had said it during every Wednesday check-in, but her father was eternally anxious. He was convinced that his daughter would get snatched up by a masked boogeyman if she took the scenic route. Or her accommodations would be infested with flesh-eating parasites. Or a rogue flame and an inconveniently placed puddle of gasoline would blow up the *Silver Bullet* with Lenny and Evan inside.

At least that way they'd die viral.

"How's the hotel?" Dad asked.

He meant to say: *Has it burned down yet?*

The lights flickered again. Dammit. Her straightener turned off. She'd plugged it into one of the two outlets in the room. Her hair was drenched in sweat, and the humidity wasn't helping calm the frizz. She had to try to make herself presentable for their Night One Investigation—if they could even do an investigation. As soon as she'd left the gift shop it started pouring and hadn't let up the whole afternoon. She had texted Bri that they'd like to do a tour when the rain stopped. But it looked like that would have to be a tomorrow thing.

"Hotel's great. Just like the pictures," Lenny answered.

"How's Evan?"

Still pouting. "He's editing," Lenny said. "There's a lot of footage to go through." Her parents still didn't know they were on a break. If it wouldn't last, why bother announcing it?

"Well, tell him hello from us!" Mom said.

Evan was hunched over a computer, headphones over his mop of brown hair. He hadn't spoken to Lenny since their fight that afternoon. Or moved, really. Every few minutes his left hand would rise from the keyboard to sip his coffee or push up his glasses. And once an hour, he'd take a hit of his inhaler. Lenny would resist asking if he felt okay. Because she knew he'd lie, and he'd only reply with some pithy remark if she told him that she thought the air felt different here. That the presence of Old Lucky could be aggravating his asthma.

We're like magnets, Evan had said in an early video. Lenny had nodded, bobbing her head like a stupid puppet. She didn't speak much at all in that video because Evan had told her she was talking too fast. It was hard to cut up footage when all her words were overlapping.

They were still magnets, but one of them had flipped poles and now they were repelling each other. As much as Lenny wanted to blame him for changing, she knew it was her own fault. They should've taken a *real* break, so she could sort out these conflicting feelings. See if she could manage to survive without him before pulling the plug for good.

But there was no time for that. They had a schedule to keep. That's showbiz, baby.

The entire caboose rattled as another burst of thunder boomed above them.

"What was that?" Dad asked.

"It's raining. And no, we didn't drive in it."

They were to pull over for bad weather, just to be safe. Lenny's father loved safe; therefore, he loved Evan. Lenny had all the ideas, but Evan had the follow-through. *We don't just fit together romantically, but creatively,* she had said in a livestream once. *We fill in each other's gaps. Evan's like my missing piece.*

The memory made her cringe.

"Well, we know you're really busy," Mom said. "Just wanted to check in. We'll let ya go. Love you!"

"Talk next Wednesday," Dad added.

"Love you."

Right after hanging up, her phone chimed with a text alert: *Have you arrived yet? Would love on-the-road pics!*

Maria: their social media assistant and secret third member of *Odd Kids.* They sent her selfies, photos of restaurants they ate at, and fans they met. Maria made the captions. She slapped on the hashtags. She altered Lenny's face with enough filters to make her prettier without being unrecognizable. All of the actual footage was edited by Evan for now, while Lenny did most of the research. She wrote the monologues, finding the *heart* in all the strange little towns they visited. Soon, that would all change. Evan wanted to hire an editor. *Every big channel outsources labor*, he said. *It's not unethical. It's smart.* He'd said the same thing when he'd told her to just use ChatGPT to speed up script-writing. *The algorithm likes consistency. Think of how much faster we can upload new content.*

Lenny wished they weren't on the hunt for UFOs. What she really needed was a time machine, so she could go back to the beginning when she was terrified that the tall kid with glasses didn't like her back. When they were making videos to find proof of something bigger, not selling VPNs and subscription boxes. She missed that sizzle inside of her, when she knew she was barreling toward something more. When she didn't have a woman she'd never met IRL telling her to ditch her platform sneakers because the shippers thought their height difference was adorable and they should lean into that.

Evan started to laugh. It wasn't the laugh he did when something was funny—that was more of a wheeze. This was his cynical cackle. He had closed his laptop and stared at his phone.

"One guess where the *Dark Unknown* crew is right now," he said.

He handed the phone to Lenny. The screen showed an Instagram post from Max Malitz, the host of *Dark Unknown*. He had his thumbs up in front of a pueblo-style house with a wavy roof, all the cacti around it brown and shriveled. Lenny didn't need the location tag to know where this was. She knew that house just as well as her own. She had a map of it in her glovebox.

"Good thing we didn't go to Harrows House, huh," she said, returning the phone to Evan.

"We were going to get there first. We would have been ahead of them."

Oh. So it was a bad thing. Lately, for Evan, everything was a bad thing.

"It shouldn't be about getting ahead," Lenny told him.

Evan hopped off the bed and studied the window. The sky looked like a bruise. The un-mowed grass quivered in the wind.

"Can you get off your moral high horse? We're a business. Okay?" he said.

Lenny laughed. She wished he just screamed it like he wanted to. She was so over that gentle, condescending tone. "That's what we are? A business?"

"I meant the channel. And it was your idea to break up, Lenny. Not mine."

"We're not broken up," she reminded him. "We're on *a break*."

"This isn't a break."

As always, he was reading her mind. But she wasn't going to give him the satisfaction of being right.

"Would it be a break if we were at the Harrows House?" she retorted.

He took a deep breath, likely debating if he would retreat or hit her back with something crueler. He could remind her that *his* business skills allowed her to travel the country, therefore she ought to let him decide where to go. Let him hire writers. Plan more con appearances. They would never have to get a real job because of *his* hard work and well-researched strategy. But a real job didn't sound so bad. Lenny thought of the girl at the counter of the gift shop: curvy with a freckled face, long blond hair with dark roots grown out. She wore cowboy boots and ripped shorts and an unbranded tank top. When Claire clocked out, she didn't have to deal with those customers. They came and went. She wasn't glued to any of them. She wasn't forced to share a bed with her work.

She had freedom.

This fight, like the storm, had been brewing since the drive. They had gone the whole road trip without a real spat; Lenny should have seen it coming. But she stupidly thought they were different. That they could take a break without breaking up. Because maybe they didn't love each other *like that* anymore, but Evan was her home planet. Without him, she was floating in space, untethered.

He could still fill in all those gaps. He had to. He was the only one who knew how.

"You need to make a decision, Lenny. If you don't want to do the show anymore just say it," Evan said.

"I didn't say anything about quitting the show. I just can't be *betrothed* before my brain's finished cooking."

She'd told him that when she had invoked the break. When he'd cried and asked why, oh why would she dump him and she searched her mind for a tangible reason. It was supposed to be a brainstorming session for the road trip. She had just pitched they go to the Winchester Mystery House and Evan had debuted his ten-year plan. *By 2030, we'll probably be married, and have at least 2 million subscribers . . .*

That's when she'd snapped. Kicking him out of her room abruptly and asking for *some time to think.*

"Betrothed?" Evan repeated now. "This isn't one of your Jane Austen novels. My God. I told you a million times I wasn't proposing when I said that, just trying to make sure our goals were compatible. Reasonable people make plans. The real world isn't just impulsively driving to the next shiny thing."

"Scarberry isn't an impulse," she said. "I've always wanted to come here."

"No offense, but have you considered that you don't have prophetic dreams? That you just latched on to this place and assigned it meaning?"

He'd tell their subscribers that their Ouija board accurately predicted the latest celebrity death but refused to believe her recurring nightmare meant anything. Had he ever believed in the places they visited? Had he ever believed in *her*? She couldn't just leave before she knew for sure.

"I never said I know what the dreams meant!" she protested. "Just that it's a gut feeling."

"Your gut feeling is making us miss out on getting actual, usable content."

Lenny rolled her eyes. She'd grown to hate that word. *Content.*

"There it is, again," Evan said. "I can feel your resentment every time we're filming. Is it me? Or is it the channel?"

It's all of it! she wanted to scream. *It's living by a script.*

Before she could answer, the dull ceiling light flickered off, and the AC stopped running. They had officially lost power. This night just had to get worse.

There was a beat of silence, and then a new sound from

outside. It was a one-note howl, long and mournful and so high-pitched it hurt. Then, another one. Another one. Overlapping, tinging, like bells.

They both froze for a moment, looking at each other as if to say, *You hear that too, right?* The wails continued. This was real. This was happening. Finally, this was happening. She was where she was meant to be.

Lenny ran outside, hearing Evan unzipping a camera bag behind her. The UFO lights around the caboose flicked on and off. The window AC started and died again. The rain had let up, but it was still dark, and the humid wind blew her curtain bangs around her eyes. She couldn't see anything, but she could feel it. Something was out there with her.

The failing electricity, the strange sound—this was exactly what was reported in the summer of '61.

Yet Lenny couldn't tell what direction the wails were coming from. She stepped away from the cover of trees, brushed her hair back, and looked up at the sky. No stars. No strange lights.

The shrieks were terrifying, but Lenny felt herself smile. Evan was wrong about this place. She had trusted her gut, and her gut had been right.

"We were about to begin our investigation when we heard a strange noise outside of our room," Evan said from behind her in his narration voice. He always spoke clearer when the camera was rolling. He was a natural, while it had taken some getting used to for Lenny. She had to train herself not to talk so fast. Not to mumble. Evan used to squeeze her hand when she got too excited. Lately, she hardly got excited. But now she felt like she was going to leap out of her skin and into another dimension.

Evan focused the lens right at her. "What do you think it is?" he asked.

Lenny pulled a strand of hair from her mouth. For the first time in a long time, she told the camera the truth: "I think it's Old Lucky."